THE KILLING
CONNECTION

THE KILLING CONNECTION

A DCI Gilchrist Novel

T. F. Muir

Constable • London

CONSTABLE

First published in Great Britain in 2017 by Constable

Copyright © T. F. Muir, 2017

1 3 5 7 9 10 8 6 4 2

A CIP catalogue record for this book is available from the British Library.

ISBN: 978-1-47212-320-6

Typeset in Dante MT by Hewer Text UK Ltd, Edinburgh
Printed and bound in Great Britain by CPI Group (UK) Ltd., Croydon, CR0 4YY

Papers used by Constable are from well-managed forests
and other responsible sources.

Constable
An imprint of
Little, Brown Book Group
Carmelite House
50 Victoria Embankment
London EC4Y 0DZ

An Hachette UK Company
www.hachette.co.uk

www.littlebrown.co.uk

For Anna

CHAPTER 1

7.35 a.m., Thursday
Last week in November
St Andrews, Fife

'Watch your feet there, sir, it's slippery.'

DCI Gilchrist could only nod, his concentration focused on picking his way with care across the rocks towards the body. From where he stood, or more correctly *stooped*, his hands palming slime-covered rocks as he worked around a particularly tricky outcrop, he could tell the woman had been dead for several days, maybe a week. But rain hammering his face at the insistence of a gale-force wind – in Scotland, a *stiff breeze* – was not making his task easier. And windswept waves pummelling the rocks were only aggravating conditions.

If they'd had any sense, they should all have stayed in bed.

'Watch yourself, sir.'

But a wave exploded at his feet before he could react, drenching him waist-high, and it took all his strength to avoid being sucked seawards. 'Bloody hell,' he gasped. 'I don't know if this is a good idea.'

'You all right, sir?'

He nodded to Detective Constable Mhairi McBride, who seemed to have found her sea legs without any effort, even though, strictly speaking, they were still on dry land – if it could be called that. 'I'm fine, Mhairi,' he shouted, thankful for her outstretched hand as she pulled him up to a higher level.

'There you go, sir. It's a bit safer here.'

Gilchrist sucked in the damp morning air, surprised to find himself struggling to catch his breath. At the end of next month he would turn fifty. Who would have thought he would have let himself become so unfit? Maybe all those pies, chips and beans were catching up on him. He hooked his fingers under his belt and gave an upward tug. Still thirty-two-inch waist and weight steady at 70 kilos – about eleven and a half stone in old money – although he had the uneasy sense that his body was taking up more space than it used to.

'Nearly there, sir.'

He followed her, relieved that the rocks provided a greater foothold at that level. To his left, the stone ruins of St Andrews Castle reared sixty feet into the dark morning sky, looking perilously close to collapse. He had to shield his face as another plume of spray burst landwards, breakers thundering the rocks with a force he could feel through his shoes – his *soaked* shoes, soaked everything, for that matter.

A burst of rain whipped his face with a force that stung; he tugged up the collar of his leather jacket and tightened his scarf. With the sea being so rough, he'd been in two minds whether to inspect the body *in situ* or not, but you never could tell what a first-hand examination might uncover. Although, as he now looked down at the woman's face, blonde hair flattened across her eyes – nature's attempt to cover the grotesqueness of fish-nibbled eyes – he wondered what on earth he could achieve.

Maybe drown himself?

'She must've been swept up here at high tide, sir.'

'I think so, yes.'

'Then been trapped in the rocks.'

He eyed the dead woman at his feet, feeling an odd reluctance to take a closer look, now he had worked his way here. She lay supine, feet crossed at the ankles, as if she'd settled down for a nap. But her left arm lay at an unnatural angle flat to her stomach, palm skywards, as if double-jointed. Her skin was scuffed and scraped and alabaster white, although it struck him that if the body had been submerged for more than a day or so, he might expect to see more damage from the thrashing it must have received from being thrown on to the rocks.

He lifted his gaze up the height of the castle wall, trying to work through the logic of the woman having leaped to her death, rather than being drowned. 'What d'you think, Mhairi?' He nodded skywards. 'Could she have jumped?'

Mhairi frowned, as if suicide by leaping off a cliff had not occurred to her. Then she slipped on a pair of latex gloves and took hold of the woman's hand. 'Don't think so, sir. I'd say she's been in the water for a couple of days or so and was swept on to the rocks overnight. If she jumped during the night, I'd expect to feel some rigor.' She flexed the hand to make her point. 'Skin's wrinkled, too. And waterlogged. Definitely come in from the sea, sir.'

Gilchrist agreed, but didn't want to sound too eager to concur. 'I'm thinking that it's too cold to have come out without a jacket or a coat at this time of year. Of course, I suppose it wouldn't really matter if your intention was to commit suicide, would it?'

'No, sir.'

'But still,' he said, 'you'd wrap yourself up. At least I think I would.'

'I think so too, sir.'

'So we both agree her body's likely been washed ashore.'

'Yes, sir.'

He pulled on a pair of latex gloves. They could conjecture all they liked, but it would be up to the forensic pathologist – Dr Rebecca Cooper – to determine cause and time of death. He kneeled on the wet rocks, leaned closer, checked her outstretched hand. No rings. He slid her sweater's sleeve up. No watch or bracelet. He did the same with the other hand, taking care not to disturb the arm in case the bone was broken. Same result. He then eked her sweater's roll-neck collar down a touch. No neck-lace. Next, he eased his hand into the left pocket of her jeans, then the right. Both empty.

He pushed to his feet.

He felt puzzled by the way her sleeves hung on her arms – maybe the material had stretched. He didn't want to pull up her sweater to check, but her chest looked flat enough to suggest no bra. Her jeans, too, had the zip partially undone, permitting a glimpse of white skin where he thought he should see underwear. And no shoes, her painted toenails looking remarkably unscathed around the scraped skin of her feet.

All of which meant . . .?

That she had dressed in a hurry – jeans, sweater, nothing else? – and scurried down to the castle to jump off the cliff? He thought not. Nor was it appropriate attire in which to take to the seas, other than in a luxury yacht or ocean liner, of course.

He turned his face into the full force of the wind, squinting against the spindrift and breaker spray. If the seas had not been as rough, or the winds as strong, would the body have turned up on these rocks when it had? Maybe not, but this spell of bad weather was now on its third day, and who would venture out to sea in conditions like these? Maybe that could be a starting point – check local harbours for anyone crazy enough to take a boat out in such a wild November swell.

With that thought, he felt a shiver course through him.

Bloody hell, he was cold. And wet.

He looked back across the rocks over which they'd scrambled. The tide might be on the ebb, but the crashing waves would make the trip for suited-up SOCOs hazardous at best – look how he'd almost been swept away. He couldn't imagine them erecting a forensic tent here either. What evidence could they possibly gather from rain- and sea-battered rocks? Everything would have been washed away. And transporting a bagged body off the rocks would be no easy task.

Was the wind slackening, or was he just imagining it? He pulled his scarf higher up his neck and blew into his hands. A bitter cold was working through his sodden clothes and doing its best to take hold of him. A cup of tea back in the North Street Office was not going to cut it. He would need to drive back to his cottage in Crail, have a piping hot shower and a change of clothes. Mhairi, on the other hand, was jotting down notes and seemed in her element. Maybe he was becoming too old for this any more.

Back to the dead woman.

What age was she? If asked, he would put her somewhere in her thirties, maybe forties, although the length of time she'd been in the sea made it difficult to say for sure. Now out of the saltwater, the body was already showing signs of bloating: skin less wrinkled, face more swollen, a general taking up of more space – a bit like himself, come to think of it.

How had she died? And what had she been doing in her final moments? Struggling against drowning seemed the obvious answer, although he knew from experience never to rely on the obvious. But why out at sea?

Fishing? Sailing? Swimming?

Her sweater and jeans told him No. But the more he thought about her attire, the more he came to see that this was no simple case of falling overboard, or taking her life by walking half-clad into the North Sea. In weather like this, you would not go out half-dressed, but what if she had stripped off her outer clothes before wading into the sea, then swam out until she tired and drowned . . .

A blast of wind whipped breaker surf into the air. He turned to shield his face from the ice-cold spray and found himself looking at the woman's hands again, puzzling over the way the sleeve of her left arm rested on her stomach. Which was when he saw what he hadn't picked up earlier.

'Is she wearing a bra?' he asked.

Mhairi slipped her notebook into her pocket, then lifted the hem of the woman's sweater. 'No, sir.'

'Knickers?'

She unclipped the top button, slid the zip down a touch more. 'No, sir.'

He waited until she re-zipped and re-fastened the button before saying, 'So sweater and jeans, nothing else?'

'No, sir.'

'In weather like this? Why would she go out like that?'

Mhairi shook her head. 'I have to say it is a bit odd.'

Gilchrist paused, as the tumblers of logic dropped into place. 'She didn't drown.'

'Sir?'

'She was killed, then dumped in the sea.'

'Why do you think that, sir?'

'No underwear,' he said. 'Someone else put her clothes on.' He nodded to the body. 'Check out the neck of her sweater. Roll it down.'

Mhairi did so.

'What do you see?'

Mhairi mouthed a perfect *Oh*, and said, 'The label. It's on back to front, sir.'

Gilchrist removed his mobile from his jacket and stepped closer to the cliff face, searching for a sheltered spot to make the call. His *in situ* investigation might not have told him all he wanted to know.

But it did tell him the woman had been murdered.

CHAPTER 2

By the time Gilchrist clambered back to the safety of the steps leading from the beach to The Scores – the road that fronted the cliffs – he'd called the Force Contact Centre in Glenrothes and logged the discovery of the body as a suspicious death. The Procurator Fiscal had been notified, too, as had the forensic pathologist, although Gilchrist couldn't see Dr Rebecca Cooper leaping across slippery rocks, and suspected that the body would need to be moved before she could officially confirm *life was extinct* – one of those odd requirements of the investigative process, even though it was often more than obvious to everyone standing around that the body they were all looking at was indeed a corpse.

Still, you had to tick all the boxes.

The SOCO Transit van was pulling up to the kerb on the East Scores behind Gilchrist's BMW as he reached the top of the steps. First out was Colin, the lead SOCO, scrubbing his chin as if to confirm he needed a shave. Gilchrist could not remember the last time he'd seen Colin clean-shaven, and could never tell if his face was sporting a couple of days of absent-minded growth or trimmed designer stubble.

Colin's eyes widened as Gilchrist approached. 'Bit cold for a swim, isn't it?'

'Your turn next,' Gilchrist said.

'At least the rain's stopped.'

Gilchrist felt so cold and wet he hadn't even noticed. Looking down on the beach and the rocks beyond, the sea looked half as wild and nowhere near as dangerous as it had close up. Even the wind felt as if it had dropped to a mild breeze. For all he knew, it could be blue skies and calm seas in an hour, even less.

'So who's with the body now?' Colin asked.

'DC McBride.'

Colin smiled, flashing a set of perfect teeth. 'You've just made my morning.'

'Well, keep your thoughts on the job.'

Colin winked, then set off down the path to the beach, seemingly oblivious to the cold and the wind, as if his body had just been energised.

In the morning darkness, Gilchrist could just make out Mhairi's figure as she crouched and prodded about the rocks. He didn't expect she would find anything, but you had to admire her tenacity. On the other hand, he was thinking no further than getting home and changing before he froze to death. With a briefing in the North Street Office scheduled for 9 a.m., he could be back in plenty of time for that.

He clicked his remote. His car flashed its lights at him.

It didn't take long for the heater to blow hot air – past the cathedral ruins and left into Abbey Street – by which time the shivering had reached his teeth. He turned the fan to high, and put a call through to DS Jessie Janes on his car's system.

She answered on the third ring. 'I thought you told me to take a day off.'

'You sound as if you're still choked up.'

'Lemsips morning, noon, and night. Already had one for breakfast. Don't know what they put in that stuff, but it's not working.'

'You should try a hot toddy with a spoonful of honey.'

'I should cut through the chaff and go straight for the whisky.' She let out a muffled sneeze. 'Although I wouldn't expect Smiler to approve. Come to think of it, I can't imagine Smiler approving of anything that came close to pleasure.'

Gilchrist chuckled. Chief Superintendent Tom Greaves had retired unexpectedly a month ago. Health reasons were rumoured, although Gilchrist suspected that a heated run-in with big Archie McVicar, the Chief Constable, over budget cutbacks had paved the way for a quick and silent exit. Greaves's position had been filled at short notice by Tayside's Diane Smiley, whose surname was already being proven to be the opposite of her personality.

Jessie said, 'But you're not calling to ask how I'm keeping. So, what've we got?'

'A woman's body at the foot of the Castle rocks. We think she's been murdered.'

'Pushed over the cliffs?'

'We don't think so.'

'Floated in on the tide?'

'More like thrown on to the rocks by storm breakers.'

A pause, then, 'Who's we?'

'Me and Mhairi.'

'How's she coming along?'

'Mhairi?'

'No, Queen Elizabeth.'

'Showing promise, taking the initiative, observant, too.'

'It's good she's fitting in,' Jessie said. 'I like her a lot. After what she's been through, the least we can do is give her a leg up every chance we get. Oh no, hang on.'

Gilchrist drove on while a series of hacking coughs barked from the speakers.

'Bloody hell.' Jessie came back, and snorted a sniff.

'That's why you should stay in bed.'

'I'm not in bed. I'm up and about. Fresh air is what I need.'

'There's plenty of that about,' he said, then stamped his foot on the brake and skidded to a halt. 'Let me get back to you.' He slammed into reverse and backed up, engine whining, and parked askew to the kerb – not quite as good as he used to be.

Maybe it was an age thing.

Out of the warmth of the car, the cold air hit him anew. He walked around the boot of his car to the front garden of the house. 'Hey,' he shouted. 'What's going on?'

The young man jerked at the sound of Gilchrist's voice, then turned from the woman and directed a 1,000-watt glare at him. A white T-shirt seemed to be all he needed to ward off the November chill. He flexed a pair of tattooed sleeves and stomped towards Gilchrist like a dog to raw meat.

'The fuck you want?' he roared.

Gilchrist held up his warrant card. 'Careful, sonny.'

But the man was over the garden railing and launching himself, giving Gilchrist next to no time to sidestep the flying assault. The man landed on all fours, his momentum carrying him onwards to headbutt the rear wheel of Gilchrist's car. Even that seemed not

11

to faze him. Up and on to his feet with the agility of an acrobat, a trickle of blood already working down his forehead – face tight with madness, fists clenched with anger.

Alcohol, that was the problem. Not that the man had drained a few pints and whisky chasers for breakfast, more like he'd been drinking all night, giving it laldie.

'I'm with Fife Constabulary,' Gilchrist said. 'And you're under arrest for—'

'Fuck that.'

This time, Gilchrist was ready, using his attacker's impetus to spin him to the ground. Even from that split second of inter-action Gilchrist knew he was no physical match for the younger man. What he did have in his favour, though, was sobriety and a fearful sense of urgency – if he didn't end the fight before it started, he would be on the receiving end of a right old beating.

Experience, too, helped, and as Gilchrist followed him down, the point of his knee thudded into the man's back with a force that should have cracked ribs. The man's breath left him in a hard grunt but, more importantly, the blow stunned him for a moment. A tug at his left wrist, then his right, and Gilchrist had him hand-cuffed before he had time to recover.

He kept his weight on the man's back and leaned down, close enough to smell the warmth of alcoholic breath. 'I am arresting you, sonny, for assaulting a police officer.'

'Fuck, I didnae mean it.'

To Gilchrist's surprise, all strength left the man at that moment and his body sagged like a puppet having its strings cut. He read him his rights, turned him over and helped him into a sitting position. The man's face was grazed where he'd hit the pavement, and smeared with blood from the cut to his forehead. Spittle and blood dribbled from a split lip.

'Stay put,' Gilchrist said, and shoved the man's back hard against the railings. A quick adjustment with the cuffs had him secured to the metal bars. But he seemed not to notice, and simply hung his head in what could have been mistaken for shameful remorse.

The garden gate opened to the strain of rusted hinges, and closed with a hard metallic clatter. A wheelie bin overflowing with carry-out detritus stood to the side of the front door which stood ajar and gave a view of curled linoleum, peeling wallpaper, children's toys.

Gilchrist walked to the corner of the property, where a boundary hedge butted against the house wall. He leaned down. Although he saw no evidence of physical injury, he said, 'Are you hurt?'

The young woman looked up at him through red-rimmed eyes, swiped her hand under her nose, shook her head.

'Are you able to stand?'

She nodded.

He held out his hand, and she took it. Her fingers could have been iced to the bone. Of course, nightdresses were not intended for outdoor winter weather. He pulled her to her feet and diverted his gaze from an unintentional slip of nudity. A tremor gripped her body and made her teeth chatter. Two crushed beer cans lay at her bare feet, and he kicked them aside. He unravelled his scarf and threw it around her neck, then took off his jacket and draped it over her shoulders.

'We'll get you inside,' he said. 'Heat you up.'

By God, he could be doing with that himself.

The hallway smelled like a snooker bar – cigarette smoke and alcohol, an underlying hint of burned food that teased the nostrils. As he led her to the kitchen, he noted a couple of fist-holes through the hall plasterboard, and a bedroom door with a split panel where there should have been a handle.

The kitchen door, too, had a cracked hole about boot high. A chipped laminate table sat in the middle of the room, a broken pottery mug on its surface, tea or coffee trailing to the floor. He sat the woman down on the closest chair, lifted one of two over-turned chairs off the floor and sat next to her.

He was about to speak, when movement to the side of the fridge caught his eye, and he felt a thud in his chest at the sight of a child, no more than a year old, seated in a high-chair. The woman caught his look of concern, and said, 'My daughter, Danette,' then rose from her seat and lifted her out of the high-chair.

While the woman rocked Danette in her arms, Gilchrist took the opportunity to call the North Street Office and report a domestic – male offender handcuffed outside main residence, arrested for assault on a police officer. When asked, the woman confirmed her address, her name, Jehane, and that of her partner, Blair, and *we're not married.*

While Gilchrist waited for support to arrive, he tried to find out about events leading to the moment when he'd caught Blair's angry face inches from a frightened Jehane's. He hadn't needed to hear what was being said to recognise a domestic in full flow.

Besides, the kitchen warmth was doing wonders for his chilled body.

He opened his notebook. 'Jehane,' he said. 'How do you spell that?'

14

She told him.

'That's an unusual name.'

'My mum's French. My dad's Scottish. Mum passed away in Nantes a few years ago. Her name was Danette.'

'Is Blair Danette's father?'

Jehane shook her head. 'Drew is. Blair's friend. We split up a year ago.'

'You and Drew did?'

'Yes.'

'Over Danette?'

'Over Blair.'

Gilchrist thought he saw the problem, but let his silence do the asking.

'Blair and Drew don't speak any more.'

No, he thought. They wouldn't.

'Blair's OK when he's sober,' she said. 'Then something just sets him off.'

Alcohol, as good a catalyst to violence as any. But Gilchrist thought it best to ask. 'So what set him off this morning?'

'He'd been out all night with a friend, and she told him I was seeing Drew again. It's not true.' She hugged Danette to her.

Gilchrist decided to fast-forward a few frames. 'Has Blair ever hit you?'

Jehane lowered her eyes, hugged Danette closer, and Gilchrist knew the next words out of her mouth would be a lie. 'No,' she said.

'Just verbal abuse?'

'Not abuse,' she said. 'Just shouting.'

Just shouting. This was the problem with most domestic incidents, one partner failing to understand the seriousness of the

15

problem, that verbal and mental abuse could be every bit as damaging as physical abuse.

The sound of feet thudding down the hallway brought Gilchrist's interview to an end. A van crew in close proximity had answered the call. He rose from his chair as PC Tomkins entered the kitchen and hesitated, as if trying to work out how anyone could have beaten him to the scene. But he nodded when Gilchrist said, 'I called it in.'

Ten minutes later, Gilchrist was back behind the wheel.

Blair had been escorted into the van without complaint, although Gilchrist thought he detected stiffness in his movements, a suggestion of pain, perhaps. They would drive him to the hospital to have his head wound checked – nothing serious, Gilchrist suspected – take an X-ray, glue the wound, maybe even take a CT scan just to be sure.

But who was Blair, and what had led to that morning's domestic?

If Gilchrist was a betting man, he'd put money on physical abuse being in Blair's history. But it was the presence of the child that troubled him, in a home with evidence of violence – holes in walls, burst door panels, broken handles.

You never want to get Social Services involved to the point where they might remove the child from its parents, particularly the mother. But everyone has a moral responsibility, police officer or not, to report concerns about any child living in violent surroundings.

He would fill out a Cause for Concern Report.

Another box he would make sure was ticked.

CHAPTER 3

Crail, Fife

Gilchrist parked his car in Castle Street and walked down Rose Wynd.

The wind had strengthened, bringing with it a touch of Arctic ice that had him stuffing his hands deep into his pockets and wishing he was flying off to somewhere warm. Wasn't that what he used to do, spend a week in warmer climes over winter months? Now it seemed as if all his time was taken up with work, that holidays and weekends were a thing of the past – like mild winters in Scotland, come to think of it. If the temperature continued its downward spiral, they could be snowed under with ice blizzards by Christmas.

Indoors, he turned up the central heating, but it would take time to work through the radiator system. In the bathroom, he switched on the shower and stripped off his wet clothes. His legs looked blue-white, as if they'd lost semblance of life – sticks of marble – and it took a minute under the hot water before he felt warmth returning to his frozen limbs.

Five minutes later, his skin looked steamed and cooked, and he felt warm enough to walk into the kitchen barefoot, wearing nothing but a towel around his waist. Having missed breakfast due to the early call-out, he intended to have a bite before returning to the Office for the kick-off briefing. Two slices of bread into the toaster, teabag into the teapot, and about to pop open a jar of marmalade when his mobile rang – ID Mo. His daughter, Maureen, was not a morning person by habit, although better than his son, Jack, for whom mornings never had daylight hours in them. But if Maureen was up early, was something troubling her?

'Good morning, Mo. Is everything OK?'

'Of course, Dad, it's just . . .'

He thought he caught a man's voice in the background, and said, 'It's just?'

'It's just that I've got some good news, well . . . at least I hope it's good news.'

Something in her tone came across as forced, warning him that he might not like what he was about to hear. But he tried to sound lively. 'If it's good news for you, Mo, I'm sure it'll be good news for me, too.'

A pause, then, 'You remember Tom, don't you?'

He did. Tom Wright. Mo's on-again-off-again boyfriend. St Andrews local. Father an English lecturer at the university. And that was about it. But last he'd heard, Mo and Tom had split up, hadn't they?

'Of course I remember Tom.'

'Good. Well . . . he's asked me to marry him.'

In the face of his immediate dismay, he said, 'That's wonderful news, Mo,' and hoped he'd hit the right note. On the one hand, having someone there for her, a soon-to-be husband who could give support during her bouts of depression, was just what the doctor ordered. On the other hand, Maureen could be the devil in disguise at times, and he hoped Tom knew what he was letting himself in for.

'Are you sure?' Maureen said. 'You're not just saying?'

'Of course not. But I have to say it depends on how you answered Tom's question.' He gave a dry chuckle to let her know he was joking.

'I said Yes, of course.'

'I know you did, Mo, and I'm really happy for you.' He caught the scratch of a hand being placed over the mouthpiece, some muffled voices, then Maureen was back.

'We'd like to take you out for lunch today, Dad. Sort of a celebration.'

Gilchrist felt his heart sink. With a murder investigation about to begin, all his time would be tied up for the next several days, maybe longer. It was unlikely that the discovery of the woman's body had made it to the local news yet, but the media had surprised him before with the speed at which they could react. So he tried, 'Have you heard this morning's news?'

'What about it?'

'I shouldn't be saying anything until after the briefing, but a woman's body washed up on the Castle rocks this morning, and it'll be full-on for the rest of the day.'

'How about tomorrow?'

Well, he supposed that was how most people would react to the news of a stranger's death nowadays. With local and global news available 24/7 at the press of a button, it seemed that citizens the world over were inured to the tragedy of sudden and unexpected deaths.

'Probably tomorrow, too,' he said.

'Saturday, then?'

Bugger it. He knew Maureen wouldn't let it go, that he would have to agree a time and place. 'How about tomorrow, then? I could maybe squeeze in a half hour or so between briefings. Provided I'm not out and about,' he added, just to give himself an exit strategy if he needed one.

Despite the obvious slipperiness of his offer, Maureen said, 'That would be great, Dad. We won't take up your time. Just a quick chat and a drink and show you the ring.'

The *ring*? Bloody hell, this was for real. Not that he hadn't thought he'd be a father of the bride one day, just that it all seemed so . . . so unexpected and – and what?

Premature?

Had Maureen fully recovered? Was she ready for this? Well, if he thought back to his own engagement – if he could call it that – he certainly hadn't been ready. Nowhere near. Of course, a knicker-dropping session in the Valley of Sin by the eighteenth green could have had something to do with it.

'How about the Central?' Maureen said. 'It's close to the Office.'

Too close, he thought, particularly with Smiler being an unknown quantity. 'How about the Criterion?' he offered. 'Now they've changed it back from Lafferty's.'

'Does twelve o'clock work?'

'Sounds good. If you don't hear from me, I'll see you there.'

'Great, Dad, love you.'

The line died before he realised he hadn't given his wishes to Tom.

Fifteen minutes later, he fired up the BMW's ignition, wiping toast crumbs off his jeans as he clipped on his seatbelt. He'd given up wearing suits to the Office, and resorted to smart trousers and casual jackets. But he'd not collected his laundry for two weeks and was faced with the choice of putting on a new pair of Levi 511s, or re-wearing his sodden trousers – he should have draped them over the radiator if he'd thought about it. The jeans won. He was running behind schedule, and called the Office to set the kick-off briefing back fifteen minutes. Then he phoned Jessie.

'Just heard you've postponed the briefing,' she said.

'How did you hear that?'

'I'm at the Office. Couldn't stand being stuck indoors any more.'

'Spreading germs?' he said. 'We could have the entire Office signed off by the start of the week.'

'You're just going to have to make sure I get out and about, then.'

'Well now you're here, get Jackie up and running on misper reports, and get a photo and distribute it around other forces. It's too soon to say where she could have come from, but I'd include Lothian and Borders, and Tayside in the first instance. Has the body been moved to the mortuary yet?'

'SOCOs are working on it.' Jessie lowered her voice. 'And you'll never guess who's just walked in.'

'Ah, shit.'

'Got it in one,' she said. 'Smiler.'

Chief Superintendent Diane Smiley was the last person Gilchrist wanted to attend his kick-off briefing. She was known for being hands-on, so he shouldn't have been surprised. But he was pissed off with himself at running late – for his own bloody briefing, for crying out loud. Not the best of starts to have witnessed by your new Chief Superintendent.

'Want me to get it going?' Jessie said.

'I'll be with you in fifteen.'

'So that's a No?'

He hung up.

As it turned out, he arrived at 9.10 – ten minutes later than his original briefing time, or five minutes early for the revised. When he entered, he sensed an embarrassed rush to silence, as if he'd been the topic on everyone's lips.

He nodded to the Chief Superintendent. 'Ma'am.'

'Good of you to come along, DCI Gilchrist.'

He took a few minutes gathering together what information was available, relieved to see photographs of the dead woman posted on a corkboard, and miscellaneous notes printed on an adjacent whiteboard: Name? Address? Age? Married? Friends? Employed? Credit Cards? Bank Accounts? – and photos of the Castle rocks, with date, time, weather, wind strength, and more printed notes: Pushed? Jumped? Drowned? Suicide? Murder?

Hadn't he already concluded that she'd been murdered?

He faced his team, irritated by CS Smiley choosing to stand to the side of the group. With her navy-blue trouser suit, white silk blouse and dyed blonde hair, she looked more the business executive than Chief Superintendent. The tiny smirk in her mouth warned him that she might know something he didn't.

'OK,' he said, eyeing the group. 'Let's summarise what we know. He tapped a photo that showed a close-up of the victim's face – hair pulled back like wet ribbon, eyes damaged from fish teeth or crab claws, skin cut and grazed and spattered with rain or sea spray. 'The body was found at the foot of the Castle rocks this morning by a Mr . . .' He searched the whiteboard for the man's name, but couldn't find it. 'Remind me.'

'Murdo,' Mhairi offered. 'George Murdo. Called it in at twenty past six.'

'Thanks, Mhairi.' He added the name and time to the board, and caught a glimpse of Smiley's smirk widen. 'We have his written statement?' he asked.

'Yes. PC Burns interviewed him. Mr Murdo was out jogging—'

'Must be keen,' Jessie quipped.

'—when he said he saw something moving on the rocks.'

'Where exactly was Mr Murdo when he saw this movement on the rocks?'

The entire office, it seemed, turned to face Chief Superintendent Smiley, who stood as still as a statue, smirk replaced by tight lips that warned everyone she meant business.

Mhairi said, 'On the East Scores, ma'am.'

'Yes, I know that, DC McBride. But what I'm asking is – how far away was he when he first saw *something moving?*'

Mhairi fumbled through her notes.

Gilchrist said, 'That's not important, ma'am.'

Smiley's eyes narrowed. 'Oh really, DCI Gilchrist? How someone happened to notice movement on the rocks in the pitch black of a winter's morning? And you don't think that's important? Did he have infra-red eyes? Night-vision binoculars? Would you care to explain?'

'What I said, ma'am, is that—'

'I know what you said.'

Gilchrist returned her look, seeing in her stiff-backed posture her need to stamp her authority on the Office. But the tension in her eyes gave her away, and the tiniest flush that crept from the collar of her blouse and coloured her neck exposed her vulnerability. Here was a woman in a mostly male-dominated profession, who had worked her way to a position of responsibility – and was rumoured to have her eye on greater aspirations – who felt the only way to command respect in her new job was to demand it.

Rather than inflame the confrontation, Gilchrist said, 'Mr Murdo walked down the steps from the East Scores and on to the beach to check what he had seen, ma'am. The weather was wild at that time in the morning, so he wasn't able to reach it. He did say in his statement that he thought it might have been a body, but it could just as easily have been a piece of flotsam.' He gave a short smile, and added, 'Moonlight. And a break in the clouds. That's what helped him notice something moving, ma'am.'

'And you've read his statement?'

Skimmed through it, more like. But he said, 'Yes, ma'am.'

She gave a tight-lipped nod. 'Carry on.'

He turned to the whiteboard and tapped the headshot. 'She was wearing nothing more than jeans and a sweater—'

'Sir?'

'Yes, Mhairi?'

'We found a black Nike running shoe close to the body. Size six. It looks like the right size, but we'll get that confirmed.'

'Laces?'

'Yes, sir.'

'Done or undone?'

'Undone, sir.'

If you were dressing a dead woman, and put a pair of trainers on her, would you tie the laces? More than likely, Gilchrist supposed, but it did lend credence to the other shoe slipping off in the sea. He carried on with his briefing, identifying priorities – ID the most critical – assigning individuals to specific tasks, and couples for door-to-door interviews. He always encouraged his team to fire questions amongst themselves, ask the obvious or outlandish if they had to. Better to engage by brainstorming, than to sit back in silence.

About twenty minutes into his briefing, he noticed to his surprise that Smiley was no longer in the room. Since their confrontation – if it could be called that – she had monitored his briefing in silence, a mute overseer taking in everything and offering nothing. He knew it should not trouble him, but it did, the fact that she had challenged him so blatantly in front of his team, then backed down with surprising non-contention.

He hoped she didn't feel as if he'd made her lose face.

For if she did, she could make his life a misery.

CHAPTER 4

By mid-afternoon, the wind had dropped, the skies had cleared, and the sea was about as calm as it would ever be for November. The SOCOs had scoured the rocks and cliff face at low tide, and found nothing of interest – as Gilchrist had suspected – and a search team had failed to find the other shoe, if indeed there ever had been *the other* shoe.

The woman's body had been photographed and examined on the rocks by the SOCOs, then bagged and transported to the police mortuary in Bell Street, Dundee. Dr Rebecca Cooper was at trial in Edinburgh for most of that morning, giving evidence over an apparent suicide – a man missing for six days had been found dead in a village stream – but insisted she would start the post mortem herself that afternoon. Despite Gilchrist's requests to have one of her assistants take over in her absence, she refused, even ending his call mid-sentence; post-affair professional relations were always a problem.

Seven months had passed since he and Cooper ended their affair, and it irked him greatly that he still found himself drawn to her. He had always seen it as an affair, the ever-present threat of it ending any moment with the soon-to-be-but-not-quite-yet-divorced Mr Cooper forever on the periphery. So, when he'd found himself listening to the tone of a dead line, he assigned Jessie to follow up with Cooper for the PM report.

Meanwhile, he would focus on trying to identify the woman.

Five teams of door-to-doors were well into their enquiries, having started at homes closest to the castle. But early reports were all negative. The discovery of the woman's body was now being reported by the media, and Gilchrist ordered an E-fit image of the woman's face, and an appeal to be put out on local and national TV news channels asking for anyone who might have seen her or have knowledge of her to contact their nearest police station. A toll-free number scrolled along the bottom of the screen like ticker-tape; callers were encouraged to use it with anonymity.

The MCA – Maritime and Coastguard Agency – was contacted for maritime charts of Fife and Tayside coastal waters, and experts consulted to determine where a body washed up in St Andrews might have originated. To add to their difficulties, an easterly wind recorded in excess of seventy miles per hour in places made calculations more difficult. Without knowing exactly how long the body had been submerged, they could be talking about a maritime area in excess of one thousand square miles.

With these numbers, they might as well stab a pin at a chart.

Hopes were momentarily raised when the same name cropped up three times within an hour – Mary Blenheim from a dairy farm near Ladybank – who had not been seen for four days. A mobile unit was assigned to check out the callers, until a woman identifying herself as Mary Blenheim phoned to confirm she had moved to Edinburgh to live with her new man. Lothian and

Borders were contacted to confirm her new address, only to report back two hours later that she was indeed Mary Blenheim, and that her likeness to the dead woman was uncanny – if the latter changed her ethnicity to black Jamaican. Gilchrist considered having one of his team follow up in a few days to charge the callers with wasting police time.

In the meantime, he had more important issues at hand.

By 5 p.m., the incident room had received calls from fifty-six people claiming to recognise the dead woman. Four were obvious crank calls, and of the remaining fifty-two, seventeen said they had seen her in some shop, or bank, or in passing, and no, sorry, they didn't know her name or where she lived. Each of the places where the woman had allegedly been sighted was marked with a red tack pinned to a map on the incident room's wall. The East Neuk village of St Monans seemed to have the most sightings.

DC Mhairi McBride was the first to put her head on the block.

'Four people say they saw her walking down Braehead here, sir,' she said, and tapped the map. 'Two, past the primary school here.' Another tap. 'But ask yourself, if she was seen at these locations, where was she coming *from*? I think she might have been living in the holiday park.' She tapped the map again. 'Here.'

Gilchrist raised his eyebrows. A caravan park might suit the profile of someone new to the area – annual visitors up for a week or two during the summer months, or for some peace and quiet during the off-season. Someone from out of town might explain why no locals had come forward with definitive ID. Still, he had limited resources, stretched at the moment on door-to-doors, and had no doubt that Smiler would be keeping an eye on the budget. But he could reassign one of the door-to-doors to the caravan park in the morning.

'I know we're tight on resources, sir,' Mhairi said. 'But I could have a look around the caravan park tomorrow.'

He nodded. That was a possibility. But he still had questions on the evidence they'd gathered thus far. 'How are you getting on with her clothes?'

'The sweater and jeans are your common or garden gear sold in a gazillion shops throughout the UK.'

He waited. 'And?'

'And that's about it, sir.'

'So you've found nothing?'

She picked up on his change in attitude. 'Not nothing, sir. But I'm getting nowhere—'

'Forget the caravan park. Finish what you were tasked to do.'

'Yes, sir.'

He waited until Mhairi sat at her desk before he turned his attention to the map again. The caravan park was intriguing, but as he stared at the map he felt annoyed with himself for snapping at Mhairi. She was showing initiative, doing good detective work, even great, and was fast becoming a valued member of his team. But he needed everyone to complete the tasks he'd assigned them, or his investigation would spiral beyond his control. Of course, he was the wrong person to offer criticism. Look at how his career had plateaued due to his own maverick approach. Detective Chief Inspector was about as high up the ladder as he would ever make, and even then he felt fortunate to have climbed that far, having escaped demotion on a number of earlier cases. He decided he would have a chat with Mhairi later, share his experience, good and bad – hopefully explain the error of her ways.

Why have two careers ruined because of maverick initiative?

As he turned from the maps, Jessie signalled him over.

'Just in from Her Highness,' she said.

'Which one? Cooper or Smiler?'

'Haven't seen Smiler since she sneaked out of here this morning. No, this is an early draft of the PM report.'

'I thought Cooper didn't do draft reports.'

'She doesn't, but I told her I was going to come to Bell Street and sit in her office if she didn't give me something by close of business today.'

Well, he could see how that might work. The urbane Cooper and the brash Jessie were about as compatible as oil and water, but managed to maintain a professional relationship – only just.

'So what have we got so far?' he said.

'Murder.' Jessie scrolled down the screen. 'Here we go. She was strangled. Cutaneous bruising on the neck consistent with compression of the throat. Cricoid cartilage fractured at the C6 vertebra, consistent with severe compression of the throat with intent to kill.' She looked up at him. 'You didn't mention bruising.'

'I didn't see any,' he said. 'But her sweater didn't help.'

'Signs of a struggle?'

'None obvious. How about toxicology results?'

'Nope. They'll come later. You're thinking she was maybe drugged and couldn't have put up any resistance?'

He *was* thinking that, and was again impressed by the speed of Jessie's thought process. If the woman had been fully conscious, being strangled face-to-face almost guaranteed a fight-back.

'What about under the fingernails?' he asked.

Jessie mumbled as she read the screen. 'Nothing about them yet.'

'Hang on,' he said, and walked to a rear window where he dialled Cooper's mobile number. Outside, darkness had settled.

Windows of homes beyond the boundary wall glowed from warmth within. How nice it must be to go home at the end of a fixed working day and put your feet up and watch the telly.

After twenty rings, he ended the call.

He dialled again. If Cooper saw the incoming call was his number, she might not pick up. But if she was still at the mortuary, working on the PM, she might see his persistence as a professional call – not that he'd been anything other than professional of late – and feel compelled to answer.

He killed the call, and dialled again.

It rang once.

'Yes Andy.'

Even from just two words, he could tell Cooper was irritated. 'Fingernails,' he said. 'Anything under them?'

'Can't this wait until I've written the PM report?'

'Preferably not.'

She let out a heavy sigh, then said, 'Nothing under the fingernails. So she didn't put up a fight.'

'Toxicology results?'

'Should have those with you tomorrow.'

'Any chance of getting them sooner?'

'None.'

The line died.

Well, he supposed he had interrupted her. He glanced at his watch. He'd had nothing to eat since toast and marmalade that morning, and was more or less free until his debriefing in the Office at 7 p.m.

'Hungry?' he said to Jessie.

'Trying to lose weight.'

'I take it that's a Yes?'

31

'Yes, I'm hungry. And no, I'm not having anything to eat.'

'Can you print out that draft PM report for me, then?' He caught Mhairi's eye and said, 'Fancy a bite to eat?'

'No, sir.' She turned back to her screen.

Well, Mhairi could huff all she liked, but she would have to learn the hard way.

Jessie handed him the draft PM report – no more than half a dozen pages – which he flipped through as he strode to the door. 'I'll be back in thirty minutes,' he said to no one.

The Criterion buzzed with the hubbub of an early Thursday evening; office workers wetting their throats at the end of a hard working day; students revelling in the possibility of an early start to the weekend; weather-beaten caddies wondering why that day's cash was already running out.

Gilchrist worked his way to the bar, squeezed in between a pair of sozzled caddies with a smile and an *Excuse me*. Scottie was at the far end serving a couple of women, giving them his patter for all he was worth. If past experience was anything to go by, he could be tied up for several rounds. Gilchrist caught the assistant bartender's eye; Martha, a history student at the University.

Gilchrist ordered a pint of Deuchars and a steak and ale pie, and managed to steal a seat at the window as a pair of American tourists – loud anoraks and white teeth a dead giveaway – settled their bill and left a cash tip. Outside, South Street pulsed with activity despite the weather. It might not be raining, but a cold wind that could cut bone was holding its own. Once seated, Gilchrist eyed the bar patrons, half-searching for Maureen and Tom. If he'd thought ahead, he could have met them here. But he was staying only until he ate his steak pie, so it was pointless calling them now.

He turned his attention to the draft PM report, annoyed that he hadn't noticed bruising on the woman's throat. Being wet and cold to the bone was no excuse, certainly not one Smiler would accept anyway, but it had contributed to his mistake. He sipped his beer. The hyoid bone wasn't damaged, which can happen when the assailant's thumbs press higher into the throat during the struggle. Damage only to the cricoid cartilage might suggest someone with strong hands – male perpetrator? – gripping the neck tight and squeezing the life from her, no need of thumbs for extra pressure. Of course, if she was drugged and already unconscious, her assailant could press his thumbs deep into her throat without fear of a struggle.

Was that unusual? He lifted the report from the table as his steak pie was placed in front of him. Just the smell of warm meat had his mouth watering. His mobile rang.

'PC Tomkins here, sir. Sorry to trouble you.'

It took a couple of confused seconds for Gilchrist to place the name – the uniformed police officer who'd responded to his call for a domestic.

'I'm calling about Mr Stevenson, sir. He's been—'

'Sorry?' Gilchrist said. 'Stevenson?'

'Blair Stevenson, sir. The man you arrested this morning.'

'Oh right, yes, how did that go? Did you alert the Social Services?'

A pause, then, 'Well, no sir, his girlfriend turned up at the station. She's now refusing to press charges. She more or less revoked her entire statement.'

Gilchrist gave a deflated curse. Abused women the world over seemed incapable of breaking free from their abuser, returning time and again to more abuse. It's not like help was not available or hard to find. Social Services and a number of charitable organisations could protect these women, but importantly, protect the child.

'But that's not why I'm calling, sir.'

Gilchrist lifted his pint. 'I'm listening.'

'Blair Stevenson was admitted to hospital this afternoon, sir, suspected broken ribs and ruptured spleen.'

Ice swept through Gilchrist's blood like a cold wind.

'Said he was kicked on the ground by the arresting officer, and that he's going to sue the police.'

'And we believe him?'

'He has a witness, sir.'

'Who?' he asked, but when the name came he was not surprised.

'Jehane Marshall. His girlfriend.'

'Thanks for calling, PC Tomkins.'

Gilchrist ended the call, and pushed his food away.

Outside, the night air burned as cold as his mood.

CHAPTER 5

10.17 p.m., North Street Office
St Andrews

Gilchrist felt an almost overpowering sense of déjà vu. Nothing had changed in the room. The desk and chairs were the same. The window blinds were the same – opened at a slight angle, raised a foot off the sill. Both bookshelves were the same, although if he was being honest, there appeared to be more books than he recalled. The same phone sat on the same spot on the same desk, its lead twisted and coiled over the edge as it always had done.

The only change was the person seated behind the desk, although it did not take much of an imagination to think that Chief Superintendent Tom Greaves might have morphed into Chief Superintendent Diane Smiley – who made a show of sniffing the air.

'Do I smell alcohol?'

'Shouldn't think so, ma'am.'

'I don't approve of drinking during working hours.'

Gilchrist thought of reminding her that the official working day was long over. But he chose to play safe, and stood silent.

'OK, DCI Gilchrist. Bring me up to speed.'

Since attending the kick-off briefing, Smiler had made herself scarce. She hadn't been seen in the incident room again, nor over lunch break, and failed to show for the debriefing at 7 p.m. Now she had asked, he wondered if he should give her the long version, or the short.

He went for the latter. 'We have no formal ID yet, ma'am.'

'What about leads?'

'We've drawn a blank in St Andrews, but have reported sightings in St Monans.'

'Where's that?'

Her question surprised him for a moment. But her professional life had been spent in Tayside, so he should not have expected her to know every fishing village in Fife. 'On the coast, south of Anstruther, ma'am.' He didn't want her to think that the entire day had been a waste of resources, so he said, 'I've been in contact with the Anstruther Office, and they're going to assist us in door-to-doors first thing in the morning.'

'I understand she was throttled to death?'

Well, so much for leads. It seemed he had Smiler wrong. She might have stayed out of sight for the day, but she'd kept abreast of his investigation on the QT. All of a sudden, he saw this meeting as something more than a face-to-face debriefing; some personal test he had yet to pass. So he said, 'Yes, ma'am,' then expanded on his thoughts of a powerful male perpetrator, aware of her eyes holding his in an unblinking stare.

'And she didn't put up any struggle,' she said.

'We're not sure about that yet, ma'am.'

'That wasn't a question, DCI Gilchrist.' She slid a folder which he hadn't noticed until then from the edge of her desk and removed from it what looked suspiciously like a PM report. She flipped through a couple of pages. 'She'd been drugged. Rohypnol. Alcohol. Both in sufficient quantities to ensure she would've been unconscious and unaware of what was happening to her, thank God.'

'When did you get that report?'

'This?' She held it up like a prize. 'About two hours ago.'

He raked his hair. Jessie hadn't mentioned anything about the PM report. Had she been sidestepped, too? 'Why didn't I receive a copy?'

'Because I instructed Dr Cooper to email it to me directly.'

Being the Senior Investigating Officer, and having a PM report withheld from him by both the forensic pathologist and his Chief Superintendent, particularly after he'd pressed so hard for an early copy, was not only tantamount to betrayal, but to conspiracy against him.

'And when were you going to let me see it?' he asked.

She could not have missed the bitterness in his tone, but she kept her composure. 'If it contained anything that required your urgent attention,' she said, 'I would've sent it to you immediately.'

'That's for me to decide.'

'Not in this instance, DCI Gilchrist.'

He exhaled a gasp of frustration. 'She'd been drugged unconscious – new information that you thought didn't require my attention?'

'*Urgent* attention, DCI Gilchrist.'

'That's not the point,' he said. 'As SIO, I need to be advised of any and all matters relating to my investigation as and when they are received. Ma'am.'

She held his look for several seconds longer than considered polite, then said, 'I wanted to talk to the Chief Constable before we had this discussion.'

Forget the alarm bells. Klaxons were sounding.

'By all accounts you tend to have an unhealthy disregard for police procedures.' Her eyes flared as they focused on his. 'I wanted to know more about your background, DCI Gilchrist. So I spoke to Chief Constable McVicar to ask his personal opinion.'

Gilchrist was still at a loss. 'About . . .?'

'About your aggressive side, DCI Gilchrist. The side of your personality that you only reveal when making an arrest.'

Gilchrist gave her his best blank look, but thought he knew where she was going with this. 'Any arrest in particular?' he said. 'Ma'am.'

'Blair Stevenson?' Her eyes burned. 'I'd like you to explain, DCI Gilchrist. From the beginning.'

So he told her, explaining how he'd noticed what appeared to be a domestic dispute while driving, and how he'd stopped to intervene. He emphasised how drunk Blair had been, and how he'd attacked Gilchrist for no reason other than the fact he'd interrupted his verbal abuse of his partner, Jehane Marshall.

'And you used no force in making the arrest?' Smiley said.

'No more than necessary, ma'am.'

'His skull was split.'

'Self-inflicted, headbutting my car's rear wheel.'

'I don't follow.'

He described it to her.

'His face and mouth were also grazed and cut,' she said.

'That happened in the scuffle to arrest him.'

'And you don't consider any of that excessive force, DCI Gilchrist?'

'No, ma'am. Only sufficient force to overpower him.'

'That's not what his girlfriend says.'

'His girlfriend was in the front garden in tears, and in no fit state to witness anything. I helped her to her feet and led her back indoors.'

'Did you take her statement?'

Bugger it. He'd taken notes, but hadn't asked Jehane to sign off on them because PC Tomkins had arrived and would take over. Or more correctly, because he'd been shivering from the cold and wet, and all he'd wanted to do was drive home, have a hot shower and change into dry clothes. Again he chose a safe answer. 'No, I didn't, ma'am.'

'Why not?'

'The van crew arrived within seconds of me calling it in, and they took over.'

'Really?'

He could tell from the glint in her eye that he was wading deeper. But now he'd started, he couldn't retreat.

'Within seconds, you say?'

'Minutes, more like.'

She took a sheet of paper from the files and said, 'Six minutes, to be exact.'

'If that's what PC Tomkins says, then I wouldn't want to argue with that, ma'am.'

'I'm not asking you to argue with it, DCI Gilchrist. What I *am* asking is for you to be honest and forthcoming when you answer my questions.' Another glare that reminded him of being pulled into the headmaster's office. If he'd been wearing short trousers, he could be there right now. 'Is that understood, DCI Gilchrist?'

'It is, ma'am. Yes.'

'Six minutes is not six seconds.'

'What I meant to say was that it seemed like—'

'After some consideration, I've decided not to assign a new SIO to this investigation, DCI Gilchrist. Chief Constable McVicar holds you in high regard, it seems.' She scowled at the file on her desk. 'But do I believe you? Or do I believe Blair Stevenson?'

He banked on it being a rhetorical question, so said nothing.

'Well I can tell you that I certainly don't believe Blair Stevenson.'

Not quite the affirmation he was looking for, but it was probably as close as he would come to receiving one from Smiler.

'Stevenson sees his threat of legal action as an easy way to make a few quid.' She lifted her eyes, and turned her hateful look his way. 'And I don't want him to succeed in that, DCI Gilchrist. Is that clear?'

'It is, ma'am, yes.'

She slapped the file shut. 'That'll be all for now, DCI Gilchrist.'

He thought of asking for a copy of the PM report, but it had been a long and tiring day, and there was nothing more he could achieve – with or without the report. Jessie could follow up with Cooper in the morning.

Without a word, he turned and strode to the door.

Outside, the car park at the rear of the Office sparkled with frost. Clouds had cleared to expose a gibbous moon more orange than white. The wind had dropped to little more than a breeze, as if that morning's storm had only been imagined.

He clicked his remote fob, and his car winked at him.

Seated behind the wheel, he thought over the events of that day.

Although his relationship with Chief Superintendent Tom Greaves had deteriorated, at least Greaves had known the physical difficulties that often had to be overcome when making an arrest. But Smiler seemed interested in doing things only by the book. Rules of arrest were all well and good, but in the heat of the moment when you were dealing with a threatening and overpowering drunk, you didn't hang around. You had to take the initiative.

Had he been too tough on Blair Stevenson? He hadn't thought so. But he would have to find out. Fife Constabulary's CCTV control centre was based in Glenrothes HQ, and headed by Mac Fountain.

He reached for his mobile. Said, 'Sorry to disturb you, Mac. But I need your help.'

CHAPTER 6

Fourteen years earlier
Portree, Isle of Skye

They didn't normally take a walk the other side of midnight, particularly when it was early March and raining, and certainly never when it rained as heavily as it was doing at that moment. In fact, when Norma thought about it, she and Bobby rarely walked anywhere together any more.

Which was so sad, as they used to be so much in love.

And not so long ago, either.

Had it been only eighteen months since she first thought she'd found the man of her dreams, the man she used to call the love of her life, her best best-friend ever, her soulmate? But something had changed in the last couple of months, or perhaps more correctly, Bobby had changed. And could she blame him? She had put weight back on, all the weight she'd lost for the wedding, and because of that, Bobby no longer found her attractive, she was sure.

But in her defence, she had never been a slim person, had always tended towards the tubby side of the equation. She'd told Bobby when they first met, that she was as slim as she'd ever been, that she'd forced herself on a diet of fruit and veg only, and small portions. But it was so hard to keep up – impossible to maintain, as it turned out – and when Bobby encouraged her to forget her diet, she jumped at the chance. You only live once, he'd said to her, and the first time they made love – for Norma it was the first time in four years, the main reason she'd gone on a diet – Bobby had told her that he much preferred a man's woman, a woman with a bit of meat in the right places.

Oh, how she had fallen for him.

But it turned out he had lied to her. Started complaining about cellulite on her thighs, and telling her to cover up her arms, wear this instead of that. After a while it began to affect her confidence, so much so that she stopped going out shopping. She would just phone the Co-op and have their weekly shopping delivered. Clothes, too, were ordered online, and mailed back when she found they didn't fit, or made her look too fat – nothing at all like the models in the ads. And nothing like some of the wives around the fishing village, who would give Bobby looks that could turn the head of a blind man.

That was when she decided to change her life, and reclaim the man of her dreams.

She bought herself an exercise bike and one of these skiing machines that toned the muscles on the arms and legs. She hired an architect to design an indoor gym – either knock down the walls between one of the six bedrooms, or add an extension. In the end, she decided to settle for extending the house, which was when Bobby learned of her plans.

And she had to say that his reaction surprised her. Instead of shouting at her, telling her she was wasting money, he warmed to the idea. In fact, he warmed to her, reminding her of how much he loved her and saying there was no need to spend all that money on a subcontractor to do the work. With him being a handyman, he would do most of the work himself. In the meantime, she could begin to recover some of her muscle tone by taking long walks.

Bobby was so encouraging, and so helpful, working around the house, buying in the food and drinks, preparing meals, serving up gin or vodka cocktails even when she thought she'd had one too many – you only live once, seemed to be his mantra.

Take tonight for example.

They'd shared a bottle of wine – well, somehow she had ended up having the bigger half – before Bobby made her one of his special cocktails. A Miami Whammy was what he called it. And she had laughed at that name. God knows what was in it, but it packed a punch for sure, and made her feel all wobbly and unable to think straight.

Chunks of her memory seemed to slip from her being, too. One second she was there, the next she was somewhere else without the faintest idea of how she'd got there. She could remember Bobby suggesting that they go for a walk together, that much was clear to her – but she had no recollection of putting on her raincoat and wellingtons, or leaving the house.

It just seemed as if she woke up from a dream, and . . .

Here she was.

'I'm tired,' she said.

'Just a few more steps, my dearest, and we can rest over here.'

His arms were around her shoulders, pushing more than helping her. She stumbled as she lifted her face into the hard rain, but Bobby was there to catch her. Oh my, what a storm it was tonight. She should never have agreed to go for a walk on a night like this. But Bobby said the rain would clear her mind – she had a vague memory of him saying that. The stiff wind felt good, so maybe Bobby was right. She took deep breaths, tried to clear the cobwebs from her mind, shift that darkening veil of sleep that threatened to overpower her.

But it all seemed beyond her.

'I think I'd like to go back home.'

'Here we go, my dearest. Just a couple more steps . . .'

Norma had no feeling of falling, only a distant sense of Bobby's arms no longer being there, and of the world tipping on to its side. Even her cry for help came out soundless, at the same instant she hit the water. The shock from the sea's ice-coldness struck her like a hammer blow, injecting her with a flurry of panic that had her struggling against the sodden weight of her raincoat and swamped wellington boots that as good as sucked her down into the mud slurry of the harbour floor.

Her last conscious thought as her brain began its terminal shutdown was a question.

Only one word.

'Bobby . . .?'

7.18 a.m., Friday
Crail, Fife

Snow had fallen overnight, a light coating that clung to Gilchrist's car like icing to a cake. He had no ice-scraper handy, so he fired up the engine and let it idle with the heater on while he returned indoors for a pair of gloves. When he sat behind the wheel again, the screen had defrosted enough to clear with a couple of sweeps of the wipers.

He slipped into gear and eased forward.

This was the time of year he disliked the most – dark mornings becoming darker as winter solstice neared. And this year, winter seemed to have kicked off with a vengeance. As he turned on to High Street South, the gauge on his dash read −5 degrees Centigrade, which only added to the feeling that it was time to have a holiday in the sun, time to soak up the heat in some quiet place where you could wear shorts and a T-shirt in the evening, without a shiver running through you. The thought that the middle of winter was still four weeks away had him cursing under his breath.

He had just cleared Kingsbarns when his mobile rang – ID Jessie.

'How's your flu coming along?' he asked.

'No worse than a hangover.' She coughed, and said, 'Just been reading the PM report emailed from Her Majesty. You seen it yet?'

'I'm heading to the Office right now.'

'I'm betting she was raped.'

The nape of Gilchrist's neck turned cold. Smiler had made no suggestion of sexual intercourse, even though Rohypnol was a known date-rape drug. 'Why do you think that?'

'Bruising of the buttocks, inner thigh and vagina, even though vaginal swabs showed no traces of semen. Of course, he could've worn a johnny', or the sea could have flushed it all out. Either way, there's nothing available for DNA.'

'Bruising of the buttocks?' he said. 'Like . . .?'

'Getting screwed from behind?'

'Well . . .'

'Rough doggie-style, you're thinking?'

'Well . . . no. I was thinking more of a beating, a kicking maybe, and not sexual.'

'Oh it's sexual all right,' Jessie said. 'No doubt about that.'

Something in the tone of Jessie's voice warned Gilchrist that he might not like what he was about to hear. He gripped the steering wheel. 'I'm listening.'

'Bite-marks. A nice set either side of the labia majora – or piss-flaps in layman's terms – as if he's taken a full mouthful and just . . . I don't know . . . tried to bite it off.'

'*What?*'

'Some serious bruising there, Andy.'

Gilchrist felt his breath leave him in a hard gush. 'Oh for fuck sake,' he said. 'She was *alive* when he did that?'

'Clearly yes, but from the levels of alcohol and Rohypnol in her blood, she was likely unconscious. At least I hope to God she was.'

Gilchrist reduced his speed and indicated left. He pulled off the road, bumped on to the verge and stopped. He checked the heat control – set at medium – but the cabin felt too hot. He took off his gloves and tore at his scarf, then opened the window and breathed in cool fresh air. He'd seen a lot in his time as a detective – battered faces, bloated bodies, writhing maggots – more than any one person should ever be exposed to, but rather than becoming inured to it all, he found it was affecting him now. The thought of some demented killer taking sexual pleasure from biting a woman's genitalia was beyond him.

Six cars passed by before he realised Jessie had gone quiet on him.

'You still there?' he said.

'You know, Andy, I hope to hell we catch this sick bastard, because I'm going to make sure I have the biggest set of secateurs money can buy, and I'm going to sneck his dick off at the roots.'

Not a bad idea, but none of this was helping them find the assailant. He forced his thoughts back into focus. 'Was the skin broken?'

'No. Just bruised.'

'Enough to ID this . . .' he wanted to use the C-word, the worst word he could think of, but in the end settled for '. . . this sick bastard from dental records?'

'Bite-marks on skin can be tricky to ID,' she said. 'But at Strathclyde we worked with a university professor – I forget his name – who helped us nail some sicko who'd been going around biting prostitutes' tits. But his bite-marks were distinctive: a couple of teeth missing, cracked incisor, that sort of thing. You want me to get hold of him?'

'Let me talk to Cooper first,' he said, and ended the call.

He kept the engine running, and stepped outside. The cold air did what it could to cleanse his mind of a sense of revulsion. His shoes crunched frosted grass as he walked around the boot. An iced wind swept over frozen fields sprinkled with patches of snow and ice. Bloody hell, it was Baltic. This winter seemed to be starting off worse than most.

He dialled Cooper's number. Seawards, the sun was still below the horizon, not up for another fifteen minutes, but already brightening the winter sky with hints of pink. Maybe it would be a good day, after all.

Cooper answered with, 'Have you checked your inbox?'

'I asked you to send me the PM report as a matter of priority.'

'I thought you'd assigned that task to your little Glaswegian terrier.'

'Look, Becky, I don't want to—'

'And I don't want to get caught up in the middle of your in-house fighting, Andy. Why don't you talk to Chief Superintendent Smiley? I'm sure Diane can give you a better explanation than I ever could.'

Cooper's reference to the Chief Superintendent on first-name terms surprised him, but he said, 'The victim was bitten.

I should've been notified immediately. We could have had someone on it, examining the bite-marks. Which is why I'm phoning.' It had been several years since he'd last sought the help of an expert in bite-marks, and it had not been a happy experience; the man had been a plonker, as it turned out. 'Didn't you tell me you went on a course somewhere on the identification and comparison of dental records to bite-marks, or some such thing?'

'I did, yes.'

'Well? Can you recommend anyone?'

She chuckled, and he could not rid himself of the feeling that she was laughing at him. 'I've already emailed contact details to you.'

He clutched a hand to his shirt collar as a gust of wind blew frosted snow across the road, stinging his face like sand. 'Anyone I know?'

'I couldn't say, but he lectures at Dundee University, and is well respected and highly regarded. His full professional name is Professor Raymond Harris, DDSc., MChD, FFGDP. I think I got all of that correct. But he answers to Ray.'

'Should all these letters mean something to me?'

'Only that he'll satisfy your requirements for a forensic expert in bite-marks.'

'OK, thanks, Becky.' He opened the car door to a welcoming blast of warm air from within. 'I'll give him a call when I reach the Office.'

'He's probably already working on it.'

Gilchrist frowned as he took his seat behind the wheel. Cooper's office was in the mortuary in Bell Street, within spitting distance of Dundee University where this Professor Harris

– call-me-Ray – lectured. Maybe Cooper and he were on speaking terms. 'Have you already contacted him?' he said.

'No need to.'

'What am I missing, Becky?'

'I thought you might already know,' she said, and trilled another chuckle. 'Ray and Diane are partners.'

For a moment, the coupling eluded him. Then it hit him. 'Diane Smiley?'

'The one and only.'

Gilchrist killed the call, and hurled his mobile on to the passenger seat. The tyres spun for grip on the verge as he floored the pedal, the sound of turf and earth splattering the underside only adding to his mood. He was being toyed with, being made a fool of, and he was damned if he was going to stand for it.

By Christ, he would make sure he didn't miss Smiler with this hit.

CHAPTER 7

As it turned out, Smiler had been called to a meeting with Chief Constable McVicar at HQ in Glenrothes and was not expected back in the North Street Office until late afternoon. Which was just as well, because by the time Gilchrist had driven through the pend into the car park, he would have been fired on the spot with what he'd decided to say to her.

But time has a habit of dowsing the fire of the wildest anger.

And so does a murder investigation.

Gilchrist threw himself deep into the task of trying to ID the dead woman.

He phoned Anstruther and secured more help in door-to-doors around St Monans, and assigned Jessie to oversee the teams. Jackie Channing, researcher extraordinaire and someone Gilchrist had come to rely on more heavily with each passing week, could find no matching fingerprint or DNA records in the PNC – Police National Computer – which meant that the dead woman did not have a criminal record on file, and was more than likely an innocent member of the public.

He spent thirty minutes going through Cooper's PM report,

which told him nothing new. The dead woman appeared to have been drugged, sexually abused, then throttled – in that order – before being dumped into the sea. Another review of the reported sightings did nothing to move the case forward, and he breathed a sigh of relief when Professor Raymond Harris returned his call and agreed to meet him mid-morning.

As it turned out, Harris was younger than Gilchrist had imagined – somewhere in his late thirties – with a strange style, too. A Beatles haircut covered his ears and forehead, and thick sideburns more suited to the nineteenth century covered his jawline, as if he'd grown a full beard then shaved off a two-inch wide strip under his chin. His grip was warm and dry, and lively brown eyes returned Gilchrist's look with professional confidence.

An image of Smiler and Harris as a couple simply failed to manifest.

In his office, Harris sat at a computer and clicked the mouse. The screen wakened to a tiled array of coloured images. He enlarged one, and a measuring tape next to a vagina filled the screen. 'If you look here,' he said, and ran a manicured finger along the labia majora, 'you can see indentations made by the top teeth.'

'You know they're the top, and not the bottom?'

'By size, and incisors. The top teeth tend to be larger than the lower.' He clicked the mouse, and the image leaped out at him. 'See there? That indentation's been made by the left incisor.' A couple of clicks and the screen shrank, then returned. 'And that, by the right. So we can tell which is up, and which is down.'

Other images came to life as Harris worked the mouse.

'On human skin,' he explained, 'it's always difficult to make an exact match due to the skin's elasticity. The crushing effect as the jaw closes can distort the bruising. Add to that the different textures of underlying tissue and you can see that it's not an exact science.'

'Can you draw *any* conclusions from these marks?' Gilchrist asked.

'I'd say they've been made by a man's set of teeth – wider than a woman's – but as to their use in helping you ID the assailant, I'd have to say they're more or less useless.'

Gilchrist frowned at the screen. The bruises might not be the clearest he'd ever seen, but they had to provide them with some information – size of the jaw at the very least, surely?

'Why useless?' he asked.

'They're too perfect.' Harris opened his mouth and ran a finger along his top teeth. 'I take care of my teeth,' he said, 'but over time, like everything else, they suffer wear and tear. This one's crooked, and this one juts out a tad. No one's teeth are perfect, particularly as one ages.'

'False teeth?' Gilchrist tried.

'Close, but no. I'd say these bite-marks were made by a set you might find as a teaching aid in the school of dentistry.' Harris reached out to a bookshelf and removed what looked like a set of plastic teeth – top and bottom – hinged with a spring to replicate the jaw opening and closing. 'Like these.' They snapped shut with a sharp click. 'Other sets might be designed to show over- or under-bites.'

'So we could be looking for someone in the dentistry profession?'

Harris shook his head. 'Not necessarily. You can purchase these online.'

Gilchrist almost groaned. Tracking purchases on Amazon or eBay or anywhere else that sold sets of teeth as training aids could keep Jackie glued to the screen for the rest of the year – provided they had been purchased online, or that Harris was correct in his assessment.

'Let me see?' Gilchrist removed the teeth from Harris's grip and opened and closed them to the sound of a click. It was possible, he supposed, to use these in the manner Harris described. But somehow, it didn't seem right. 'Why would you do that?' he said. 'Place them over a vagina, then squeeze them shut. Sexual pleasure? Sadistic satisfaction? Or what? I don't get it.'

Harris shrugged.

'There's no chance you could be wrong?' Gilchrist asked.

Harris tugged one of his sideburns. 'There's every chance I could be wrong. Someone somewhere could have the perfect set of teeth. It happens. But . . . I don't think so.'

Back outside, a grey sky sucked the heat from a wan sun. It could be a dead star for all the warmth it was providing. Before firing the ignition, Gilchrist checked for messages, but either everyone was busy, or had nothing to tell him. He exited the university parking and was about to enter the lane for the Tay Bridge when he decided to pay Cooper a visit in the Bell Street police mortuary.

He found a parking spot, then powered down his mobile.

Cooper greeted him with a nod of her chin and a slack smile. Not quite the welcome he hoped for, but he supposed she had to make the point that there was no way they would ever get back together. He thought she looked tired, as if she'd been up most of the night.

'Body's this way,' she said.

He followed her into the cold room.

To his left, the body of a young man, stiffened from rigor mortis, seemed to grapple the air with outstretched arms. On the next gurney, a woman's body with frizzled blonde hair lay on its side – at least he thought it was female – skin black and crisp like barbecued meat.

Cooper veered to the right, and unzipped a body bag.

Gilchrist placed a hand to his mouth and nose as a waft of putrefaction fouled the air.

Cooper seemed not to notice. 'I don't take kindly to being instructed to rush my PM examinations,' she said. 'It's how mistakes happen, or in this case, how things get missed.' She lifted the woman's arm. 'Where the skin was exposed, it suffered scrapes and cuts from being washed on to the rocks. Her jeans gave some protection to her legs and buttocks, but her torso and arms were scratched despite being covered by a woollen sweater.'

Gilchrist leaned closer. 'Missed, you said. As in, not included in your PM report?'

'I woke in the middle of the night,' she said, 'with this niggling feeling that I'd missed something. So I came in early and went through my notes again, then re-examined the body.'

'And found what you'd missed?'

'See here?' She turned the arm so that the palm was face up, then ran a finger along the skin. 'Numerous cuts and abrasions, the lack of bruising around them confirming they occurred post mortem.'

Gilchrist could only agree, although it seemed that the victim's body looked more battered than it had been on the rocks. Of course, breaker spray and spindrift in addition to poor light had not helped his initial examination.

'Not like the broken wrist,' Cooper said, 'which is swollen and bruised, the injury having been inflicted prior to death.' She pressed a finger into the woman's arm and said, 'And not like this, either.'

Gilchrist peered at a small bruise on her skin, no larger than the diameter of a pencil, close to the tip of Cooper's forefinger. 'From a needle?'

She nodded. 'I've gone over the rest of the body and found only one injection site.'

'Not a junkie, then?'

'Nowhere close.'

'You're thinking . . . maybe benzodiazepine?'

'More than likely, yes.'

'Like Rohypnol?'

'Yes.'

'But why not slip it into her drink?'

Cooper replaced the arm gently, laying it along the woman's side, then re-zipped the bag. 'Any number of reasons,' she said. 'It's one of the most common date-rape drugs and used to come in the form of a 2-milligram tablet that was clear when dissolved, making it almost impossible to detect in a spiked drink. It's since been reformulated to turn blue when dissolved in light-coloured drinks. Of course, if dissolved in a dark cock-tail it's again almost impossible to detect.' She shrugged. 'Or maybe she'd had enough to drink, and didn't want any more,' she said. 'Or maybe she didn't trust the man she was with. There could be a hundred different reasons for her assailant to resort to an injection.'

Gilchrist nodded. The fact that the date-rape drug had been injected into the woman's system, rather than being taken orally, did not change the thrust of his investigation. What it did do – when you also considered the vaginal bite-marks and her broken

56

wrist – was tell him that whoever killed this woman took pleasure from inflicting pain.

'You find anything else?' he asked.

Cooper shook her head. 'That's it, Andy.' She walked from the room. 'I'll email you a modification to my PM report. It should be with you by midday.'

On the walk to his car, he switched on his mobile and was surprised and pleased in equal measure to see that his son, Jack, had finally deigned to give him a call. When had they last spoken? A couple of weeks ago? Longer?

He could not say for certain.

Jack answered with his customary, 'Hey, man.'

'It's been a while,' Gilchrist said.

'Well, heh, what can I say, been busy, man.'

Gilchrist had never really understood how being an artist could keep his son busy, particularly when Jack seemed to spend most of his mornings asleep, and his waking hours in the pub. This side of midday could be an early rise, for all he knew. Still, he thought it best to play it safe with, 'That's good to hear.'

Jack chuckled, as if he knew his father's take on his profession. 'Got some good news,' he said. 'Jen's going to exhibit my work.'

'Who's Jen?'

'See? That's your detective mindset overriding your common sense again,' Jack said. 'Anybody else's old man would have said – Hey, Jack, that's great your work's going to be exhibited. And hey, when's it going to be shown?'

'But I'm not like anybody's old man, am I?'

'You can say that again, man.'

'Well, congratulations are in order, but I do need to ask – when and where?'

'One week's time in Jen's new studio on South Street. And she's keeping my stuff up for an entire month.'

Gilchrist wasn't sure if that was the norm for exhibitions, but could tell from the tone of Jack's voice that he was excited about it, regardless. 'So, does this mean you're going to buy a house with all your money, and settle down?' he tried.

'No way, man.'

Gilchrist chuckled along with Jack, letting him know he was joking, when his mobile beeped – ID Jessie. 'Listen, Jack, got an incoming call. But let's get together for a pint to celebrate. Get back to me with a time and place. OK?'

'Will do, Andy.'

Gilchrist took Jessie's call. 'Any luck?'

'Yes and no,' Jessie said. 'Got one teenager who lives in St Monans, name of Jock Fletcher, who says he's positive he's seen her around, no doubts about it. In the bar in the Mayview Hotel. But he doesn't know her name.'

'Did he talk to her?'

'Tried to chat her up, according to him.' Jessie snorted. 'Bumfluff City, for crying out loud. Young enough to be her son.'

'So he doesn't know anything about her?'

'The square root of eff all, I'd say. But he said his mate definitely knows her pal.'

'The dead woman's pal?'

'Yes. Says her name's Kandy. With a K.'

'Kandy who?'

'He doesn't know, but says his mate might know.'

'Have you spoken to his mate?'

'Not yet. He's just spent the night in jail for being drunk and disorderly. Does the name Alex Wilson ring a bell?'

It took a couple of seconds to make the connection. '*Lex* Wilson?' Gilchrist said. 'Wasn't he jailed for producing and distributing videos of young girls?'

'Which he still continues to deny.'

'And he's supposed to know who Kandy is?'

'According to Fletcher.'

Gilchrist grimaced. This sounded like wasted effort. 'Lex's word isn't worth a spit in the wind,' he said.

'Maybe so. But he's the only lead I've got so far.'

'Bugger it,' he said. 'I'm on my way.'

CHAPTER 8

Lex Wilson was in deeper trouble than Jessie had suggested, and was being held in custody pending his appearance at Kirkcaldy Sheriff Court on Monday. So they arranged to interview him in Anstruther police station.

Jessie sat next to Gilchrist, in charge of the recorder.

When the door opened and Wilson entered, Gilchrist almost gasped.

Five years earlier, he'd thought Lex Wilson was the ugliest man he'd ever seen. Since then, time had not been kind. Where his face had pockmarked skin as ruddied and bald as a whipped arse, several days' worth of growth dotted his cheeks and chin like white skelves. What little hair he had was yellow-white and greasy, and lay flat on a skeletal skull like strips of lard. Swollen bags under eyes as small as beads gave the impression of a man who hadn't slept in ten years.

'Well well well,' Wilson said. 'If it isn't Mr Gilchrist.'

'You've got to stop flashing your cock around town, Lex. You're scaring the locals.'

Wilson's mouth opened to reveal teeth as yellow as a sewer

rat's. 'What's the harm in that? I'm only airing my privates, that's all.'

It annoyed Gilchrist that Wilson was taking pleasure from what he perceived as shock value, so he decided to keep it short. He nodded to Jessie, who clicked on the recorder.

'We're going to record this interview.'

'Anything to save the trees, Mr Gilchrist.'

As a matter of formality, Gilchrist gave his and Jessie's name and rank, adding that Lex Wilson had, 'Agreed to be interviewed of his own free will. And I am obliged to inform you, that you do not have to answer any questions and are free to leave any time you like. But it would be helpful if you could assist us.'

'Always here to help my friends in Fife Constabulary.'

'Kandy,' Gilchrist said. 'With a K.'

'Oh yeah?'

'Oh yes indeed.'

'What about her?'

'I was hoping you could answer that.'

'Answer what? Youse huvnae asked a question.'

'Do you know her?'

'Yeah. Why?'

'Do you know where she lives?'

'Huvnae a clue.'

Well, it was worth a shot. 'When did you last see her?'

'A week ago. Why?'

'Where?'

'In the Mayview Hotel.' Wilson's eyes sparkled. 'Did some-body plug her?'

'Plug her?'

'Yeah, give her one against her wishes.'

'Why do you say that?' Gilchrist leaned closer. 'You know something, do you?'

Wilson backed off. 'See? This is why I don't trust youse lot. Youse're always trying to fit me up.'

Gilchrist raised his hands in surrender. 'Nobody's trying to fit anybody up, Lex. So why don't you stop asking questions, and just answer mine? That way, nobody'll get upset, and we'll be out of here in a jiffy. OK?' He waited for the hint of a nod then said, 'When you saw Kandy with a K in the Mayview Hotel, was she with anyone?'

'A boyfriend, like?'

'Anyone.'

'She had a mate with her. A right tidy bird. Slim. Nice shape.' He ran his hands over an imaginary waist and hips. 'Tits not too big, not too small.'

Which could be the woman on the rocks, or a good percentage of women in Fife.

'Stein fancied her rotten.'

'Stein? Who's Stein?'

'My mate, Jock.'

'Jock Stein?'

'Jock Fletcher. Stein's his nickname. After the Celtic manager, Jock Stein. Get it?'

Jessie opened a file and slid the E-fit of the dead woman across the table. 'Is this the right tidy bird Kandy with a K's mate with the nice tits?' she said.

Wilson's gaze slipped sideways as he took in the photo. 'Could be,' he said, 'but I widnae be sure. I wisnae paying *her* much attention. No my type. I prefer my coffee with nae milk.' He winked. 'If youse get my drift.'

Gilchrist caught the emphasis. 'Are you saying Kandy's of ethnic origin?'

Wilson sniggered. 'Of ethnic origin? I like that.' He leered at Jessie's chest. 'Kandy has a right pair of tits on her, too, with nipples like plum saucers.'

'How would you know?' Jessie said, which brought Wilson back to earth.

'She puts it about a bit.'

'Certainly not your way, by the looks of things.'

Wilson scowled and scrubbed his chin, as if stung.

Gilchrist said, 'So what ethnicity is Kandy?'

'Indian.'

'She here on a visa?'

'Naw, she's as Scottish as youse lot.'

'And she lives in St Monans?'

Wilson picked his nose, shook his head.

'I take it that's a Don't know.'

'Aye.'

'So, if we wanted to find this Kandy with a K,' Gilchrist said, 'where would be the best place to look?'

Wilson shrugged. 'Fucked if I know. Ask around. Somebody'll be plugging her.'

Despite Wilson giving them a basic description of Kandy – average height, neither fat nor thin, brown eyes, big tits – without a photograph or surname, they could be chasing shadows. The staff in the Mayview Hotel confirmed that several *ethnic* women drank there from time to time, but none of them knew a Kandy – with a K – or recognised the E-fit image.

'I don't think either of them are from here,' Jessie said.

Gilchrist nodded. Jessie was right. His murder investigation was going nowhere fast.

Back in St Monans, they spent the next hour being debriefed by each of the door-to-door teams. A number of locals thought they recognised the dead woman, but when pressed, seemed to lose confidence in their recall. The team assigned to the caravan park – WPC Anne Bryson and PC Craig Morton – confirmed that about one in four caravans were occupied, with the others locked up, and that no one they spoke to recognised the E-fit.

'Right,' Gilchrist said to Jessie. 'Get Jackie to make a list of the caravan owners – names, addresses, phone numbers, the works – and the names of recent and current tenants, short-term, long-term, holiday rentals, whatever. And get her to check the voting register.'

Then he turned to Bryson and Morton. 'Visit local property management companies, and see if they've got anyone from out of town on their books. Start with companies in St Monans, then move to Anstruther, and let me know how you get on by close of business.' He glanced at his watch – after 4 p.m. – and said, 'Make that midday tomorrow. So jump on it. We're looking for this woman, Kandy with a K, which can't be common.'

Jessie ended her call to Jackie, and faced Gilchrist. 'You know, I'm thinking that we're putting a lot of trust into Lex Wilson's statement.'

That was always the problem, relying on the statement of a petty criminal like Wilson, known by the local police for being drunk and disorderly and flashing his cock in public, not to mention a prior conviction for underage prostitution. Bloody hell. He could be leading them up a blind alley just for the sake of having someone to talk to.

'Don't think I haven't thought of that,' he said. 'If Kandy with a K lives around here, we'll find her. But if Lex is making her up, then he won't have to worry about being charged with flashing his cock in public ever again, because I'll have it *and* his balls deep fried.'

'Ouch,' Jessie said.

Then a sudden thought hit him, the clarity of its logic so simple that he wondered if his brain was losing its ability to join two disparate but coherent thoughts together.

He turned to Jessie. 'Kandy with a K?'

'That's the one.'

'And Jock Fletcher told you that?'

'Yes.'

'Why?'

She frowned at him. 'Because I asked him?'

'No. I mean, why – with a K? You meet a woman in a bar, you introduce yourself to her – and then what happens?'

'Are we talking about Jock Fletcher meeting Kandy with a K for the first time?'

'We are.'

'Well, let's see. If I was being chatted up by baby-face Fletcher, I'd say – piss off, and come back when you can grow a beard.'

'But what if Kandy didn't give him the cold shoulder. What would she have said?'

'Hi. I'm Kandy with a K—'

'That's it. Right there. You wouldn't say that. You'd say – I'm Kandy.'

'So how would he know it began with a K?'

'*Exactly.*'

One beat, two beats, then, '*Shit,*' Jessie said. 'She gave Jock a business card.'

'And if he got her name, he's got her address and number, too.'

'That wee bastard,' she hissed. 'He never mentioned that.'

'Give me directions,' he said, and slid in behind the steering wheel.

CHAPTER 9

But Jock Fletcher wasn't at home.

A young woman with jet-black hair and matching tights that covered anorexic legs answered the door – no wedding ring. Fletcher's girlfriend? 'He's probably gone to the pub to get pished again,' she said. Air as fetid as a blocked sewer pipe wafted down the hallway. A child wailed from the depths of the home. She turned and shouted over her shoulder, '*Shut it*, you. Or I'll bloody well gae you something to cry about.'

The child cried louder.

'Which pub?' Jessie asked her.

'Do I look like I'm a fucking psychic?'

'But if you were,' Gilchrist intervened, 'what pub would you put your money on?'

'The Ship.'

'In Anstruther?'

'And when you find that good-for-nothing drunk, tell him his dinner's getting served to the dug.' The door closed with a hard clatter.

But Jock Fletcher wasn't in the Ship Tavern. Or Legends. Or the Old Bank House either. They struck lucky in the Dreel Tavern, or more correctly, as they were searching for a parking spot. Gilchrist had just pulled off the road on to a tiny parking area that fronted the pub, when Jessie said, 'That's him,' and leaped from the car before it came to a stop.

Gilchrist followed, catching up with her as she grabbed a slip of a lad by the shoulder and brandished her warrant card. 'Hold it there, Jockie boy.'

Panic flashed across Fletcher's face. 'What the fuck . . .?'

Gilchrist said, 'Got a minute?'

'Do I have a choice?'

'You've always got choices,' Gilchrist said. 'Just don't make mistakes with them.'

'I done nothing wrong.'

'Is that a fact?'

Fletcher looked down, scuffed his shoes on the ground. When he next looked up at Gilchrist, his eyes had welled. 'Is it Lex that done me in?'

'Why would you think that?'

But Fletcher only shrugged his puny shoulders.

'We can talk here, or in the car,' Gilchrist said. 'Your choice.'

Another shrug. 'Here's fine.'

'Is the child yours?'

'Whit child?'

'The child crying its eyes out back home.'

Fletcher gobbed off to the side. 'Wee bitch trapped me.'

Jessie said, 'It takes two to tango, Jockie boy.'

'Aye, well, fuck that.'

'Lex said you chatted up Kandy with a K.'

Fletcher frowned. 'He would know, wouldn't he?'

'How come?'

'He'd shag anything that moved, so he would.'

'And you wouldn't?'

He sniffed, ran a hand under his nose.

'Why Kandy with a K?' Gilchrist said.

'How the fuck would I know?'

'Did she spell it out to you?'

'Naw.'

'Did she write it down for you?'

'Naw.'

Gilchrist waited for Fletcher to return his look. 'Be very careful how you answer this, Jock.' He held Fletcher's gaze until he sensed his bravado waver, then said, 'Did Kandy give you a business card?'

Fletcher's eyes flicked back to the ground. 'She might've.'

'No might have about it, Jock. She did, and I want to see it.'

'It's at home.'

'Where your girlfriend can find it?' Gilchrist shook his head. 'I don't think even you're that stupid, Jock. We can take you to the station and book you for obstructing a police investigation, or you can hand over the business card, and we'll leave you to continue searching for a pub.'

Fletcher's eyes widened at the sight of an escape route. 'Might be in my pocket.' He dug a hand into his jeans and removed a pile of loose change, crumpled banknotes and pieces of paper. He flicked through them, one piece of paper blowing off in the wind, then said, 'Here it is.'

Gilchrist took the dog-eared card from him and read the name.

Beneath the name, in bold print, a mobile number and website.

'Can I go now?'

'In a minute.' Gilchrist held the card out to Jessie. 'Pull up that website.'

Jessie tapped her mobile, and within seconds made the connection. She enlarged the image using her thumb and forefinger, then turned the screen to Fletcher. 'Is that her? Kandy with a K?'

'Looks like her. Aye.'

Gilchrist eyed the screen, saw the smiling headshot of an attractive Indian woman, eyes wide, teeth sparkling. He would put her somewhere in her late thirties, early forties, the same age bracket as the dead woman on the rocks.

Jessie said, 'Isn't she a bit old for you, Jock?'

Fletcher shrugged.

'So why would she give her business card to a nice young lad like you?'

'Told me what she did for a living and I pretended I was a writer.' He chuckled.

'Lex put you up to that, did he?' Gilchrist again.

Fletcher belched. 'Can I go now?'

Jessie said, 'I wouldn't go home. Your dinner's being fed to the dog.'

'Whit?'

'Beat it, Jockie boy, before I find something to book you with.'

Fletcher cantered off, shoulders hunched against an ice-cold wind, then vanished down a side street.

Gilchrist said, 'Is there a contact address on that website?'

Jessie scrolled down the screen. 'Doesn't look like it.'

'Call her number.'

Jessie did, but it failed to connect. She tried again. Same result. 'It's switched off or needs charging.'

'I'd bet the latter,' he said. 'Text Jackie. Give her Kandy's full name. We need her home address.'

As he opened the car door, his mobile rang – ID Mac. He answered it with, 'Give me good news, Mac.'

'Sorry, Andy. Can't help you. We're short of coverage in that area. And what we have is too distant. The recording's out of focus and more or less useless.'

Shit. Without photographic evidence of Blair Stevenson's arrest, Jehane's reversal of her account of events was as good as career-ending fodder for Smiler. He thanked Mac for his efforts, switched on the ignition and powered out of town.

They were driving past the Inn at Lathones when Jackie came back with an email to Jessie. 'Don't you just love her?' Jessie said. 'Manikandan Lal is a freelance copy-editor who works with numerous mainstream publishers and has written a number of self-help booklets—'

'Did she find an address?'

'Hang on, Mr Grumpy.'

Gilchrist eyed the road ahead. Locating Kandy Lal was key to his investigation. They needed to find her, talk to her, but her mobile number was unobtainable, which raised other, more troubling possibilities. Two friends – one dead, the other unreachable. You didn't have to be a genius to work out the obvious.

'Here it is,' Jessie said. 'Manderley Cottage,' and rattled off the street address.

Gilchrist tightened his grip on the wheel. 'You need to give me directions again.'

CHAPTER 10

Manderley Cottage was not a cottage *per se*, but one of a row of terraced houses just south of St Monans Holiday Park. Curtains were drawn on the dormer window. Ground-floor windows were dulled with sheer blinds. Gilchrist cupped a hand against the lounge window and peered inside. But night was settling, and the interior was too dark to make out anything other than a sofa that backed against the window.

'You see anything?' he asked Jessie.

She stepped back from the window on the other side of the front door. 'No lights on anywhere. She's not in.'

Gilchrist had to agree, but rang the doorbell anyway.

He let a minute pass before trying again.

'Maybe she's not back from work yet,' Jessie said.

'She's a freelancer. Wouldn't she work from home?' He stepped away, mobile in his hand. 'Check with the neighbours. See if they know where she might be, or if they can ID our woman.' He crossed the road, breath steaming in a frosted wind that felt as if it was chilling by the second. Night had not crept up on them, it had arrived with equatorial abruptness. Streetlights lined the road like ghostly sentinels, and a haar was moving in off the sea. It could be thick fog in a matter of minutes.

Jackie answered with her customary grunt. A civilian who worked from the Office and sometimes from home, she provided research services to Fife Constabulary. Cerebral palsy inhibited her mobility, but she could throw herself around the Office with surprising agility – *throw* being the operative word. But what stumped her every time was her stutter, which was so bad that she'd almost given up speaking. Between them, she and Gilchrist had devised a system to relay instructions to her.

She would recognise his number. 'Do you have a pen handy?' he said.

'Uh-huh.'

'I want a copy of the title deeds for . . .' he read out Kandy Lal's address '. . . and I need you to give me the name and phone number of the owner.' If it was a rental property the owner could grant them access if Kandy was out of the country – maybe in India, visiting relatives for all he knew. Once inside, he hoped to find a photograph or an address book, something that might help ID the dead woman. 'Text me as soon as you find anything. OK?'

'Uh-huh.'

'Thanks, Jackie. You're the greatest.' He gave a loud *Mwah* down the line, and felt a smile tickle his lips at the sound of her laughter. 'Catch you later,' he said.

'Uh-huh.'

He caught up with Jessie.

'Kandy's been living here for four years,' she said, 'but no one knows anything about her.' She scowled at him. 'I think it's to do with the colour of her skin. I mean, which century are we living in?'

'And the E-fit didn't ring any bells?'

'Nada.'

On the walk back to his car, he mentally summarised what they'd accomplished that day. But despite the early promise, he had to confess that it was close to eff all. He had just driven through Kingsbarns when his mobile beeped – a text from Jackie.

He handed Jessie his mobile. 'Can you read it out?'

'Title deeds are in the name of Manikandan Lal,' she said. 'Ten-year mortgage with RBS at four hundred and sixty-five pounds a month.' She read out the mobile number they already had from her business card and said, 'Doesn't really help us, does it?'

No, it didn't, but he kept his thoughts to himself, and drove on.

Back at the North Street Office in time for his debriefing, he wrote Lal's full Indian name on the whiteboard with her shortened name beneath it, adding *with a K*. He tacked her business card to the corkboard, next to a quality headshot, which Jessie had downloaded from her website. A smiling Kandy gleamed fresh-faced at him, and he prayed he was wrong.

He eyed his team. Despite the door-to-doors, no one had anything positive to report. It seemed that Lex Wilson and Jock Fletcher were not just their best bet, but their only one. He tapped the photograph. 'Kandy Lal. With a K,' he said. 'We need to locate her as a matter of urgency. She could be the last person to have seen our victim alive. We know where she lives, but her neighbours haven't seen her for several days.'

'About the same length of time as our victim's been dead, sir?' Mhairi asked.

Gilchrist had already thought of that. But it was too early to share fearful assumptions.

'Could be,' he said. 'But we don't know. So let's find her and ask her.' He scanned the faces before him, making sure he had their full attention before continuing.

'Kandy's a freelance editor and writer, so get on to all the publishing companies and magazines she's written articles for. Find out if she has a current deadline for any, and if so, what that article is. We might track her down if she's writing an article on pubs in Kirkcaldy, for example. You get the gist, I'm sure.'

The next hour was spent reading reports, looking for anything that might have been overlooked. But nothing jumped out at him. He'd tasked PC Morton with visiting Lal's home on the hour, but the latest report confirmed that her house was still unoccupied. This was leading nowhere with a happy ending. Why else would Kandy not answer her phone, return their texts, or respond to the string of emails they'd sent through her website? His dark thoughts were interrupted as Mhairi approached him.

'I've managed to track down the victim's sweater, sir. It was purchased in Frasers in Glasgow about three weeks ago.'

'Well done, Mhairi.'

'But it's not going to get us anywhere, sir. Looks like it was a cash sale.'

'Nobody uses cash nowadays, do they?'

Mhairi grimaced.

'How much did she pay for it?'

'Eighty-nine ninety-nine, sir.'

Bloody hell. The most he'd ever spent on clothing was his leather jacket, which had set him back just over three hundred quid. But that was aided by a rare win at the bookies – not that he gambled a lot – when a caddie in the Central convinced him to place money on Tiger Woods to win the Open at St Andrews.

So, who would spend that amount on a sweater? A high earner? Or a visitor from a foreign country where Scottish sweaters were valued, or where salaries were comparatively greater? And if she'd paid cash for her sweater, she'd probably paid cash for her jeans, too. So any leads he'd hoped to find from her clothing were dead in the water – so to speak. But the phrase *foreign country* somehow had him thinking of another possibility that seemed so basic, he wondered why they hadn't thought of it sooner.

'Follow me,' he said to Mhairi.

He was surprised to find Jackie still at her desk, so focused on her monitor that she jerked when she noticed him. 'I want you and Mhairi to work together,' he said. 'Tomorrow, make a list of travel agents and find any flight bookings in the name Manikandan Lal.'

'She might have arranged her flights online by herself, sir.'

'She could have, but let's tick the boxes. Travel agents first, then airlines.'

'Got it, sir.'

'OK, Jackie?'

Jackie nodded, her bob of rust-coloured hair bouncing as if on springs, her freckled face creased with pleasure. He'd seen less enthusiasm announcing a piss-up for the team in town. By contrast, he sensed stillness in Mhairi's posture, and he turned to catch Smiler standing in the doorway.

'You got a minute, DCI Gilchrist.'

'I do, ma'am, yes.'

She walked off without another word.

'Call or text me if you find anything,' he said, then followed Smiler's trail of perfume along the corridor and into her office.

Once inside, he was again struck by how little had changed, although he did notice the corner of a cardboard box on the floor at the side of her desk. She took her seat and motioned with her hand for him to sit opposite.

'I'll stand,' he said.

'Suit yourself.'

No love lost there. Which could work both ways. He tried to reinvigorate his emotions with some of the anger he'd felt earlier, but he'd been so caught up in his investigation and the possibility of Kandy Lal leading them to the identity of the victim, that all sense of earlier grievance had evaporated.

'What's the status of your investigation?' she said.

He spent fifteen minutes bringing her up to date, but chose not to mention that he'd met Professor Harris-call-me-Ray. Smiler had made no mention of any bite-marks last night, so he was interested to see how that would come to light, if at all.

When he ended his debriefing, she seemed pleased, offering a show of teeth for a split second. 'We shouldn't mention Ms Lal's name to the media, in case she turns out to have no knowledge of the victim. After all, you could be putting far too much faith in the word of a convicted porn dealer.'

He could not disagree, and gave a nod. 'Ma'am.'

She adjusted her writing pad, as if trying to align it with the edge of her desk, then looked up at him. 'You met my partner, Ray, I believe.'

'This morning, yes. Bit of a surprise,' he added.

'In what way?'

'That he'd already been asked to examine the bite-marks.' Gilchrist glared at her. 'I didn't particularly care for that, ma'am.'

She pushed her chair back as if to stand. 'When we met yesterday, DCI Gilchrist, you should know that I was undecided whether to let you continue as SIO or pull you off the case. Until I made my decision, I decided to take care of some matters myself, one being the bite-marks, bearing in mind that Ray is an expert. And another being your replacement.'

Well, there he had it. About to be kicked off to a flying start – emphasis on the *kicked off*. 'Anyone I know?' he asked.

'I had a meeting with the Chief Constable yesterday.' She smiled, a quick parting of her lips. But he saw no pleasure there. 'Like me, he had difficulty believing Blair Stevenson's complaint, that someone with your years of experience would resort to unnecessary violence while making an arrest. But we failed to agree on what course of action to take.'

Gilchrist almost held his breath. Was he being suspended, or not?

'The Chief Constable can be stubborn once his mind is made up, and not one to back down in the face of confrontation.'

'No, ma'am.'

'He's of the opinion that replacing you as SIO of such a high-profile investigation at this point of time would only be seen as a sign of weakness, an admission of guilt, as it were, and not something he would be willing to countenance. We've already received Stevenson's formal complaint, some legal firm in Cupar, can't remember the name. Not that it matters.'

'No, ma'am.'

'It's making its way through the system, so no doubt you'll hear from the Complaints and Discipline Department in due course. In the meantime, DCI Gilchrist, it looks as if you're still on the case.'

Well, well, well. Friends in high places, right enough. Smiler had wanted to replace him, but being new to the job had first sought approval, then been overruled. Greaves might have had his failings, but at least he'd been open and honest.

Gilchrist said, 'Will that be all, ma'am?'

'For the time being, DCI Gilchrist.'

He was about to leave her office when she said, 'For all our sakes, DCI Gilchrist, I hope Stevenson's formal complaint turns out to be unfounded.'

He nodded, and closed the door behind him.

CHAPTER 11

Rather than drive straight home, Gilchrist decided to have a pint in the Central Bar. A short walk along College Street, and he had a pint of Deuchars settling within fifteen minutes of leaving Smiler's office.

Halfway through his pint, he rang Maureen.

She answered on the second ring. 'Busy day?' she said, without introduction.

'And then some.'

'Tom and I had lunch in the Criterion.'

Bugger it. He'd completely forgotten. 'Sorry, Mo. I'm at the start of an—'

'You do have to eat, right?'

'Yes. But I skipped lunch.'

'How about tea?'

'That, too.'

'So you've had nothing to eat all day, is what you're saying?'

Not strictly correct. He'd had a slice of DS Baxter's leftover pizza. So, rather than wade deeper into the swamp, he said, 'How about tomorrow?' But Saturday could be a busy day at the Office. 'Or definitely Sunday?' he said. 'The Criterion – one o'clock?'

'That's what you said today.'

'Sunday's quieter.'

She said nothing for the longest moment, as if giving his words some thought, which helped him see how much she didn't trust him. If he was half the father he told himself he was, he would offer to take her and Tom out for a nightcap. But he'd had a difficult day, a long one at that, and all he wanted was to drive home and crawl into bed.

'OK, Dad. You promise?'

'I do.'

'I'll see you then.'

'Goodnight, princess.' But the line was already dead.

He whispered a curse. Of his two children, Maureen was the one who'd always been able to wriggle her way around him, make him do what she wanted, with a tongue that could cut steel, just like her late mother – cold and heartless when it suited her. Jack, on the other hand, seemed to have grown up all of a sudden, and was actually earning a living from his paintings now. More importantly, he was off drugs for good – if you believed him, that is.

Gilchrist pushed his half-finished pint away, and headed to the Office car park.

He was still a couple of miles from Crail when his mobile rang – ID Mhairi. He made the connection through his car's speaker system. 'You're not still at the Office, are you?'

'Yes, sir.'

'It's late.'

'I'm sorry to trouble you, sir, but I thought you should know that we . . . well, actually, Jackie did . . . she found a Ryanair booking to Tenerife in the name of Manikandan Lal.'

Gilchrist flexed his grip on the steering wheel. 'I'm listening.'

'But it was subsequently cancelled.'

'She never took the flight?'

'No, sir. She cancelled it. She didn't pay for the ticket.' A pause, then, 'Two tickets, actually, sir.'

Electricity zapped his spine. 'I'm listening.'

'One seat in the name of Manikandan Lal, and the other in the name of Alice Hickson. We've already run the name through the PNC, sir, and come up with a blank.' A pause, then, 'But we thought we should bring that to your attention, sir.'

Gilchrist lifted his foot from the accelerator, let his speed drop. The rain had stayed off and the road surface was dry, but his headlights barely pierced a thickening sea haar.

His thoughts could be as fogged as the road ahead.

If Alice Hickson was their victim on the rocks, and Kandy Lal was not returning their messages, did that mean both women were dead? But why book flights, then cancel them? Too many questions, not enough answers. So what next? Carry out a search of the Electoral Roll for Alice Hickson, DVLA records, too? But without a birthdate or home address, they could be searching for the proverbial needle.

'The booking,' he said. 'Any passport information on it?'

'No, sir, they just used Kandy Lal's address.'

'For both of them?'

'Yes, sir.'

Ah, shit. Something sank deep into his gut. If Alice was the woman on the rocks, and she lived at the same address as Kandy Lal, then it did not bode well for finding Kandy alive. Were they now looking at a double murder? But he needed more.

'They were planning to fly to Tenerife,' he said. 'So why would they cancel?'

'Change of heart, sir?'

He couldn't shift the thought that they couldn't take the flight because they were both dead. But he forced himself to think positively. Mhairi used the word *cancelled*. You didn't cancel your flight for the convenience of being murdered.

'Maybe they found a cheaper deal to some other destination,' he tried.

'That's a possibility, sir.'

'We could search the manifests for other flights to Tenerife.'

'*If* they went to Tenerife, sir.'

A big *if* at that, he realised. 'That could be our starting point,' he said. 'If nothing turns up, we could then search other Ryanair flights.' But even as he was speaking, the size of the task he could be setting his team ballooned in his mind's eye. How many daily flights to how many different holiday destinations? And why would he expect Kandy Lal to cancel a flight one day, then select another flight to somewhere else on the same day?

All of a sudden, the task seemed ridiculously man-hour intense.

He glanced at the clock on the dash – almost 11.30 p.m. 'It's getting late, Mhairi. You and Jackie head off home, and we can discuss this tomorrow.'

'I'm quite happy to make a start on it tonight, sir.'

'It's often better to sleep on some things. Tomorrow morning we can tackle the problem with a fresh mind.'

'Very well, sir. Thank you, sir.'

When the line died, he drove on, deep in the misery of his thoughts. Was Kandy Lal dead? Would searching flight manifests be an impossible task for a team of his size? Would doing that blow his budget in a matter of days, maybe even hours?

By the time he parked in Castle Street, and stepped into the bitter November chill, he was none the wiser. Off in the distance, the heavy rumble of surf broke the fogbound silence. Rose Wynd lay before him, curtained lights spilling into the night haar like warm mist. The grumbling of the surf and the stillness of the street seemed incongruous somehow, as if you could have only one, and not the other.

He slipped his key into the lock and shivered off a chill as he stepped inside.

After turning up the heat, he walked into his kitchen, removed a packet of dried cat food from the cupboard and opened the back door. In the far corner by his garden shed – even in the dimness of the night haar – twin pinpricks stared back at him. He strode down the path, shaking the carton, whispering, 'Here, puss puss.'

He owned a cat – if he could call it that – a long-haired moggy that he named Blackie after she'd turned up in his back garden six months ago, tail broken, black fur clotted, chunks of skin missing from her left side and front right leg. She'd been mauled by a dog, maybe a fox, and managed to escape – at least that was his theory – but despite his best efforts to befriend her, Blackie refused to let him any closer than six feet.

Unable to pick her up, and worried over her physical condition, he had called the vet to his cottage. But Blackie vanished before the vet arrived, as if she, too, had a sixth sense, and she didn't return that night, or the next. Not sure if she had gone for good, he continued to leave fresh food and water by his garden hut, and five days later he was relieved to find some food nibbled, and a wide-eyed Blackie peering out from the safety of the back of his shed. From that point on, he resigned himself to the fact that he had effectively adopted a wild animal as a pet.

He washed out both bowls using the garden hose as usual, then filled one with water, and the other from the carton. He eyed his shed and whispered, 'Here, puss puss.' But Blackie had either fled, or was watching him from some other safe and hidden spot.

Back indoors, he locked the door then went through to his lounge. He eyed what he jokingly called his cocktail cabinet – nothing more than a silver tray, left by mistake when his wife stomped from the marital home with both his children all those years ago – on which stood an assortment of bottles of Scotch. He was not a great whisky drinker, but enjoyed the occasional night-cap, or a cheer-me-up, particularly when the nights were long and cold. He glanced at the window, felt an involuntary shiver course through him. November nights were long and cold, so why not?

He switched the TV on to the BBC News channel, opened a bottle of The Aberlour, a Speyside whisky he'd first tasted at a gallery event last year – some of Jack's sculptures had been on display – and poured himself a measure.

He settled into his chair and took that first delicious sip, relishing the fiery bite as the whisky worked its way down his throat.

His mobile rang – ID Jessie.

He switched the TV to mute. 'Missing me already?'

'I wish,' Jessie said. 'Just found out through the Glasgow grapevine that my mother died earlier tonight.'

This was a first – Jessie mentioning her mother, even if it was to announce her death. Rather than pry, he said, 'I'm sorry to hear that, Jessie.'

'Aye, well, the bitch had it coming, I can tell you.'

'Do you know what happened?'

'No one knows for sure yet, but it's looking like murder.'

'What?' He pushed to his feet, placed the tumbler on top of the TV.

'Her body was found in Anchor Lane. Skirt up. Knickers to her ankles. A fucking whore to her dying day.'

'Jessie, I'm sorry—'

'Christ, you've no idea how fucked up our family was when I was growing up. And that bitch would hit us across the face with a leather belt. We were bloody kids. I mean, a leather belt?'

'Jessie.'

'I know Tommy and Terry are criminals and that, but can you blame them? They had to stand up for themselves. Christ, they were beaten at home, and beaten at school. Terry used to come home from school with a black eye every week—'

'Jessie.'

'Every week. Christ on a stick, I mean, can you imagine putting up with that? And what comfort did he get when he got home? None from that bloody bitch. Just another smack across the head with that leather belt. I had to get away. That's why I joined the police. Did I tell you that? No, I suppose not—'

'Jessie.'

'But I—'

'*Jessie*,' Gilchrist said, louder than intended. But it did the trick. The line went silent for several beats, making him think she had hung up, until he heard the scrape of a hand over the mouthpiece, thought he caught muffled mewing. He waited for her to come back to him, but realised she was through talking. 'Are you OK, Jessie?'

Silence.

He thought of just hanging up, but how could he do that when she'd called to seek his support? And if not him, who else could she speak to?

'Jessie,' he said, 'losing someone is never easy . . .'

'But I hate the bitch.' She sniffed, exhaled into the mouthpiece. 'For crying out loud, what the hell's wrong with me? Why am I crying over that fucking bitch?'

'Because she was your mother.'

'Who I *hated*.'

He let a couple of seconds pass, then said, 'You're upset over what could've been, Jessie. You had a rough start in life. And maybe your mother was to blame for that. But no matter how you remember her, she was the woman who brought you into this world, the woman who gave you—'

'She gave me bugger all, the *bitch*.'

'She gave you the chance to be a mother yourself.'

He waited for some cutting comment, but his words seemed to have settled her. So he pressed on. 'You had a terrible relationship with your mother. But because of that, you know what doesn't work, and you now have a great relationship with your son.'

She sniffed, cleared her throat, but said nothing.

'Robert loves you,' he said. 'And you love him. And he loves you because you're a good mother.'

Another sniff. 'I'm sorry, Andy. I'm sorry . . . I shouldn't have—'

'Yes, you should. That's what I'm here for.'

A pause, then, 'I can't believe how it's affecting me. It's just . . . it's . . .'

'It's normal,' he said.

'Jesus.'

'Your mother was a huge part of your life, without you ever realising it.'

'I'm not sure what I'm going to do,' she said, her voice stronger, more like the Jessie he knew. 'I mean, whether I should go to her funeral.'

'Sleep on it,' he said. 'You'll know what to do in the morning.' A few seconds went by, then he said, 'How did you find out?'

'Phone call from Strathclyde. A Detective Sergeant I used to work with.'

He thought silence as good a response as any.

'I'm sorry, Andy. Sir. It's late. I'll talk to you in the morning.'

'Take the morning off, Jessie.'

'I can't.'

'You can.'

The line filled with the rush of digital silence, then she said, 'G'night.'

'Goodnight.' He held on until the line clicked.

He switched off the TV and picked up his whisky. The mood for a nightcap had left him. Rather than decant it back into the bottle, he slid the tumbler into the fridge, the memory of his father's fearsome words – *whisky's a warm drink* – bringing a smile to his lips. He'd not had a good relationship with his father, far from it. Nothing like Jessie's with her mother, but his father had governed his home with strict Presbyterian authority – and look where that had got him.

He stripped off his clothes and washed the day's coldness from his skin with a stinging hot shower. He turned the heating down before slipping between the sheets, shivering at the smooth

88

cotton coldness. He picked up a notepad and pen from his bedside table, to jot down a few ideas for tomorrow morning's briefing.

But sleep pulled him down, and his last waking thought at the end of that long Friday was a memory of Jessie's mother shouting down at him from her Easterhouse home, the air almost sparking from the language, and her brother, Terry, rushing at him, eyes wild with drink and anger, muscled body tattooed as if dipped in ink.

And of Jessie sitting quietly in his car, tears welling in her eyes.

CHAPTER 12

Saturday
North Street police station

By mid-morning, Gilchrist's investigation was stalling. As predicted, checking manifests for flights to Tenerife and other destinations was proving to be a waste of manpower. Even though he had managed to pull in IT support from Anstruther and Cupar, the task of searching hundreds of holiday flights to hundreds of destinations seemed endless.

His first break came a few minutes before 1 p.m., when PC Sweeney took a call on the hotline number, and signalled for Gilchrist to pick up the other line.

'She kept saying, I know who she is, I know who she is, then she broke down. I'm sorry, sir, I can't make her out now.'

Gilchrist picked up his landline to the sound of a woman sobbing. 'This is Detective Chief Inspector Gilchrist,' he said. 'Who am I speaking to?' But the caller continued to sob. He asked again, more forcefully, but the woman was beyond listening. Then he turned to Sweeney. 'Can we get a fix on this number?'

'Already got it, sir. It's a mobile.'

Back to the phone. 'I want you to hang up,' he said. 'Do you hear me? I'll give you a call back in exactly ten minutes. Ten minutes. You got that?' He thought he heard her gasp something, but the connection was poor. Then the line died.

He replaced the handset in its cradle and faced Sweeney. 'Let's have it.'

'She said she picked up a British newspaper in a grocery store in Xàbia, saw the picture and recognised the woman. I know who she is, she kept saying. I know who she is.'

'So who is she?'

'I couldn't make her out.'

'And where's Xàbia?'

'Spain, sir. Mediterranean coast. North of Benidorm. Here, let me play the tape back for you.'

A woman's voice burst from the speaker – Scottish, was about all he could tell – and by the time his own voice cut in, he was none the wiser. He switched it off and said, 'Give me that number, including the international dialling code.'

Sweeney jotted it down.

Gilchrist pushed from his desk. He found Mhairi in Jackie's office.

'Xàbia, in Spain,' he said. 'Where's the nearest international airport?'

'Alicante, sir. My parents have been there.'

It seemed that everybody had been to Xàbia bar himself. 'See if Kandy Lal was on any flights to Alicante from Edinburgh or Glasgow. Start off with budget airlines. Let me know as soon as you have a hit.' It was a long shot, he knew, but he needed something to be done while he watched the clock tick off ten minutes.

He returned to his desk, sat down – six minutes to go – then got to his feet again. He filled a paper cone from the water cooler, drained it, then scrunched it up and threw it into the wastepaper bin. A quick look into Jackie's office offered nothing new, and he walked back to his office, where he flipped through a file. But his eyes scanned the words, while his mind took nothing in.

One minute to go – close enough. Making sure the recorder was on, he picked up his landline and dialled the international code, followed by her mobile number. He fretted as he listened to a phone ringing. Had he been too hasty in hanging up? Should he have stayed on the line until she pulled herself together? The line clicked as the connection was made . . .

To voicemail, and an automatic recording.

'Shit.' He killed the call and tried again.

Same result.

'Third time lucky?' he muttered, and hit the redial button.

The call was answered on the first ring. 'Hello?'

The connection was strong, her voice clear. 'This is Detective Chief Inspector Andy Gilchrist of Fife Constabulary,' he said. 'You called the hotline number. You can remain anonymous if you'd like, but it would be helpful if you could give me your name.'

'Manikandan Lal.'

He almost punched the air. 'How do you spell that?'

She rattled it off with a thick Scottish accent – Glaswegian, he thought.

'And your home address?'

She gave it to him – Manderley Cottage in St Monans. So far, so good. 'You were upset on the phone earlier,' he said. 'Can you talk now?'

'I think so, yes.'

He caught a slight tremor in her voice. He would have to stay in control, keep her talking, prevent her breaking down. 'You recognised the woman from a newspaper, you said. Do you know her name?'

'Alice Hickson,' she said, and spelled it out for him.

He pressed the phone hard to his ear. All the pieces were clicking into place. 'And how do you know Alice?'

'We're friends, she's a journalist . . .' a pause, then '. . . *was* a journalist.'

He carried on, keeping her focused. 'When did you last see Alice?'

'Monday night. We'd had a few drinks at my place, then she walked home. We were flying to Spain the following morning, and sharing a car to the airport.'

'Sharing a cab?'

'No. A car.'

'A friend's car?'

'Yes. Scott Black. Alice knows him. But I got a text from her in the morning, saying she'd make her own way to the airport and just meet me there.'

'Did you ask her why?'

'No. She's independent that way. I thought nothing of it.'

'And she didn't show up at the airport?'

'No.'

Something didn't fit. 'So you just flew off on holiday by yourself?'

'What could I do? I had my ticket. And she texted me again at the airport to tell me she'd fly out later that day.'

'Did you get any other texts from her?'

'No. That was the last one. I texted her, phoned her and emailed her, but I got no reply. I was worried sick. And then, when I saw her photo in the newspaper . . .'

He could sense she was about to lose it. 'That last time you saw her,' he said quickly, 'you'd had a few drinks, then she walked home.'

'Yes.'

'By herself?'

'Yes.'

'So she has a place of her own?'

'She rents.'

'Do you know where she lives?'

She gave him an address, which he jotted down, scribbled *search warrant* next to it, and passed to PC Sweeney.

'Was Alice married?'

'No.'

'Next of kin?'

A pause, then, 'I don't know.'

'No brothers or sisters?'

'I don't think so.'

'Parents alive?'

'I don't know.'

His rapid-fire questions were keeping her mind in focus. 'Was Alice in a relationship with anyone?'

'I don't know if you'd call him a boyfriend,' she said, 'but Scott sometimes did some work for her.'

'Scott Black?'

'Yes.'

Now he was getting somewhere. 'Do you have an address for Scott?'

'Not off the top of my head.'

'OK. You texted and phoned Alice. Can you give me her mobile phone number?'

'Oh no.'

'What's up?'

'My battery's low. I don't know how long I've got.'

Oh no indeed. 'Where are you staying? I can call your hotel.'

'I'm flying home tonight. I can meet you tomorrow if you'd like.'

'You got a pen and paper?'

'No.'

He rattled off the address anyway. 'It's the only police station in St Andrews,' he said, 'so you can't miss it.' He didn't want to mention the possibility of her ID-ing the body in case that set her off again, so he agreed a time of 11 a.m. the following day – Sunday – at the North Street police station.

The phone beeped.

Then the line died.

He pushed his chair back and smiled. He'd had more questions, but they could wait until the morning. At last he felt positive about his investigation, and he spent the next ten minutes replaying the recording, jotting down more notes in preparation for their Sunday-morning meeting.

He walked to Jackie's office, surprised to see Jessie, elbows on the desk, face to the monitor. She seemed her normal self, nothing like the woman on the phone last night. Catching his puzzled look, she said, 'Can't keep me away,' then nodded to Mhairi who handed him a printout.

'We got a hit on Manikandan Lal,' Mhairi said, 'on a return flight to Edinburgh from Alicante on easyJet.'

'She's flying back tonight,' he said.

Mhairi's smile evaporated. 'You already knew that, sir?'

'Just off the phone with her. We've got a meeting set up for tomorrow. She's ID-ed our woman as Alice Hickson. So well done, everyone. I've also got Alice Hickson's address, and have applied for a search warrant. We should have it later today.' He turned to Jackie. 'I want you to do a search for a local handyman. Scott Black. Start in St Monans. Then spread out if you have to. Work and home address, mobile number, the lot.'

'And Scott Black is who?' Jessie asked.

'Alice Hickson's . . .' He clawed the air. 'Boyfriend?'

'And the last person to have seen her alive?'

'That's what I'm thinking.' He brought them up to speed with his phone call with Kandy, ending: 'Alice was alive on Tuesday morning, because she sent Kandy a couple of texts.'

'Or someone sent them using Alice's mobile,' Jessie said.

'If they did, then that's our killer. But until we find that phone, we won't know.'

'You don't have a number for it, do you?'

'We got cut off before I could ask.' He raked his hair in frustration. 'Flat battery.'

'It's a woman thing,' Jessie said.

'Right,' he said, as Jackie waved at him. Her printer clicked alive and spewed out a single sheet.

He picked it up, a single mobile phone number for Black and a couple of addresses, one physical, the other a website for SB Contracting. 'Can you access the website, Jackie?'

She grinned, and nodded to her monitor.

'You've already got it up?'

'Uh-huh.'

'Well done,' he said, and squeezed her shoulder in appreciation. Then he leaned down to the screen and tapped *About* on the bar menu at the top of the page. 'Can you open that page for me?'

The screen shifted to half a page of text.

He ran his eye down it – generic contracting language: fences, walls, flooring, tiling, renovation – you name it, SB Contracting did it. He had Jackie access every page on the bar menu, but the website was basic, nothing but text in poorly written English, no hyperlinks, no photographs of previous work, and no images of the owner, Scott Black.

'How are you feeling?' he asked Jessie.

'Good enough to kick some contractor's arse.'

He handed Mhairi the printout. 'Chase up that search warrant, and contact me the instant you get it.' Then he walked to the door, Jessie beside him.

'I'm giving you directions again?'

'Got it in one.'

CHAPTER 13

Once Gilchrist hit the A915, he upped his speed to eighty.

Hedges, fences, grass verges whipped past in a dizzying blur.

Jessie sat silent, staring out the window, for once seemingly oblivious to the speed.

Gilchrist hadn't yet told her that he'd phoned DCI Peter 'Dainty' Small of Strathclyde Police first thing that morning. Not a big man – five six as best Gilchrist could recall – Dainty had gone on to carve out an impressive career for himself. He'd joined Fife Constabulary at the same time as Gilchrist, but then moved to Glasgow. They'd kept in contact, exchanging information as the need arose. And after Jessie's phone call last night, the need most definitely had arisen.

According to Dainty, Jessie's mother was a known user, and fresh needle-marks in her arms suggested hard drugs had caused her to overdose. Toxicology results to confirm exactly which drugs had not come back yet.

'But the fucking question is,' Dainty had said, 'were they self-administered?'

'You're thinking she was murdered?'

'The way she was found? One breast hanging out, underwear down to her fucking knees. I'm thinking she'd been posed to make it look like a sexual attack gone wrong.'

'What about CCTV?'

'Fucking everywhere. But half the bastards are battered to fuck. We're doing the necessary, calling in favours, checking out what's what.'

'Any suspects?'

Dainty lowered his voice to a conspiratorial whisper. 'Our difficulty is that Jeannie Janes was on closer than speaking terms with big Jock Shepherd, if you get my meaning. If she's been dumped in the lane to get back at Jock, we could be filling up the morgue by the middle of next fucking week.'

'What about Tommy and Terry?' Gilchrist had asked, and been assured that Jessie's criminal brothers were under the watchful eye of Strathclyde Police. He had ended the call by asking Dainty to contact him if he found anything. Another look at Jessie warned him it was best to keep quiet about his call to Dainty.

At least for the time being.

They had just passed the turn-off to Cameron Reservoir when Jessie turned from the window. 'Life's just like one never-ending uphill struggle,' she said.

'And then you die?'

She coughed out a laugh, a bit forced, he thought. 'My family's fucked up, and I've done what I could to keep them away from Robert. My bitch for a mother tried to contact him when I first came up to St Andrews. Nothing to do with wanting to see him, more wanting me not to have him. That's the twisted rationale of a psychopath. But it was always at the back of my mind that Robert might meet her somehow, and she'd get her hooks in.'

'But she's gone now,' Gilchrist offered.

'But Tommy and Terry are still around.'

Gilchrist eyed the road ahead.

She blew her nose, then said, 'I'd always thought that if that bitch would just pop her clogs, then I wouldn't have to worry about Robert if anything happened to me, because my family would be out of his reach, and the world would be bright and rosy.' She coughed, and said, 'How wrong can a woman be?'

Silent, Gilchrist drove on.

'I can't imagine what it must be like not being able to hear your own voice, or any music, or a crowd roar when a goal's scored.' She wiped a tear from the corner of her eye. 'Or hear your wee mum tell you – I love you.' Her voice broke at that, and Gilchrist eased his foot off the pedal, and let his speed drop to the forties.

About a mile farther on, he glanced across at her, saw cheeks damp with tears. He'd known Jessie for about a year now, but she'd never allowed him into her private life, only letting the odd snippet slip here and there. But something seemed to be troubling her, nothing to do with her mother's death, he thought.

'Is Robert OK?' he tried.

'Not really.'

'What's happened, Jessie?'

'No, no, nothing's happened. It's just that nothing's ever going to happen.'

He thought he could guess the problem, but approached with care, just in case. 'His operation's still on, isn't it?'

'Therein lies the problem.'

'Bloody hell, Jessie. Don't tell me it's off.'

'Got it in one. That plonker of an ENT consultant that Robert and me met last year? Turns out he knows the square root of eff all. The useless wanker.'

'I thought you'd gone through all the tests—'

'I thought so, too. But Robert had a pre-op assessment last week which confirmed that his hearing nerves are dead.' She pressed a hand to her mouth. 'They're now saying they never developed from birth, the ones that connect the cochlea to the brain. Without them, it's like trying to make a phone call without a connection.'

'I'm sorry, Jessie.' It was all he could think to say.

'They've cancelled his operation,' she said. 'There's nothing they can do. My wee boy's going to be stone deaf until the day he dies.'

He negotiated a couple of bends, then said, 'How's Robert taking it?'

'I haven't told him yet.' Tears spilled from her eyes. 'And I don't know how I can.'

Gilchrist looked over, wanted to say something, but found himself lost for words.

Jessie turned away, back to staring out the window.

Silent, he drove on.

St Monans is about thirteen miles due south of St Andrews, situated on the Fife coast overlooking what is effectively the Firth of Forth – almost ten miles wide at that point. It was a few years since he'd last visited the small fishing village, which on a clear day offered views across the dark waters to North Berwick, on the coast east of Edinburgh.

That day, grey skies hung low, hugging a weather-beaten horizon that might not have seen the sun in weeks. Gilchrist listened to his Satnav as he navigated the narrow streets of the old Scottish village.

As it turned out, the offices of SB Contracting consisted of a cottage that sat close to the sea. The front garden had been replaced by brick pavers that were in need of a weed-killing exercise, and doubled as parking space for a dark blue 1990s Land Rover Discovery and a rusting trailer, on which sat a small day-sailing yacht, twenty foot long, at a guess, with a cuddy cabin and retractable daggerboard, and a 40hp Evinrude outboard motor.

The driveway was narrow, and they had to squeeze between the garden wall and the Land Rover to gain access. A glance through the passenger's window revealed a dust-ridden seat covered with plans and drawings, and a footwell packed with a toolkit that displayed chisels, screwdrivers, saws, a pair of leather gloves.

The vestibule lay open to a glass-panelled front door through which Gilchrist could see the length of a bright hallway. He rang the doorbell, and stood back as a well-built figure walked towards him.

The inner door opened to reveal a bearded man with thick black hair, 1970s-style long, and wide shoulders that almost filled the doorway. 'If you're selling, I'm not interested.'

'Scott Black?'

'Yeah?'

Gilchrist introduced himself and Jessie, showing their warrant cards, and asked if Black could answer a few questions that might help them in an ongoing investigation.

'Sure,' he said.

Gilchrist nodded to the yacht. 'You take it out often?'

'Now and again.' Black stepped outside on to the pavers. Although he stood the same height as Gilchrist, six-one, where

Gilchrist was slim to the point of skinny, Black's build gave the impression that he was used to hard work.

Strong hands, too, Gilchrist noted.

'You take it out any time last week?' he asked.

'In all that bad weather?' Black shook his head. 'Seas were too rough.' He cast his gaze seaward, his thick hair ruffling in the wind, and Gilchrist had a sense of narcissism, of a man knowing he was handsome, adopting an affected posture to show off his best features.

'So that's a No,' Gilchrist said.

'I'm a fair-weather sailor, Mr . . .' He turned to Gilchrist.

'Gilchrist. DCI Gilchrist.'

Black smiled, showing white teeth as even as a dentistry teaching aid. 'I only take her out in the summer,' he said, 'and even then only when the seas are calm.'

Gilchrist was intrigued by a twin line of weeds in the brick paving that appeared to have been flattened by wheels rolling over them. 'Looks like you've had the trailer out in the last few days.'

Black followed Gilchrist's gaze and said, 'Got to clean the Evinrude for the winter.'

'So you pull the trailer all the way out the driveway just to do that?'

'I give everything a final going-over. The outboard, the trailer, the wheels, the tow-hitch, the lights. Preparing it for the winter months.'

'It's cold enough to be winter now,' Gilchrist said, and ran a hand over the outboard motor's casing. 'You didn't do a good job at cleaning,' he said, and held up his thumb and forefinger, rubbing salt between them.

'Chased back indoors because of the weather. Besides, it's in the air.' Black inhaled deeply, as if to prove a point. 'Living by the sea, saltwater gets everywhere.'

'It certainly does.' Gilchrist turned to Jessie.

'Alice Hickson?' she said to Black.

Black looked down at her. 'What about her?'

'You know her?'

'I do, yes.'

'When did you last see her?'

Black bared his teeth, sucked air through them with a grimace. 'Sunday?' he said.

'Asking or telling?' Gilchrist said.

'Sunday for sure.' He narrowed his eyes at the horizon again. 'I went to her home to finish a job and collect payment.'

'Collect anything more than payment?' Jessie again.

'Like what?'

'You tell me.'

Black smirked at her and Gilchrist stepped in with, 'Finish what job?'

'Skirting board in the kitchen. Had to be replaced due to water damage.'

'Insurance claim?'

'Preventive maintenance.'

'Anybody see you?' Jessie said.

'See me?'

'Yeah. Anyone who can corroborate your story?'

Black didn't rise to Jessie's close-to-the-bone snipes. He shrugged. 'Neighbours, I suppose. But Alice keeps herself to herself, so I really couldn't say.'

Gilchrist noted the present tense – *keeps* – and had a sense of

Black telling them more than they asked for, and all for effect. 'Do you know Alice well?' he asked.

'Not really. Just see her from time to time.'

'But well enough to know she keeps herself to herself,' Gilchrist said, 'and well enough to offer her a lift to Edinburgh Airport.'

Black never so much as flinched. 'Not *offer*. I was going to charge them for the lift. Not as much as a regular taxi. But I'm a businessman, and a businessman has to make a living.'

'Them?' Gilchrist said.

'What?'

'You said you would charge *them* for the lift.'

A hint of uncertainty slid behind Black's eyes, as if he were only now seeing Gilchrist for the first time. 'Alice and her friend,' he said.

'Does the friend have a name?' Jessie asked.

Black held her look with a stare of his own, then his face relaxed into a slow grin. 'What is this?'

'Do you watch the TV?' she said.

Gilchrist added, 'It's been on all the news channels.'

'Don't watch the news,' Black said. 'Nothing but doom and gloom.'

Jessie stepped closer. 'You never told me Alice's friend's name.'

'Kandy Lal,' Black said.

'You do work for her, too?' she asked.

'From time to time.'

'Like what? More preventive maintenance?'

Black's smile widened. 'As I said, the saltwater gets everywhere.'

'So you drove her to Edinburgh Airport last week?'

'Yeah.'

'Without her friend?'

'Yeah.'

'In the Land Rover?'

'Yeah.'

'Your Land Rover's in good condition,' Gilchrist said.

'Want to buy it?' Black chuckled, as if amused by the change in tack.

Gilchrist ran a hand over the tow-hitch, intrigued by a shiny glint of worn metal where the trailer had ground against the tow-bar, which confirmed – at least in his own mind – that Black had moved it recently. But to do what? Not to have it cleaned. He thought he knew that much.

'You had the trailer long?' Gilchrist asked.

'Couple of years. Bought it from a local. *Sundancer* came with it.'

'*Sundancer?*'

'My yacht.'

Gilchrist gave a tight grin, and nodded with his chin to the Land Rover's cabin. 'Is that a dashcam?'

Black nodded. 'You get an insurance rebate if you have one of those.'

'Linked to your computer, is it?'

'Wi-fi.' As if that explained it all.

'Where do you launch *Sundancer?*' Gilchrist asked. 'Once the weather clears up?'

'Down by the harbour. There's a concrete ramp.'

'Just back up and float her off?'

'Yeah.'

Gilchrist turned to the trailer. If he half-closed his eyes, he could imagine a waterline on the metal. And spots of white that clung to the wheel-rims like dried salt. He leaned down, ran his fingers over them, rubbed flakes of dried salt off. 'Down by the harbour, you say?' He pulled himself upright.

'Find what you were looking for?' Black said.

Gilchrist returned Black's firm look with a friendly stare. 'Getting there,' he said, then turned to Jessie. 'Do you have any other questions you'd like to ask Mr Black?'

'No, I think he's pissed me off enough for the moment,' she said, and walked back to the car without another word or a backward glance.

Gilchrist was conscious of how close Black was standing to him, almost cornering him against the end of the trailer. Not exactly *in his face*, but his personal space was being violated. That close, he felt the warmth of Black's minty breath. Red veins in the whites of his eyes suggested a night of little sleep.

'Thanks for your time,' Gilchrist said, and made to step past him.

But Black didn't move.

Gilchrist didn't think it appropriate to push him out of the way. 'Do you mind?'

'There's nothing stopping you from walking around me.'

'No, there isn't, is there?' he said, and gave Black a wide berth as he headed to his car. When he fired up the ignition, Black was still staring at him.

He chose to ignore Black as he reversed up the narrow street.

But it was too much for Jessie, who gave a toodle-doo wave and a deadpan smile, and muttered, 'See you later, dickhead.'

CHAPTER 14

Gilchrist parked in a half-empty car park and switched off the engine.

'He's lying to his back teeth,' Jessie said. 'See him posing like a haddy? And the way he looked at my tits?' She let out a hard gush of breath. 'Give you the bloody creeps.' She opened the door, pulled her scarf around her neck as a gust of wind whipped in off the sea. 'What is it about the east coast?' she snarled. 'Is it closer to the North Pole or something?'

Gilchrist followed her as she stomped her way down the concrete ramp.

At the water's edge, the harbour air was thick with the heady stench of fish, kelp, oil, petrol. The water lay flat and still. A fishing boat puttered towards the open sea, spluttering water, trailing grey exhaust. Gulls strutted the harbour walls, some stretching their wings like fledglings, others pecking at spilled rubbish from an overturned bin.

'And did you see him?' Jessie said. 'Face to the wind. Flexing his muscles like he's God's gift to women. Christ,' she hissed, 'I hate bastards like that.'

'I'd have to say he was handsome in a rugged sort of way.'

'I've seen better-looking chimpanzees.'

'So you'd turn him down if he asked you out?'

She smiled at that, and it struck him that he'd not seen her happy in days. But it didn't last. She scowled at the ramp, the concrete walls, the frothy scum on the water, the industrial detritus of a busy harbour.

'Is this where he would launch his boat?' she said.

Gilchrist eyed the ramp. Rusted rails ran like tramlines into the water. To the side, an expansive concrete area permitted boat owners to back their trailers to the water's edge. He remembered as a teenager helping a friend's father pull his dinghy from the sea. The wind had been blowing, the waves choppy, and the dinghy had a 75hp outboard. But what he remembered most about that day was how difficult it had been pulling the boat from the water. Single-handedly, you would have to be strong to launch a yacht the size of Black's from a pier like this. And Black was strong.

'Could be,' he said.

Jessie looked at the harbour buildings. 'I don't think so. Not here. Too many houses and people around. Not exactly Sauchiehall Street, but it's too open. Even in the middle of the night, someone could see him.'

In the short time he'd known Jessie, he'd found her intuition to be second only to his own. But you couldn't make an arrest based on intuition. 'So you're thinking what I'm thinking? That he was the last person to see Alice Hickson alive, and took his boat out during the storm last week to dump her body?'

'His story about cleaning it for the winter doesn't wash, excuse the pun.'

'We'll ask around, find where else you could launch a boat.'

'Maybe we should just get a warrant to give his excuse for a yacht a thorough search. The SOCOs could put the whole thing to bed in a matter of hours.'

Gilchrist had already thought of that. Black was someone he would want to talk to again, no doubts about it, but it was all too soon, the link too tenuous, to throw limited resources into a forensic examination of Black's boat and his premises. 'Let's see what Hickson's place turns up first.' He called Mhairi for the status of the warrant.

'Just had it signed off,' she said. 'Was about to call you, sir.'

'Meet us there,' he said, 'while I drum up a joiner to help us gain access.'

Ten minutes later, they stood at Alice Hickson's address, a cottage on the outskirts of St Monans, within sight of the caravan park. A look through the windows revealed no broken furniture, shattered glass, pools of blood, or anything that would permit them to break down the door in advance of the warrant – just a tidy home with a tidy garden, at the end of a quiet cul-de-sac.

Jessie whistled. 'It's bloody brass monkeys out here.'

'Thought you said the fresh air would do you good.'

They both turned to the sound of a high-revving engine as a white van raced down the street towards them. It screeched to a halt at the end of the cul-de-sac, the driver not quite judging it. Its front wheels mounted the kerb with a hard thud. A quick tyre spin had the van reversing on to the road. The driver's door opened and a young man wearing paint-spattered overalls stepped out. Shorn head, tattooed neck and studded ears gave the impression that he was a painter-decorator only just freed from jail.

He strode towards them, carrying a crosscut saw. 'S'is it?' he said.

'Thought I'd called for a joiner, not a painter,' Jessie said.

He held up the saw like a rifle. 'S'is look like a paintbrush to you?'

She turned to Gilchrist and said, 'Does this look like a joiner to you?'

Gilchrist ended the verbal tussle with, 'We're still waiting for the warrant. So it'll probably be another five minutes.'

The young guy flexed the saw like a weapon. 'I can get youse in right now.'

'I'm sure you can,' Gilchrist said, 'but we need the warrant.'

'Suit yoursels. Youse're on the ticket anyway.' He ran a hand down the edge of the front door, then peered in the gap by the lock. 'S'no deadbolt. Youse're in luck.' And with that he returned to his van, wobbling the blade, and slid in behind the wheel.

Gilchrist thought he was going to drive off, until the hard bass beat of some reggae music spoiled the country silence.

'Is it just me?' Jessie said. 'Or are kids becoming thicker?'

In response, Gilchrist phoned Mhairi. 'Where are you?'

'Just driven through Pittenweem, sir. So I'm almost there.'

Gilchrist ended the call and said to Jessie, 'Another few minutes.'

Jessie slapped her hands together and blew into them. 'We could always get Wonder-chippy to let us in before the warrant arrives. Wouldn't be the first time,' she said.

He and Jessie had entered premises before without a warrant, but had always agreed on their story before doing so. But he was reluctant to do so in this instance, not because the joiner had

111

already arrived, but because Smiler was still an unknown quantity.

Ten minutes later, Mhairi arrived in her Vauxhall Vectra.

'About bloody time,' Jessie said. 'My feet are like ice. Let me check on the DJ in the van.'

Mhairi walked up the path and said, 'Sorry, sir. I took a wrong turn.'

'Not a problem.' He read the search warrant, making sure it had the correct name, address and reason for issue, then stood back as the joiner took over.

'Here youse go.' He slipped the blade of the saw between the door and the frame, and slid it down and out. The lock clicked, and he pushed the door open. 'S'stupid no having a deadbolt. Don't even need a saw, so youse don't. Any bit of flat plastic'll do the trick.' He presented Gilchrist with a slip of paper and a pen. 'Sign here, and that's youse done and dusted.'

Gilchrist did.

The van's tyres were spinning before Gilchrist had his latex gloves on.

When he stepped inside, the first thing that struck him was the heat. A check on the thermostat in the hall gave him his answer. He turned it down to 20 degrees, walked into the kitchen, and noted the new skirting boards, surfaces planed smooth and glistening with clear varnish.

The second thing that struck him was the cleanliness of the place, the air redolent of lemon and floral spray, as if Alice had been an OCD freak. The stainless-steel sink shone like new. A finger along the windowsill pulled up no dust. A mug tree held six ceramic mugs that looked as if they'd never been used. He opened a kitchen drawer to reveal rows of shining knives, forks, spoons.

The next drawer down contained stacks of plates, teacups, saucers. Pots and pans were hidden in a small cupboard.

He picked up several days' worth of mail from a tight space behind the front door, where it had been shoved when they had entered. Mostly generic advertising, the usual stuff punted through letterboxes to try to persuade you to buy something you didn't want, or need. But strangely, or so he thought, not one letter – eleven in total – had Alice Hickson's name in the address line.

Two were addressed to The Occupier, four to Mrs Susan West, two to G. Bray and three to Mr K. Bradford. For one confusing moment, he wondered if they were in the wrong house, then realised that in a coastal village, the cottage would have been rented out over the years, and that these names more than likely belonged to previous tenants.

But why no Alice Hickson?

Because she hadn't been living here long enough?

And if not, for how long? Days? Weeks? A couple of months?

He had no way of knowing, and made a mental note to ask Kandy Lal when they met in the morning. He walked through to the lounge. 'Anything?'

Mhairi said, 'It's strange, sir. I don't know about you, but I'm getting the feeling that the house has been professionally cleaned.'

Jessie entered from the rear hall. 'Two bedrooms, never been used by the looks of them.'

'This is where Alice Hickson lived, right?'

'According to the records, yes.'

'Any computers, laptops, mobile phones?' he said. 'Chargers? Anything?'

Mhairi shook her head. 'Not yet, sir.'

'Well, let's find them,' he said, as a thought struck him. 'If she was going on holiday, where's the suitcase, the carry-on luggage, the handbag, the purse? And how about holiday clothes?'

The house was not large, consisting of a kitchen, two bedrooms, living-cum-dining room, one bathroom, and a small hall that led to the back door. The furniture looked like it had been purchased from IKEA – modern, plain-coloured, easy-to-assemble flatpacks. Ten minutes later, each of them had come up empty. For all intents and purposes, the house could have been cleaned and prepped, ready for a new rental. Other than the mail crammed behind the door, they found nothing. Even the wardrobes in the bedrooms were empty except for wooden hangers hooked over the rails. The bathroom cupboards, too, were bare – sink and WC sparkling, shower room clean and dry, toilet-roll holder with a full roll of paper.

At least the *Mary Celeste* had evidence of having been abandoned.

Maybe Kandy Lal could provide the simplest of explanations in the morning.

Outside, darkness had settled and a mixture of rain and snow whipped the air, as if nature was doing what it could to depress his mood. But the day had not been a waste, far from it. Scott Black had come across as a potential suspect and with a boat he said hadn't been to sea in recent weeks. The SOCOs might have something to say about that. And Kandy Lal was on a flight from Spain, and would be in the Office in the morning.

'Do you want me to put tape across the door, sir?'

Doing that might attract unwanted attention, he thought. 'No need, Mhairi. Just close it. It should lock itself.'

Mhairi pulled the door shut, then tried the handle – locked.

As he followed Jessie and Mhairi down the path, Gilchrist's mind was working, deciding on his next step. He would have Jackie carry out a search on Scott Black, see what she could find on the man. But it was comforting to know that Jessie's intuition was in tune with his own.

When they next met Black, he would be better prepared.

CHAPTER 15

Ten years earlier
Oban, west coast of Scotland

Janice threw back another flute of Bollinger '95, then reached for the bottle again. She sploshed some over the new granite worktop as she filled up her third glass – or was it her fourth – who was counting and what the hell did it matter anyway? – struggling against the surge of her rising temper. And oh God, how it was rising. Penny had warned her, not once, not even twice, but over a dozen times, for God's sake. But oh no, she had known better. She was in love with James, madly so, deeply so, like a love she'd never experienced before, and she so desperately wanted to marry him.

'It's your second marriage,' Penny had told her. 'And it's too soon after Bernard's passing. If you love James, time will tell. There's no reason to rush into marriage, darling. Trust me, Janice. I love you, too, but have you considered you're marrying each other on the rebound?'

That was the word that stuck in her craw the most – rebound – and almost ended their friendship. Rebound? She was in her thirties – well, just turned forty – old enough to know her own mind, for God's sake.

And by God did she tell Penny that. They didn't speak for four weeks after that confrontation, and when they made up, one night at a dinner party James had laid on as a surprise for her, no expense spared, she'd since felt that Penny never quite trusted her, that some part of their friendship, that special part that made some friends so much closer than others, had simply evaporated.

But Penny had been right, and she, Janice the know-it-all, Janice the lover who had found her soulmate, was wrong.

Oh my God, how she was wrong.

She took another sip, almost finished the flute, and had to take a couple of deep breaths to try to settle her nerves. It was no use getting too drunk to speak sensibly, or getting over that limit that she'd seemed to be exceeding more frequently of late, because tonight was the night she was going to tell James it was over, that she'd made a mistake, one of the gravest mistakes of her life. She'd loved him once, she would tell him that, soften the blow that way. But he'd changed since they'd married. They both had. That's what she would say. Even in those short eighteen months since they had first set eyes on each other at a summer buffet, as if drawn to each other by pure chance – although she had always harboured an uneasy suspicion that James had targeted her that day – her feelings had moved on.

James had shown a side to her, a dark side that he'd kept hidden and which . . . well, quite frankly, frightened her. But in his brighter moods, there was no one quite like James. He was loving, considerate, gentle, kind – like he had shown himself to be the last couple of weeks, as if he'd known she was reaching the end of her tether, that something needed to change, and he would have to make amends to correct it.

This evening, for example. The surprise bottle of Bollinger, her favourite, and the reservation at the Highland Hotel, for no reason other than to tell her that he loved her.

117

But it was too little too late, and she would tell him that.

She sipped her flute, dribbled some down her chin – how had she managed to do that? Oh dear, and where was her handkerchief? She turned in surprise as James entered the kitchen, and tried to look up at him. But her head was too heavy all of a sudden, and her eyesight seemed blurred. And what on earth was he wearing? She gave out a tiny chuckle, tried to tell him that he looked ridiculous, as if he were ready to paint the house.

Then his hand was on her shoulder – why was he wearing gloves? – and a glass was placed in her hand. 'There you go, my dearest. Drink this. It'll make you feel better.'

She tried to resist, tried to say No, but for some reason her arms had no strength. She felt so tired, so damned tired all of a sudden. She didn't need anything else to drink. He must have sensed her resistance, but the glass pressed to her lips regardless, her head tilted back, and liquid as tasteless as water slipped down her throat.

'There there, my dearest. Go to sleep now. You'll feel better in the morning.'

'Sleep,' she managed to say as her head lay against the cold kitchen tiles, and the light faded like the sun setting on this mid-December night, becoming dark, and darker still, until all that was left was the tiniest spark of light in the centre of her vision.

Then . . .

Complete and utter blackness.

Silent and solid.

11.30 a.m., Sunday
North Street police station

Jessie had already called Edinburgh Airport and confirmed that last night's flight from Alicante had landed on time and that

Manikandan Lal had been on the flight manifest. But Kandy hadn't turned up for their eleven o'clock meeting.

Jessie said nothing as DCI Gilchrist dialled the number for the fourth time, only to be dumped into voicemail again. He slapped the handset on to the cradle. 'That's it,' he said, and jumped up from his chair.

She managed to keep up with him as he skipped down the stairs and opened the door to the car park at the rear of the Office. She slid into the passenger seat as he fired the engine and accelerated on to North Street as if his life depended on it. She never liked to see her boss this frustrated, but she knew from experience that you messed with him at your peril.

And Kandy Lal was messing with him big time.

'There might be a simple reason she's not turned up,' she said. 'Maybe she got pished on the flight and is in bed nursing a major hangover. I've done that before.'

As if to show her what he thought of that, he accelerated past a Mini Countryman dilly-dallying at walking speed, indicated right, then sped down South Castle Street. She thought of reminding him that South Castle Street was for access only, then decided against it.

'I should've pulled Black in for questioning yesterday,' he said.

'Well you can pull him in for questioning this morning. And at the speed you're going, that could happen within the next thirty seconds.'

He smiled, a flash of white teeth. 'Sorry,' he said, and eased his foot off the pedal.

'So, talk to me,' she said. 'What are you thinking?'

'It's – I don't know. Kandy Lal was so upset when she called the hotline yesterday. I mean, she should've been gagging to meet us

119

this morning. And now we can't reach her? Something's not right.'

Jessie had to agree. It certainly was odd. 'You know what I'm thinking?' she said. 'If Black ran Kandy to the airport, he'd probably arranged to pick her up from her return flight.'

'Exactly,' Gilchrist said. 'And he must have known about it when we met him. Which is why we need to pull him in for questioning today. Try Kandy's number again.'

Jessie did, but it kicked her into voicemail. 'Nada,' she said.

Gilchrist clenched his jaw and upped his speed to seventy.

They had just thundered past the intersection with Station Road when Jessie's mobile buzzed. The incoming number came up on the screen – 0141, a Glasgow number – so she made the connection with a firm, 'DS Janes.'

'This is DCI Joe Donaldson from Strathclyde Police, DS Janes. I'm the SIO on the investigation into the death of your mother, Jeannie Janes.'

Jessie had the vaguest recollection of having met Joe before – freckled face, a tad on the plump side, sandy hair as tight as wire, and a lopsided smile, the result of having his jaw broken while trying to make an arrest.

'DS Young told me he'd spoken to you,' Donaldson said. 'I'm sorry for your loss.'

Jessie said, 'Thanks for that.'

'But I'm afraid I've got some more bad news for you.'

A cold hand swept the length of her back.

'It's your brother, Terry,' he said. 'He's been involved in an altercation and been taken to hospital. He's critically ill.' A pause, then, 'He's currently undergoing emergency surgery, but we've been advised that he's not expected to survive. I'm sorry, DS Janes.'

120

Jessie dabbed her eyes, embarrassed by the nip of tears. What the hell was this about? Why the tears? She couldn't remember the last time she and Terry said a kind word to each other. They'd never been close. They might have had the same mother, but that was it.

'What happened to him?' She was conscious of the car slowing down, the indicator ticking.

'Several stab wounds to the chest. He's lost a great deal of blood. I'm sorry, DS Janes, but I don't think he's going to make it.'

'OK,' she said. 'That's it, then.'

'I'll let you know as soon as I hear anything, but in the event your brother passes, we would ask you to make a formal identification.'

Jessie felt a flush of anger. 'What for?' she said. 'Get my other nutcase of a brother to do that.'

'That's where we have a problem, DS Janes. We believe it was Tommy who stabbed Terry. We have CCTV footage of him leaving the scene, but we can't find him. We now have an All Ports alert out for him. He's on the run.'

'Oh for fuck sake,' Jessie said. 'I can't do this right now. Not right now.'

She killed the call, aware of the car pulling off the road, slowing on to the grass verge, drawing to a gentle halt. Then a warm hand holding hers.

She pulled free, opened the door, stumbled outside, fell on to the grass. Water seeped through the knees of her tights, squeezed through her fingers. She looked up at the sky, surprised at the sleet stinging her face. Her vision darkened, and she couldn't seem to pull in enough air. She turned around, sat on the wet grass, and looked up as Gilchrist approached her.

Then his hands were on her arms, gripping her biceps, hauling her to her feet. 'Over here,' he said, and she was aware of the stone wall being hard and uneven, and a cold dampness seeping through her backside.

'Head down. Deep breaths.'

She did as she was told, conscious of the motion of his hands on her back, rubbing warmth into her, just the way she used to do with Robert as a baby. A beeping sound came from somewhere by her ear, and on automatic she tapped her pocket for her mobile.

'It's mine,' he said.

'Take it. I'll be all right.'

He did, said, 'Andy Gilchrist,' then walked to the front of his car. The engine was still running. It would be hot inside. But just that thought sent a spasm to her stomach, and she slumped on to her knees and threw up – once, twice, then a third time, which seemed to do the trick. She wiped her hand across her mouth, cleaned her fingers in the damp grass, aware of Gilchrist returning.

She struggled to her feet, flapped his hand away. 'I'm all right now,' she said. 'Just took a funny turn there. Don't know what came over me.'

He stood by her as she took a couple of deep breaths and blew them out.

'Must've been something I ate.'

'I heard most of what was said.' He held her gaze. She thought he looked sad as he returned his mobile to his pocket. 'That was Dainty,' he said. 'He's just spoken to DCI Donaldson.'

'The man gets around.'

'Donaldson didn't get a chance to explain it all to you.'

122

'Yeah, well, I wasn't up for it at the time.'

'Are you up for it now?'

She trusted Andy. He would not be pressing her if he didn't think what he had to say was important. 'Let's have it,' she said.

'I'll tell you on the way,' he said, and helped her into the car.

She smiled as he opened the door and she took her seat again – his way of making sure she was sitting down when he told her. Still, she'd had the worst of it all by now, she was sure of that. She clicked on her seatbelt and waited while he walked around the bonnet, then got inside, behind the wheel.

When they'd gone about a mile or so, he said, 'It's to do with your mother again.'

'Don't hear from her in months, and now she's making a bloody nuisance of herself.'

He smiled at her silly joke, then said, 'And Tommy.'

'A match made in hell, let me tell you.'

Gilchrist's lips tightened for a moment, then he said, 'Dainty asked me to let you know that they suspect Tommy was involved in your mother's death, too.'

A surge like an electrical jolt powered through her. For a moment, her world seemed to stop, and she heard herself say as if from a distance, 'Tommy? They think Tommy killed her?'

'Not for sure,' he said. 'They need to find Tommy first, and question him.'

She stared out at the countryside. Fences, bushes, hedgerows passed by in a grey blur. Time could have stopped, or be speeding up, she couldn't tell, but her memory retrieved stop-start images of herself as a child, when she and her brothers were innocent children, before all this hatred, before the world turned the years on, before they grew up into criminals . . .

'I can drive you home, if you'd like.'

'Let's keep going,' she said. 'I'd probably open a bottle of plonk too early for the good of my health.' She tried a laugh, but it sounded forced, even to her ears.

'Any idea where Tommy might have gone to?'

'How the hell would I know? I haven't spoken to him in years.' Then she turned to face him. 'Is that why Dainty called? To ask you to find out if I knew where Tommy might run off to? Bloody hell, Andy. I thought you knew me better than that.'

Several silent seconds passed, before Gilchrist said, 'That's not it at all, Jessie.'

'Yeah, sure it isn't.'

'Listen to me. It's important you understand what's being said here. Dainty's far from stupid, and he's thinking that if Tommy killed his mother, and then Terry, well . . . you don't have to be a rocket scientist to work out that you might be next on his list.'

She turned to Gilchrist, searching his eyes and mouth for any hint of a joke. But he was deadly serious. She placed both hands to her chest, gripped the seatbelt tight, and held on to it. 'Bloody hell, Andy. Is this really happening?'

He eyed the road ahead. 'I'm afraid so.'

CHAPTER 16

Gilchrist rapped the letterbox, then held his finger down on the doorbell. From deep within, a melodic ringing echoed back at him. He held it down to the count of twenty, then tried the letterbox again, rattling it against the frame.

Jessie pulled her face back from the living-room window. 'She hasn't come home.'

Gilchrist kneeled and peered through the letterbox, but saw nothing except the inner door, its lack of glass panels casting the vestibule into darkness. He stood up and stepped into the middle of the narrow street. The dormer windows still had their curtains half-drawn. The house looked no different than it had last night.

'Let's see if any of the neighbours heard anything,' he said. 'I'll try this side.'

He pressed the next-door's doorbell, and was about to press it again when the door opened with a sticky slap. He flashed his warrant card at a haggard woman, rollers wrapped to her head like a protective helmet. 'Your neighbour, Ms Lal, was flying home last night from holiday. Did you hear her arrive?'

'Sorry, son. I widnae've heard a thing once I took out my hearing aids.'

'Does anyone else stay here with you?'

'Naw, just me and Erchie.'

'Is Archie here?'

'I widnae waste your time, son. Erchie'd had a few in the Mayview, being Saturday an' that. And once he's had his tea, that's it. Off snoring for Scotland.'

He thanked her, and tried two more doors – same result. No one had heard a thing.

Jessie walked back to him, shaking her head. 'I don't think she's turned up.'

He phoned Mhairi. 'Check that Ryanair manifest again, and see if Kandy Lal really was on that flight from Alicante.'

'Already done that, sir. She was.'

'Pull CCTV tapes from Edinburgh Airport. If she was on that flight, we need to track her.' He ended the call. 'Right,' he said to Jessie. 'Let's see what Scott Black has to say about this.'

The drive to Black's cottage took less than five minutes, but even before he parked, Gilchrist knew something was wrong. He stepped into the cold sea air and eyed the brick-paved driveway. The Land Rover and trailer with its day-sailing yacht were both gone.

'So much for being a fair-weather sailor,' Jessie said.

'I don't think he's taken it out for a sail.'

The temperature felt close to freezing. An easterly wind whistled in off the sea. The Firth of Forth could be a black canvas dotted with white specks. In a matter of hours, they could be battling a gale-force storm, or as weather forecasters say in Scotland – *a light breeze with some scattered showers*. No wonder whisky was downed by the gallon.

'Check the front door,' he said, and pulled out his mobile as Jessie strode up the path. When Mhairi answered, he said, 'Put out an All Ports for Scott Black, and place a trace marker on the PNC. Dark blue Land Rover Discovery. You got the registration number on file?'

'I do, sir, yes.'

'His yacht's gone, too. So check with the coastguard and other harbours for a white yacht called *Sundancer*. He can't have gone far.' But even as he spoke, his mind was working out the hours from yesterday to the present, multiplying the answer by fifty – which could be a conservative average speed if it was all motorway driving – and reached the conclusion that if Black had left shortly after they'd called on him, and driven through the night, he could already be in France.

As he watched Jessie walk away from the front door and push open the gate that led to the back garden, he added, 'And apply for a warrant to search Black's home.' He gave her the address. 'Then contact Colin and tell him to get his team ready for a forensic investigation. Get the IT techies on to Black's website and see what they can come up with. And send copies of Kandy Lal's headshot to all forces in Fife, Tayside, Lothian and Borders, Central and Strathclyde. We need to find that woman.'

On the off-chance that Black had only moved his boat to storage for the winter, he asked for Black's mobile number, then dialled it. But as the connection was being made he knew he was wrong.

The number you are calling is no longer in service.

Well, there he had it. He ended the call, slapped the roof of his car. How stupid had he been? How fucking stupid to have let Black slip through his fingers like that. He looked up as Jessie reappeared through the garden gate.

'He's gone,' she said. 'Place is locked up. Looking through the windows, I'd say he's gone for good, and left in a hurry.'

'Ah, fuck.' Gilchrist strode to the end of the street and faced the sea, letting the wind and the freezing rain batter his face as punishment. And how he deserved to be punished. He wanted to scream to the sky, and curse at the top of his voice. They'd had him. *He'd* had him. He'd had Scott Black in his hands, and ignored his gut feeling, that sixth sense of his that had helped him over the years.

Just *fucking* ignored it.

Now Black and Lal were both missing, and you didn't need a sixth sense to know that the outcome didn't bode well. And he was to blame. 'Ah *fuck*,' he shouted, and stomped back to Black's cottage.

Jessie registered the look on his face. 'What are you doing, Andy?'

He reached the front door, and removed his wallet. A quick look around to confirm no one was watching, then out with a credit card, into the gap, pull it down, press it through a bit of resistance at the lock, then . . .

'*Voilà*.' He opened the door.

'Warrant's on its way?' Jessie said.

'I'm concerned over Kandy Lal's well-being,' he said. 'There might be something in this property that could give us an insight into where Black has taken her.'

'That'll work,' Jessie said, 'although I'd like us to agree that we won't disturb a thing until we have the warrant.'

He handed Jessie his car keys. 'Stay outside, and keep an eye open. Only one house has a direct view of this door.'

'Back garden's different,' she said. 'Keep away from the rear windows.'

He slipped on a pair of latex gloves, entered the house and closed the door behind him. He was taking a risk. Without a search warrant, any evidence he happened to find would be deemed inadmissible. But if he argued that he believed Kandy Lal's life had been in danger, that might possibly mitigate the damage.

In the hallway, he heard nothing, and walked into the lounge.

A grey phone sat on a side table. He picked it up – dead. He replaced the receiver, ran his gaze along the lead to the wall connection. It looked OK, so it was possible that Black never used a landline, but phoned exclusively on his mobile.

He walked to the middle of the room.

Jessie was correct. Black had left in a hurry.

A wooden coffee table with several drawers opened squatted in the corner of the lounge. One of its drawers had been pulled right out, its contents strewn on the carpet – table mats, carry-out menus, electrical leads, a webcam with a clip for fixing to the screen of your computer, and . . . an old Nokia mobile phone.

He was no expert in mobile phone technology, but knew enough to access the SIM card. He slid the plastic cover off the back, and whispered a curse.

The SIM card had been removed.

Well, what had he expected? A signed confession?

He replaced the Nokia on the floor, then entered the kitchen. A peek into a poorly stocked fridge suggested that Black must eat out, or have food brought in. He depressed the waste-bin's pedal and the lid opened to reveal a pizza box and a foil carton from an Indian takeaway.

Upstairs, he entered Black's bedroom. He knew it was Black's bedroom, because the other two bedrooms had a funereal look to them; they smelled of dust and polish, single beds made up as if no one ever slept in them.

But Black's bedroom was a mess.

Bedsheets lay scattered on the floor, alongside a crumpled bath towel and a bathrobe that had seen better days – too threadbare for Black to take with him? The bathroom was cluttered with toothpaste, toothbrush, soap, all items that could be purchased anywhere, anytime. But they could provide good DNA samples, so it was important that he and Jessie secured a formal search warrant, and followed protocol.

Back to the bedroom.

The wardrobe lay open, clothes ransacked, empty hangers strewn across on the floor. The bedside table, too, had been pulled from the wall, revealing a skirting board covered in dust. A single drawer lay upturned on the carpet. He was about to return downstairs when he glanced out the window at a panoramic view of a sandy beach and grass-covered rocks, beyond which lay the black waters of the Firth of Forth.

It was not nature's beauty that stilled him, but the sight of an abandoned trailer.

He ran down the stairs and out of the front door, making sure to secure it behind him.

Jessie looked up from her mobile, and he signalled for her to follow him.

She caught up with him as he stepped on to the beach. 'Anything?' she said.

He nodded ahead. At that level and angle, the trailer was out of sight, and he realised Black had abandoned it there in an attempt to hide it. 'Black's trailer.'

Jessie squinted against the wet wind. 'Where?'

'Along here.'

By the time the trailer came into view, they had walked over two hundred yards along the beach. Windswept dune grass offered some cover at ground level, but from the way the trailer had rammed into the sand, it looked as if it had been parked there with force. Tyre-marks and deep ruts caused by spinning wheels confirmed that Black had launched his yacht, then reversed his trailer into the dunes.

Which begged the question, where was his yacht?

'You sure this is the trailer?' Jessie asked.

Gilchrist ran a hand over the wheel rim, the same wheel he'd checked out yesterday – black paint peeling off red lead primer where rust was setting in. He then walked to the rear of the trailer and scraped his shoe across the sand, and deeper still until he uncovered the number plate. He had an excellent memory for numbers, and nodded when he read it.

'This is it,' he said. 'Looks like he's abandoned it, and we're supposed to think he's sailed off into the horizon.'

'And do what?' Jessie said. 'Beam up his Land Rover?'

'Maybe he had someone help him.'

'And maybe he thinks our heads zip up the back.' She glared at the sea. 'He's done a runner, Andy.'

Gilchrist could not disagree. Scott Black was a loner. He thought he knew that much. But launching a yacht singlehand-edly in waters as rough as these – small as the craft was – would take some strength. Yesterday, the sea had not been as wild as it was today, but even so. 'I'm thinking he backed the trailer into the sea when the tide was in,' he said. 'Then locked the yacht's tiller, fired up the outboard, and let it go.'

'He couldn't have done that without getting in it, could he?'

'Once he'd set it on its way, he'd jump overboard and swim ashore.'

'So what's that going to hide?' she said. 'It'll eventually turn up somewhere.'

'Not if he's punctured the hull.'

'To destroy evidence?'

'Alice Hickson's DNA, I'd say. From dumping her overboard.'

'Possibly Kandy's, too?'

Gilchrist felt his heart slump. It really didn't bear thinking about. If he'd acted sooner, none of this would have happened. Black would be in custody, and Kandy Lal would still be alive. He shivered off a sudden chill. He could surmise all he liked, but that wouldn't get him anywhere. Black had got rid of his yacht and abandoned his trailer.

The key now was to find the Land Rover Discovery.

He phoned Mhairi. 'Any hits on Black's Land Rover?'

'Nothing yet, sir.'

'We need to up the search for it,' he said. 'If you haven't already done so, run the registration number through the ANPR. We need to find it as soon as.'

When he ended the call, Jessie said, 'A horrible thought's just occurred to me. If Black collected Kandy Lal from the airport last night, she might be on that yacht.'

Gilchrist found his gaze drifting seaward. If Kandy had been killed, or drugged and tied up inside the yacht, Black would have scuttled it, taking Kandy to the bottom of the Firth of Forth. But he found himself shaking his head.

'Too risky,' he said. 'The sea's too unpredictable. And if his yacht was found with her body on board, there's only one person we would go after.'

'So where is she?'

'That's what we have to find out.'

He gave a brief smile, then walked back along the beach.

Ice-cold spindrift rose off the waves like mist. He struggled to lift his mood. By going on the run, Black had shown his guilt. Gilchrist felt as though he could take that positive point from today's work, at least. But it didn't help. His whole being was leaden with the thought that they were already too late to help Kandy.

Way too late.

CHAPTER 17

On the road back to the North Street Office, Gilchrist had just driven past the entrance to Stravithie Castle when his mobile rang – ID Mo.

'You forgot,' she said. 'Didn't you?'

Gilchrist sucked air through his teeth. Bugger it. Their lunch appointment at the Criterion. What could he tell her? His usual excuse that he got tied up at work was now so lame it was beyond the point of recovery.

'I'm sorry, Mo,' he said. 'But what are you and Tom doing right now?'

'We've already eaten, Dad.'

'But I haven't.'

She let out a heavy sigh. 'You said you'd meet us today. For lunch. Which means at lunchtime. Not four o'clock in the fricking afternoon.'

'I know, Mo. I'm sorry. What can I say?' But his words echoed with the electronic hiss of digital silence. 'I'm heading to the Criterion right now,' he lied. 'If you're still there, I could buy you and Tom a drink, or you could watch me eat a burger.' He chuckled to let her know it was a joke, but she wasn't for laughing. He thought of hanging up, pretending the connection was lost.

'How soon can you get here?' she said.

Here? So they were still in the Criterion. 'Ten minutes?' He caught Jessie flapping her hands and mouthing *twenty*. 'To be honest, it'll probably be more like twenty by the time I find a parking spot.'

'OK, Dad. See you then,' she said, and hung up.

He glanced at Jessie. 'It's less than twenty minutes to St Andrews from here.'

'This is where you guys always screw up, promising more than you can deliver. Have you got her an engagement card yet?'

Bugger it. 'I didn't have time to buy one.'

'You have now. You've built in a ten-minute fluff factor. And slow down, will you. You always drive too fast.'

He braked as he approached Brownhills Garage, then kept his speed at a sedate forty on the downhill run into St Andrews. The skies opened at that moment, and he had to slow down even more as his wipers struggled with the deluge. In late November the sun set before four o'clock in the afternoon. But with clouds as thick as smog, the sun could be a make-believe star.

In South Street, rain bounced off his car like liquid bullets. Headlights coming towards them were blinding. He pulled off the road, opposite the Criterion.

'You'll get a ticket,' Jessie said.

'Park it in the Office car park. If anyone asks, I've had a family emergency.'

He covered his head with his hand as he scurried across the street in the pelting rain and entered the potpourried ambience

135

of J&G Innes. He took several seconds to establish his bearings – card-shopping was not top of his list – then found what he was looking for. Five minutes later, he paid at the till, wrote a personal note in the card, and sealed it.

The Criterion adjoined J&G Innes, and it took no more than a quick trot for him to enter the pub in reasonable dryness. He squeezed through the early-evening throng, past students, locals, visitors, a couple of red-faced caddies – were they still golfing on the Old Course? – all vying for a better spot to watch the TVs, or place an order at the bar. A roar went up, and a glance at the action replay on the screen told him Manchester United had just taken a 1-0 lead over Arsenal.

He caught Maureen standing by herself at the end of the bar. He thought she looked tired, her face pale as if a couple of days in the sun was what she needed. She smiled as he approached her, the crinkling of her brown eyes, the pull of her lips so like the mannerisms of her mother that he almost stopped in his tracks. Then his arms were around her, and her voice was in his ear, telling him she was so pleased he could come and meet Tom, and, 'What do you think of the ring?'

She thrust out her hand, palm down, ring up.

He held the tips of her fingers. 'A solitaire?' he said. 'I'm impressed.'

She giggled. 'As if you would know.'

He wasn't sure if he should ask how many carats the diamond was, or where Tom had bought it, so he chose safety in, 'Where's Tom anyway?'

'Gents.' Her gaze shifted over his shoulder as her eyes lit up, telling him that the man of the moment was on his way. A hand clasped his shoulder, and he turned.

The first thing that struck him was that Tom was taller than he remembered – six-two, maybe -three – and more masculine, too, as if he'd gone to bed one night and woken up in the morning with a heavy growth. The second was that he'd supped more than his fair share of alcohol that day; his eyes were glazed, almost struggling to focus. Of course, if he'd been in the Criterion since one o'clock to meet his future father-in-law, a DCI with Fife Constabulary no less, he might be excused for having one too many in search of Dutch courage. On the other hand, Maureen seemed alert and ready to carry on, although he'd long known that both of his children could hold their drink, a trait they seemed to have inherited from their late mother.

'Mr Gilchrist,' Tom said, sliding his hand off Gilchrist's shoulder and reaching for a handshake. His grip was too firm, a *mano-a-mano* squeeze that tried to convey . . . what? That he was man enough to look after Gilchrist's daughter?

'I'm sorry I didn't seek your permission before asking for your daughter's hand in marriage, sir,' he said, pumping Gilchrist's hand. His speech was made with sincerity, and without stuttering, which suggested he'd spent time practising it. 'I hope you don't mind, sir.'

Gilchrist kept his rictus smile going, and managed to extract his hand from Tom's, aware of Maureen's eyes on him. It seemed that Tom wasn't the only one being put through a test here.

'Well, Tom,' he said, 'I don't know anything about you, other than what Mo has told me.' Tom seemed to hold his breath. 'But if you're half as nice as Mo says you are, then I'm sure I'll have no worries at all.'

Tom gripped his hand again, a two-handed pumping action this time. 'Thank you, sir. I'll look after your daughter, sir.

Don't you worry about that, sir. I love her so much, sir, that I . . . eh . . . I . . .'

'Why don't I buy a round to celebrate?' Gilchrist said, recovering his hand a second time.

'No, sir. Let me. I'll get that.'

'Tom.' He gave a stare that froze the lad to the spot. 'This is my round, OK?' He waited for Tom's nod of agreement. 'And one other thing, Tom?'

'Sir?'

'Stop calling me sir. Andy will do just fine.'

Relief washed over Tom's face – like watching butter melt on a hot roll. Gilchrist smiled, then turned to Maureen and whispered, 'I'm very happy for you,' and pecked her on the cheek. He took their order – pint of Tennent's for Tom, ice-cold; dry white wine, small, for Mo – a change from the usual large. Maybe marriage would suit her, after all. Even though he knew he shouldn't, he ordered a pint of Deuchars for himself.

His mobile vibrated in his pocket as he watched the pints being poured. He checked the screen – ID Jessie – glanced at Maureen and Tom, who seemed deep into some tender conversation, then squeezed from the bar to take the call in relative quiet.

As he reached the door, he said, 'Don't tell me you scraped the Beemer.'

'You wish,' she said.

He stepped into the entrance vestibule, staying out of the rain. The storm might have slackened, but not by much. The pavement hissed with complaint. He said, 'Come on – let's have it.'

'They've found the Land Rover,' she said. 'Near Montrave House.'

He'd heard of the place, but that was about it. 'Where's that?'

'North of Leven, south of Cupar.'

Well, that covered a lot of ground. 'Abandoned?'

'They told me you were good. I've arranged for the SOCOs to give it a going-over,' she said. 'But that's not all.'

He cupped his hand over his other ear to block out the ambient din.

'*Sundancer*'s been found, too. It ran aground on the Isle of May.'

He struggled to place the island – somewhere in the Firth of Forth was all he could come up with. But if *Sundancer* had run aground, was that a mistake? Had Black hoped it would capsize in rough seas and sink? Had he not breached the hull?

'I'd say that's an unexpected find,' he said. 'What about DNA?'

'The boat's in bits. Any DNA will have been washed off by the sea.'

'We've got his Land Rover,' he said. 'Don't tell me it's in bits, too.'

'It's intact. And if there's any DNA to extract, Colin's team will find it.'

He knew they would find Kandy Lal's DNA all over the Land Rover – Black had driven her to Edinburgh Airport, after all – but if they found Alice Hickson's DNA, then that would go some way to avenging her murder. Gilchrist realised the main thrust of his investigation had changed. They were no longer trying to solve Alice's murder, but attempting to locate Kandy Lal before it was too late and she, too, was killed. But even as these thoughts filtered through his mind, his gut instinct told him that Kandy Lal was already dead, that her body was rotting away, returning itself to the ground.

He glanced back inside the pub. He needed to get on with his investigation. But he'd only just arrived, and couldn't leave right away. 'Listen, Jessie, come and get me in fifteen minutes.' He slid his mobile into his pocket and returned to the bar.

He paid for the round and passed over Tom's and Maureen's drinks. Picking up his own, he said, 'A toast.' He chinked their glasses. 'To a happy and healthy marriage.'

Tom repeated it, then did his best to finish his pint in the one sitting.

'Steady on,' Maureen said. 'There's no rush.'

Gilchrist detected a nip in her tone, but thought it wise not to comment. 'So tell me, Tom. What have you got planned for the future?' he said, and felt puzzled when Tom looked at him like a deer caught in headlights, then buried his mouth in his pint.

'We're going to emigrate to Australia, Dad.'

Gilchrist almost stopped mid-sip, but forced himself to finish. He licked his lips, and said, 'East coast or west?'

'West,' Tom said. 'Perth.'

Gilchrist nodded, trying to quell his rising panic. This was something he'd not given thought to. Not at all. Maureen marrying was one thing. Emigrating to the other side of the planet was something else entirely. Not that he hadn't expected his children to marry, start a family, have lives of their own. He just hadn't expected it to happen so soon, and with such carefree finality in the announcement of a distant destination.

Australia?

'I hear it's a beautiful place to live,' he said.

'We've never been, of course.' Tom shook his head with wisdom. 'But from what we've seen and read about it, it certainly is beautiful.'

It struck him that, since blurting out her intentions, Maureen

140

had gone silent. Her wine glass was clamped to her lips as if to prevent anything else slipping free.

'It has to be one of the most remote cities on earth,' Gilchrist suggested.

Tom gave a nervous chuckle. Maureen sipped her wine.

'When you think about,' he continued, 'thousands of miles of ocean to the west, the same to the north, Antarctica to the south, and four thousand miles of desert to the east—'

'And your point is?' Maureen snapped.

He couldn't say it, but his point was that he didn't want her to leave. Why Australia, for God's sake? Glasgow had been bad enough. But now she'd returned to St Andrews – they both had, she and Jack – he'd somehow taken it for granted that they would remain there, the pair of them, himself, too, his whole family, together again at long last. He'd missed so much of their lives growing up; the relentless demands of the job, the necessary but hated overtime to pay the bills, climbing the career ladder of success – and look where that got him; stuck at DCI with no hope of promotion – that he'd thought he would spend more time with his children in later years, now they were together again.

But reality was different. He still worked too many hours, still didn't spend enough time with them, still missed arranged appointments – today being the perfect example. He felt his face warm with the knowledge that he had failed as a father, not been there for them back then, and not making the effort to be in more regular contact with them even now.

He smiled at Maureen. 'No point,' he said. 'Just an observation. But you will invite me to come and stay, I hope.'

'Of course, sir, I mean . . . Andy. Of course we will. Won't we, Maureen?'

Maureen's eyes never left Gilchrist's, as if they were searching his soul. Even when he gave Tom a quick smile, her eyes were waiting for him.

'Here,' he said, and retrieved the card from his inside pocket. 'To wish you well.' He handed it to Maureen, who passed her drink to Tom, then eased the envelope open, as if not wanting to tear the seal. She removed the card, read the printed cover, then flipped it open.

Silent, he watched her eyes dance over his words.

Without looking at him, she held up the card for Tom to see. 'I can't believe my baby is getting married,' she read. 'It seems that it wasn't so long ago that I was doing the same. I wish you and Tom a long and happy life together. If he loves you only half as much as I do, then you truly are a lucky woman. I know Mum would have been so proud of you. Love you, princess. Forever. Dad, and two kisses.'

'That's lovely, Mr Gilchrist . . . Andy. That's nice. It really is. Thank you.'

Tom gave him a hug, which Gilchrist managed to reciprocate without spilling his beer. He hadn't expected Maureen to read his words out loud, and oddly felt disappointed by her lack of emotion. But that detached coldness was a trait inherited from her mother, so he shouldn't have been surprised. With a watchful eye, he sipped his beer while she returned his card to the envelope and placed it with care into her handbag.

She looked up at him then, her eyes glistening, then stepped forward and put her arms around him. 'I love you, Dad,' she whispered. 'And I'm sorry.'

He hugged her in response, feeling her lips against his cheek, confused as to why she was sorry. Sorry for the problems she'd given him as a child? Sorry for marrying Tom, someone he barely knew? Sorry for announcing their intention to emigrate to Australia? Sorry for snapping at his comment about Perth? Sorry about what?

But he was saved by his mobile vibrating. He gave an apologetic smile as he retrieved it – a text from Jessie – and placed his unfinished pint on the bar.

'Got to go?' she said.

'I'm afraid so.' He shook Tom's hand again, gave Maureen a quick peck and a, 'Love you, princess,' then headed for the door.

CHAPTER 18

Gilchrist parked his car behind the SOCO Transit van and switched off the engine.

Dragonlights lit the scene like a summer party. If not for a sharp-eyed cyclist, Black's Land Rover could have lain abandoned half in and half out of a shallow ditch for the rest of the night, and not been discovered for days, maybe even weeks. Finding it had been a stroke of luck. The number plates had been switched, which explained why nothing had come up on the ANPR – Automatic Number Plate Recognition System – but it had been confirmed as Black's from the Vehicle Identification Number.

The recovery vehicle had not yet arrived, and the SOCO team had all the doors wide open, dusting the cabin for fingerprints. One of the SOCOs was crawling in the back, searching the boot carpeting for the tell-tale blue glow of luminescence from the reaction of luminol with iron in blood haemoglobin. Despite being forensically suited up, Colin was recognisable from his slender build.

'Black might not have a criminal record,' Gilchrist said to Jessie, 'but he's done this before.'

She glanced at him. 'You think so?'

'Who keeps a spare set of number plates handy just in case they have to do a runner?'

'He probably changed them on the beach when he was launching his boat.'

'Out of sight?'

'That's the idea.'

It irked that he'd missed his chance to pull Black in for questioning. And it angered him that he had walked around the man like a scared dog, when confronted. He should have told him to step out the way, maybe egged him on a bit. The fire in Black's eyes had warned him that the man might have been about to do something he would later regret. But if he had, then Black would now be in custody instead of scuttling yachts and abandoning cars.

Or worse, murdering another woman.

With that thought, he could not shift the gut-wrenching sense that whatever danger Kandy Lal had found herself in, he had done nothing to prevent that. It might even be argued that their visit to Black's home had forewarned the man. And by not arresting him, they had simply let him carry on with getting rid of the evidence.

Christ, it didn't bear thinking about.

He stepped into the frosted chill and walked towards the Land Rover.

Colin slid from the back and pulled down his mask. 'A couple of specks of blood,' he said, 'but I wouldn't hold my breath. It's been thoroughly cleaned. Also found strands of black hair trapped in the door hinge.' He pushed the cargo door wide open as far as it would go, and pointed with a gloved finger to the bottom hinge. 'Found them here,' he said.

145

Jessie said, 'So you're saying they could've been trapped by the hinge if he'd thrown a body into the back and closed the door?'

'I'm saying no such thing. I'm just telling you what I found.'

'How about ethnicity?' Gilchrist said. 'Can you conclude anything?'

'Not until I'm back in the lab.'

'Indian?' Gilchrist tried.

Colin shrugged. 'Wouldn't rule it out.'

Gilchrist nodded to the Land Rover. 'Cleaned, you said. So no fingerprints?'

'Mostly smeared from cleaning. But we've managed to lift a few partials. Maybe enough to piece together a full print. But I wouldn't bank on it.'

'Let me know what you find,' Gilchrist said, and walked to the edge of the dirt-tracked lane.

Surrounding fields lay in blackening silence. A burst of wind shivered the hawthorn hedgerow, flicking water from its branches, causing him to step back. He stared off beyond rain-flattened grass that faded into a dark horizon. Out here, in the middle of nowhere, what would Black have done after abandoning his Land Rover?

It was a long walk back to town, far too long for someone on the run from the law. So, how had Black left? He was a loner – Gilchrist was already convinced of that. Everything he had seen so far told him that Black was a man who liked solitude; his home at the end of a dead-end road; his fridge with barely enough food to feed one; his yacht, large enough for two perhaps, but not for bigger parties; his spare bedrooms with their smell of dust and emptiness; his Land Rover with its tattered passenger seat covered with plans and drawings and . . .

And . . .?

Something else that his eyes had caught, but his brain hadn't registered.

He forced his mind back to that first glance through the Land Rover's window.

Then thought he saw it. In the opened toolbox.

Thick leather gloves. Not workman's gloves. But . . .

Motorbike gloves.

He retrieved his mobile and phoned Mac Fountain, the CCTV Manager.

'I need you to check CCTV footage for a motorbike on the Cupar to Leven road.'

'What make and model?'

'Don't know.'

'Registration number?'

'Don't know.'

'Travelling in which direction?'

'Don't know.'

Mac let out a sigh, and Gilchrist could only pinch the bridge of his nose in despair. 'You're not making it easy,' Mac said. 'Cupar to Leven's what – ten, fifteen miles? Through open country? We don't have cameras out in the country. If you could pin it down to a time, Andy, I could maybe give it a better shot.'

Gilchrist whispered a curse. 'Let me get back to you,' he said.

He found Jessie by the Land Rover, texting on her mobile. He sliced a hand across his throat, and she dropped it into her pocket.

'Yes, sir?'

'Get on to Mhairi and Jackie and find out if Black has a motorbike registered in his name. I want make, model, registration number, the works.'

'What kind of motorbike?'

'One with two wheels.'

Without a word, Jessie turned away, mobile out again and pressed to her ear.

Gilchrist walked to the rear of the Land Rover and squatted. The registration number plate looked scraped and dented, and dotted with specks of rust. Close up, it was obvious that the plate did not belong to the Land Rover. But a passer-by, or anyone driving past, would be none the wiser.

'They belong to a 1976 Reliant Scimitar,' Jessie said.

Gilchrist jerked a look at her.

She held up her mobile. 'Just in from Jackie.'

He grunted as he stood, knees stiff from the cold, or from getting older.

'Been registered as SORN for the last ten years.'

Statutory Off Road Notifications were used by owners who did not want to sell or scrap their vehicle, but garage it without paying road tax. Which meant the vehicle was not allowed to be driven. With a SORN you could hold on to a car you might wish to restore in future years. A 1976 Reliant Scimitar would fit that bill. But importantly, a SORN recorded ownership details.

'Did Jackie give an address?' he asked.

'John Smith, Kingsbarns,' she said. 'One out of ten for originality.'

'You think it's a fake?'

'Don't you?'

'Let's go.'

The address in Kingsbarns led Gilchrist and Jessie to a tidy cottage with white walls and a red pan-tiled roof. They entered the property through a wooden gate and walked up to the front door. A coach light warmed the white paint.

Gilchrist nodded to the nameplate – *Smith*. 'Not fake, after all.'

'You could be in luck then.'

'How come?'

'Maybe he's related to the John Smith of Yorkshire fame, and you could sign up as a taste-tester for all that real ale.'

'Right.' He pressed the doorbell.

'I thought you liked real ale.'

'I certainly do.'

'What're you moaning at, then?'

He was saved by the door opening with a hard click. An overweight man with ruddy cheeks and wild red hair that reminded him of Jackie from the Office, stood in the doorway in pyjamas and dressing gown. A bit early to go to bed, but it was Sunday, after all.

'Yeah?' the man said.

Gilchrist held out his warrant card, and introduced himself and Jessie.

'And?'

'And do you know Scott Black?' Jessie said.

'Aye, I know that Black bastard. You strung him up by his fucking balls yet?'

'Why would we want to do that?' Gilchrist tried.

'You tell me. Youse're the ones asking the stupit fucking questions.'

'You shouldn't swear on a Sunday,' Jessie said.

'Oh, aye? How about I tell youse to fuck off out of it?'

Gilchrist stepped in with, 'Let's start again, shall we? We'd like to speak to John Smith. Is that you?'

'That's what it says on the nameplate.'

'Do you own a 1976 Reliant Scimitar?'

Smith's eyes widened and he glanced at a wooden garage at the side of a neat lawn, in front of which sat a silver Ford Fiesta, as if not permitted entry.

'It's in there, is it?' Gilchrist said.

'It fucking well better be.' Smith tore the keys from the inside lock, then was out the door and past Gilchrist, slippered feet crunching gravel. 'If that Black bastard's stole it, I'll fucking have him this time.' The padlock rattled as Smith wrestled with the key, then he unclipped it and opened the door wide enough to step inside and click on a switch.

'Oh,' Smith said, surprised.

Gilchrist stood in the tight space of the garage doorway. A blue protective car cover, tailored to measure, stood in the shape of a 1976 Reliant Scimitar. Not that he knew what a Reliant Scimitar looked like, but he would be willing to bet that was what was under it.

'You sound surprised,' he said, just to gauge a reaction.

Smith eased back the bottom corner of the cover, as if to ensure he was not being tricked. 'No, that's it,' he said.

'See what jumping to conclusions does for you,' Jessie said.

'I thought it was stolen.' He turned to Gilchrist and scratched his head. 'Why did you want to know if I had a Scimitar?'

Gilchrist shrugged. 'What's its registration number?' he asked.

Smith rattled it off – the same number as on Black's abandoned Land Rover.

'You might want to check the plates,' Jessie said.

Smith frowned, then lifted the cover back. 'What the fuck?' He peeled it up to reveal the front end, as if expecting the number

150

plate to be lying on the bonnet. 'Fuck,' he growled, and squeezed his way to the back of the garage. He sank out of sight as he checked the rear plate. 'What the fuck?' he shouted.

Gilchrist waited for him to work his way to the front, then said, 'This time?'

Smith scowled at him. 'What?'

'You said you'll have Black this time.'

'If he's taken them plates, I fucking will, I'm telling you.'

'Lock up the garage,' Gilchrist said, and stepped into a cold wind that ruffled his hair with icy fingers. 'You're shivering.'

'It's fucking freezing.'

'Well let's have a seat inside where it's dry and warm. And you can tell us all about what happened between you and Black . . . *last* time.'

CHAPTER 19

The living-room heat hit Gilchrist like a blast from a furnace. Logs roared in an open fire in front of which sat a woman in a dressing gown, hair in curlers, knees tucked under her. At the sight of Gilchrist and Jessie, she turned the TV to mute. Smith introduced her as *the wife* – no name – and she smiled and nodded, not embarrassed by being caught in her night-attire, nor seemingly offended by the off-hand introduction. But when Smith said that Gilchrist and Jessie were *a couple of polis here to talk about thon Black bastard*, she looked as if she could spit molten nails across the room.

Smith stood by the fire, his back to the fireguard, close enough to set his dressing gown alight, Gilchrist feared. 'Pour us a cup of tea, pet, will you?'

'Not for me,' Jessie said.

'Me neither,' Gilchrist added. 'We won't be staying long. We only want to ask you about Scott Black.'

That did it. Smith's wife slunk into the kitchen and closed the door. Gilchrist raised an eyebrow at the sound of drawers being slammed, cutlery chinking. If he didn't know better he'd have thought someone was ripping the place apart.

'She still gets upset about it,' Smith said, as if that explained all.

'We're listening,' Gilchrist said.

Smith took a deep breath, and said, 'He done some work for us over a year ago. Fitted new bathroom units, sink, WC, and a new shower cubicle.'

'Cowboy contractor?' Jessie said.

'No, no, nothing like that.'

Gilchrist raised his hand to keep Jessie quiet, and Smith pressed on.

'He done a great job. I'll gie the bastard that. The wife was right pleased, so she was. And I was, too, to a certain extent. But I'm fussy, ken? So the wife keeps telling me. I cannae stand it when fittings are no square, or no plumb, or there's a wee gap where there should be a right tight fitting.' He gritted his teeth. 'Does my nut in, so it does.'

'And . . .?' Jessie said.

Smith looked at her.

'The tea'll be cold by the time you get round to it,' she said.

Gilchrist said, 'Take your time, John.'

'The bastard said he'd come back in a month just to be sure there were nae leaks or nothing, which I thought was dead good of him, following up like that. You don't get great service nowadays, so you don't. I mean, you want to see some of the crap that gets built in some of they new housing schemes. Cheap as fuck, so it is.'

Jessie shifted her stance, cleared her throat.

'Aye, well, me being OCD like, so the wife says, I seen a wee bit of loose mastic at the edge of the sink, where it butts against the tiles. So I went down on my knees for a better look – and that's when I seen it.' His lips pressed into a white line. 'Boils my fuck-ing blood just thinking about it, so it does.'

'Thinking about what?' Jessie again.

'The fucking webcam.'

'The *what*?' Gilchrist said.

Jessie was ahead of him. 'Bastard,' she hissed.

'Bastard right enough,' Smith snarled. 'At first I couldnae believe it. I just sat there, looking at the thing, realising we'd been on fucking *Candid Camera* for the last couple of months. The wife went mental when I showed it to her, ken? It was aiming right into the shower cubicle.'

'Did you report it to the police?' Gilchrist asked.

'Did I fuck. I ripped it off and took it round to that Black bastard to shove it right up his arse.' He clammed up as the kitchen door opened and his wife walked in with a tray of tea and biscuits.

Gilchrist noted three mugs.

She placed the tray on a side table by the sofa and said, 'How do you take yours?'

Gilchrist declined, as did Jessie.

Smith's wife poured tea into a mug, added a fair helping of milk and three spoonfuls of sugar, then handed it to her husband.

'Thanks, pet,' he said, cupping his hands around it as if trying to heat himself up.

Gilchrist thought Smith had to be close to toasting himself by now. No one spoke while his wife gave a tight smile on her way out.

When the kitchen door closed, Smith said, 'The wife cannae talk about it.'

'Did Black deny it?' Gilchrist said.

'Absolutely fucking denied it, so he did. Asked me if I'd had any visitors since it'd been fitted. And if so, it had to be one of them.'

'And had you?'

'A few friends. It was summer, ken? And we were planning to have a barbecue.'

'And Black knew that?'

'We'd paid a bit extra to get the job done in time. So, aye, the bastard knew.'

'So he blamed it on one of your visitors?' Jessie again.

'Aye. But I knew he done it. None of our friends are IT whizz-kids. They can handle a laptop and mobile phone and stuff, but that's it. And it takes time to fit that stuff up, ken.'

'So you've no doubts it was Black?'

'Absolutely fucking none. I should've gave the bastard a right doing.'

'How did it end?' Gilchrist said. 'Your confrontation with Black.'

'Told me he was going to his lawyer to see about getting a written apology, or else he was going to sue me for slander.'

It took a few seconds before Gilchrist realised Smith was waiting for a question. 'And did you give him a written apology?'

'Did I fuck.'

'Did you hear from his solicitor?'

'Not a squeak.'

'Scare tactics,' Jessie said.

Smith said nothing, took a gulp of tea, as if ashamed by the outcome of his showdown with Black. But Gilchrist had felt the same, as if a force field emanated from Black, warning those close enough to threaten him to back off.

'How did Black know about your Reliant Scimitar?' Gilchrist asked.

'I bring it out for an airing a couple of times a year. I'd been getting it ready for the barbecue, to show it off, so I'd just gave it a good waxing and polishing when he turned up. When he seen it, he offered to buy it. But I told him no fucking way.'

Gilchrist waited, but it seemed as if Smith had said all he was going to say. He glanced at Jessie. 'Anything else?'

She said, 'No,' then surprised him by reaching for Smith's hand. 'Thanks for your help,' she said.

Smith shook her hand and nodded – somewhat sheepishly, Gilchrist had to say.

Outside, the cold air hit Gilchrist as he crunched his way over the gravel to his car. The locks clicked, just as the skies opened. Jessie leaped into the passenger seat, as Gilchrist fired up the ignition and switched on the windscreen wipers.

'How do you do that?' she said.

'Do what?'

'Click that remote fob thingie and the rain starts. Can you turn it off, please?'

He chuckled. 'Now that would be something worth inventing.'

'Especially in the land of the horizontal rain.'

Neither of them said another word, both lost in their own thoughts, until Gilchrist turned on to the A917 and cleared the village limits, heading for St Andrews.

'He's a cocky bastard, that Black,' Jessie said, and shifted in her seat so she faced Gilchrist. 'And he's into voyeurism? Bloody hell, I didn't see that one coming.'

'Me neither. But the question is – why?'

'He's into spying on naked women, that's why.'

'He installs a webcam in a client's bathroom, then returns in a month to make sure it's all right, and removes it. By which time he's got all he needs for blackmail.'

'But Black didn't threaten Smith with blackmail. He denied it to his back teeth.'

'So, what else would he do with it?'

'Maybe it depends what he catches the person doing. You know? Smith and the wife hard at it.' Jessie laughed. 'Now that would be a sight for sore eyes.'

Gilchrist slowed down as he neared St Andrews. The rain hadn't been as heavy there, but the road surface glistened with ice from a cold wind that whistled in from the North Sea. 'Maybe you're right,' he said. 'Maybe Black would be selective in who to blackmail. Only those in a position where public opinion matters, perhaps? But what would he do with those he doesn't blackmail?'

'Post them online? Sell them?'

'Is there a market for that?'

Jessie lowered her head and eyed him over a pair of imaginary specs. 'My dear Andy, there's a market for *anything* to do with sex.'

'Really?' he said. 'I didn't know that.'

She laughed, and said, 'Mr Squeaky Clean, right enough.'

They said nothing more until he drove through the pend in North Street and parked his car. 'I'm going to see if there's anything for me in the Office, before heading home.'

'And I'm off to see my wee boy. He'll be starving.'

'He'll have made himself something to eat, a sandwich or something?'

Jessie guffawed. 'When he's got a mum to do that for him? I don't think so. He'd rather starve first.'

'If anything comes to you,' Gilchrist said, 'give me a call. Any time.'

'Will do.'

The car park was sheltered by the police station itself. Despite high boundary walls, an ice-cold wind swirled through it like a mini-whirlwind. Jessie jumped into her car, pulled the door shut and switched on the engine. Her Fiat 500 was a great wee car for getting around town and saving money on petrol, but with a small engine it took forever for the cabin to heat up. She switched the fan on, and texted Robert as she waited for the heat to kick in.

Home soon. Fancy a curry?

Fifteen seconds later the reply came.

Chicken pakora spicy onions lamb madras

Jessie sighed. 'What happened to please or thanks?' But Robert's favourite food was an Indian curry, and all she wanted was to make her wee boy happy. A curry also let them sit at the table together, and might allow her to bring up the subject of his operation. But just the thought of that had her stomach churning as she phoned the Indian restaurant for a delivery.

A minute later, it was all done. The chill had gone from the cabin, and she switched on the radio to catch some 1970s song about love being in the air. She tapped her fingers on the steering wheel as she indicated to turn right into Union Street and work her way back to her home in Canongate. But even during that short drive, she could not shift the sickening feeling in her gut, and she thought of putting off telling Robert about his operation. Maybe best to do that first thing in the morning, or when she got home from work tomorrow night.

158

The closer she got to her home, the worse she felt.

How could she tell her wee boy such awful news without breaking his heart?

She pulled her car into the driveway and switched off the engine.

The place settled into blackness.

She was so deep in thought, still undecided about what to say and when to say it, that she failed to notice the figure creeping along the driveway. When the passenger door opened, and a balaclava-clad man slipped in, and a knife flickered before her eyes with a steely glint from its wickedly pointed blade, and she knew she was about to be killed . . . her first thoughts were for Robert. *What will become of him? How will he cope?*

The blade pressed against her neck with a touch as cold as ice.

'Not a fuckin word,' he said.

CHAPTER 20

Recognition choked a grunt of disbelief from Jessie.

Then fear flashed through her with a desperation that had her struggling to open the door and run. But a hand like a grapple hook gripped her, and a fist like a rock hit the back of her head. Her world darkened. She was aware of the dashboard tilting, and hands on her shoulders, pulling her down.

When she came to, he was looking at her.

In the cabin darkness, she couldn't make out his face, only that he'd removed the balaclava. She rubbed the back of her head where a dull pain throbbed, then ran a shaking hand across her mouth. 'Where's the knife?' she asked.

'In mah pocket.'

'They said you were going to kill me.'

'The bastards would, wouldn't they?'

Despite the inferred assurance of being out of danger, Jessie's heart thumped in her chest like a caged animal. 'So why are you here, Tommy?'

'Ah'm being set up.'

'What is it about you?' Anger gave her strength. 'You never

160

listen to a word I say. I'm asking you, why are you *here*, Tommy? *Here*. In St Andrews.'

'Ah need your help.'

'My *help*?' she scoffed. 'Why don't I just arrest you?'

'Ah'll no let you.'

She said nothing as the darkness brightened to the click of a cigarette lighter, and her brother's face appeared before her in hard relief. Sunken cheeks and haunted eyes piled years on to him, closer to fifty than his thirties – she had never known his exact birthdate.

He held the cigarette out to her. 'Want a puff?'

'I gave up smoking.'

'*You?*' He rasped a laugh. 'Wonders'll never fuckin cease.'

Fear and anger were morphing into deep irritation. She'd never been close to any of her family, but if she was asked who had been the least unfriendly to her, she would choose Tommy. 'You want my help?' she said. 'What does that mean?'

The cigarette glowed red as he did what he could to finish it in one hit. 'Ah didnae kill Terry,' he said. 'And Terry didnae kill the auld dear.'

'No, Tommy. They think *you* killed the old dear.'

'That's what they're fuckin supposed tae think. Ah told you, ah'm being set up.'

'Why should I believe you?'

'Fuck sake, all ah'm looking for's your help. Is'at too much for you to take in?'

'You've got a funny way of asking for it.'

'What the fuck am ah supposed to dae, eh?'

'You could've phoned.'

'That'll be right. You'd shop me in it. Or they'd trace the call.'

'They?'

'Maxwell and his lot.'

Hairs on the back of Jessie's neck chilled. 'Chief Superintendent Victor Maxwell?'

The cigarette glowed red once more, then died as Tommy crushed it between his thumb and finger. 'Yeah. Maxwell.'

Jessie had met Victor Maxwell once before, when she was with Strathclyde Police before transferring to Fife. She remembered thinking he was full of it, how he fancied himself as a ladies' man, how she'd squirmed under his X-ray gaze. Maxwell headed up the BAD squad – Battle Against Drugs – and was rumoured to have bought a couple of Spanish villas with the backhanders he was creaming off to turn a blind eye. But rumours and facts were at opposite ends of the same equation, and Victor Maxwell was an expert in deception.

'So why is Maxwell after you, Tommy? You're not dealing in drugs, are you?'

'No me. But the auld dear was.'

Nothing would surprise her about her bitch for a mother. When Jessie was growing up, Jeannie Janes had taken her along with her to meet clients, some of whom she'd do a turn with, usually out of sight. But on more than one occasion, Jessie had watched her mother having sex with a stranger. Even though she'd been too young to comprehend what was happening, these images seared into her mind with such indelible force that by the time Jessie was in her teens, she had clear recall of what her mother had done. Which was why she'd gone to such great lengths to protect her son, Robert, from the toxic contamination of his grandmother.

Although Jessie had last seen Terry and her mother about a year ago, she had no idea when she'd last seen Tommy. Three years ago? Four? Longer?

With Tommy's cigarette finished, Jessie's night vision had recovered. Where she had a fine nose, Tommy's was crooked and battle-thickened. He could be handsome, she thought, if you ignored the scars and the missing lobe on his left ear where it had been bitten off in a street fight. Rumour had it that Tommy had retaliated by biting the man's bottom lip clean off.

Jessie shuffled in her seat. 'How did you find out where I live?'

'Friend of a friend.'

'You know I could lose my job if we're seen together and I don't arrest you.'

'We'll no be seen thigither.'

She could not fail to catch his anger, which shimmered off him like heat from rock. His temper had been the architect of his life of crime. If he'd not been so wild-headed and lightning fast with his fists and boots, he might have become a decent family man. On the other hand, having a drink- and drug-addled prostitute for a mother, all chance of an honest life had been lost to him at the moment of his birth.

'You know, Tommy, despite all the shit you've done in your life, I never thought you were stupid. You were never the brightest, right enough. But you had street smarts.'

'Fuck sake, Jessie. Whit's wi the fuckin degree in psychology?'

'You don't need a degree to know I can't help you.'

'You're all ah've got,' he said. 'We're the same flesh and blood, Jessie. There's only you and me now. That's all.'

'As far as I'm concerned, there's only me and Robert.' She regretted mentioning her son's name the instant it slipped from her mouth. She tensed as Tommy's dark shape shifted, felt her car move under the transfer of his weight. Was she about to witness first-hand his infamous temper? Was he going to take his knife to her?

Then she breathed a sigh of relief as his face lit up, and a cigarette glowed like a beacon of truce. He held it out to her. 'Take it.'

'I don't want it.'

'Go on. Take it. It's only nicotine.'

She obliged, but didn't put it to her lips. He lit another, took a deep pull and exhaled in her direction. She breathed in his second-hand smoke, loving its acrid taste. On impulse, she placed the cigarette between her lips.

She inhaled, and felt faint as that first burst of nicotine worked into her system. For a moment her vision threatened to vanish, but smoking was a bit like riding a bike – you never lost the habit. She took another pull, held it in her mouth for a long second, then said, 'Get real, Tommy. How the hell do you expect me to help you?'

'You'll help me,' he said. 'Ah know you will.'

She could sense his smile of victory, almost see the tilting of his head, the narrowing of his eyes, a stance he took when he was about to overpower an opponent. The gap between them flickered in shades of greys, one moment dull, the next clear. The fragrance of cigarette smoke could be a drug that smothered them like an ethereal cloud. If she closed her eyes, she could be floating in a dream. She was about to take another pull when she realised what she was doing. She opened the car's ashtray, and killed the cigarette.

'Fuck off, Tommy. I'm not going to help you.'

The speed with which he closed the gap shocked her. She jerked back, thumped her head against the window. His face was tight to hers, the stink of cigarettes and sweat almost over-powering. Spittle splashed her mouth as he said, 'Don't play high and fuckin mighty with me, Jessie, just 'cause you're in the polis. Ah'm no goin down for something ah never done. You got that?'

Jessie held her breath.

'Have you? Eh? Have you *fuckin got that?*'

At the metallic click of a flick-knife, Jessie tried to push herself back. But there was nowhere to go. 'Don't, Tommy, don't.'

The point of the blade dug into her fleece jacket with a force that should push it through the material and straight into her heart.

'Tommy, please.'

His breath hissed in and out of clenched teeth.

'Please, Tommy. Robert needs me.'

The mention of Robert's name was like clicking a switch.

Tommy stopped breathing, as if his lungs had been turned off. Five seconds, maybe more, passed in silence. Then the scene rebooted, and he pushed away.

'Go,' he said. 'Just fuckin go.'

Jessie opened the car door. Night air rushed in, fresh and cold, sweeping away the stench of sweat and fear. She was about to step out when she turned and faced him. He hadn't moved, as if he intended sitting in her car overnight.

'What will you do?' she said.

'Run. Hide. It's what ah'm good at.'

The words were out before she could stop herself. 'What d'you want me to do?'

His eyes were tight beads that brightened with surprise. He removed something from his pocket and held it out to her.

She took it. 'What is it?'

'Names.'

'Of?'

'Them that done it.'

'Murdered Mum and Terry?'

'Yeah.'

'You have proof?'

'Naw. Only what's there.'

'Why not hand this in yourself?'

'Don't act the daft cunt, Jessie. Who'd fuckin believe me?'

'And when they ask me where I got this, I'm going to tell them I just woke up and there it was, lying on my pillow? I don't think so. They'll put two and two together, Tommy. And once they do, I'll be in deepest shit.'

'Won't be the first time, will it?'

Headlights swept the driveway behind them.

Tommy's head jerked, his flick-knife clicked, and his whole being tensed like a rabbit ready to sprint from danger.

'It's no one, Tommy. Only our curry.'

'Get rid of the fucker.'

She met the delivery boy halfway down the drive, positioning her body to prevent him from seeing someone in her car. 'Keep the change,' she said, and waited in the driveway as the van drove off.

She returned to her car and pulled the passenger door open. 'I'd invite you in. But I've only got two straws.'

Tommy stepped out, and she closed the door behind him.

'I can give you some naan bread—'

166

'Naw, ah'm fine.' He stood in the dark, hands deep in his pockets, breath fogging the night air. Then, without a word, he turned and strode down the driveway, into the shadows.

Jessie's fingers shook as she tried to insert the key into the lock.

When she pushed the door open, she stumbled inside and managed to carry the curry into the kitchen without spilling it. She removed the note from her pocket, and for a moment thought of just binning it. Who could she give this to? But more troubling, if anyone found out that Tommy had given it to her in person, she could be suspended, maybe even charged with aiding a wanted criminal, perverting the course of justice.

She stuffed the note back into her pocket.

For the time being, she would do nothing.

Well, not exactly nothing.

She opened the cabinet and removed a bottle of Glenfiddich Toasted Oak Reserve, a decent whisky she had intended to give to Angie as a present for all the times she looked after Robert. She opened it and sloshed a goodly measure into a tumbler, conscious of her hands shaking as she took a large gulp. The next mouthful drained the glass, and she poured another.

'Bloody hell,' she said. 'What on earth am I doing?'

CHAPTER 21

7. 33 a.m., Monday
North Street police station
St Andrews

Gilchrist played the CCTV footage DS Baxter had retrieved from Edinburgh Airport.

Together, they watched Kandy Lal leave the terminal at 10.25 p.m. and walk across the pedestrian access to the passenger pick-up point. A Land Rover Discovery bearing the same registration number as Black's abandoned Land Rover pulled in, and Scott Black – Gilchrist could tell it was Black from his physical stature alone – took the suitcase from Lal and lugged it into the back.

Then the Land Rover drove off.

'Let's go through it again,' Gilchrist said.

As they replayed the footage, what troubled him was that Kandy Lal seemed not in the least wary of Black, which told him she had no suspicions of his involvement in Alice Hickson's murder. Had Kandy Lal walked straight into the arms of her own killer?

'We were able to track them all the way to St Monans,' Baxter offered. 'They got back just before midnight on Saturday. Then we lost them in the fog.'

Despite the UK having more CCTV cameras than anywhere else on the planet, many villages, small towns, and much of the Scottish countryside did not have them installed. And every now and then Sod's Law would kick in, with the camera not focusing on the area they needed, or the one camera that would have caught all having been vandalised. Then there was the Scottish bloody weather, with its driving rain, heavy winds, or plain old fog that could turn a CCTV camera blind.

Christ, it was enough to drive a sober man to drink.

Gilchrist pushed away from the monitor. 'Have you seen Jessie?' he asked Baxter.

'Not yet, sir.'

So Gilchrist phoned her. 'Got the search warrant for Kandy Lal's place in my greasy little mitts,' he said. 'I can pick you up, or meet you there.'

'Meet you there in thirty minutes,' she said. 'And mine's a tall latte.'

Before leaving, he spent ten minutes checking the latest with his team. But he might as well not have bothered. No news on Black's whereabouts; and Kandy Lal was still uncontactable. He instructed his team to go through any and all CCTV footage in the vicinity of Montrave House where Black's Land Rover had been abandoned.

If Black had a motorbike, he wanted to know about it.

By the time he arrived at Kandy's, Jessie was already there, pacing the street, mobile to her ear. As he walked towards her, she finished the call.

'That was DCI Joe Donaldson,' she said. 'Confirmed that Terry fell off the perch last night.'

He grimaced. 'I'm sorry, Jessie.'

'I'd already marked him down as murdered.' She stared off along the street. 'We didn't have a normal family upbringing. So I can't blame Terry for turning out the way he did.'

'You turned out fine.'

She faced him, her eyes glistening. 'For Terry and Tommy it was worse. They were a right pair of hard cases,' she said. 'But they stood up for each other, and would stand back to back against all comers.'

Not quite Gilchrist's recollection of Terry. But Jessie was hurting, trying to find some rationale in what appeared to be a pair of senseless killings, much too close to home.

'Donaldson wants me to ID his body.'

'When?'

'Today, if possible.'

Gilchrist nodded. 'Take whatever time you need.'

She gave a tight-lipped smile and said, 'Did you forget the coffees?'

'In a rush. Sorry.'

'Just as well your head's screwed on.' She rubbed her hands together. 'Could've done with one to beat the chill.'

'Come on,' he said. 'Maybe the heating's on.'

Together, they crossed the road.

At the door, they pulled on latex gloves, and Gilchrist held the doorbell down for ten seconds. 'She's not here,' he said, and pulled a key from his pocket. 'Courtesy of the next-door neighbour.'

'Clever clogs.'

The lock was stiff, and he had to wiggle the handle to release it.

With a helpful nudge from his shoulder, the door opened to a gentle waft of heat.

The first thing that struck him was that something was not fresh, nothing he could pin down, just . . . not quite fresh. '*Anyone?*' he shouted, in case Kandy Lal was in bed and not answering her phones or door.

Silence came back at him.

The house had been renovated, with a dividing wall knocked down to create an open-plan living space. A room to the side – an original bedroom? – had been turned into a master bathroom with a glass wet room that glistened like new and still had its original seals attached like strips of plaster printed with the name and address of the manufacturer.

'Take a note of that,' he said. 'Find out if Black installed this.'

The kitchen, too, had been upgraded, with new cabinets that slid in and out on silent runners. A brightly coloured rug covered a length of the laminate flooring, which flexed a tad under his weight. He laid the key on the breakfast bar, then opened the fridge – well stocked with basics, but more suited to someone who ate out rather than dined in.

Stairs in the hallway led to an attic that had been turned into two bedrooms, one with a pair of dormer windows that over-looked the street, the other with a skylight and a view of a waste-land of a garden that could do with being rotovated and turned into a potato field.

Only one bedroom showed signs of having been slept in. A wardrobe full of clothes told him that wherever Kandy Lal was, she had not left town with Scott Black. No, this place was all ready for a woman to return to from holiday.

Back downstairs, Jessie had her ear to the landline. 'Anything?' he asked her.

She replaced the handset. 'Nothing on the answering machine. And the last incoming call was one of these sales calls you can't phone back.'

He spread his arms out and slowly turned around the room. 'What do you see?'

'A house that's far from being a home?' She pointed to a framed picture on the wall. 'Who lives in a home with only one picture on the wall? And not a house plant in sight. What does that tell you?'

'That she's not into gardening?' He sniffed the air. 'Do you smell anything?'

'Can't smell a thing. I'm all blocked up. Why?'

He screwed up his face. 'Something's off.'

'Maybe it's something in the kitchen.' She found the rubbish bin under the sink and flipped it open. 'Nope. Been cleaned before she went on holiday.' She closed it and sniffed the air. 'Still nothing. Maybe the place just needs an airing, or something.'

'Or something.' He walked back to the lounge, mobile in his hand, and called Colin.

'What are we looking for?' Colin asked.

He almost shrugged. Nothing seemed out of place. 'Check for bloodstains,' he said. 'And bag any personal items. There's no evidence of a crime, but until we know what's happened to Ms Lal, we need to be careful on this.'

He ended the call, and Jessie said, 'Fancy that coffee now?'

'I fancy finding that motorbike.'

'I'm still not convinced,' she said. 'Someone could've picked him up and driven him off. That seems the sensible thing to do.'

'But he's a loner.'

'He wasn't such a loner that he couldn't do without women's company,' Jessie said.

'What does that mean?'

'Hold on there. Don't shoot the messenger. I'm only brainstorming here.'

Gilchrist realised he was glaring at her. 'Sorry,' he said. 'Just thinking.' He tried a smile, but didn't think he pulled it off. 'Come on,' he said. 'There's nothing more to see here. Let's get that coffee.'

They were almost at the front door when he slapped his jacket pockets.

'On the breakfast bar,' Jessie reminded him.

'I knew that.' He returned to the kitchen and picked up the keys. As he turned back to the hall, his gaze tripped up on something on the floor, by the kick-plate under the cooker. He leaned down, swept his hand over the flooring, held his fingers up to the light.

'What've you got?' Jessie asked.

'Sawdust?'

'So you're thinking this means . . . what?'

'It's fresh.' He eyed the rug that ran the length of the kitchen, then pressed his foot on it, hard. The floor creaked. Down on his knees now, peeling the rug back, pushing it to the side, until . . .

He saw it, a rectangular panel cut through the laminate flooring.

'Jesus,' Jessie hissed.

'Get me a knife.'

She opened a drawer and clattered her fingers through cutlery. 'This do?'

He pushed the blade into the saw-cut close to the panel's corner, and tried to prise it up and off the floor. But the wood was too tight for proper leverage, and the knife bent.

'Give me another one,' he said.

She did.

He pushed that into the flooring on the other edge of the panel, and wiggled both knives together. Still too tight, but he felt the panel move.

'Stand on that corner,' he said, 'and when I edge it up, press down.'

Jessie positioned herself at the corner.

Gilchrist pressed the knives in and twisted. 'Now,' he said.

She leaned forward, and the flooring eased up. 'A bit more,' he panted, and managed to slide one of the knives under the panel as it lifted clear. He gripped it with his free hand, and lifted it up and out, and slid it on to the floor.

A waft of *something not quite fresh* rose from the opening.

Gilchrist felt his anger smoulder as he stared at Kandy Lal's body crammed into a tiny space between floor joists, too small for her to be laid lengthwise. He couldn't see her face, but knew from the colour of her skin that they were looking at Kandy Lal.

He pushed himself to his feet, and tried to work out what had happened. No signs of blood, so she'd likely been throttled to death – Black's *modus operandi*. Her body had been folded up, knees and arms bent at impossible angles, then jammed into her makeshift grave. He could almost make out the boot-marks on

174

her clothes, from Black stomping down on the body to squeeze her in.

He removed his mobile and called Colin.

'Change of plan,' he snarled. 'We need the works. The whole shooting match.'

CHAPTER 22

By midday, Gilchrist and his team were no closer to finding Scott Black. The DVLA had no record of any motorbike registered in his name, and Gilchrist was now having serious doubts over his rationale. Had Black really abandoned the Land Rover and driven off on a motorbike? Or was it all conjecture and wishful thinking on his part?

Was Jessie correct? Had there been another vehicle? Another person?

CCTV footage on the outskirts of Cupar and Leven captured seven motorbikes on the southbound A916, and ten heading north, all within the estimated time frame. But they could be hours out, and had no way of confirming if any of these bikes had originated from the area around Montrave House.

And they hadn't even considered roads leading inland or to the coast.

Christ, he could quadruple his team, and they would still be short on manpower.

There had to be some other way of finding Black, as another thought struck him: the post office might be able to help. The

Royal Mail was legally obliged to deliver mail to the noted address, whether the addressee was the registered occupant of that address or not. So, he instructed Mhairi to visit St Monans' post office and the Royal Mail sorting office in Anstruther to find out if they had any record of delivering mail to Black's home address, but in some other addressee's name.

A long shot, he knew. But so far his team were spinning their wheels.

Next, he phoned Cooper.

Preliminary findings on Kandy Lal's body confirmed extensive bruising on her arms and thighs, which had Gilchrist asking the staggering question, 'Could she have been alive when she was put under the floor?'

'Shouldn't think so,' Cooper said. 'Heavy bruising around the neck, and fracture of both the thyroid and cricoid cartilages, suggest death by manual strangulation. So I'd say she was throttled first, then hidden.'

Thank God for small mercies. 'And the other bruises?'

'Cutaneous cuts and abrasions from defending herself, probably. I've also managed to scrape skin tissue from under the fingernails, which suggests that our Ms Lal put up one hell of a fight.'

Gilchrist pinched the bridge of his nose. What chance would a woman have against a brute of a man like Black? None, came the answer, and an image of Kandy Lal being booted around the kitchen floor hit him with such force that he had to walk to the window and press his forehead against the cold glass.

'You still there, Andy?'

'Sure, Becky. It's just . . .'

'It doesn't get any easier, does it?'

He closed his eyes. 'No, it doesn't.'

'I should be able to get a good DNA profile from the skin tissue under the fingernails, and compare that to the samples from Black's toothbrush and razor.'

Gilchrist gave a quiet sigh of relief. After entering Black's home without a warrant, he and Jessie made sure their stories matched. With a subsequent search warrant issued, Black's personal effects had been bagged and sent for DNA testing. He caught a glimpse of Mhairi walking past his office door and said, 'Got to go, Becky. Get back to me as soon as you have a match.'

He caught up with Mhairi in the incident room.

'Any luck?' he asked.

'Yes and no,' she said. 'St Monans post office confirmed that they deliver mail to Black's home slash business address for a Mr Scott Black and SB Contracting only. They have no record of delivering mail to that address for any other person.'

'So that's the No. What about the Yes?'

'I asked if they had a Post Office Box in his name.' A pause, then, 'They don't.'

'But . . . ?'

'But if Black wanted mail delivered to him under some other name, he wouldn't use a local PO Box where he might be known, would he? So I drove to Anstruther post office, and showed the staff Black's photo, and that's when I got lucky. One of them – Liz Murray – said she recognised him, but not as Scott Black. She knows him as Robert Kerr.'

'She's sure it's him?'

'No doubts.'

'And there's a PO Box in that name?'

'Yes, sir.'

'Find out how he pays for it, and if he's got a bank account. Credit and debit cards, too. And see if he's got a Social Security number, then get on to the Inland Revenue. Maybe he's paying taxes. Who knows.' Another thought struck him. 'This Liz Murray, would she know if mail's delivered to that PO Box on a regular basis?'

Mhairi smiled. 'This is the Yes bit, sir. The return address is mostly from the Standard Chartered Bank in St Helier, Jersey. I was about to contact them.'

'Don't,' he said. 'Without a warrant, you're wasting your time. Get on to the FIU in Glenrothes, and have them jump on the paperwork. We need access to all accounts in the name of Robert Kerr as a matter of priority. And make sure they understand that he's wanted for questioning on suspicion of double murder.'

'I'll do that right away, sir.'

He returned to his office, enthused for once. A bank account in the Channel Islands might give his investigation the injection it needed. The Financial Investigation Unit should be able to fast-track the paperwork, particularly at the mention of double murder.

He was scribbling down his thoughts when a knock on his door interrupted him.

Jessie stood there, face pale and drawn. 'Have you got some time, sir?'

'If you've got the money,' he joked. But whatever was troubling her seemed to have stifled her sense of humour.

'I was going to drive to Glasgow this afternoon to ID Terry.'

He almost cursed at his thoughtlessness. Recent events must have had her tottering on the edge. 'I'm sorry, Jessie. Of course. Take whatever time you need.'

'Thank you, sir.'

He held her gaze, expecting her to leave, but she just stood there, eyes tearful.

'Can I help?' he said.

She jerked a smile. 'I've been stupid.'

'Who hasn't?'

'No, Andy, I've been *really* stupid. Tommy came to my house last night.'

Ice zapped his spine. He recalled Dainty's words of concern, of Jessie being next on her brother's list of people to kill. 'Did he threaten you?'

She slipped a hand into her pocket. 'He wanted my help. But I can't do that. So I'm just going to pass this on.' She laid Tommy's note on Gilchrist's desk.

Gilchrist stared at it, not sure if he should bag it as criminal evidence. But being given a note from a criminal brother – albeit one wanted for questioning on suspicion of murder – was not criminal in and of itself, although he could already hear the legal arguments.

'Have you looked at it?' he asked.

'It's some names.'

'Whose names?'

'I think you should have a look yourself, sir.'

'Where's Tommy now?' he asked.

'On the run. Said he wasn't going down for something he didn't do.'

'Meaning . . .' He hesitated, tongue-tied as to how best to phrase it. 'Your mother's and brother's . . .'

'Yes.'

'So he's saying he's got nothing to do with either of them?'

'Yes.'

'And you believe him?'

'Yes.' She blinked, and a tear spilled down her cheek.

He sensed that what she was asking him to do was beyond what anyone could expect to be reasonable. But he couldn't let her down. 'So this list is presumably the names of those responsible for the crimes for which Tommy is wanted for questioning?'

'I think so, sir, yes.'

He felt helplessness swell within him. He would never have taken Jessie for a fool, but she was being as gullible as any fool he'd ever come across. 'You do realise, don't you, that Tommy could be spinning you a line.'

'He's not lying. I know he isn't—'

'He's wanted on suspicion of a double murder, Jessie. He'll say anything to get out of it. He'll lie to his back teeth if he has to.'

'He's not lying, Andy.'

Well, there he had it. Blood really was thicker than water. Even bad blood.

'Tommy's been in and out of prison all his life,' he said. 'He was charged with GBH and got away with it before. He's perfectly capable of killing, so it's not unreasonable to suspect he's responsible for . . .' Jesus Christ, here he was again, trying to tiptoe on eggshells around the obvious. 'For murdering your mother and brother,' he said.

'Yesterday you were worried that I could be next on Tommy's list. Last night he had his chance to kill me. But he didn't. Is that not convincing enough?'

'If he had, there was no turning back for him. He now sees you as his only chance of staying out of prison.'

'I know he's not lying, Andy. I just know it.'

Well, the mood Jessie was in, it was pointless continuing to argue. He pulled the note closer. 'And this will prove Tommy's innocence?'

'No. It'll give them some other names to consider.'

'By *them*, you mean . . .?'

'Someone only *you* can trust.'

He nodded. She was implying Dainty. Over the years, he and Dainty had confided in this, shared in that, none of it ever illegal, but all of it played close to their chests. If Gilchrist had to trust someone with his life, Dainty would be his go-to man.

He unfolded the note, ran his eyes down it, then grimaced.

She nodded. 'That's what I thought.'

'OK,' he said. 'Let's have it from the beginning.'

CHAPTER 23

An hour later, Gilchrist phoned DCI Peter 'Dainty' Small of Strathclyde Police.

'Keep it short,' Dainty said. 'I'm up to my oxters in fucking alligators and horse shite and Christ knows what else.'

'What's the latest on Tommy Janes?' Gilchrist said.

'Not being handled by me. Like me to pass you over to Victor?'

'Would that be Chief Superintendent Victor Maxwell of the *BAD* squad?'

Dainty hesitated, but caught the emphasis. 'What've you got, Andy?'

Gilchrist smiled. 'A few names you might like to have a look at.'

'To do with Tommy Janes?'

'Correct.'

'Names you don't want Maxwell to look at because . . .?'

'Because Tommy Janes could be innocent, and is being set up.'

'Says who?'

'A friend.'

The line filled with electronic silence long enough for Gilchrist to worry that Dainty had hung up. But Dainty harboured a mistrust of phones and all things digital, and would be considering how to carry on without mentioning a snitch's name over a phone line that could be – as unlikely as it seemed – compromised.

'Do you want to meet?' Dainty said at length.

'Probably easier if I arranged a delivery to your preferred address.'

'You got my home details?'

'I have.'

'Tonight. Between seven and eight. I'll be there.'

The line died.

Gilchrist wrote a brief summary of Jessie's incident with Tommy, then inserted that and the note into an envelope addressed to Dainty's home in Bearsden, north of Glasgow. He then spent the next hour reading fresh reports, before catching Ted Baxter sneaking a smoke in the Office car park.

Baxter ground out his dout when he saw Gilchrist approaching. 'Sir?'

'Any advance on the motorbike footage?'

'Not yet, sir.'

'Keep hard at it.' He held out Dainty's envelope. 'You've got family in Glasgow, haven't you?'

'I do, sir, yes.'

'And you're familiar with Bearsden?'

'Yes, sir.'

'I want you to deliver this in person between seven and eight tonight.'

Baxter took the envelope. 'Do you need a signed receipt for it, sir?'

184

'That won't be necessary. I'll be talking to DCI Small later.' He levelled his gaze at Baxter. 'And it would be useful to have something positive on that motorbike when I do.' He caught a look of puzzlement creep across Baxter's face – what does Strathclyde Police have to do with a search for a motorbike in Fife? Nothing, if he had to be told the truth. But it was as good a kick up the arse as any. 'Can you manage that?'

'Yes, sir.'

Gilchrist found Mhairi in Jackie's office.

'I got hold of the FIU like you said, sir, and they jumped on it. Standard Chartered has one account for a Robert Kerr, sir, but the home address they have for him isn't St Monans, but Alloa.'

Gilchrist didn't like the sound of that. Did he have it wrong? Were they chasing down some other Robert Kerr? 'Do you need to speak to Liz Murray again?'

'No, sir, there's no doubt it's him. Standard Chartered *does* mail monthly statements to the Anstruther PO Box, sir. In his name.'

'So Alloa is where Black lived before changing his name and moving to St Monans?'

'I think so, sir. Standard Chartered also confirmed a change in mailing instructions three years ago.'

'About the time Black arrived in St Monans?'

'Yes, sir.'

Now they were on track. 'But why not change his address to St Monans?'

'Don't know, sir. Maybe he didn't want the bank to know where he's moved to.'

Gilchrist's mind crackled with possibilities. 'Whose name is on the title deeds of that Alloa address?'

Mhairi smiled, to let him know she was one step ahead. 'Jackie's already done a title search, sir, and it was transferred into some holding company three years ago.'

Again, about the same length of time Black had lived in St Monans. 'Does that holding company have a name?' he asked.

'Butterworth Holdings.'

The name meant nothing to him. But they were now uncovering some historic trail to Black – or was it Kerr? – and he was itching to reassign his team from tracking an imagined motorbike, to digging deeper into the fresh tracks of Black's past. But experience had taught him that murder investigations were not solved by simple flashes of inspiration, but through persistent plodding and relentless pursuit of the mundane and the boring.

No, better to continue with two fronts for the time being.

'Get on to Companies House and find out what you can on Butterworth Holdings – who its directors are, what its value is, how it earns its keep, is it privately owned, et cetera. You know the score.'

Back in his office, he called Cooper again.

'You're becoming impatient,' she said. 'I don't expect the DNA results today.'

'Speed it up if you can, Becky. I need to be one hundred per cent certain that it's Black's DNA under Kandy Lal's fingernails.'

'I'll do what I can.'

He spent the next thirty minutes being brought up to speed on his motorbike theory. But no one had any luck interviewing the motorbike riders captured on CCTV, and by late afternoon he was about to abandon that line of enquiry once and for all when his mobile rang – ID Jack.

'Jack,' he said. 'This is a rarity.'

'Me calling you during daylight hours, you mean?' Jack gave a dry chuckle, then said, 'Are you busy, man? You eaten yet?'

Jack's question made Gilchrist realise he'd had nothing to eat all day, just a cup of coffee. A late lunch might reinvigorate his tired brain cells. 'Could do with a bite.'

'And a pint?'

'Wouldn't say no.'

'Just walking into the Central. Want me to order a Best?'

'That'll work.'

'Better get here before it goes flat, then.'

Outside, the day was dying. A stiff wind chilled North Street with its ice-cold breath. The middle of winter was still five weeks away, but no one would call you a liar for saying it had already arrived. He turned into College Street, now pedestrianised, not much more than a single lane. His footfall echoed off the old stone buildings either side. Damp cobbles glistened with an early frost. Ahead, Market Street glowed like a welcoming beacon.

He pushed through the Central Bar's side door, into the hubbub of a busy town pub. Only Monday evening, and it seemed as if the crowd was already practising for the weekend. He located Jack at the bar, pint in hand, talking to a woman he would place somewhere in her forties, maybe even fifties. A full pint of beer stood next to an empty shooter glass – Jack's double vodka?

Jack surprised him by holding out his hand – not the usual high-five – then turned to the woman by his side and said, 'Jen, I'd like you to meet the old man.'

Jen flickered a smile, a flash of whitened teeth that could do with being straightened. 'Does the old man have a name?' she said.

'It's Andy,' Jack said.

'Not Andrew?'

'Andy will do just fine,' Gilchrist said, then nodded to the beer. 'Is that mine?'

'It's got your name written all over it,' Jack said.

Pint safely in his hand, and that round-robin chinking of glasses done, he took a first sip that brought it almost to the half-way mark.

'Thirsty?' Jack said.

'Could say.' He noticed Jack's pint was barely touched, and he had the unsettling feeling that he had interrupted some private moment between his son and Jen. He caught Jen giving Jack a wary look, as if warning him not to let their secrets slip. So he stepped in with, 'Tell me, Jen, how do you know Jack?'

'She's exhibiting my work,' Jack said.

'In your South Street studio?'

Jen's eyes flared. 'How do you know I have a studio in South Street?'

'Don't you?'

'I do. Of course. Only had it about a month.' She reached for her glass.

Jack did likewise.

Gilchrist let a few seconds pass, then said, 'So how does that work?'

'How does what work?'

'Artists. Studios. Who pays what to whom?'

'Fifty-fifty, man. Just the norm.'

'No money upfront?'

'Is that what you think I would do?' Jen said.

Her look reminded him of an eagle's – piercing, wide-eyed, direct – and he wondered why he'd taken an instant dislike to her.

Because she was so much older than Jack? He couldn't say, and thought it best just to pull back from any confrontation.

'Not at all. I'm just interested in how the process works.' He sipped his beer, caught Jack's what-the-fuck look, then said, 'Didn't Jack tell you that I'm with Fife Constabulary? A policeman.'

'He did mention that,' she said.

'Well, there you go. Bad habit of mine. Asking too many questions all the time.'

Jack laughed, chinked his glass against Jen's, then gulped back some beer.

Gilchrist felt relieved that whatever mini-crisis he might have caused seemed to have evaporated. He took another mouthful of beer, and said, 'Are you going to surprise me by telling me that Jack's the next Picasso?'

'Hey, man. Steady on. I'm good, but not that good.'

'So how good is he?' he asked Jen.

She pursed her lips, rocked her head from side to side. 'As in life, beauty is in the eye of the beholder. What appeals to one art-lover might not appeal to another. So any piece of art, be it a sculpture or a painting, has no intrinsic value attached to it.'

'So you're saying that Jack's paintings are only worth what someone is willing to pay for them?'

'Any artist's paintings, for that matter.'

'Other than Picasso or Van Gogh?'

'Well, they've already made their name, and their works command exorbitant prices. But when Van Gogh was alive, he was penniless, and was able to carry on with his art and eke out a living only through his brother's generosity.'

'It seems unfair,' Gilchrist said.

'Yeah, man, when I go, all my stuff'll be worth a mint, then you'll be rich.'

He tilted his pint towards his son. 'I'd rather hope I'd be dead and buried long before you.'

Jen offered a lopsided smile in condolence.

'You never answered my question,' Gilchrist said to her.

She held her glass to her mouth and said, 'Jack's work is exciting and colourful, solid and competent, and . . .' She glanced at Jack as her eyes crinkled in imitation of a loving smile. '. . . without putting my head on the block, mostly worth somewhere in the low- to mid-five figures. But . . .' she said, and cast her arm wide in an expansive gesture – without spilling a drop, he noted. 'Who knows? In a few years, Jack's work could command six figures, even more. Seven. You never know.'

Jack beamed. 'Now you're talking, Jen.'

She buried her face in her wine again.

Gilchrist thought *solid* and *competent* were adjectives that did not inspire much confidence, and had the distinct impression that he'd just listened to a sales spiel by someone who lacked the expertise of a salesperson. 'But with a bit of luck,' he said, 'Jack could die young, and his work might then become priceless.'

Jack guffawed. 'Didn't I tell you the old man had a warped sense of humour?'

Jen nodded, and edged closer to Jack.

'And what about Chloe's paintings?' Gilchrist asked.

'Jen's going to exhibit them alongside mine.'

It hardly seemed credible that three years had passed since the nightmare of Chloe's death. Jack had inherited her paintings against the wishes of her parents, who had wanted to sell them,

190

even destroy them. But Jack had vowed never to sell her paintings, only to exhibit them from time to time.

Gilchrist was no art aficionado, but to his eye Chloe had been talented, a gifted artist whose paintings could evoke emotion in a way that Jack's never could – although he would never dare share these thoughts with his son. He took a sip of beer, and eyed Jen.

'So how much do you think Chloe's paintings could sell for?'

'They're not for sale,' Jack said.

Gilchrist thought Jen looked less convinced. 'In theory,' he added.

'About the same,' she said.

'The same as Van Gogh's, or the same as Jack's?'

Jack guffawed again, then downed his beer and thumped the empty glass on to the bar counter, catching the barman's eye with a nod for another round. 'You crack me up, Andy, so you do. I tell you what, man, I'm hungry.' He grabbed a menu from the bar, then threw an arm around Jen's shoulder. 'Ready to eat, pets?'

She almost spilled her wine freeing herself from Jack's grip, and made a show of dabbing her lips with a tissue she pulled from her sleeve. 'Order for me, Jack,' she said.

'The usual?'

'I'll be back in a tick.'

Gilchrist watched Jack watch Jen squeeze through the throng, heading to the Ladies.

Then Jack turned to him with a smile, and said, 'What do you think?'

'I think I'll skip lunch.'

'No. About Jen.'

'Oh.' He sipped his beer. He didn't want another. 'I think she knows her stuff.'

'And she's good-looking, too.'

191

'Well, I can't dispute that, although she seems a bit older than you.'

'We're not a couple,' Jack said. 'Yet.'

Gilchrist raised an eyebrow.

'But I tell you, man, with age comes maturity. And experience. As you say, she really knows her stuff.' Jack nodded at the wisdom of his own words. 'Lots of contacts, too. Big names from London. Even Paris. Hey man, New York, too.'

'How about China?'

Jack frowned, then grinned. 'You're at it, man. But I tell you what, I'm just champing at the bit to get this exhibition going.'

The barman plonked two beers on the counter, and Gilchrist said, 'I can't stay, Jack. I've got to get back.'

'I just got you a beer, Andy.'

'I'm sure you won't let it go to waste.'

'Waste not, want not. That's what Mum used to say.'

Gilchrist didn't bother to finish the remains of his pint, just placed it on the bar and pushed it away. 'Give my apologies to Jen, but I've got to go.'

'Will do, man.'

'Do you happen to have one of her business cards?'

'Sure.' Jack removed a shiny leather wallet from his back pocket. 'Like it?' he said. 'Present from Jen.'

'Very nice.' He took a card from Jack.

Then Jack gave a chest-high high-five with a reverse hand-shake, managing to pull Gilchrist into him for a hug. 'Love you, man.'

Despite his surprise, Gilchrist said, 'Love you, too, Jack.'

He eased his way through the evening crowd and exited on to Market Street. Through the window he caught Jen returning to

Jack, her face breaking into a smile when Jack told her that his *old man* had to return to the Office.

In College Street, he had Jen's business card in one hand, his mobile in the other. He dialled the Office and got through to Mhairi.

'I'd like you to do a favour for me.'

'Of course, sir.'

'It's off the record,' he said, 'but I need you to get Jackie to check out a company for me.' He read the name on the business card. 'Jen Tinto. The Tinto Gallery.' Then an address in London.

'Anything we're looking for, sir?'

'Whatever you can find on the owner. If it's a genuine business or not. How long it's been around. How it earns its keep. That sort of thing.'

'Will do, sir.'

He ended the call and quickened his pace. He never understood how that sixth sense of his worked, how his gut twinged when something didn't seem right. Jack had never been materialistic, was more into his painting than anything else. Which was his weakness, if you thought about it, too willing to take people at face value, too eager to befriend anyone who appreciated his work. And always far too trusting when it came to money.

Gilchrist had no idea who Jen Tinto was, or what she was about.

But he would make a point of finding out.

CHAPTER 24

Jessie hadn't set foot in Glasgow's Mortuary for well over a year, not since she'd insisted on witnessing a post-mortem of a drug mule to confirm there were no last-second switches with the mule's delivery. When the package, half a kilo of uncut heroin in small bundles of tightly wrapped plastic, all the better to swallow, had been removed from her stomach – one bag having leaked, and the cause of death – only then had she signed off on the body.

And here she was again.

This time to ID the bodies of her bitch for a mother, and lunatic for a brother.

She walked up to the first of the two gurneys, surprised by how small her mother's body looked under the sheet, as if death had come in overnight and stolen not only her soul, but half her body mass, too.

Dr Fotheringham gripped the edge of the sheet.

Jessie took a deep breath and said, 'Let's get it over with.'

Fotheringham lifted the sheet, pulling it back with care, easing it down and over the dead woman's face, to fold it neatly across the body's shoulders.

'Jesus,' Jessie said, and clapped a hand to her mouth. She closed her eyes for a brief moment, then forced herself to look, willing all that hatred and anger she'd built up over the years to transfer itself into the wreck of the woman who lay before her, dead and stiff and marble-white.

Jeannie Janes had lived hard and tough. She'd struggled against drink and drugs all of her life, the pain of that battle printed on her face in scars and wrinkles for the world to see. It seemed that her mother's transition from the land of the living to that of the dead had been every bit as difficult. Her lips were bared in a rictus smile that revealed capped teeth rooted in black gums. A rugged graze on her cheek, deep enough to show bone, looked as if someone had scraped her face down a roughcast wall. Her left eye was swollen closed and purple, her right half-open to reveal the thousand-yard stare of the dead.

'DS Janes?'

'Roll it down.'

'Are you able to confirm if this is—?'

'All the way down. Please. I need to see.'

Fotheringham frowned, then pulled the sheet back to reveal a string of floral tattoos that ran from each shoulder down her arms. The irony was not missed on Jessie. Her mother never had a garden, never wanted one, and never brought flowers home, as if their fragrance would chase the preferred filth from her life. And here she was, arms tattooed like a human trellis. Fotheringham lowered the sheet past a pair of breasts as flat as potato scones. Jeannie Janes had never been overweight, and the sight of her ribbed torso helped Jessie understand that her mother must have been averse to eating. Her skin was blue-white, veined like marble, as if her body had never seen the sun.

195

Jessie lifted her gaze and looked at Dr Fotheringham. Why anyone would choose forensic pathology for a career defied logic. A slender woman, closer to the beginning of her working life than the end, Fotheringham returned her gaze with calm brown eyes that seemed at odds with the gruesome nature of her job. Dyed blonde hair cut short accentuated the roundness of a face that seemed destined to defy age and wrinkles.

The woman who lay between them could have been a different species.

Jessie nodded. 'She's my mother. Jeannie Janes.'

Fotheringham gave a sad smile, then pulled the sheet up and over the body.

Jessie walked to the second gurney and waited for Fotheringham to join her.

Fotheringham eased the sheet back without prompting, folding it down to a whippet-thin waist. Where her mother's body had been pale to the point of alabaster-white, Terry's was tanned as if he'd just returned from a month's frying on the Costa del Sol. A full-body tattoo, more colourful than a Yakuza gangster's, told stories of knives and mythical beasts, overladen with the names of women he'd bedded, or worse, murdered. Even in death, Terry looked fit and lean and street-fighter hard. The invincible image was spoiled by a twelve-inch slash – maybe longer – that ran diagonally across his belly-button, and had Jessie wondering how Terry had managed to prevent his guts from spilling on to the street.

But strangely, or so Jessie thought, she felt nothing, absolutely nothing. Not even a sliver of a hint of sadness over Terry's wasted life. Not even the tiniest flicker of regret that she and Terry had failed to form any familial bond whatsoever. Growing up, they could have been two strangers living in the same household. As adults, they hadn't spoken to each other for over fifteen years – if you discounted face-to-face swearing, that is. Instead, she looked down on her brother's body with a dispassion that almost frightened her.

Shouldn't she feel something? Shouldn't she be wishing they'd at least made some kind of effort to get to know each other? This was her brother, for crying out loud, her own flesh and blood. Christ, the man before her had been Robert's uncle – a scary thought that brought her back to her senses.

She nodded to Fotheringham. 'That's my brother, Terry Janes.'

She didn't wait for Fotheringham to pull the sheet over the body. She didn't wait to be accompanied from the mortuary, or to be invited to Fotheringham's office for a parting cup of tea. Instead, she turned on her heels and headed for the door.

When she walked out on to Saltmarket, the wind had stilled, and the air felt nowhere near as cold as it had on the east coast. She took a long breath, tasting that west coast dampness that could seep into every part of your clothing and being, and chill you to the marrow if the wind picked up. She felt the oddest sense of being unclean, as if just being in close proximity to her family was contamination enough. Another couple of breaths, deep and quick, voided her lungs of any remnants of air from the mortuary.

She took out her phone.

Gilchrist answered on the third ring. 'How did it go?' he asked.

She stared off along the busy street, at cars and buses and people all going about their business, not knowing that her mother and brother were lying in the City Mortuary behind her, dead for the rest of eternity. She started walking.

'All done and dusted,' she said.

'You'll be glad that's over.'

'You have this habit of understating things.'

He pushed a dry chuckle down the line. 'Heard anything more from Tommy?'

'Nada. He's gone into hiding, like he said he would.'

'I've sent Baxter down to Glasgow to hand-deliver that note to Dainty. So nothing's going to happen until tomorrow at the earliest.'

'And then the shit hits the fan?'

'Could do,' he said. 'But my advice to you is to back off from it, and let it lie. You've done what you can, so it'll be up to Dainty and others to move things forward if – and it's a big if – they take on board what Tommy's given them.'

'I hear you,' she said.

'I'll see you first thing tomorrow.'

Jessie slipped her mobile into her pocket, and strode into town. She felt tense, from anger or frustration she couldn't say. It was to be expected, that information provided by a known criminal would be viewed with the deepest suspicion – a guilty man trying to save his own neck. But deep down, she knew Tommy had been speaking the truth. Not like that snake of a dead brother of hers. Nor that demented witch of a mother. Tommy might have been the hardest of her family, but he'd held on to that almost forgotten mantra – *you don't harm friends and family*. Not that his and Jessie's relationship had been anywhere close to sibling love, but he had never hurt her – well, not much.

Jessie found herself traipsing west along Argyle Street, as if her mind was leading her back to her former place of work,

Strathclyde Police HQ. But halfway up Buchanan Street, common sense prevailed, telling her not to make a fool of herself, not to have it out with past work associates who were better off left alone, and forgotten. She hadn't asked for a transfer to Fife Constabulary because she was in love with Strathclyde. No, she left Glasgow to get rid of the mistakes of her past, clean her life of her criminal family and, more importantly, make a new life for herself and her son, Robert.

But just being in the city centre again, with its constant background rush of business and pleasure, its damp streets teeming with the end of Monday work crowds, and lit up with lights set for Christmas, sent a thrill through her. Buskers strummed guitars, or sang tuneless songs. Street artists twisted balloons, or stood as still as statues.

A whole year had passed since she'd last set foot in the city centre by herself, and almost eighteen months since she and her friend Fiona Lawson had last spoken. They texted each other from time to time, but as she was now in Glasgow she should at least make contact.

'Hello?'

Jessie thought Fi sounded wary, as if a call from an unknown number signalled only bad news. 'Fi?' she said. 'It's Jessie.'

'Jessie Janes?'

'How many Jessies do you know, for crying out loud? Of course it's me.'

'God, Jessie. It's been, what – a year? Where are you? Are you in St Andrews?'

'I'm walking up Buchanan Street, and my stomach's grumbling.'

'How long are you here for?'

'I'm driving back tonight.'

'Ditch the car. You're staying at mine. I'll meet you in the Rogano in ten minutes.'

'But I've got to—'

The line died.

CHAPTER 25

Gilchrist moved back from his computer, stood up and stretched his arms. He glanced at the time – 19.08. Christ, they were getting nowhere. He turned to the window and looked outside. The night sky was covered by clouds as dark as his mood. He could be staring at the results of his investigation for all he could see.

A knock at his door had him spinning on his heels. 'Yes, Mhairi.'

'I think you should look at this, sir.'

Something in her eyes gripped him. Hope sparked as he followed her.

In the incident room, her monitor came alive to an image of an expansive gravel area that fronted what looked like a row of stables. Off to the side, where a hawthorn hedgerow ended, the gravel opened on to a country road.

'What's this?' he said.

'Angus Graham's farm near Craigrothie. About four miles north of Montrave House, sir. PC Norris brought this in this afternoon.'

At the mention of Montrave House, Gilchrist leaned closer.

'Mr Graham was troubled last year with vandalism, so he installed a webcam under the eaves of one of the buildings opposite. Quality's not great, but it does the job. And it also picks up passing vehicles on the road.' She worked the mouse, and the screen jerked through a series of staccato images as first one car, then several more, drove past.

Then the monitor froze, and she zoomed in.

Gilchrist peered at the locked image. 'It's a motorbike,' he said.

'Heading north, sir. But it's not just any motorbike.' She flicked open a stapled pile of A4 sheets – registration numbers, names, addresses, highlighted in yellow, struck through in red pen. 'This is the list we've been working from: sixteen motorbikes picked up by CCTV on the outskirts of Leven and Cupar.' She tapped a finger at the screen. 'That number's not on the list. Check it out.'

Gilchrist scanned her list. An error might have been made if one of the numbers had been mistaken for a letter – 5 for an S; 8 for a B, that sort of thing. But within forty seconds, he'd been through them all. None came close to being similar.

'Is this webcam set to the correct time?'

'PC Norris checked it,' she said. 'It is.'

'So if this bike's not on the list—'

'It's because it never made it to Leven or Cupar, and it's still in the area, sir.'

He could see what Mhairi was getting at. But that motorbike could have been making a short journey from one farm to another, or could have turned off on to any number of roads between Cupar and Leven, beyond CCTV range. Whatever hope he'd built up evaporated in an instant. This proved nothing.

'We ran the number through the ANPR system,' Mhairi said, 'but it's not been picked up. So we checked DVLA for ownership, and it's registered in the name of Kerr Roberts.'

Gilchrist jolted. 'Kerr *Roberts*?' he said. 'Not Robert Kerr?'

'Kerr Roberts, sir.'

Robert Kerr? Kerr Roberts? One and the same, or just coincidence? But if you didn't believe in coincidence, where did that get you? 'What's the registered address?' he asked.

Mhairi gave him a knowing smirk. 'Same address in Alloa.'

Gilchrist's world stuttered for a split second. His mind was crackling with too many options. He needed to find that motorbike, expand CCTV footage, check the Alloa address, dig into bank accounts, tax records, credit cards, utility bills, maybe even try to uncover other vehicles registered in the name of Robert Kerr or Kerr Roberts.

He took a deep breath to steady his thoughts.

'Pull everyone into the Office,' he said. 'And put a marker on the PNC for that bike. Can we get someone to ID the make and model?'

'It should be on the DVLA records, sir.'

'Of course.' He was thinking too fast, and not with a clear mind. But by Christ they might just have smoked Black out of hiding. And with these thoughts, he came to see that in Scott Black he was dealing with a devious killer expert in the art of deception.

The PO Box in Anstruther; the number plates nicked from a 1976 Reliant Scimitar; the abandoned Land Rover; the replacement motorbike – make and model to be confirmed; the Channel Island bank account; the surprise address in Alloa. And with Black's historic trail now being uncovered, you didn't have to be a genius to reach the troubling conclusion that if he'd fled the scenes of two recent murders, there was every chance he'd fled the scenes of past murders.

Why else would he change names, change home addresses, confound bank accounts, obscure mailings, abandon boats and vehicles, and live alone in a quiet cottage by the sea? The thought of Black being a serial killer on the run, to keep hidden a murderous past, hit him with such force that his heart shuddered. They needed to find this man before he established a new identity and settled into some other, unsuspecting community.

Or worse . . .

. . . killed again.

'Prepare an appeal for national TV,' he said. 'And forward Black's photograph to all police forces – Scotland only for the time being. That motorbike was heading north. He won't be expecting us to be looking for it. So I'm banking on him not making a run to England or the Continent, but north to the Highlands, maybe one of the islands. Contact the Ports Authority, ferry terminals and airports. Let's make sure that bastard can't leave the mainland.'

Mhairi was scribbling like mad. 'Yes, sir.'

Another idea struck him, that if Black changed his identity with such regularity, then it might be interesting to see what names appeared on other documents. 'Did you have any luck with Companies House on Butterworth Holdings?' he asked.

'Not yet, sir. We should have something through in the morning.'

'Let me know what you come up with.'

Jessie watched Fiona Lawson bustle into the Rogano, a look of expectation creasing her face, which swept into a radiant smile when their eyes met. She rushed over and gave Jessie a hug that almost crushed the air from her lungs.

Then they faced each other.

'Jeez-oh, Jessie, you look amazing. Just amazing. Have you lost weight? Oh, I really hate you. I just need to look at food and I put on pounds. How do you do it? I bet you're on some secret diet that you're never going to share.' She rubbed her arms. 'Gosh, it's so cold outside. Not even December yet. Are you not cold? What're you having to drink?'

'I'll stick to soda water. I'm driving.'

'No, you're not. You're staying at mine.' She glanced at the glowing gantry, then said, 'I'm going to have a wine.' Then she dug into her handbag and removed a flower wrapped in plastic. 'Here,' she said. 'That's for you.'

Jessie held it to her face. 'It smells lovely, Fi. What is it?'

'A weed from my window garden,' she said, and burst out laughing.

Jessie couldn't help herself, and she joined in. With her infectious laugh and contagious effervescence, Fi lived life as if she were the most carefree person in the world.

But it hadn't always been that way.

Fi had been the only girl in a family of four brothers, whose alcoholic mother could do nothing to stop the sexual abuse Fi suffered at the hands of her abusive father. As if that wasn't bad enough, when Fi was ten her mother died – choked to death on her vomit – and Fi became the skivvy, a replacement mother to her brothers, a slave who cleaned the house, did the washing, cooked the meals, then was screwed by her father whenever the mood took him. It hadn't taken long for the brothers to catch on, and by the time Fi turned sixteen, she was being passed around the house like a sexual toy.

That was when Jessie first came across her.

As a fresh-eared PC with Strathclyde Police, Jessie had been the youngest member of a team investigating the fatal slashing of a local hoodlum. She had been assigned to door-to-door interviews, checking with neighbours who might have known the victim, or witnessed the offence taking place. She had rapped on the Lawsons' door as part of a routine process, and had to exchange words through the closed door before it was finally opened.

Old man Lawson stood before her, sweat beading his forehead. 'Fucking screws,' he said. 'What the fuck're you bastarts wanting now, eh?'

Jessie held out her warrant card, and explained that she was making enquiries with respect to a fatal attack on a resident of the block of flats. She was returning the card to her top breast pocket, when she caught movement in the hallway. Lawson shifted his stance to block her view. Even so, she glimpsed a girl over his shoulder, in T-shirt and knickers, running across the hallway. Her back was to Jessie, but as she entered the room, she cast a tearful glance Jessie's way.

Then she was gone, the door closed behind her.

'Who's that?' Jessie asked.

'Who's what?'

'The girl.'

'What's it to you?'

'Just asking.'

'Thought you were here to ask about thon fuckin murder.'

'I am, but maybe your daughter saw something.'

'Who says that was my daughter?'

'Isn't she?'

Lawson's eyes danced, as if unsure about admitting he had a daughter, albeit running about half-naked, or coming up with some other story. In the end, he settled for the truth. 'She is, aye, but she's fuckin stupit. Widnae've seen a thing.'

'Who else lives here?'

'The boys.'

'How many?'

'Four.'

'And your wife?'

'Deid.'

'I'm sorry to hear that.' Jessie flicked a smile. 'Can I speak to your boys?'

'They're no in.'

'Out working, are they?'

'Something like that.'

'So it's just you and your daughter that's in all alone, then?'

Lawson narrowed his eyes. 'What the fuck're you saying, eh?'

'Just trying to ascertain who lives here.'

'Aye, well, fuck that. You want my help answering questions, you fuckin wee cow, you'd better get a fuckin warrant, then. Eh? *Fuck* you.'

The door slammed.

Later that night, at the conclusion of her shift, Jessie did some work on her own. The look that girl had given her stayed with her. Although she could guess what was going on, without any evidence of abuse her Office would not assign already depleted resources to investigate. So, Jessie sniffed around, but found nothing on the PNC associated with the Lawson household. A talk to a friend in Social Services also confirmed no reported incidents.

But the girl's look haunted Jessie. If she closed her eyes, there it was. If she tried to sleep, it came to her in her dreams. She pleaded with her superiors to take action, and a mobile unit was eventually sent to the address, but reported nothing untoward. She met with Social Services in person, and someone was sent to talk to the girl – Fiona – but nothing seemed out of order. Jessie might not like Fiona being the only female in a household of five males, but that was no reason to take action. Jessie realised that it needed more than the memory of a furtive glance from a half-naked girl for something to be done.

So she decided to take matters into her own hands.

It took her six days, watching that house at night, after completing her shift. But she struck lucky on a Saturday when she spotted Fiona walking to the local Tesco supermarket. She followed her into the store, and made a point of bumping into her in one of the aisles.

'Sorry,' Jessie said, then added, 'you look familiar. Have we met before?'

Fiona lowered her eyes and walked away.

'*Fiona.*'

She stopped at the sound of her name, and turned to Jessie, eyes glistening.

Jessie walked up to her. 'I know what's going on, Fiona. Let me buy you a coffee. Will you let me do that? Please? And we can talk. I'm only trying to help.'

'You can't help,' she said.

'Fiona. Look at me. Look at my eyes.'

Her eyes flickered to Jessie, struggling to return her look.

Jessie reached for her hand. 'It doesn't need to happen, Fiona. I know it doesn't. We can stop it. No, don't, Fiona. Listen to me.

Please.' She tightened her grip as Fiona tried to pull away. 'We can stop it, Fiona. I know we can, because it happened to me.'

Fiona's eyes searched Jessie's, pleading for the truth.

'I can help you, Fiona. But to do that, you must help me.'

Without another word, Fiona fell into Jessie's arms and sobbed her heart out.

Two days later, Joe Lawson and his four sons were arrested and jointly charged with multiple counts of performing sexual acts with a minor, rape, and physical and mental abuse. Jessie was praised for her standalone efforts, and it was that single incident that changed her career, and put her on the path to becoming a detective.

Fiona was placed in a foster home, and she and Jessie kept in regular contact, up to and beyond the trial. All would have ended well, if not for one disappointing outcome, which came from one of Jessie's own. DS Brian Wheelan, who worked out of the Rutherglen police station, provided character references for Davie and Joey Lawson, Fiona's oldest brothers. He accused Jessie of making a scapegoat of the Lawsons for being sworn at during her door-to-door enquiries all those months earlier. His statements almost brought down the case, but in the end were sufficient only to mitigate the charges against Davie and Joey, who escaped custodial sentences. Joe Lawson was sentenced to ten years, and his other sons, Billy and Freddy, to four years each.

All that happened twelve years ago.

Fiona applied to the courts for a non-harassment order against her family, and as far as Jessie knew, that order was working. It was helped, of course, by Fiona's brothers having since left Glasgow; one to London as a sales rep with a major beverage distributor, two to Saudi Arabia as corporate security advisors

– thugs, in other words – and one to Australia as a computer sales-man. Her father, too, left the area, marrying some unfortunate Dutch woman and moving to Amsterdam. Fiona now worked with Strathclyde Police, in the payroll section, and was always a good source of gossip – and other information.

Jessie finished her soda and said, 'Want another glass of wine?'

Fiona shook her head. 'I shouldn't, should I? Are you having one?'

'I've got to get back for Robert.'

'How is your wee boy?'

'He's not wee any more.' The thought of the conversation turning to Robert's deafness had Jessie rushing on with, 'He's doing great at school, and my friend Angie – she's a part-time English teacher – helps when I'm not there. But she's got a hubbie to get back to.'

'So you can't stay at mine.'

'Sorry, Fi.'

'Well, have a wine then.'

'Maybe later. But that should't stop you having one now.'

'Go on, then. I'll worry in the morning about having a sore head.'

Jessie placed the order – large house red, soda water – and said, 'So what's the gossip, then? Do you ever come across Brian Wheelan?'

'He's still a DS. Nobody'll have him.'

'Other than Victor Maxwell, that is,' Jessie said.

'Scum of the earth, they are. I don't know why they don't get fired. Rules for us, then there's rules for them.'

Jessie leaned closer, gave a conspiratorial look around the bar, then cupped her hand to her lips. 'I know it's been a while, but did you ever get to the bottom of why he stood up for your brothers, Davie and Joey?'

'Why're you asking that now?'

Jessie shrugged. 'Just something I'm working on.'

Their drinks arrived then, and Fiona clamped shut.

When the waitress left, Fiona said, 'Freddy phoned when he got out of jail. Wanted to meet me. But I was having none of it. Besides, he's not allowed within fifty yards of me, or he'd be in breach of the non-harassment order. So I told him to eff off.'

Jessie chinked her glass against Fiona's. 'That's my girl.'

'He was really pissed off that he got sent to jail while Davie and Joey got away with it. Said he couldn't prove it, but he was sure Wheelan was their supplier.'

Jessie gave a tight smile. She had always suspected Wheelan was dealing drugs. But suspecting and proving could be on opposite poles of the planet. 'So when it came to crunch time, Davie and Joey had Wheelan by the curlies,' she said. 'And if he didn't put in a good word, they were going to dob him right in it.'

'Good and proper,' Fiona agreed. 'But I don't think Wheelan's ever stopped. He's got a big villa in Spain somewhere. You can't afford one of those on what a DS earns, I can tell you. And I should know.'

Jessie's mobile rang. She looked at it – ID Boss – glanced at Fiona and mouthed, *Got to take this.*

'We've got an early start in the morning,' Gilchrist said.

She pushed through the door into Exchange Place. 'When and where?'

'Briefing in the Office at seven a.m. Then we're going for a drive.'

'What's on?'

'I was right about Black's motorbike,' he said. 'It's been picked up on the ANPR in the small hours of Sunday morning, heading west on Clackmannan Road.'

'Where's that?'

'Outside Alloa. But then we lose him again.'

'Are you going to put a team on it?'

'No. Too much manpower to cover too wide an area. Until we get a better fix, it's going to be just you and me. I'll pick you up at quarter to seven.'

'Won't give me time to put on my make-up.'

He chuckled and said, 'Come as you are.'

The line died, leaving Jessie to shake off a shiver – from a frigid north wind, or from a sense of dread, she couldn't say.

What she could say, though, was that she wouldn't be staying over at Fiona's.

CHAPTER 26

Tuesday morning

Despite his intention to hit the ground running, flooded roads from an overnight sleet storm delayed Gilchrist on his way to the Office. At least it hadn't snowed, or the entire Fife coast would have needed ploughing out.

He started his briefing at 7.20 a.m., and sorted out his teams with a vengeance.

Mhairi was tasked with tracking down Butterworth Holdings, with Jackie assigned to work with her exclusively. Review of CCTV footage was paramount, particularly west in the direction of Alloa. Two teams were assigned to bank accounts, credit cards and tax filings for Robert Kerr and Kerr Roberts, working hand in hand with the Financial Investigation Unit in Glenrothes.

Next, he shoved a stick of dynamite up the IT techies' arses, telling them they were missing a beat. There had to be a lead in SB Contracting's website, he was sure of that – *so get the hell on with it.* Baxter was tasked with organising the appeal to the public; if Black wasn't dead, then he was buying food to stay alive, so someone must have seen him. Others were to liaise with Port authorities and harbour masters on the Fife coast. Airports, too, were to be alerted, and other local police forces contacted. Until they knew more about that motorbike, Gilchrist wanted to play it safe, stop Black at source if he ever decided to make a run for it overseas.

He ended the briefing with, 'Any questions?' When no one responded, he clapped his hands. 'Right, let's get cracking. We need to find this nutcase before he harms anyone else.'

He and Jessie set off for Alloa at the back of 8.00 a.m., only to be delayed by flooding on the outskirts of St Andrews, and construction works before Guardbridge. Intermittent storms and violent downpours forced him to slow to a crawl while his wipers did what they could to clear the windscreen. But traffic was relatively light, and Jessie used the time to bring him up to speed with her visit to the morgue, finally sharing her thoughts with him on DS Wheelan.

'Victor Maxwell knows how to pick them,' was all Gilchrist offered.

'Nothing back from Dainty?' she asked.

'It's too soon.'

When they reached Kinross, Jessie ordered him to stop for a coffee *before my tongue turns to cardboard*. With the last of her latte downed, she crammed her polystyrene cup into the space between the side of her seat and the console.

'Feeling better?' Gilchrist asked.

'Don't know how they lived in the Stone Age without coffee.'

'Who says they didn't have coffee back then?'

'Didn't know Costa Coffee had been in business that long.'

Gilchrist chuckled, and drove on as his phone rang – ID Cooper.

214

He put it through his car's speaker system. 'Yes, Becky?'

'Good morning to you, too, Andy.'

Jessie rolled her eyes, but said nothing.

'I rushed the DNA tests as you requested. You were right, Andy. It's Scott Black's DNA under Kandy Lal's fingernails.'

'So he killed her.'

'I'll get the PM report to you by the end of the day.'

He thanked her, but the line was already dead.

Jessie said, 'What side of the bed did she get out of this morning? She can say good morning, but can't say goodbye? The *bitch*.'

Silent, Gilchrist drove on, boosted by the knowledge that Black had been careless in disposing of Kandy Lal's body. Had he made his first mistake?

Or were they about to find out he'd made many others?

By the time he turned right at the roundabout and on to the A907 towards the town of Alloa, it was half-past nine already and the temperature had plunged. Ahead, in the cold mist, Alloa stood silhouetted like a fortified mound. Beyond, the Ochil Hills seemed to overlap in darkening greys and rounded peaks capped in white.

As he approached town, Gilchrist said, 'We're coming to where the ANPR picked up Black's motorbike.' He pulled his BMW off the road, killed the engine, and stepped out into a frosted Clackmannanshire morning.

The wind had stilled. Frozen mist blanketed the horizon. An articulated lorry thundered past, engine roaring, startling a cluster of starlings that fluttered to the air in waves. He walked to the front of his car and compared the scene before him with the CCTV image in his hand.

'What are we looking for?' Jessie said.

'Just getting a feel for the place.'

'Well see if you can get a feel for the weather heater, and turn it on. I'm freezing.'

'You're always cold.'

'That's because it's always cold up here.'

'Up here being Scotland?'

'Up here being north of Glasgow.'

'Here we're mostly east.'

'That, too.'

'Right.'

He stared towards town.

The only CCTV image picked up on the ANPR system was the image he was holding. Somehow that warned him that Black was a formidable foe. Every move Black made, he did so to cover his tracks. CCTV cameras watched over most of Alloa's thorough-fare. Gilchrist had confirmed they were all working, which begged the question – if this was the only CCTV image they had, and Black had not driven into town, then where the hell had he gone?

He crossed the road, Jessie behind him, and walked to a gap in the hedgerow where a pedestrian path petered off across the fields. Several hundred yards in the distance, a woman was walking the flattened trail, a Golden Labrador criss-crossing the fields with its nose to the ground. Gilchrist crouched down, ran his fingers over flattened grass.

'OK, Tonto. What've you found?'

He stood. 'Too much rain.' He eyed the fields. Beyond, the land seemed to swell like a rising wave up to the Ochil Hills. The dog-walker changed course as she followed the path. From where he stood, it was impossible to see the path itself, but if he looked past the dog-walker, towards where she was heading, he thought he saw an opening in another hedgerow that led to a copse of trees.

'Let's go,' he said, and stepped onto the pathway.

Without walking boots, the path was slippery, and his feet slid out from under him a couple of times. He managed to prevent himself from falling, with quick reactions, using his hands. But Jessie seemed to be having no trouble.

'It's these shoes you wear,' she said, 'all polished with leather soles. You need a pair of these.' She stamped the ground, leaving indents as deep as moon-prints. 'Only five quid on eBay.'

'You buy second-hand shoes?'

'I didn't say that.'

'Well, seeing as how you don't need your hands, find out if Mhairi's had any news back from Companies House.'

'A bit early for that, isn't it?'

He walked on, leaving her to it with her mobile to her ear. She might have no need of hands when walking, but she seemed unable to use her legs while on the phone.

Ten minutes later, he pushed through the opening in the hedgerow into a wooded area, thankful to find the ground drier there. The air seemed warmer, too, the trees acting as wind-breaks. But if he thought drier ground would make it easier to find tyre tracks he was sorely mistaken. The path branched off in any number of directions, fading into the woods. He was no forensics expert, and certainly no scout, and realised he was searching for a trail that in all probability didn't even exist.

It took Jessie a couple of minutes to reach him, her face red from the effort of trying to catch up. 'Bloody hell, I'm knackered,' she said.

'Exercise is good for you.'

'It's all right for you, being skinny as a rake. Try walking about humping this lot.' She put her hands to her chest and heaved upwards.

'Any luck?' he said.

She smirked. 'Scott Black is the nominated director of Butterworth Holdings, and his registered address is a PO Box in Alloa.'

This was news. 'Get Mhairi on to the post office and—'

'She's already on it,' Jessie interrupted. 'But here's the good bit. Kerr Roberts is the company secretary. And his address is in Alloa, too.' She handed him her mobile. 'You're going to love this.'

A Google Maps layout with a red location arrow filled the screen. He zoomed out to get his bearings, but lost the screen. Jessie recovered it, and handed it back to him. He fiddled with the screen again, got his bearings, and stared off across an adjacent field that rose to a line of bushes, then fell away on the other side.

'Christ,' he said. 'It's over that hill.'

'Want me to call it in?'

'No, let's ca' canny, and have a look first.'

He set off, Jessie traipsing after him.

Once out of the copse, the land rose before them in a steepening slope to a rounded peak. The address they were looking for should be on the other side. If Black and Roberts and Kerr were one and the same person – and he had little reason to doubt that now – the pieces were slotting into place: the escape on the motorbike, the ride across fields to avoid being picked up by CCTV cameras in Alloa, and ending at a new address – his safe house? – to lick his wounds. Or plan his next move.

218

But with that logical summary came worry.

So far, his team had found nothing criminal under Black's name, or his aliases. But for all anyone knew, the man could have a hidden cache of weapons at this address. Even so, it was too early to call it in. They would first need to ascertain whether he was there or not.

They plodded on, like a couple of hikers in line.

The going was easy at first, the grass thick and uncut, which allowed Gilchrist to stomp in his shoes for grip as the slope steepened. But what had looked like a gentle slope from the outset was turning into a steeper gradient, the closer they got to the row of bushes. Over the last few yards, Gilchrist had to grip tufts of grass to pull himself up, avoiding dormant thistles that seemed to thrive on that spot.

He reached the flattened peak, then turned to lend Jessie a hand.

'Bloody hell,' she said. 'I've just been spiked by a thistle.' She scrubbed the back of her hand against her jacket. 'It's sore.'

'You'll survive.'

'I think you need to work on your bedside manner.'

'Nearly there.'

He pushed through a thinning gap in the hedgerow into another field that plateaued for fifty yards before rearing into the Ochil Hills to their right, but rolling over and down into a small valley on their left, from which a wisp of smoke rose into the still air like a grey mast.

'Let's see that phone of yours again,' he said.

Jessie pulled up Google Maps. 'There's only one house,' she said. 'So that smoke's from the address we're looking for—'

'Which means Black's in.'

'Or someone else is.'

He frowned at her. 'You think he's got an accomplice?'

'With this dickhead, nothing would surprise me.'

From where they stood, the cottage was hidden by the crown of the slope. But if they stood on the crown, they would be silhouetted against the backdrop of the Ochil Hills.

Anyone in the cottage could see them.

He looked around him, his gaze drifting down the hill, all the way back to his speck of a car parked on the edge of the road. It looked miles away. Had they really walked that far? Which made up his mind for him. They would keep moving forward.

Ahead, he noticed a hillside burn, its slopes thick with undergrowth. He pointed to it. 'We'll take a look from there,' he said. 'And stay out of sight.'

The wind shifted then, breaking the column of smoke, twisting it as if it had collapsed under its own weight. The sky had turned an angry grey that threatened snow.

'Let's go before the heavens open,' Jessie said.

As they stole towards the hillside undergrowth, Gilchrist could not shift the unsettling feeling that they had missed something, that Black was always one step ahead of them.

And that they were walking into a trap.

CHAPTER 27

Before Gilchrist and Jessie reached the burn, the chimney stack came into view.

As they, eased closer, the roof deepened. Closer still, guttering appeared, followed by roughcast walls. He raised his hand to keep Jessie from stumbling on. Another few steps and they would be fully exposed before they reached their vantage point.

'We need to keep back from the edge,' he said.

He changed tack, turning towards the foothills, keeping the bushes as a visual barrier between them. Even so, he trod with care. Clumps of hawthorn and ferns provided cover, but other saplings – chestnut, ash, oak – had lost their leaves for the winter, and offered next to no cover at all.

He folded into a crouch, and had to sink to his knees over the final yards. From there, they had a clear view of the cottage. If Black happened to look out one of the windows, and his gaze found its way up the hill, against the backdrop of the Ochil Hills he would not notice Gilchrist and Jessie – provided they remained still.

Cold dampness seeped through Gilchrist's trousers, sending a chill into his thighs. He heard Jessie scuffling behind him, felt the warm gush of her breath as she pulled level.

'What've we got?' she said.

'I don't see the motorbike.'

'You think it's here?'

'See that hut?' he said. 'It could be in there.'

The cottage stood at the end of a narrow asphalt road that stretched off to Alloa in the distance. Closer to the town, houses stood either side of the road, but thinned out as the road rose to the foothills, until only fields, stone walls and hedgerows lined both sides. The road rose steeply over the closing quarter-mile. The hillside burn, which provided fertile banks for bushes and saplings, slipped past the back of the cottage in a deep cut that became a narrow stream which hugged one side of the road.

The cottage itself reminded Gilchrist of a smallholding constructed in the 1940s, with roughcast walls painted weather-worn white. But where smallholdings were mostly square in shape, this cottage was longer, more rectangular. Two windows at the gable end had curtains drawn. A single chimney stack sprouted two chimney pots, one of which oozed smoke. A flat-roof extension had been constructed by the back door, which he figured was a utility room. Even from where he kneeled, the extension looked in dire need of a coat or three of paint, or being ripped out altogether.

At the bottom of the slope stood the garden hut, relatively new, its wooden structure a golden varnish, and large enough to store a complete array of gardening tools, although he saw no signs of a garden, vegetable or otherwise. Interestingly, or so he thought, the hut had a small window on the rear wall. He turned his attention back to the cottage, searching for movement within. But it could be derelict for all he could see.

'It seems awful quiet,' Jessie said. 'D'you think he's here?'

'Well, the fire's on.'

'Maybe he's gone into Alloa for shopping or something.'

'And left the fire untended?'

'He could've used one of these metal cage-type thingies.'

'A fireguard?'

'That's the word I was looking for.'

He'd seen too many deaths from fires started through domestic carelessness to put his trust into something as flimsy as a fireguard. When he'd renovated Fisherman's Cottage, he tore out the original fireplace and installed a gas fire – convenient, clean, and easy to light with the click of a switch. Somehow, that thought told him that Black would not have left for town with a fireguard for safety.

'I don't see a car,' Jessie said.

'Because he's got a motorbike.'

'Or driven a car into town.'

'Get hold of Mhairi,' he said. 'See if she's found anything.' While Jessie made the call, he checked his own phone for messages – two only – but neither had any bearing on his investigation. He slipped it back into his jacket as Jessie ended her call.

'Anything?' he asked.

'The IT techies are twitching over some server details,' she said. 'Something to do with SB Contracting's website.'

'What've they found?'

'She's not sure, but they might have something by the end of the day.' She nodded to the cottage. 'So what are we waiting for?'

Somehow the thought that Black might be down there, barricaded inside, armed to the teeth and just itching to resist arrest, sent a tremor through him. Or perhaps he was shivering from the cold.

But Jessie was right. It was time to make a move.

'Turn off your phone,' he said, scanning the hillside that overlooked the cottage. He imagined he saw the makings of a worn pathway through the ferns, which ran along the face of the hill. If they took that path, it was as good a way as any to the cottage.

He pushed himself back, knees shuffling through wet grass, until he was far enough from the top of the slope to stand without being seen from the cottage. He brushed his legs, slapped off water, leaves, bits of grass, and waited for Jessie to join him.

'Ready?' he said.

'What's my hair like?'

'This way.'

The pathway turned out to be no path at all, but a rabbit- or hare-run that zig-zagged through a cluster of wild ferns. Gilchrist trod with care along the side of the hill, conscious again of how unsuitable his shoes were, until he reached a point that overlooked both the hut and the gable end of the cottage, with its two curtained windows.

If they went down the slope at that location, no one could see them from the cottage. It also gave him the perfect opportunity to peek through the hut window.

'It's steep,' he said. 'Think you can manage?'

'I'm all right.' She dug her boots into the ground. 'It's you I'm worried about.'

'OK, let's go.'

But Jessie was right, and he found himself on his backside in short order, slithering through damp grass, fingers clawing the ground to control his descent. He managed to stop the downhill rush, but slipped again when he took another step. When he reached the bottom of the slope, he pulled himself to his feet and cleaned his hands in the damp grass. Jessie was still only halfway down the slope, working around tufts of grass, clumps of ferns, patches of thistles.

'You look a mess,' she said to him, but he was already walking to the hut.

He peered through the small window. Although the hut looked new, spiders' webs clouded the glass like sheer curtains. But he let his eyes adjust to the dark interior, and ten seconds later had his answer.

Garden tools littered one wall, hanging from nails or hooks screwed into the wooden framing. But on the opposite side, a tarpaulin or canvas sheet took up most of the space, its angular shape and size suggesting it was covering a motorbike.

Had they really found it?

He turned to Jessie. 'We need to get inside.'

'It'll be locked.'

'I'm sure it will.'

Without a warrant, he could compromise evidence. But he needed to see for himself, just to make sure that his wild assumptions had been correct. If so, then they could apply for a search warrant, secure in the knowledge that the motorbike was here.

'We could call the local Office for backup,' she said.

Jessie was right, he knew. But it still felt too early to involve others. He first needed to know what they had. 'I'd rather check inside the hut first.'

Jessie grimaced. 'Well, if you're going to try the door at the front of the hut, you can be seen from the house.'

Which was Gilchrist's dilemma.

He needed to confirm the motorbike was the one they were looking for, before calling for backup. If he contacted the local Office, or requested a search warrant, and was found to be wrong – well, that was just the sort of waste of resources that Smiler would use against him. And the memory of Black facing him down on his driveway told him that he needed to make sure of his facts before he went in for the arrest.

'Stay put,' he said. 'And keep me posted if you see anyone.'

He crept around the corner of the hut, aware of being in full view of one of the windows at the front of the cottage – maybe the lounge? He was gambling that Black was in the kitchen or some other room, and that the lounge was for TV in the evenings. But he saw no satellite dish or aerials on the roof or walls or fixed to the eaves, and it struck him that maybe he had it all wrong.

No time to waste.

At the front of the hut, the door was secured with a padlock and hasp. He tugged the padlock – locked – which left him only one option. The four screws that fixed the hasp to the doorframe had rusted, and one of them appeared to be loose. A quick dig under the screw using his car key, and he was able to wriggle it out and confirm it was only a half-inch long – a bit short, he thought – which worked in his favour.

He checked the cottage for signs of life, but it could have been deserted.

He turned back to the hut door, put his shoulder against it, and pushed.

The door creaked against the framing.

He tried again, keeping pressure on the door, stressing the metal hasp.

The strength of a padlock hasp is that if you try to force the door open by pulling it, you are confronted with a lock mechanism as good as a metal bar. But if you force the door inwards against the frame, consequent stresses work against the hasp fixings, and something has to give.

Well, that was the theory. But the problem he now faced was that the doorframe was stronger than he'd thought, too strong to push the door inwards to the point where the hasp would tear the screws free.

He put his shoulder to the door again, and gave it a quick thump.

The door creaked. The hasp strained. He was about to give it another thump when—

'Andy.'

He froze for a split second, then slipped around the corner of the hut.

Jessie said, 'There's a woman.'

'What?'

'She just opened the door and walked outside and placed a potted plant on the step. It's a wonder she never saw you.'

Gilchrist peeked around the corner of the hut and there she was, with ill-fitting jeans and an anorak that had seen better days, fiddling with clumps of purple and yellow pansies in a glazed pot large enough to hold a small conifer.

'Is she with Black?' Jessie said.

It took a second for him to make up his mind. 'Only one way to find out.'

As he and Jessie walked towards the cottage, the woman froze at the sound of their footfall. Then she saw them, and tucked a trail of dyed black hair behind her ear with a dirt-covered hand.

Gilchrist saw no fear in her eyes, only puzzled curiosity.

'Can I help you?' she said.

He would put her in her fifties, with an attractive face that seemed prematurely lined. The closer he neared, the more decrepit her appearance became – scuffed brown shoes, toes white from lack of polish; jeans faded at the knees and several sizes too large, tied with a belt knotted like string; anorak shiny and smooth and fit for the bin. Maybe she was wearing old clothes for gardening. Warrant cards held out, he introduced Jessie and himself, then said, 'We'd like to ask a few questions, if you have a moment, Ms . . .'

'Kerr,' she said. 'Martha Kerr.'

Gilchrist thought he kept his surprise hidden, then tried, 'Is Mr Kerr here?'

'Not at the moment.' Which confirmed that Black was now Kerr.

'Where is he?' he said.

'Gone into town to get some shopping.'

Electricity zipped his spine. Black-call-me-Kerr was here. In Alloa. They had him. All they had to do was wait. He thought of calling the local Office for assistance in making the arrest, but could not shift the worry that he was still missing something. Which brought him full circle to the hut and the motorbike. If the registration number was the one they were looking for, then they had Black good and proper.

'When do you expect him back?' he asked.

She shrugged. 'An hour or two, perhaps.'

That would work. It gave them time to check out the motor-bike, then arrange for backup. He nodded to the hut. 'Do you mind opening that for us?'

'Why?'

'We're looking for a motorbike,' he said, intrigued as to how she would react.

But she seemed uninterested, as if it was the most natural thing for policemen to want to see a motorbike. 'Wait here while I get the key,' she said.

He almost told Jessie to follow her inside, then decided against it. Doing so, without invitation, might alert Kerr to their high level of interest in talking to Black.

'Is this for real?' Jessie said.

'We'll know for sure once we see that motorbike.' He glanced at his watch – 10.20. 'Get on to Mhairi, and get her started on a search warrant for this place. And have someone liaise with the local Office here, and let them know we might need their assistance.'

Jessie had her mobile in her hand, and was waiting for the connection to be made when she said, 'What's keeping her?'

Gilchrist eyed the open door. How long had she been gone? One minute? Two? What was she doing? He walked on to the top step, peered inside. The hallway was dark, with flecked wallpaper that had to have come from another era. He thought he caught the metallic chinking of cutlery, voices talking – a TV in the kitchen? – and was about to step inside when Mrs Kerr appeared in the hallway, key in hand.

'Problems?' he said to her.

'No. Why?'

He said nothing as he followed her to the hut, her feet cracking ice. He held his breath as she slotted the key into the padlock, worried that she might notice the missing screw. She struggled to unclip the padlock, and he stepped in to give her a hand. 'Probably a bit rusted,' he said, removing it from the hasp.

He pulled the door open to the smell of petrol and oil masked with woody freshness. On the floor by his feet, a five-gallon plastic container seeped petrol from a recent purchase. To his right against the wall, a tarpaulin covered what looked suspiciously like a motorbike – handlebars high at the front. He gripped the edge of the tarp and eased it up to reveal a pair of black leather gloves and a burgundy crash helmet with a black visor on the motorbike's seat.

He eyed the plate on the mudguard, his lips reciting the number he knew by heart.

It matched. Black was here.

CHAPTER 28

Gilchrist put on his best poker face as he replaced the tarpaulin. He said nothing as he closed the door, slipped the padlock into place and locked it with a click.

That motorbike was going nowhere.

'Is it what you were looking for?' Mrs Kerr asked.

Gilchrist ignored her question. 'Where does Mr Kerr do his shopping?'

'Tesco in town. Why?'

'Why wouldn't he take his motorbike?'

She shielded her eyes from a sudden burst of sunlight. 'It doesn't have a pannier.'

For just that moment, with her face lit up by the sun, he thought he had never before seen eyes so dark – pupils as black as irises. But he was also struck with a sense of déjà-vu, that he had been here before, questioning someone who knew more than she was letting on. He eyed the cottage, seeing for the first time its lack of overhead wires, and as if in slow motion the tumblers in his mind slotted into place.

He almost hissed a curse. How could he have been so stupid, so bloody stupid?

'Do you have a phone?' he snapped.

She reached inside her anorak pocket and produced a black Nokia.

'No landline?'

'Only mobiles.'

'You phoned him when you went inside for the hut key.'

'Just to tell him to hurry back, that you wanted to look at his motorbike.'

'Ah, fuck.' He ran towards Jessie who was standing at the property entrance, mobile to her ear. She turned at the sound of her name. 'He knows,' he said. 'She's already phoned him. Get on to the local Office and give them a description, if they don't already have one. He's in Tesco. Approach with extreme caution. Arrest him on suspicion of murder.'

He eyed the road leading to town – at least a mile long, probably more. Shit and fuck it. Even if he ran flat out, it would take him over five minutes to reach town, longer to find Tesco. He could call a taxi, but how long would it take to reach the cottage?

Another glance at Mrs Kerr made his mind up for him.

He jogged back to her. 'Let me see your mobile.'

She held it out.

'I'm confiscating this,' he said. 'The key for the motorbike. Do you have it?'

'It's in the ignition.'

'Open the hut,' he said, and almost tore the key from her as she tried to insert it into the padlock. When the lock clicked, he pushed her out of the way, removed the padlock and entered. He ripped off the tarpaulin, spilling the helmet and gloves to the floor. He reached for the handlebars, tugged the motorbike upright, surprised by its weight. He kicked the stand, and it clicked into place. But the hut was too tight to wheel the motor-bike outside, and he had to drag the rear wheel across the floor before he could pull it into the open.

'What are you doing?' Mrs Kerr said.

'Going to find Mr Kerr,' he said, mounting the bike. A turn of the key, and it fired first time. He pulled in the clutch, revved the engine, feeling the power beneath him. It had been years since he'd last driven a motorbike – well, a Lambretta scooter if he was being honest, and as a teenager. He slid into gear, eased out the clutch, and worked his way around ice-covered puddles until he reached Jessie standing in the middle of road.

He handed her Mrs Kerr's mobile. 'Check out the number she called him on, then have the Office track it, see what mast it pinged.'

'You realise that you've compromised evidence by riding his motorbike.'

'Helmet and gloves are in the hut on the floor. And we have CCTV footage.'

'Right,' she said, but she didn't seem convinced. 'I spoke to a DS Whitby in the local Office here, who's despatched two mobile units into town. Jackie's emailing them a photo of Black even as we speak.'

'Get back on to Whitby. Tell him they need to be armed.'

He revved the engine, was about to release the clutch when Jessie said, 'Do you know what you're doing, Andy?'

What could he tell her? That he was fired up because he'd let Black slip through his fingers once again? That he needed to nail him before someone else was killed? That he knew he was no physical match for the guy, but had no option but to take him on? He couldn't say. All he knew was that he had to get into town and arrest Black when they had the chance. He would even run the bastard over with his own motorbike, if he could get him in his sights.

'I won't do anything silly,' he lied.

'Want me to ride pillion?' Jessie said.

He shook his head. 'Keep an eye on Mrs Kerr. Other than the bike being garaged in the hut, why this cottage? We're missing something, but I don't know what. And prioritise that search warrant for this place.'

Then he released the clutch, and the motorbike leaped forward.

He took his time over the first hundred yards, working through the gears, changing down again, just getting the hang of it all. Even though it had been years, it all came back to him – well, it was just like . . . riding a bike.

He accelerated to thirty, forty, fifty, and once he felt he had it under control, opened the throttle and accelerated downhill into town.

He reached the main road, the A907, indicated right, then powered into town. Even in that short time, without gloves his hands were already frozen, his face cold enough to lock his lips into a determined grimace. He came to a roundabout and went straight through. At the next roundabout, he clocked Morrisons on the left and had an almost overwhelming urge to check out the car park – if you walked into town to do shopping, would you not stop at the first store you came to? But Morrisons wasn't Tesco, so he carried on.

He kept well back from an articulated lorry in front as he negotiated the roundabout, aware of traffic entering from his left. The lorry veered off into the Morrisons complex, and Gilchrist was accelerating when he caught a flash of movement in his wing mirror, some car exiting the complex at speed. Within seconds he had his speed back to fifty – in a thirty-mile-an-hour limit – intent on finding Tesco.

He had no idea where it was, and pulled kerbside at a bus stop to ask for directions – *next roundabout, and turn left, you cannae miss it.* He set off again, struggling to stifle the niggling feeling that he had it wrong. This was too far to walk for shopping.

The next roundabout opened up to an Asda store off to his right, but he turned left as instructed and accelerated uphill on to Auld Brig Road. When he reached another roundabout, and saw Tesco Extra off to his left, he knew he had it wrong. Who in their right mind would walk all the way up here, instead of shopping at the first store they came to?

He stopped and rang Jessie. 'Anything?' he asked her.

'No sightings,' she said. 'But there's been an altercation in Morrisons.'

'Ah, fuck it. I knew it. It's Black. It has to be. Get me the details.' He flicked the tail end as he did a quick U-turn, almost losing his balance, then headed back the way he'd come.

When he reached the Morrisons roundabout, the flash memory of a speeding car had him powering through it, accelerating on to Clackmannan Road. The wind whipped through his hair with claws of ice. He gritted his teeth against the fierce wind chill, squinted his eyes as he accelerated to seventy. He felt his mobile vibrate in his jacket; he pulled on the brakes and skidded to a halt.

'Who's this?' he said.

'It's Jessie. You were right, Andy. A man matching Black's description attacked a woman in Morrisons car park and stole her car. We're now looking for a silver Ford Fiesta.' She rattled off the registration number. 'The reg is now on the PNC, and I've put out an alert on the ANPR.'

Gilchrist grimaced. The Automatic Number Plate Recognition system was invaluable in tracking vehicles – provided the plates hadn't been changed or discarded. He didn't need to think hard to know that Black was an expert in criminal deception. Even in that short time, the Fiesta's number plates would likely already be changed, or discarded altogether. False plates could help evade the police initially, but once they knew the changed number, they could track it through the ANPR.

'Shit,' Gilchrist said. 'Put a call to all police forces to look out for that Ford Fiesta. And get cracking with the ANPR.'

'Already on it.'

'Get back to me if you come up with anything.' Up ahead, he saw his BMW parked off the side of the road where he'd abandoned it earlier.

He kicked into gear and drove towards it.

He discarded the motorbike, resting it against a hedge, then clicked his car's remote. Inside, he fired up the ignition and turned the fan to high. Cold air blew at him. Even though the engine had not yet heated it felt warmer than outside. He was shivering, and couldn't stop his body jerking with spasms. The temperature gauge on his dashboard confirmed it was 1 degree Centigrade outside, but riding a motorbike at speed was as good as a sub-zero wind chill. A glance in the mirror reflected blue lips and a red-tipped nose, and strained eyes that looked years older. He palmed the air vents, revved the engine. 'Come on, come on.' But it would take several minutes for the warm air to work through the system and he had no time to waste. He could warm up later.

He slipped into gear and did a fast U-turn.

On his drive to Alloa earlier that morning, he remembered going through a five-way roundabout on the outskirts of town. As he approached it, he felt his heart sink. Black could have taken any one of four roads. His peripheral vision caught sight of something glittering in the grass on the side of the road, and he skidded to a halt.

He stepped out of his car to the angry blast of a car horn. But he was too focused to be troubled, and raised his hand in apology. He stepped into frosted grass and stared at a car's registration number plate. He didn't need to pick it up to know whose plate it was.

He stared off to the Ochil Hills in the distance while he worked through the rationale. Rather than let the ANPR track him to the roundabout ahead, Black had removed both plates, prepared to risk being pulled over, rather than being tracked by the ANPR system, even for part of the way. The timing, too, was deliberate. Once he reached that roundabout, he could go anywhere in the country.

Gilchrist called Jessie. 'He's discarded the plates, so put an alert out on all channels for a silver Ford Fiesta without number plates.'

'Which way's he heading?' Jessie asked.

He eyed the roundabout. Which way indeed? Eeny, meeny, miny, moe seemed as good a choice as any. First left put him on the road to St Andrews, Dundee, Perth, and any number of country roads in between. Straight ahead to Dunfermline, and more country roads. Next exit put him on the road to Kincardine, which could take him to Edinburgh, or the bridge across the River Forth and south-east to Glasgow. The final exit tracked back to Alloa through the village of Clackmannan.

His mind crackled alive with possibilities. Think, for crying out loud. *Think.* Which way? Black would have had no time to think. He was on the run, driving a stolen vehicle without any registration number plates.

But for once in his life, his sixth sense let him down.

'Find out if the local Office has CCTV cameras in the area,' he said to Jessie. 'There can't be too many silver Ford Fiestas driving around with no number plates. Alert Kincardine and Dunfermline. If he crossed the Forth, he might be heading for Glasgow, maybe Falkirk or Stirling. Alert these Offices, too.' He was struggling to recall his geography, but he did know that the Scottish road network could put you in the back of beyond in no time at all.

Scott Black could be anywhere in a matter of hours.

Gilchrist cursed under his breath. 'I don't have a bloody clue where he's heading, Jessie. But the longer we talk about it, the less chance we've got to find this guy. We need whatever help we can get. CCTV. ANPR. Mobile units. All Ports Alert on all channels. Get working on a TV appeal for this evening.'

'I'm on it,' Jessie said.

'Oh, and one more thing.'

'Yeah?'

'Send someone to pick up Black's motorbike. It's on the side of the road where we parked the car earlier. The key's in the ignition.'

'What're you going to do, Andy?'

'Try to find that silver Fiesta.'

CHAPTER 29

In the end, Gilchrist chose the road to St Andrews and Perth, secure in the logic of his struggling rationale that Black would have headed north, and nowhere else. He accelerated to seventy, thankful for the heat blowing through the air vents. He kept his speed up, touching eighty in places. But the A977 was not designed for fast driving, and he had to slam on his brakes and tuck in behind slower-moving vehicles a couple of times.

He powered through Rumbling Bridge, held a steady sixty through Crook of Devon – renowned for speed traps – then leathered it on the final stretch to Balado before reaching the interchange for the M90. Again, instinct told him to head north, and he floored it to well over the ton – touching 128 mph at one point. But by the time he had to make another choice – exit left for St Andrews, or continue on the M90 to Perth – the Ford Fiesta was nowhere to be seen.

He made a snap decision and gave it one last shot, keeping to the M90. He pushed his speed through the ton again, but after a couple more minutes, realised he was literally spinning his wheels. He pulled on to the hard shoulder, and slithered to a halt.

He phoned Jessie. 'Anything?' he asked.

'Zilch, Andy. The ANPR's picked up nothing, and we've had no reported sightings of any car without number plates.'

For a moment, he wondered if he'd got it wrong, that Black had not thrown the plates away but simply swapped them for another pair. But he'd had no time to do that, and no one had reported stolen plates, so Gilchrist felt that he had to go with his logic.

'They must have something on CCTV footage,' he said.

'We've got him in Morrisons, with a clear recording of the assault. When we arrest him, he'll go down for that. As for the Fiesta, we've got it leaving Alloa, then it disappears and doesn't resurface.'

'He has to be somewhere, for crying out loud.'

'I know that. You know that. We all know that. But *where*, is the big question.'

'Let me get back to you.'

He hissed a curse. Christ, he'd been so close. If Martha Kerr hadn't alerted Black, all they had to do was wait for him to return from his shopping, then arrest him. He gripped the steering wheel with a force that threatened to bend it. Shit. And fuck it. He slapped his hand against the dashboard, once, twice, then took a deep breath.

Getting angry solved nothing. He had to think back to what had happened, use clear and rational thought. He had to figure out how Black had manufactured his escape, force his way into his head, think like the man himself.

The five-way roundabout was the critical point. That's where he'd made his mistake, chosen the wrong exit. In his mind's eye, he replayed the scenario – Black pulling the Fiesta to a halt, stepping on to the road, ripping off the plates, throwing them away, driving off. But that roundabout could be a busy intersection, so someone may have seen something. They could put out an appeal on national TV that night. But it would have taken Black less than a minute to remove the plates, and how many cars had passed in that time? Or more to the point, how many of these drivers had paid any attention to what Black had been doing?

Not many, and none, came the answers.

Which told him that the TV appeal was a long shot.

Back to the five-way roundabout. Seeing it in his mind's eye, Black driving up to it, slowing down, the choice of which direction to take already made. He put himself in Black's shoes: on the run; no number plates; a need to stay off main roads; search for a hiding place and lie low . . . and ever so slowly the fog began to lift.

Lie low was the key. Keep hidden until the dust settled. Taking the quietest route was the answer. Which meant Black would have taken the Dunfermline exit, a road through open country where he would likely not come across traffic police.

He dialled Jessie again. 'Any news?'

'Jeez, Andy, give me time. No new reports in the last five seconds.'

'I got it wrong,' he said. 'He's taken the Dunfermline Road.'

'You sure?'

Oh, he was sure all right, as sure as he was that he would live to one hundred and ten. But what could he tell her? That it was only a hunch, a sixth sense conclusion backed up by warped but logical thinking?

'Look,' he said, 'I took the Perth–St Andrews road, and didn't hang about. If Black had been on it, I'm sure I would've caught him. And the road to Kincardine would have put him into heavy traffic. So, by process of elimination, that leaves the Dunfermline exit.'

'So you want me to tell the local Office . . . what?'

What indeed? 'Get them to check for CCTV footage along that road, and if they can spare a couple of mobile units, send them that way. I suspect Black will have cut off on a side road, maybe parked in a farm track or some quiet lane. So they might get lucky.' He fired the ignition and pulled back on to the M90. 'I'm on my way. Probably be a good twenty minutes,' he said, as another thought hit him. 'Are you still at the cottage?'

'Scrounged a lift into town. I'm at the local Office.'

'What about Kerr?'

'Being detained under caution on suspicion of harbouring a criminal and for attempting to pervert the course of justice.' Jessie let out a heavy sigh. 'But I'm telling you, Andy, there's something not right with that woman. She's giving off all the wrong signals. It's like she doesn't understand the seriousness of the situation. And if she asks me one more time if I would like to buy that fricking motorbike, I tell you, I'm going to clock her one.'

'Stay calm,' he said. 'And don't interview her without me.'

Gilchrist picked Jessie up from the Alloa police station in Mar Place, but rather than head straight for the interview room, he decided to join the hunt for Black. The search-party needed all the help it could get. He reached the five-way roundabout and raced through it, while Jessie kept in touch with the local Office, getting an update on the mobile units.

When she hung up, she said, 'They're a good bunch to work with. Four mobile units they've put on it, and they've called everyone in from leave and are setting up door-to-doors.'

Door-to-door interviews were useful for flushing out the latest information, but more often than not were man-intensive for little result. All Gilchrist could do was drive around the area, search for farm tracks and off-beat roads not marked on maps, then check them out. But Black was at least an hour ahead of them now. He could be over sixty miles away, parked in some hidey-hole in the back of beyond. And the more time that passed, the deeper he would slip into hiding. The likelihood of their finding him that day was zero to twenty below.

Half an hour later, the futility of it all had become fact. Black had slipped the net. They could criss-cross the countryside, drive up and down dead-end dirt tracks until they ran out of petrol, or were blue in the face, for all the results they were achieving. But he kept at it until 4.30 p.m., by which time he'd racked up 120-plus miles, checking out dead end after dead end.

Time to call it a day.

'Phone the local Office for an update,' he said.

But no one had fared any better. No sightings were reported on any CCTV footage or the ANPR system. No new results from door-to-doors. Police units in surrounding counties – Clackmannanshire, Kinross-shire, Perthshire, Fife, Stirlingshire, West Lothian, Midlothian, and even as far afield as North Lanarkshire – all came up blank.

It seemed as if Black had completely vanished.

Well, he still had one point of contact.

'What did you find out about Martha Kerr?' he asked Jessie.

'She's lived in that cottage for the last twelve years. Before that, I couldn't say. She has no criminal record, no driving licence, and

243

seems to have no friends or family. Said her parents were killed in a car crash when she was sixteen. Never married. Lives alone. Keeps herself to herself. The local Office said they see her about town from time to time, walking down the street, carrying her shopping—'

'Where from?'

'Where from what?'

'Her shopping. Where does she shop?'

'Never got that far with her,' she said. 'And she seems perfectly happy to be locked up waiting for her interview.'

Gilchrist could detain Martha Kerr for a maximum of twelve hours. After that, he had to charge her, or release her. But he found her puzzling. According to Jessie, Kerr was simple-minded, but the ease with which she'd phoned Black behind their backs and warned him off – innocent or deliberate? – and the simplicity of her answer, warned Gilchrist that she was nowhere near as dumb as she was making out.

He had Jessie call to arrange a duty solicitor for her.

'He's here at the moment, DS Janes,' she was told. 'Representing another detainee.'

'Don't let him leave. We'll be with you in fifteen.'

As it turned out, it was closer to twenty-five minutes by the time they reached Alloa. On the way, he and Jessie had discussed how to interview Martha Kerr. Jessie was tasked with establishing her personal background, and Gilchrist would focus on what, if anything, she knew about Black's present whereabouts.

He followed Jessie into the interview room and took his seat.

Kerr sat opposite, humming a tune as if she had not a worry in the world. She still wore the same baggy jeans, but the anorak had been discarded, or binned, and been replaced by a moth-eaten cable-knit sweater. Her solicitor sat next to her, a man in his thirties with a shorn head and the tell-tale tip of a tattoo peeking from the collar of his grubby white shirt.

He slid a couple of business cards across the table. 'Tom McGarry.'

Gilchrist slipped a card into his pocket without comment, while Jessie began the introductions, advising Kerr that she was being interviewed under caution, and that the interview was being recorded.

She gave her full name as Martha Margaret McFarland Kerr, and her home address as Raven Cottage, Alloa, Clackmannanshire.

'No street address?' Jessie said.

'Never use it.'

'Why not?'

'No need.'

'Are you married?'

'No.'

'So you live in Raven Cottage all by yourself?'

'Yes.'

'So what's your relationship with Mr Kerr?'

'He's my brother.'

Gilchrist tried to hide his surprise, but was not sure he'd pulled it off.

Jessie said, 'Older? Younger?'

'Younger.'

'How much younger?'

'Eight years.'

'Is he Robert or Bobby?'

'Bobby, of course.'

'What do you mean – of course?'

'Well, Robert is such a false name, isn't it?'

Jessie raised her eyes, but kept her tongue in check. 'OK,' she said.

Gilchrist placed his hands on the table to let Jessie know he would take over. 'How often do you see your brother, Bobby?' he asked.

'Every now and then.'

'Before today, when did you last see him?'

She shrugged. 'March? April?'

'Were you surprised to see him, just turning up like that?'

'Not really. That's what he's like.'

'Explain to me,' he said. 'What exactly is Bobby like?'

'Impulsive.'

He let several seconds pass, before saying, 'And?'

She shook her head. 'He's impulsive. That's exactly what he's like.'

'You called him on your mobile when you went for the key. Why did you do that?'

'I told you.'

'Tell me again.'

'To let him know you wanted to talk to him about his motorbike.'

Not strictly correct, but at that point it didn't matter. 'Why do you live in Alloa?'

'Bobby had a business close by.'

He noted the past tense. 'What business was that?'

'I don't know. I never asked.'

They were being toyed with, he felt certain of that. But he stayed calm. 'Where do you shop in town?'

'Morrisons.'

'Why?'

'Because I need to buy food.'

'I meant, why Morrisons, and not some other store?'

'It's closer.'

'The first supermarket you come to if you walk into town, you mean?'

'Yes.'

Gilchrist frowned with confusion. 'So why did you tell us that Bobby was shopping in Tesco?'

'Because that's where he said he was going.'

'But he didn't go there, did he?'

'I don't know.'

'He went to Morrisons, the first supermarket you come to if you walk into town. But you knew that, didn't you?'

'No.'

He held his focus on her, to let her know he didn't believe her. But she lowered her eyes to some spot on the table between them, and started humming again. 'I suspect you're lying to protect Bobby,' he said. 'So be careful how you answer this question.'

She frowned at the table.

'What do you get out of it?'

Her gaze flickered to Gilchrist, shifted to Jessie, then returned to the table. But for just that split second, Gilchrist caught her vulnerability. 'What's Bobby's full name?'

She shrugged.

'We can easily find that out, but it would help your situation if you told us yourself.' He added, 'So that we know you're telling us the truth.'

She lifted her head. 'Robert Matthew Kerr.'

'You said earlier that you lost your parents when you were sixteen. They were killed in a car crash. So Bobby would've been only eight.'

She nodded. 'Yes.'

'You must have been like a surrogate mother to him when he was growing up. Is that why you never married? Because you had to look after Bobby?'

'Not really.'

'Is that why Bobby never married, too?' he said, just to gauge a reaction, which came in the next second.

She stared at Gilchrist, her mouth moving with indecision. 'I . . . I . . .'

Gilchrist waited, aware of Jessie holding her breath.

McGarry looked as if he was about to interrupt.

'I . . . I don't know.'

For a moment, Gilchrist thought he'd managed to pierce her simpleton façade, but her answer trumped that. 'Scott Black,' he said. 'Does that name mean anything to you?'

She frowned harder at the table.

'Scott Black,' he said again.

McGarry leaned forward. 'Who's Scott Black?'

Jessie said, 'That's what we're trying to find out. We ask the questions, and she gives the answers. Got it?'

McGarry scowled at Jessie.

'Martha,' Gilchrist said. 'The name Scott Black means something to you. It's written all over your face. We can see it in your eyes.'

She shook her head.

'How do you know Scott Black?'

The moment passed, and she lifted her gaze over his shoulder and started humming.

Gilchrist stood with a suddenness that startled McGarry. 'We're taking a break,' he said to him. 'You've got five minutes to bring your client up to speed with the seriousness of the trouble she's in.'

Jessie suspended the interview for the record.

But Gilchrist had already left the room.

CHAPTER 30

Gilchrist walked to his car.

Darkness had fallen, and the town's thoroughfare sparkled like a Christmas oasis at night. Shop windows glowed with warmth from within. Festive displays enticed passers-by to step inside, come out of the cold. An iced wind shuffled over roads and pavements, rattling bin lids and threatening snow. Specks of frost glittered like diamonds.

Jessie caught up with him. 'A penny for your thoughts?' she said.

'She's making a fool of us, by acting the fool herself. But she's hiding something.' He shivered against the wind, found himself fighting off the inexplicable need for a cigarette. 'She's full of shit. I mean, who in their right mind would act like that? I don't get it.'

'You think McGarry will get her to come clean?'

'Wouldn't that be nice?' he said. 'But I don't think McGarry's got it in him to help our cause. Did you see the way he looked at her, almost willing her not to be helpful?'

'We could charge her as an accessory to murder,' Jessie said. 'That might get their attention.'

Gilchrist shook his head. 'I don't think she cares.'

'How about just throwing the book at her?'

'I'm thinking more along the lines of letting her go.'

Jessie rubbed her arms. 'Is it just me, or is it getting colder?'

'It's getting colder.'

'Well, I think the cold's freezing the thinking part of your brain.'

'What will throwing the book at her achieve? That's not going to help us find Black, is it? And you know what? I don't think she knows where he's gone.'

'So, what . . . we just let her go?'

'I'm thinking we release her, yes, but keep tabs on her mobile. It's how she and Black communicate.'

'He's not going to phone her,' Jessie said. 'He must know we'll be watching her.'

Gilchrist found an idea pushing to the front of his mind. 'What if we keep her name from the press?' he said. 'What if we don't mention that we've interviewed her? What would Black do then?'

'I don't follow.'

'Curiosity'll get the better of him. I'm willing to bet that after a few days, he won't be able to resist contacting her to find out what went on.'

'I don't know if that's a good idea.'

Gilchrist stamped his feet on the ground, trying to force some warmth into his system. Jessie was right on a couple of points: firstly, it always seemed to be colder this side of the River Forth and secondly, not charging Martha Kerr as an accessory wasn't a good idea. 'Well,' he said, 'when you come up with something better, let me know. But in the meantime, here's how we're going to play it.'

★   ★   ★

251

As expected, the second interview offered nothing new. If anything, Gilchrist would have to say it was even less productive than the first. All their questions were answered with a *No comment*, and when Jessie accused McGarry of giving his client incompetent legal advice, McGarry simply shrugged and grinned at her.

Jessie excused herself, and made a point of leaving the interview room loudly.

'DS Janes has a bit of a temper on her,' McGarry observed.

'She's frustrated by your client's refusal to answer.'

'My client's not refusing to answer. No comment *is* her answer.'

Gilchrist shuffled his papers, preparing to bring the interview to an end.

Sensing this, McGarry smiled, pleased with the outcome.

It never failed to amaze Gilchrist how obstructive some solicitors could be, using every legal tool at their disposal to clear their client's name, even though it was obvious to everyone present, including the solicitor, that their client was guilty. Often court cases were not about determining right from wrong, but about finding some legal technicality to twist the interpretation of the law to one party's advantage.

'We won't be pressing charges at this point in time,' Gilchrist said, 'although we would advise your client that she may be called in for further questioning.'

McGarry reached across the table and squeezed Martha's fingers.

She seemed not to notice.

Gilchrist ended the interview for the record, and switched off the recorder.

Outside, he found Jessie in the car park, pacing up and down in the chill wind, mobile to her ear. He threw his papers on to the back seat of his BMW, then fired the ignition. By the time Jessie clipped on her seatbelt, the car had warmed up quite nicely, thank you.

'You get it sorted?' he asked her.

'All done,' she said. 'Now all we've got to do is wait.'

Gilchrist drove from the car park, keeping to the speed limit as he headed out of town. Neither of them said a word as he drove along Clackmannan Road. The Ochil Hills rose into the night sky to their left, and he found himself searching the dark backdrop for the tell-tale light of Raven Cottage. But he couldn't locate it.

He passed the spot where he'd abandoned his car that morning – Black's motorbike, too – and drew to a halt at the five-way roundabout, again testing his rationale for Black's escape. Flashing headlights from a car behind forced him to nudge forward.

He took the road north.

They had gone only five miles when he said, 'Are you hungry?'

Jessie glanced up from her texting. 'I'm always hungry.'

'Like to stop for a bite to eat?'

'Can't, Andy. I've got to get something in for my wee boy.' She shook her head. 'Don't know what it is with boys. If their mums don't feed them, they'd starve to death, I swear.'

'You need to teach him how to boil an egg.'

'So he can set the house on fire? I don't think so.'

'Tea and toast?'

'Just as bad.'

'How about Rice Krispies?'

'Now you're talking.' She giggled at the screen. 'Do you want to hear a joke?'

'One of Robert's?'

'I think so.' She chuckled again, then read the text. 'My granny is eighty years old and she doesn't need glasses. She just drinks straight from the bottle.' She slapped her hand on her knee and guffawed – a bit forced, he thought. 'Don't you just love him?'

'He's got a great sense of humour,' Gilchrist said, then eased into the next question. 'I take it the *granny* mentioned in the joke is a generic granny?'

'Of course it is.'

He hadn't intended to broach the subject, but the opportunity had just presented itself. Now seemed as good a time as any. 'Have you told Robert about what happened to his . . . his real granny?'

'He's never had a real granny,' Jessie said. 'So let's end this conversation right now, before it starts.' She glared at him. 'OK?'

Gilchrist drove on, in silence.

The most difficult issue with Jessie was not her criminal family, but her reluctance to talk about her personal life. He should have known not to mention Robert's name in the same sentence as her mother. But even so, he made a mental note to give Dainty a call, to find out if he'd uncovered anything about the list Jessie's brother Tommy had handed her.

It took fifteen minutes of driving in silence, and another offer to stop off for a bite to eat, and a tea or coffee – or something stronger – before she said, 'Sorry, but you know I can't stand you talking about my family.'

'I do indeed.'

'And especially when you bring Robert into it.'

'That, too.'

'So why do you do it?'

'So that I don't stick my foot in it when I see him.'

'But you hardly ever see him.'

'I know,' he said. 'But when I do, I want to make sure that I don't tell him something I shouldn't have.'

It took another mile of countryside darkness before Jessie said, 'Has anyone ever told you that you can be a smarmy bastard?'

'Not in as many words, no.' He was saved by his mobile ringing – ID Mhairi. He took the call through his car's speaker system. 'What's the latest?' he asked.

'Just got a message from Dunfermline. A Mr Thomas Loughlin reported that the number plates on his wife's Mini were stolen today.'

Gilchrist snapped his fingers, instructing Jessie to take notes. 'I'm listening.'

'She's a member of Canmore Golf Club, just north of Dunfermline, and he thinks that's where they were removed.'

'He *thinks*?'

'His wife spent the day at a ladies' outing, and drove home without realising her plates had been stolen. Mr Loughlin says he only noticed when he was driving his own car into the garage.'

'What's the Mini's number?'

Mhairi told him. Jessie scribbled it down.

'Anything on CCTV or the ANPR?'

'Not a thing, sir.'

Gilchrist frowned. 'When did his wife arrive at the Golf Club?'

'She's been there all day, sir.'

'From early morning?'

'Mid-morning, sir.'

'So Black could have taken her plates shortly after he discarded the ones on the silver Ford Fiesta.'

'Yes, sir.'

'Thanks, Mhairi. And spread that number around the local police stations.'

'Already doing that, sir.'

He disconnected.

Jessie said, 'Why rip off one set of number plates so you can steal another?'

'Because he's going on a long journey, and couldn't risk driving around without any number plates.'

'But he must've known we'd find out he'd stolen new plates.'

'Of course, but the number's not been picked up by the ANPR system, has it?'

'So what am I missing?'

'Read out that number to me.'

She did.

'Now write down variations of it by changing letters and numbers – S to an 8, 5 to a B, that sort of thing. Imagine you've got black tape to change any letter or number.' He glanced at the registration number again. 'That C could be an O or a zero.'

'If he had white tape,' she said, 'he could blank out a letter or two.'

'He certainly could,' Gilchrist agreed.

'Even change that zero to a C,' she said. 'So it's limitless.'

'Not quite. But try to think like Black. You don't have time. You've just nicked a pair of plates, so you don't want to hang about.'

'Got three already,' she said.

'Keep going. When you get half a dozen, call Mhairi and have her run them through the ANPR. All we're trying to do is get a hit on a silver Ford Fiesta. Once we have that, we can track him.'

'Sounds simple when you say it quickly.'

Gilchrist gritted his teeth. Nothing about this investigation was simple. Scott Black was proving to be devious and slippery, an elusive killer with a high intellect, and prepared to do whatever was necessary to avoid being arrested.

Even kill again if he had to. Which told Gilchrist they were running out of time.

CHAPTER 31

By the time Gilchrist dropped Jessie off at her home in Canongate, she'd had Mhairi feed sixteen variations of the number into the ANPR system. But so far, they'd had zero hits.

Back in his office, Gilchrist tried playing with the numbers himself, and realised there were many more he could create without too much effort. Simply placing strips of white tape over part of some letters could change B to P, or J to I, or to T if you added a strip of black tape. And it didn't help that the original number contained seven digits in total. For all he knew, that might have been why Black stole that number plate in the first place.

He put another six numbers through the ANPR system, and was almost rewarded with an immediate hit on a silver Ford Fiesta in Cupar. But a mobile team from the Cupar Office confirmed the plate was genuine, and that the Fiesta belonged to an upstanding and long-term resident of the old market town.

By 9 p.m. they still didn't have a hit. Scott Black could be anywhere in Scotland, or England for that matter. Gilchrist stared at the number, forcing his mind to think like Black. Which letters would he change? And once he'd changed them, where would he go? But by 10 p.m., he was as good as washed up, and none the wiser.

Time for a breather, or more to the point, time to go home to bed.

But first, a bite to eat.

He walked past the Central Bar and crossed Market Street, intent on having a pint and a pie in the Criterion. But when he turned in to South Street, the night air throbbed with the sound of electric guitars. He'd forgotten that Tuesdays were open mic nights, and the bar would be packed to the rafters with students and music-lovers wanting a slot in that night's short-lived spotlight. Any other Tuesday he would have been happy to stand at the bar and enjoy the raw sounds of eclectic jamming, but that night all he wanted was to sit in some peace and quiet, and try to put his thoughts into place.

He doubled back to the Central Bar.

Although the Central heaved with the swell of student revelry – how could they afford to drink and eat out during the week? – it was much quieter. Muted TVs high in the corners showed the highlights of some football match, Liverpool and Chelsea, as best he could tell. He managed to find a spare stool at the back of the bar and ordered a pint of Fosters – lager for a change – and a bowl of soup.

He checked his mobile, and found a missed call from Mo. He thought of calling her back right away, but with the ambient din, he would have to make the call outside. Instead, he took a sip of his pint, removed his notes from his pocket, and studied the letters and numbers again, trying to work out what he was missing.

When his soup arrived with a side-plate of bread, he had reached the conclusion that he was wasting his time. In addition to adjusting some digits, Black might have deleted one or two completely – the end ones either side, for example – which multiplied the number of variations by a factor of three, or of that order.

No wonder he hadn't found the sneaky bastard.

He took a few spoonfuls of soup, but felt out of sorts, and spread dollops of butter over the bread and finished that off, instead. He shoved his half-finished soup and pint of lager – next time he'd stick to real ale – and left the bar.

In College Street, on the walk back to the Office, he phoned Maureen.

'Hi, princess. Sorry I missed your call. Is everything all right?'

'Yes and no.'

He stopped mid-stride. 'I'm listening.'

'It's nothing serious, Dad, it's just . . .'

He pressed his mobile hard to his ear, waited for her to continue.

'It's just that Tom got a call from the company that offered him the job, and they're keen for him to start as soon as possible.'

'In Australia?'

'Yes.'

'Well, that's good, right? Great, even.'

'Well, yes . . . but Tom being Tom won't be pushed into anything without checking it out first. So he dug in his heels, and they've offered to fly both of us out to have a look at the place – the city, the office where he'll be working, and where we might want to live. If Tom likes it, then he'll stay on while I fly back to sell the flat.'

'If *Tom* likes it?'

'Yes.'

'Don't *you* have to like it, too?'

'Yes, of course I do, Dad. You're misconstruing my words. And missing the point.'

Gilchrist frowned. 'And the point is?'

'That we're flying from Edinburgh in a couple of days.'

'This week?'

'Thursday or Friday.'

'To Australia?'

'Yes.'

Gilchrist puffed up his cheeks, and exhaled. 'Well, that's sudden.'

'That's why I called, Dad. To let you know.' A pause, then, 'You're not angry, are you?'

'Why would I be angry?'

'I don't know, I just thought . . . in the bar, when we said we were emigrating to Australia . . . I thought you didn't want me to go.'

What could he tell her? Of course he hadn't wanted her to go. He wanted her to stay here, in St Andrews, so they could be a family, stay in contact, meet each other for a chat. On the other hand, he knew she had to make a life of her own, and he couldn't stand in her way.

'It was all so sudden, Mo. I mean, one second I'm finding out you're engaged to Tom. And the next that you're emigrating.' The hiss of digital ether had him worried that he'd been too blunt. He softened his tone. 'Is that what you want to do, Mo? To emigrate to Australia?'

'I think so, yes.'

'And do you want to spend the rest of your life with Tom?'

261

'Don't say it like that, Dad. You make it sound like some prison sentence.'

'Force of habit,' he said, then chuckled to let her know he was joking. 'What I meant was, do you truly love Tom?'

'Yes.'

'And do you want to marry him?'

'Yes.'

'Then go to Australia, and don't you worry about leaving your old dad on his own for a single second. As long as you're happy, Mo, then I'm happy, too.'

'Aw, Dad, you're absolutely brilliant.'

'But I have to warn you about one thing.'

Silence for a couple of beats, then, 'What's that?'

'Box jellyfish.'

'Box what?'

'Jellyfish. In the sea. You get them mostly in Australia, the deadliest poison of any sea creature.'

'Are you serious?'

'I am, yes. But you don't have to worry,' he said, wishing he'd never brought up the topic in case she saw it as his underhand way to make her change her mind. 'You just have to be careful, that's all.'

'I'll have Tom to look after me.'

'Yes,' he said, struggling to remain cheerful. 'Tom'll look after you.'

'Will you come and see us off at the airport?'

Oh, shit. He squeezed his eyes shut. Of all the times to ask. 'I'd love to, Mo, but it all depends on the job.'

'For crying out loud, Dad, can't you just take a day off? It's not like they don't owe you the time.'

If only it were that easy. But being deep into a double murder investigation, when all hands were needed on deck, so to speak, it would not go down well. 'I'll try,' he said, but his heart wasn't in it.

Maureen picked up on his lack of commitment. 'How often does your only daughter fly out to Australia?'

'Twice,' he said.

It took her a couple of seconds to catch his joke – she was coming back to sell her flat if she and Tom liked Perth – and she chuckled, and said, 'You're silly.'

'I know. But I love you, Mo.'

'I love you, too, Dad.'

'Let me know your flight details, and I'll do what I can to see you both off.'

Back in the Office, he was surprised to see Mhairi still at her computer, and a scruffy young man in a T-shirt and gravity-defying jeans standing by her side. Their attention was so focused on her monitor that they failed to notice his arrival.

'Hope I'm not interrupting anything.'

Mhairi almost jumped. 'Sorry, sir. I didn't see you come in.' She pulled back from the screen to reveal a close-up of a woman's bare thighs and black pubic hair. Then she clicked the mouse, and the thighs seemed to shiver as the video fast-forwarded. She looked up at the man by her side. 'This is Matt Duprey of our IT section. Matt, this is my boss, Detective Chief Inspector Gilchrist, the SIO of this investigation.'

Matt sniffed, ran a hand under his nose. 'Sir.'

Gilchrist nodded in response. 'So what're we looking at?'

Matt leaned forward, took control of the mouse. The thighs continued to shimmer, then shifted all of a sudden as they strutted away from the camera to reveal a naked woman about to sit on the toilet.

The mouse clicked. The screen froze.

'We started off with SB Contracting's website,' Matt explained. 'From there, we were able to identify the IP address, the Internet Protocol responsible for addressing, delivering and routing all online search requests. But that address is actually assigned to a computer by an Internet Service Provider, and can be static or dynamic. We lucked out in a way, because SB's IP address is static, which makes it easier to track historical activity.'

'Can anyone do this?' Gilchrist said. 'I mean, track historical activity like that.'

'No,' Matt said, as if that explained it all. 'We have software that interfaces with the transmission control protocol, which is a higher level protocol that runs on top of the IP, so all datagrams passing through that IP address and—'

'Hold it.' Gilchrist had his hands in the air. 'I don't need to hear the technical mumbo jumbo.' He nodded at the monitor. 'What's this?'

'One of over seventy voyeur videos we've located on SB's server.'

Gilchrist mouthed an *Ah-hah*. 'We suspected Black hid webcams in people's homes during renovation works. Maybe for blackmailing. We got as far as that. But how does this video of a naked woman help us find him?'

Mhairi said, 'We're trying to ID her, sir.'

'I guessed as much, Mhairi. But how will that help us find Black today, right now?'

Mhairi seemed put out by his rebuke, but Matt said, 'What I was trying to tell you, sir, is that we've uncovered an entire library of webcam videos and more, much more.'

'Define more.'

'Other platforms. Other ways of extorting money. Let me show you.' Matt worked the mouse again, and the naked woman shrank on to the menu bar. A couple more clicks, and another page swelled on to the screen.

Gilchrist leaned closer. 'Is this Facebook?'

'It is.' Matt typed the keyboard, clicked the mouse, and the page shifted to a detailed profile page. Another click pulled up another profile page.

'You've lost me,' Gilchrist said.

'These are Scott Black's alter egos, if you like,' Matt said. 'The sites he uses to date women online, and lure them into sending him money.' He clicked a name, and a message box lifted off the bottom of the screen. 'This is Anita. She's online.' He typed Hi Anita. How r u? then sent it. His message appeared in a blue cloud in the message box, and a few seconds later a reply appeared in a white cloud.

Missing you big guy xx

'Who's big guy?'

Matt placed the cursor on the blue cloud. 'That's us.' Then he typed Missing u 2. Got to go. Talk later. He sent the message, and shut the box down.

'Won't she know it's not Black?' Gilchrist said.

'There's no way she'd suspect anything. Certainly not from what I've just sent her.' He clicked on another name – Mary C – and another message box appeared. 'Mary's offline at the moment,' he said. 'But read these.' He clicked the mouse, and a stream of messages scrolled down the small window like a water-fall of words, too fast for Gilchrist to read.

Then they stopped.

Matt fiddled with the cursor, until he found what he was looking for.

Then he stood back. 'What do you think?'

Gilchrist leaned forward.

'Use the mouse to scroll down,' Matt said.

Gilchrist took hold of the cursor, and read the messages.

Ta Mary u r a darling

You're welcome, big guy.

uve no idea how greatful I am

There's more if you need it.

R u sure

I said I trust you.

Gilchrist said, 'What're they talking about here?'

'About sending him money.'

'She fell for all his bullshit?'

'Not just her. Many others.'

Gilchrist eyed the screen. 'Bloody hell. How much did she give him?'

'Scroll back a few messages.'

Gilchrist streamed the messages down the screen, looking for the words that would tell him what he needed to know. He thought he found them, and leaned closer to the screen.

U r such a darling I luv u xx

Oh, you're saying all the right things, big guy.

Lets meet up soon

Just say the word.

266

I,ll pay u back with interest u no I will

I know, big guy.

Gilchrist backed through earlier messages, then whispered a curse.

It didnt work darling they want a bigger deposit

How much this time?

R u sure

I said I trust you. How much?

I hate to ask u but another 30k

So that'll be 60k down, leaving a joint mortgage of 340k?

They need ur signature

We should meet.

We will but after 60k is down.

Gilchrist pulled himself upright. 'Are they purchasing a house?'

Matt gave a twisted grimace. 'She thinks they're buying a home together. Meanwhile he's just banking her money.'

'You know that for sure?'

'Earlier messages give her his sort code and account number.'

'Over the Internet?'

'Through Facebook.'

Gilchrist raked his hair. 'For fuck sake. And she's fallen for it?'

'Hook, line, et cetera.'

'Who is she?'

Mhairi said, 'We haven't ID-ed her yet, sir. We're just trying to collect any info we can on him at the moment.'

Gilchrist turned to Matt. 'You said there were many others.'

267

'Best I can tell,' Matt said, 'there's another eight who've parted with cash. But it's early days, and I expect we'll find more.'

'So what're we talking about, money wise?'

'From a couple of thousand to Mary C's sixty grand.'

Gilchrist hissed a curse. 'All to the same account.'

'Yes, sir.' Mhairi looked at him. 'But it's an account that's new to us.'

'I thought we had all his accounts.'

'Apparently not, sir.'

'Bloody hell,' he said, and eyed the screen as an idea came to him. 'Is there any way Black would know we've accessed his Facebook page?'

'No.'

'What about that message you sent Anita?'

Matt took hold of Mhairi's mouse, found his last message to Anita, and deleted it.

Gilchrist held his gaze. 'Have you sent any other messages?'

'Only that one as a demonstration.'

Gilchrist nodded. 'So, Black doesn't know we've accessed his Facebook account, and he doesn't know we have details of this new bank account.'

'No, sir.'

'So what's to stop him withdrawing money from that account?'

'Nothing, sir.'

He squeezed Mhairi's shoulder. 'Get hold of the bank's head office and tell them to freeze that account, and to let us know the instant anyone tries to access it. We're looking for the location of whatever ATM he tries to pull cash out of.'

'Yes, sir.'

He turned to Matt. 'And I want a printout of every single Facebook message on that account,' he said. 'How long will that take you?'

'Could be a couple of hours.'

'On my desk for seven in the morning.'

He nodded to both of them, then headed for the door, mobile to his ear.

CHAPTER 32

Wednesday morning

Gilchrist jerked awake.

He didn't move as his mind struggled to push through sleep-laden thoughts and work out where he was. The back of his neck felt stiff, and he lifted his hand to rub it, surprised to find that he was sitting. He turned his head and stared beyond the dining-room window on to the darkness of his winter garden.

What the hell?

He gripped the arms of his chair, and the TV remote slipped off his knee on to the floor. 'Bloody hell,' he said. He had a vague memory of watching the BBC News, then switching it off. But he must have fallen asleep before he managed to go to bed.

He made it to the kitchen without knocking anything over, but groaned when he caught the time on his microwave – 05.44 – pointless going to bed now. Almost time to get up.

He filled the kettle, and poured a glass of sparkling water from the fridge. It tasted cold and refreshing, but did little to clear the coating of sleep from his teeth and tongue. He popped a couple of teabags into the teapot, then walked to his bedroom and stripped off.

A strong hot shower always worked for him, bringing him awake, jump-starting his system. Today he would find Scott Black wherever he might be, and arrest and charge him with the murders of Kandy Lal and Alice Hickson. The key to accomplishing this was in Black's Facebook messages, he was sure of that. They would find something in them, some innocent comment that could lead them straight to Black's hideout. Or maybe this latest bank account had a physical address, one they didn't currently possess. Either way, Gilchrist wanted to be there at the moment of the man's arrest, so he could look him in the eye and tell him exactly what he thought of him.

That morning's briefing was scheduled for 8 a.m. He would distribute copies of Black's Facebook messages to his team, and ID and locate the women who'd fallen for his romantic extortion. Maybe one of them had met Black in person, or knew something about him that no one else did.

In the kitchen, Gilchrist picked up a carton of cat food, opened the back door and stepped into the cold. He didn't waste time trying to look for Blackie or befriend her, just scattered pellets into the bowl by the hut, then scurried back indoors.

'Jesus,' he hissed. 'Where's summer when you need it?' As he poured himself a cup of tea, his mobile beeped, and he picked it up – a text from Jackie.

New South Wales Police, Australia, confirmed that Alice Hickson is an investigative journalist who has lived in Sydney for 15 years. She has 3 true crime books published, and is well known as an advocate for women's rights. She is not married, and had a sister, Janice, who lived in Oban and committed suicide 10 years ago. Both parents died in a boating accident in Sydney harbour 2 years ago.

So, Alice was an Aussie. No wonder they'd struggled to ID her. He read on.

Close friends of Alice say she flew to Scotland 2 months ago to find out the truth about her sister's death. Alice said Janice would never have committed suicide, but all attempts to speak to her husband, James Crichton, have failed. James left Oban after Janice's death, and has not been in contact with Alice since.

Gilchrist walked from the kitchen to the dining room and stared out the window. In the dark morning shadows he thought he caught the reflective pin-pricks of Blackie's eyes. But he could not be sure. One second they were there, and the next gone.

He read Jackie's text again.

James left Oban after Janice's death, and has not been in contact with Alice since.

Fingers of ice stroked his neck.

Alice said Janice would never have committed suicide.

Did she suspect that Janice had been murdered? By her husband, James? With whom Alice had since lost contact? But if Janice allegedly committed suicide, there must have been a post mortem and a police report.

He texted Jackie back.

I need a copy of the PM and police report on Janice Crichton's death.

He sent it off, and within seconds Jackie replied.

Already on your desk.

Gilchrist texted her a smiley face and a couple of kisses. Not polit-ically correct, he supposed, but who cared? He'd often told Jackie she was the best researcher in the world, and boy, was she proving it. He took another sip of tea, almost drained the mug, and returned to the kitchen for a refill.

As he tipped the teapot, his thoughts fired alive with questions. What were the odds on Alice visiting Scotland to search for the truth about her sister's suicide – think murder – only to be murdered herself? Slim to zero came the answer. And once in Scotland, the first thing Alice would have done was locate James Crichton. Why had he never been in contact since her sister's death? That alone set off alarm bells. But the most intriguing question was, of all the places to go in Scotland, why did Alice Hickson turn up in Fife, on the east coast, in the small fishing village of St Monans?

As an investigative journalist – one of a breed renowned for their relentless tenacity in uncovering the truth behind suspicious events – Alice would have left no stone unturned in her quest for answers. But why turn over stones in Fife?

And why did her path cross with Black's?

By coincidence? Or intention?

His thoughts turned over.

And over . . .

And arrived at the obvious conclusion.

Jessie placed her mobile phone on the kitchen table, then took a sip of tea.

But her stomach was churning so much, she couldn't even taste it. She glanced at the Collins & Sons wall clock, a present from Angie, God love her – what would she do without her? – and realised she would have to leave for the Office in the next ten minutes.

But first she had to talk to Robert. She couldn't put it off any longer. She had to tell him that his operation was not going ahead, and that he would remain stone deaf for the rest of his life. Just that thought had acid nipping her gut.

She had planned to tell him last night when she got home, but she'd been knackered, and just didn't have the will to face it. Robert had been in his bedroom, on his computer, deep into some story he was developing. From past experience, she knew not to interrupt him. Not that he would be upset, rather she would disturb his train of thought and put him off his writing.

Another glance at the clock.

Oh God. Nothing for it, but to get on with it.

She pushed Robert's bedroom door open, and breathed in the musty smell of sleep. Curtains hung open either side of the window, the room warm from the radiators. At the far side of the single bed, a laptop sat open on a corner desk. A banker's lamp brightened the keyboard, casting shadows into the corner.

The night had always been a fearful time for Robert. From a young age he slept with the curtains open, and all the lights on. At first, it had been every light in the room, even the door ajar and the hallway light on, too. But as he had grown older, his need for total brightness had diminished, until only a few lamps had to be left on through the night.

Jessie had never quibbled over that, just accepted that for a child who had been born deaf, the blackness of night had to be a terrifying place, creating the sensory illusion of being deaf *and* blind.

She entered his room, and squeezed herself on to the edge of his bed.

Just the gentle rocking of the mattress was enough to waken him.

He turned his head, caught her eye, and gave her a tired smile.

Her heart spilled open for her boy. That was what she loved about him. Despite having never heard a sound since birth, he always had a ready smile for her. She pushed her hands through his dark-blonde hair, scrunched it up, thick and soft – when had her hair last felt like that? – and thought it needed a cut.

Robert rolled on to his back, wide awake now, his hands signing.

I've written a letter to an agent and I'd like you to read it before I mail it.

Right now? Jessie signed back.

Yes.

Before Jessie could respond, Robert pulled himself from bed – stripped to the waist, boxer shorts on. His body was no longer that of a scrawny teenager, but was developing the toned muscles of an adult. And where on earth did he get his height from? Not from her, for sure. And not from that wee shithead for a father he'd never known.

But as she looked into her son's hopeful eyes as he handed her a single sheet of paper, the draft letter he wanted her to review, she knew she couldn't tell him that morning.

She could not break his heart, ruin his day, even his entire life.

She took the draft from him, fighting back the tears that stung her eyes.

★   ★   ★

Gilchrist sat at his office computer, spoiled for choice.

Jackie had delivered Janice Crichton's PM report and a copy of the Oban Office's police report to his desk. And Matt Duprey had printed out Black's Facebook messages, which lay before him, as thick as a Ken Follett manuscript.

Gilchrist decided to go for the thinner of the files.

Janice Crichton's PM report stated cause of death as drug overdose, with enough alcohol in her system to floor a horse – four times over the legal limit. Apparently Janice had been found unconscious in bed by her husband, James, who had tried but failed to revive her. He had immediately dialled 999 for an ambulance, but she was pronounced dead at the scene by the paramedics.

As Gilchrist read on, he learned that Janice had been taking medication for a sleeping disorder for five years prior to her death. He had read enough PM reports in his time as a DCI to recognise some of the names of the pills she'd been prescribed – Xanax, Ambien, Zopiclone – but his antennae twitched at the sight of Diazepam. The other pills were mostly prescribed for someone who had difficulty sleeping – as simple as that. But Diazepam could also be taken for anxiety disorders or to counter the symptoms of alcohol withdrawal. If taken in accordance with the prescription dosage, these pills were safe enough. But for someone determined to end their own life, these pills, together with a high alcohol intake, could be as deadly a cocktail as any.

Back to the police report.

James Crichton had been questioned under caution over his wife's death by the Oban Office of the Strathclyde Police Force, but released when he told them his wife suffered from panic disorder – which explained the Diazepam – and had threatened to take her own life on a number of occasions. Crichton had persuaded her to see a local psychiatrist who, when questioned by the police, not only confirmed Crichton's statement, but said he had put Janice on a course of cognitive behavioural therapy to treat her disorder. The results of that treatment were not what the psychiatrist had hoped, so he had prescribed Diazepam, which Janice had been taking for six months at the time of her suicide.

Gilchrist's phone rang. He thought about ignoring it, then picked it up. 'Gilchrist,' he said.

'Good morning, DCI Gilchrist. Do you have a minute?'

He needed to prepare for that morning's briefing, and in light of the reams of paper presented to him by Matt, he was thinking of assigning two of his team – Mhairi and Baxter – to review the printouts first, parse the text, and copy only the relevant sections.

'I'm a bit busy at the moment, ma'am.'

'We all are, DCI Gilchrist. You know where my office is.'

The line died.

Gilchrist flicked through the pages of the police report, and swore under his breath when he couldn't find a photograph of James Crichton. Of course, if the man hadn't been charged with a crime, there was little likelihood of his DNA, fingerprints, or even just a common or garden photo being included.

He picked up his phone, and got through on the second ring.

'Jackie?' he said.

'Uh-huh.'

'I need you to access the archives of the local Oban newspapers, the *Oban Times* or whatever it's called, and get me copies of any articles or reports about Janice Crichton's suicide. You got that?'

'Uh-huh.'

'But what I really need is a photograph of James Crichton. Anything you can find would be helpful. You think you can do that for me?'

'Uh-huh.'

'Thanks, Jackie. You're a darling.' He gave her a loud *Mwah* – again not pc, but who was listening? – and got a chuckle in response. 'As soon as, Jackie.'

When he entered Smiler's office, it was just as it had been the other day, as if she was not interested in personalising her working space.

'Take a seat, DCI Gilchrist.'

'Andy will do just fine, ma'am.'

'I prefer to keep our conversations formal.'

He gave a tight smile in acknowledgement, and remained standing.

'I've had the Alloa Office on the phone this morning, expressing concern about being compensated for assistance with resources.'

Money. It was always about money.

'I hear you racked up a tidy bill,' she said.

'They did offer to help, ma'am.'

'I'm sure they did, DCI Gilchrist. Rather than sit around twiddling their thumbs up their proverbial arseholes, they're more than happy to assign whatever idling resources they had sitting around doing nothing, so they could be paid for your sorry escapades.'

'Escapades, ma'am?'

'Oh for God's sake, DCI Gilchrist, don't act the idiot. I've been told you hijacked half their bloody mobile units and sent them traipsing over most of bloody Clackmannanshire in search of some phantom figure—'

'Scott Black,' Gilchrist said. 'We had him in our hands, but he escaped.'

'Yes, he did, DCI Gilchrist. He did indeed escape.' She sat back and eyed him with thinly veiled contempt. 'Any idea where he is at the moment, then?'

'No, ma'am.' Well, what else could he tell her?

'Any guesses?'

'Plenty of guesses, ma'am. But I wouldn't want to waste valuable resources running around—'

'Stop right there.' Her eyes blazed. Her lips quivered. She palmed her desk as if to make sure she couldn't claw his eyes out by accident. Then she took a deep breath and said, 'I'd been warned about your impudence, but by God I never believed you would be so brazen as to—'

'Scott Black has killed at least two women, possibly many more. It seems to have escaped everyone's attention that we are trying to track him down and arrest him.'

Her face paled, and she pushed her chair back as if to stand.

It seemed that cutting Smiler off mid-sentence only inflamed her. But Gilchrist gave her a tight look of his own, and before he could think it through, said, 'We've only just uncovered evidence that gives me every reason to suspect that Black has killed before.' As he watched the meaning of his words nuzzle into Smiler's mind, he wished he'd engaged his brain before letting off with his mouth. This was the sort of rash statement that ended careers, sent well-respected DCIs – maverick or not – into the grazing fields, or punted them straight into touch and out of the game for good.

'Explain,' she said.

Well, what had he expected? Nothing quite like putting your head on the block to give clarity of thought. 'We've had it confirmed by New South Wales Police that Alice Hickson was an Australian investigative journalist whose sister, Janice Crichton, committed suicide under suspicious circumstances while living in Oban.' He brought Smiler up to speed with his investigation, bending the truth a little to favour his argument, and ending with the revelation that they'd uncovered an entire library's worth of voyeur videos – not strictly correct, but he felt he'd earned the right to use poetic licence – and fraudulent Internet romance sites that Black was using to extort money from innocent victims, and possibly lure them to their death. Another quantum leap, he knew, and no proof to date, but it was possible.

Throughout it all, Smiler's eyes never left his.

When Gilchrist finished, she studied her hands for a long moment, then stared at him with a look that could burn through reinforced concrete. 'And what proof do you have that this missing James Crichton and Scott Black are one and the same?'

The truthful answer was *No proof at all*, but he was in so deep that it seemed silly not to compound his problems. 'We should have photographic confirmation within the hour.'

Smiler glanced at her watch. 'Let me know the minute you do.'

He nodded.

'That'll be all, DCI Gilchrist.'

'Ma'am,' he said, and turned on his heels.

He found Jackie at her computer, fingers typing with the speed of a woodpecker. 'Any luck with that photograph from the *Oban Times*?' he asked her.

Her rust-coloured hair wobbled like a loose Afro.

'I need it within the hour,' he said. 'Think you can do that?'

She turned to her computer, and waved him away.

Back in his office, he walked to the window, pressed his forehead against the cold glass. Below, headlights brushed the car park. Tyres splashed slushy puddles that glistened for a moment, then settled into blackness. He recognised Jessie's Fiat pulling into a parking spot. Even in the early-morning darkness, he had a sense of the sky being low, the rainclouds close enough to touch if he just reached for them. November on the east coast of Scotland.

For all anyone knew, daylight could be an imaginary state.

He watched and waited, while the hammering in his chest settled down.

What a bloody mess he'd made of it.

And all to prove . . . what?

It had been a long shot, he knew, one of his longest, and he struggled now to work through the rationale that had seemed so logical only moments earlier. James Crichton and Scott Black were one and the same. That's what he'd claimed. That's what had been so clear to him only minutes earlier. Why else would Alice Hickson have crossed paths with Black or, more to the point, why else would Black have murdered her? The logic was crystal clear, and he wondered why it had taken him so long to work it out.

Except . . .

Except that it wasn't crystal clear at all. Or obvious. In fact, it was as far-fetched an idea as he'd ever come up with. He realised that now. How in hell had he let himself be so stupid, so bloody fucking stupid? And now he had hung his investigation, his reputation, his career, *everything*, the whole fucking shooting match, on the stupid assumption that James Crichton and Scott Black were one and the same.

He turned from the window and picked up his phone.

'Any luck, Jackie?'

'Nuh-uh.'

He replaced the receiver.

Christ, this was it. It was finally about to happen.

Shot down by friendly fire. His very own gun.

He picked up Black's Facebook messages and flicked through them.

But his heart wasn't in it.

CHAPTER 33

Gilchrist brought his briefing to an end with, 'We know Black's gone into hiding, but we don't know where, and we don't know for how long. What we do know is that we need to find him, and we need to find him soon, before he kills again. So let's get cracking.'

His team dispersed, some leaving the room, others returning to their desks.

Mhairi caught his eye and said, 'Sir? Do you have a moment?'

Gilchrist followed her to a corner of the room where they could talk in comparative privacy without being heard by everyone in the office. 'Yes, Mhairi?'

'I've got some feedback on the Tinto Gallery, sir, like you asked me to.' She shook her head. 'The address doesn't exist. I've tried different variations of it, Avenue, Road, that sort of thing, sir, but nothing comes up for London. Closest I could find was a Crescent in Tadcaster, York.'

Gilchrist felt his heart stutter. What the hell had Jack got himself into? 'Keep going.'

She shook her head. 'And nothing on Jen Tinto either, sir. I ran a check on the mobile number on the business card, but it's pay as you go.'

'So Jen Tinto could be anybody,' he said.

'I'm afraid so, sir. Yes.'

'There's no mistake about the address, is there?'

'None, sir. I've got a friend in the Met, and I phoned and asked him to check it out. He came back to me with the same result, sir. The business and address don't exist.'

He thanked her, told her that was the end of it, and walked back to his office. He was about to sit down, when Jessie stuck her head in.

'Heard anything more from the Alloa Office?' she said.

He groaned. 'Only their invoice for services rendered, which Smiler was happy to tell me exactly how far up my arse she was going to shove it.'

'Ouch. That'll make your eyes water.'

He picked up movement to the side, and turned to see Jackie in the hallway, clutching her walking stick with one hand and waving a printout with the other. He couldn't tell from her face if it was good news or bad.

'S . . . s . . . s . . .' she tried, and handed him the printout.

He took it from her – a grainy image of a woman in her late twenties, early thirties, wearing a twin-set and corduroy trousers, sunglasses on her face, the frames deep enough to date the photograph somewhere in the 1990s, maybe 1980s. She was standing on a gravel drive of sorts, backside pressed against some luxury car that glistened showroom new – Jaguar or Daimler, he couldn't say. At her side stood a clean-shaven man in his mid-thirties, with a gaunt face and neat, short hair, white at the temples, giving him a distinguished look – lord of the manor, it seemed. Corduroy trousers could be order of the day, and a burgundy and white check shirt, open neck stuffed with a cravat, somehow spoke of champagne and salmon for breakfast, and unearned income – lots of it.

Gilchrist felt his heart slump.

He'd got it wrong, oh so fucking wrong.

The caption beneath the photograph read *Woman found dead in luxury villa*. The background looked distinctly Scottish – pine trees, black loch, cloud-covered sky – which had him puzzling over the term *villa* – more of a continental term, he thought.

The accompanying article offered nothing new, other than the fact that Crichton ran his own business – a local building contractor. Gilchrist stopped at that, and read the words again. Then he stared at the photograph, narrowed his eyes and tried to imagine Crichton ten years older, hair longer, dyed black, heavy beard, thick moustache, and twenty – make that thirty – pounds heavier.

Could it be?

The picture was too grainy to be conclusive, but the longer he studied it, the more he came to see that he could be looking at a younger, slimmer, fitter version of the Scott Black he'd confronted at his cottage by the sea. But it was the shoulders that did it for him – sculpted and wide, with long arms that hung by his sides, and wide hands and thick fingers that hinted of powerful muscles covered by the sleeves of his shirt.

'Is this the only photo you could find?' he asked Jackie.

She wobbled her head.

'Can you give me another one? A cleaner copy?'

'Uh-huh,' she grunted, and hobbled off, shoulders lurching, hips heaving, with the effort of simply walking.

He watched her go, his heart swelling for her, a young woman in her early thirties who lived by herself, who had no social life and who spent every waking hour, it seemed, working as a researcher for Fife Constabulary. He took a deep breath, and turned away.

He found Jessie and Mhairi at Jessie's desk, both of them riffling through a pile of paperwork. He placed Jackie's photograph in front of them. 'Recognise anyone?' he said.

Jessie scrunched her eyes. 'Where did you get this?'

'Who does it remind you of?'

Mhairi said, 'Scott Black, sir, but twenty years younger.'

Jessie leaned closer. 'Now you mention it, I'd recognise that ugly face anywhere.'

'Who's the woman?' Mhairi asked.

'Alice Hickson's sister.'

Both Jessie and Mhairi jerked a look at him.

'What?'

'Sir?'

He'd mentioned nothing at the briefing of the NSW Police identifying Alice Hickson, nor that her sister, Janice, once lived in Oban. It seemed more sensible to hold off until he had feedback from Jackie on the *Times* article. If the photo had proved him wrong, Smiler would announce that he'd been removed from the investigation, or suspended, or even fired, and she could give them all that interesting bit of news to go on. But now it was positive, or at least appeared to be so, he was able to bring both Jessie and Mhairi up to speed.

'That's it right there,' Jessie said. 'His motive for murdering Alice. She tracks him down and confronts him. They argue, he kills her, takes her out on his boat, then dumps her body into the sea.'

'Confronts him with what?' Gilchrist said, searching for the side of the argument so he could compare it with his own. 'Her sister committed suicide.'

'Sure she did,' Jessie said. 'Is that what the police report said?'

'Accidental overdose was the general conclusion.'

'You know what I think?'

Gilchrist cocked his head in a silent question.

'I think that bastard's got a history of killing women.' Jessie studied the photo. 'How old is he there? Thirty? And Alice's sister? Twenty-something?' She slapped the image. 'You don't wake up one morning and say, Hey, I think I'm gonna kill my wife.' She scowled. 'No, sir. That ugly face right there is the face of a serial killer, someone who's murdered before, and will murder again.'

'And all we have to do,' Gilchrist interrupted, 'is find and arrest him. I want the pair of you to dig out everything you can on Crichton. Check the PNC for any previous. Contact the Department of Work and Pensions, the DVLA, and HMRC for starters. If Crichton really is Black, and he was playing happy families back then, he would have a financial history, tax returns, National Insurance stamp in his or somebody else's name . . .'

'Like Bobby Kerr?' Jessie said.

'Maybe,' he said. 'But if so, then he seems to have more identities than . . . than . . .'

'Than a chameleon?' Jessie offered.

'That'll do. But you get what I'm saying. If he's a serial killer with a past, then there's a strong possibility that he lived under someone else's name, maybe even married and had a whole different family before he married Alice's sister.'

'Want me to look into that, sir?'

'No, Mhairi, I need you and Jessie to work on building a history for Crichton. If he's got a driving licence or paid income tax, then I'd love to know what address he'd given. For all we know, he might be back-tracking through his past.' He nodded to the photo. 'Email a copy of that, and a photo of Black, to Glasgow University's Dr Heather Black – no relation. She works in the Computer Science Department and Turing Institute, as best I recall. Ask her to carry out a digital facial comparison, and get back to me today with the result.'

'Is she expecting it?' Jessie asked.

'No.'

'That's asking a lot, is it not?'

'In what way?'

'To send stuff to her out of the blue and tell her you want a comparison back pronto.'

'Say please, then.' He turned and strode from the room.

Back in his office, he called Mac Fountain. Not only was Mac responsible for CCTV cameras throughout Fife, he was also in charge of the exchange and coordination of CCTV footage with other regional forces. Gilchrist had spoken to him yesterday evening about the taped-over and altered registration numbers for Black's Ford Fiesta.

'Anything?' Gilchrist asked.

'Not a thing, Andy,' Mac said. 'Nothing's come through on the ANPR. And we've had no response to the marker on the PNC.'

'He can't just have vanished,' Gilchrist said.

'He could've changed number plates again,' Mac said. 'Picked them up from any old banger off the side of the road. He's done it once, so why not twice? Or three times for luck, if you think about it.'

'Thanks, Mac. You know how to make a man happy.'

Mac chuckled.

'Keep me posted.'

'You'll be the first to know.'

Gilchrist turned to the window.

Outside, the sleet had stopped. Puddles littered the car park like slivers of glass that reflected a white sky. Somehow, finding that photograph of Crichton had energised him, set his mind alight with possibilities. Alice Hickson had come to Scotland to uncover the truth about her sister's death, but in so doing had managed to get herself killed. And her friend, Kandy Lal, just happened to be in the wrong place at the wrong time. But why had Black killed Kandy? Because Alice had told her something, or given her something that could identify him as the killer of Alice's sister, Janice?

But if so, what had she said to Kandy?

He was missing something. He could feel it, almost touch it.

It was there for him to bend down and pick up. If he could only find it.

For Black to kill Alice, she must have confronted him and threatened to report him to the police. But what had she confronted him with? What had she found? And if she'd found something, where was it now? The SOCOs had carried out a forensic search of her home and found nothing – no laptop, no mobile phone, no camera, no flashdrive, no digital equipment of any kind. Not even any notebooks or handwritten notes, which an investigative journalist would use as a matter of necessity. Black must have swept her house clean and destroyed – more likely dumped in the sea – all her digital and personal belongings. But before dumping computer hardware into the sea, would he have first deleted all content? Would any of the content be recoverable after being in the sea? Gilchrist thought not.

But you never knew what today's IT experts could recover.

Just that slight change in tack had him questioning his logic.

No investigative journalist would keep digital content on a computer without making a backup. And Alice Hickson would almost certainly have created a backup of whatever she had found on Black. Had she kept it all on a removable flashdrive? Or would she have backed it up in another file on her computer?

Gilchrist turned from the window and eyed his office computer. Not exactly the most up-to-date, but it served its purpose. It provided him with access to police files, emails, and contact with others in the Office. But if he ever needed to keep a backup of some important personal files, would he create another folder on that old dinosaur?

He didn't think so.

Was storing digital files the answer? Had Alice brought a flashdrive with her all the way from Australia? And in that moment, the answer to Alice's dilemma came to him with such clarity that it almost stunned him into immobility.

Almost.

He strode from his office.

Jackie looked up as he rapped her door and entered. 'Get me the phone number for the New South Wales Police Office in Australia, and the person who identified Alice Hickson.'

Jackie leaned to the side, removed a sheet of paper from a tray, and handed it to him.

He ran his eyes over the contact details – Senior Sergeant Stu Pierson – and saw that she had also obtained a home address for him, and a mobile number. 'Well done,' he said.

He was halfway down the steps to the main door when he got through.

'Yup?'

Even from that one word, Gilchrist could tell that Pierson was Australian born and bred. 'Senior Sergeant Stu Pierson?' he asked, and received another Aussie *Yup*. Gilchrist introduced himself, and apologised for contacting Pierson on his mobile, and at that time of night – eleven hours ahead of the UK. Then he thanked him for identifying Alice Hickson, and getting back to the St Andrews Office so quickly.

'Least I could do,' Pierson said. 'Did you get the bastard that done it?'

'Not yet,' Gilchrist said. 'But we're getting closer.'

Pierson coughed. 'Still can't believe it. The wife's read every one of Alice's books, and I tell you what, she's spot on.'

Gilchrist wasn't sure if Pierson was talking about his wife or Alice being *spot on*, but he said nothing as he left the building. He turned to his right as he listened to Pierson rattle off the titles of Alice's books. When he stepped into Muttoes Lane towards Market Street, he realised he had no destination in mind, just needed to breathe fresh air and let his thoughts fire alive.

'You make it sound as if Alice is famous,' Gilchrist interrupted.

'Not famous, just popular. Her books got to number one in the Amazon charts, so the wife tells me. She's a big fan of hers.'

Gilchrist wanted to force the conversation on to his reason for calling, but he needed Pierson's help. So he listened to him ramble on until he reached Market Street, then said, 'Alice lived alone, right? She wasn't married, was she?'

'No, mate.'

'What's happened to her personal possessions?'

'Still in her home, I'm guessing.'

'Well, here's the scoop. I've got our forensic guys going through her home here, and so far they've come up empty-handed. We can't find her computer, her mobile phone, or anything else that would give us information on her, and help us understand what story she was working on. Which is important, because I believe that whatever she was working on got her killed. But we can't find any backup files, no notes, *nothing*. Her house has been cleaned and her personal effects removed, we think by her killer. Which is why I'm calling you.'

'Sure, mate. How can I help?'

'We need someone to carry out a forensics search of Alice's home in Sydney to find out what she was working on. If I was a betting man, I'd put money on the story being about James Crichton, her late sister's husband, but I don't know. What I do know is that for Alice to have made that journey from Australia to Scotland, she must've had something more than just a hunch, something she'd uncovered in Australia, something powerful enough to make her fly halfway round the world for an answer. It's that *something* that I need you to find for us. Are you able to help?'

'Let me run it past my bosses,' Pierson said. 'And I'll get back to you.'

CHAPTER 34

Wednesday evening

Gilchrist's mobile rang – ID an unknown number.

He took it with a grumpy, 'Yes?'

A woman's laughter rang out, then turned into a chirpy voice that said, 'You sound as if you hate cold calls, Andy. Don't worry, I'm not selling anything. Just calling back with the results of my comparative analysis on the photographs your office sent me earlier today.'

'Heather,' he said. 'I'm sorry. I didn't recognise your number.'

'That's because I'm calling from home. We're about to go out for the evening, so I'll keep it short. It's a match, Andy. Not one hundred per cent, but the quality's poor. If you can send me any other images, I'd be happy to look at them.'

'That's it, I'm afraid. But you've given me all I need to know. Many thanks, Heather.'

'Happy to be of help, Andy. I'll get a formal reply to you first thing in the morning. But I've got to rush. Talk later. Bye.'

Gilchrist returned his mobile to his pocket, cheered by Heather Black's call.

Surely now the noose was tightening.

But by 8 p.m., they were no further forward. No silver Ford Fiesta with a number resembling any of the variations logged on to the ANPR, and no hits reported on the PNC. The Alloa Office managed to find CCTV footage of the silver Fiesta on the road to Dunfermline – minus its number plates – which proved Gilchrist's theory.

But after that, the Fiesta was as good as gone.

'I'm thinking he's swapped cars again,' Jessie said.

'We've had no reports of a stolen car,' Gilchrist complained.

'Maybe the owners are on holiday, or maybe Black just got lucky.'

'Or maybe he had some other home to go to,' he said, 'with some other Martha on the go.' Not that he thought that was likely, but as the day progressed with no sightings of the Fiesta by anyone, Gilchrist found himself struggling to discount that possibility.

The trace they put on Martha Kerr's mobile phone turned up nothing either. She might have had a mobile for her own convenience, considering where she lived, but for all the times she used it – once to phone her local bank – she might as well not have had one. If Gilchrist had hoped for a lead from Black calling Martha, he was well disappointed.

And attempts to uncover details of James Crichton were getting them nowhere. They managed to establish that Janice Hickson had returned to Scotland from Australia at the age of twenty-five to marry her then-boyfriend, Alexander McKay, the youngest son of a family who ran a fleet of fishing boats. Despite that marriage ending in divorce after only two years – Alexander's infidelity being the reason – Janice did not return to Australia. By all accounts, her settlement milked Alexander for all he was worth, and she stayed on in Oban, living the life of a woman of leisure until she was swept off her feet by Crichton, a business-man new to the region, but who was already making a name as a hard-nosed competitor, willing to work long hours to establish his start-up contracting business.

Shortly after that, things turned for the worse for Janice.

Although Mhairi and Jessie managed to recover a history of personal tax returns and NI contributions for Janice, her new husband, James, seemed to have been nothing more than a ghost in that regard. Tax records filed by his contracting company – JC Contracting – showed it made a loss of sixty thousand pounds in its first year of operation, and no returns had been filed since. Gilchrist was intrigued by the company being named after the owner's initials – just as Scott Black had done with SB Contracting – which had his sixth sense telling him he was on the right track. But with-out proof, it didn't matter how hard your instinct twitched.

It was nothing more than a guess.

And Butterworth Holdings yielded nothing new. The Kerr Roberts whose name was registered in Companies House as the owner proved to be one more fictional character. No tax records or NI contributions existed for him, and even though the FIU managed to freeze all assets in the RBS Jersey Account, Gilchrist had the distinct feeling that they were all doing too little too late, and that Black really had slipped the proverbial noose.

Gilchrist heard his stomach rumble, which reminded him that he hadn't eaten since breakfast – once again. He was about to set out for a pint and a bite when Jessie appeared in his doorway.

'Unless you've got anything urgent for me to do,' she said, 'I'm going to head home and feed my wee boy.'

'Nothing in from Stu Pierson?' he asked.

'Not a squeak. Want me to call him?'

'No. On you go. I'll follow up with him later.' She was about to leave his office, when he said, 'Is everything all right?'

She stopped, pressed a hand against the doorjamb. 'Not really.'

'Want to talk about it?'

She shook her head. 'I haven't told Robert about his operation yet. And I can't put it off any longer.'

Gilchrist knew how close Jessie was to her son, and how young Robert had longed to make a career as a stand-up comedian. But being stone deaf from birth, the lad never had any chance to get off the starting blocks.

'Do you need to take time off?' he asked.

'Thanks, but no thanks. You can't afford to lose any staff.'

'Are you sure?'

'Positive,' she said. 'I'll be in first thing tomorrow, but if anything crops up . . .' She placed her thumb and pinkie by her ear '. . . give me a bell, OK?'

He nodded in agreement, but he had no intention of phoning her. They might need every set of hands they could find, but calling someone in when they had personal issues to resolve would do none of them any favours. He was about to check up with Jackie, when his mobile beeped – ID Mo.

He took the call with, 'Hey, princess.'

'Just calling to let you know the flights are all organised, and that we're leaving from Edinburgh tomorrow afternoon.'

'That was quick,' he said.

'I told you yesterday that it would be Thursday or Friday.'

'I know, I know, I don't mean anything. It's just that talking about it, and then getting an actual flight time, it suddenly hits you that it's for real.'

'I'll be back, Dad,' she said. 'Probably in a couple of weeks, once we've decided where we're going to live.'

He thought she sounded more positive than she had yesterday, as if she and Tom had committed to making a go of it, come whatever. 'You want me to do anything with your flat when you're gone?' he asked.

'That's OK, Dad. Tom's got it covered. And a lift to the airport, too.'

Well, what had he expected? He'd not really been in their lives of late, so why should he expect anything different now? But he found himself not wanting to ask how Tom had it covered, in case Maureen thought he was interfering, so just said, 'That's good to hear. If there's anything I can do, just let me know.'

'See us off at the airport, Dad?'

St Andrews to Edinburgh Airport was a good hundred miles round trip, and with the status of his ongoing investigation, he didn't think he could afford to take the time off. Maureen would be expecting more than a quick hug and a teary cheerio, and if he hit any kind of traffic, the whole trip could take four hours out of the middle of his day. Shit, and bugger it. Still, how many times did your only daughter fly to Australia?

'I'll do what I can, Mo,' he said.

'That sounds like a No, Dad.'

'It's not, Mo. I've got some juggling to do. Just text me the flight details,' he said, 'and I'll get something sorted out tonight. Does that work?'

'Sure.'

He could tell from the tone of her voice that she didn't believe him, that she thought he was setting up a good excuse not to make it to the airport. But just to be on the safe side, he said, 'What are you and Tom doing this evening? Other than packing,' he added with a chuckle. 'I'd be happy to take you out for dinner.'

'We can't, Dad.'

'You're always telling me that I have to eat, right?'

'We've already eaten, Dad. Tom's parents took us out to the Vine Leaf.'

Hearing that deflated him. He knew he had no right to be upset at not being invited to join them. After all, Tom's parents would want to spend some private time with their son and future daughter-in-law. Still, it nipped, if he was being honest, made a tad more bitter by the Vine Leaf being one of the more upmarket restaurants, with a reputation for excellent food, but one he seldom visited, preferring cheaper fare. More worrying was the possibility that if he didn't see Mo tonight, he might not see her for a couple of weeks, until her return from Perth.

'How about a quick pint, then?' he said. 'In the Criterion. Just along from your flat.'

'I don't think so, Dad. We're up to our ears.'

'Is that what Tom says, too?'

'I don't need to ask Tom to know that he doesn't want another pint.'

Another pint. So they'd already had a few in the Vine Leaf. Defeated, he said, 'OK, Mo. I'll see you tomorrow, then. All right?'

'Sure, Dad.'

'Love you, Mo.' But the line was already dead, leaving him with the feeling that she had only given him lip service.

Before heading home, he walked to the incident room and eyed the whiteboard, not confident of finding anything different from an hour earlier. As it turned out, he was right. No sightings of Black or of the Ford Fiesta had been noted. No new information from the Alloa Office. Nothing from HMRC or the DVLA. No new notes on Martha Kerr or Butterworth Holdings. As he stood there re-reading his scribbled comments, he felt a burgeoning sense of failure, that his investigation was not only coming up against a brick wall, but was about to be halted in its tracks.

The only spark of hope came from his thoughts on James Crichton.

He slipped his mobile from his pocket and dialled Senior Sergeant Stu Pierson. But after five rings, it dumped him into voicemail. He gave his name and left a short message – *Anything new? Give me a call* – then hung up.

He eyed the whiteboard again.

His investigation was stalling. They had nothing new to go on.

Up until that moment, the thought that Black could outfox him, and stay hidden for so long, had never truly seemed a possibility. But as he turned away from the incident room, his heart heavy with the cold sense of defeat, he couldn't even raise a glimmer of a smile.

Jessie pushed the bedroom door wide.

Soft light from several table lamps cast a warm glow around the room, settling the corners into shadow. Robert was on his laptop, not playing games like most teenagers, but writing. It was what he wanted to do, become a novelist, a writer of comedy, of funny stories, anecdotal quips and tales, anything and everything that could put a smile on your face.

He looked up as she approached. *You look sad*, he signed.

I've got something I have to tell you. Something sad.

He frowned as she sat on the edge of his bed, next to his writing desk. *Are you ill?*

She shook her head and gave him a tired smile. She'd asked for, and received, a copy of his medical records, which included the results of these latest tests. But she had decided to tell Robert the outcome, rather than have him read the results for himself.

It's about your operation for your hearing, she signed.

Alert now, concern etching his forehead.

These latest tests they did. She held his questioning look. *They say there's nothing they can do.*

I don't understand. What do you mean?

Your hearing nerves don't exist. They never developed. That's why there's nothing they can do. The operation's been cancelled. Her son's face shimmered as tears flooded her eyes. *They say they can't fix your hearing. No one can. I'm so sorry.* She reached for his hand, but he turned away and stared at his monitor, mouth tight, jaw rippling as he fought back tears of his own.

She stood up, put an arm around his shoulder and hugged him tight as his head lolled against her chest. She ran her fingers through his hair, unable to speak as her son sobbed his heartfelt tears, his voice moaning in the toneless cry of the deaf.

CHAPTER 35

Thursday morning

Gilchrist woke to the sound of electronic beeping.

He reached for his mobile phone, confused but a few seconds until he realised he was receiving a series of incoming messages from Stu Pierson.

He clicked on the first message and tried to open it. But it failed. He tried again, but got the same result. His mobile beeped as another message arrived. He checked the time – 5.17 – which might explain why Pierson was sending messages rather than just phoning.

Another attempt at opening a message failed, so he dialled Pierson's number, only to be sent to voicemail. Rather than leave a message, he killed the call, then stumbled through the bedroom darkness into his bathroom.

He clicked the switch. Light exploded into his brain.

A quick look in the mirror assured him that he looked more tired than hungover, although he did have a faint memory of opening a bottle of The Aberlour. He slid open the cubicle door and switched on the shower. As he waited for the water to heat up, he heard his mobile beeping, receiving more messages from Down Under.

Just the act of standing under the hot water, running a razor over his face, fingertips searching for unshaved patches, brought his thoughts to life and the memory of last night's dream out of its sleep-ridden shadows.

He'd been outside a cottage on the side of a hill, riding a motorbike round and round in the pouring rain, all the while keeping his distance from a woman in a threadbare shroud who reached out to him with grappling hands each time he passed. She couldn't catch him, and she tore off her shroud in anger, to reveal the hard musculature of a man with long arms that rippled with sinewed muscles, and strong hands with thick fingers that clutched at the air. He had the vaguest recollection of groaning with fear, stirring awake, only for sleep to pull him down again.

He squeezed a dollop of shampoo on to his palms and worked the cream into his hair and scalp. What did it mean, that dream? Was it his subconscious trying to tell him that Martha Kerr was not who she said she was? But if so, who was she?

By the time he'd rinsed his hair, he was none the wiser.

Back in his bedroom, he checked his mobile again. The messages had stopped coming in, and appeared to be attachments only, with no supporting text. He tried again to open them, but still failed. He would need someone in the Office to download them for him.

In the kitchen, he switched on the TV and filled the kettle. A local weather report warned of freezing fog, snow, and dangerous winds. Through the rain-speckled window, the morning could be midnight-black. Beads of sleet slithered across the glass from a gathering storm. As if these last couple of months had not been cold enough, it looked as if winter was now intending to batter the place into frozen submission.

On the TV he caught a glimpse of Morrisons car park, and a photo of Scott Black in the top right corner, despite that incident of assault being two days old. He had just removed a carton of cat food from the cupboard, and was about to open the back door to feed Blackie, when his mobile rang.

He picked it up – ID Jessie.

His first thought was that she was phoning to say she wouldn't be in the Office for a couple of days. But instead she said, 'Have you checked your messages?'

'Not yet. Why?'

'Aussie Stu's sent a bunch of messages through to me. They're all copied to you.'

'I can't open them,' he confessed. 'I've tried, but something's not working.'

'Probably don't have enough memory on that dinosaur of yours.'

'So what's got you excited?'

'Stu's come through with the goods. Looks like he searched Alice's home and found loads of stuff that's of real interest – copies of handwritten and typed notes, tree-loads of the stuff, articles, photographs, police reports, witness statements and more. I tell you, Alice was one hell of an investigative journalist. She was at least ten steps ahead of us in identifying Scott Black.'

Gilchrist felt the hairs on the back of his neck stir. They were getting to the heart of the matter. 'So who is he, exactly?' he asked.

'Jury's still out. Looks like he had more aliases than a cat's got lives, but from what I've read of Alice's notes, it seems she knew nothing about Martha Kerr being his sister.'

'But why would Black run to her cottage?'

'To hide his motorbike?'

He chuckled. 'Seriously.'

'It's a safe house?'

Well, he might be prepared to buy that. But something niggled, telling him that there had to be more to it than that. Black had taken an enormous risk launching his yacht single-handedly and setting it off across the Firth of Forth. Then to abandon the trailer on the beach, and his Land Rover in a farm lane, then bike it fifty miles in freezing conditions, these were the actions of a desperate man. Or were they the actions of a determined man, someone who knew exactly what he was doing with every assured step?

But no matter how Gilchrist looked at it, something just didn't fit his sense of logic.

'I can't get past that cottage,' he said. 'Why head there? Why not somewhere else? There has to be a reason for it.'

'Well, when you work it out, let me know,' Jessie said. 'I just think Black knew he could hole up there for a few days, longer if he had to, because he knew it was safe.'

'Maybe that's what we're supposed to think.'

'You're forgetting we're not supposed to think anything about the cottage, Andy. We weren't supposed to find it at all.'

But they *had* found it. And now they had to act on that. 'Check up on that warrant for the cottage,' he said. 'And get on to the Alloa Office and tell them to send someone to it and bring Martha Kerr in.'

'On what charges?' Jessie said.

'On suspicion of being complicit in the murder of Janice Hickson.'

Jessie gasped. 'Jeezo, Andy, that's a quantum leap and a half.'

It was more than a quantum leap, he knew. It was a step through a black hole and into another universe. That's how much of a leap it was. On the other hand, it was also a leap of faith. Martha Kerr might come across as hapless and innocent, but everything about her warned Gilchrist it was just a façade. She was up to her skinny little neck in it, and about to be sucked down into the steaming depths of deepest shit.

'Martha Kerr,' he said. 'She's the key. Trust me.'

'I'd like to, Andy. But if you're wrong?'

Therein lay the problem. There was no turning back. Not now. 'I've been wrong before,' he said.

'That's comforting, I must say.'

'On the other hand,' he said, 'what have we got to lose?'

'Our careers?'

Well, there was that, he supposed. Still, he could take some limited precautions.

'Before we go in all guns blazing,' he said, 'we need to go through everything Aussie Stu sent us. Maybe Alice's notes might give us a clue.' A gust of wind battered hailstones against his kitchen window, as if in ominous forewarning. 'Get hold of everyone,' he said. 'I want them in the Office within the hour. We need to find out who Scott Black is, and where the hell he is now.'

'I'm on it,' Jessie said.

'And arrange for Martha Kerr to be brought to the Glenrothes Office. You and I are going to give her a right good grilling.'

305

CHAPTER 36

Alice Hickson's files had taken years to prepare.

By late morning, Gilchrist and his team had established that James Crichton had inherited his late wife's estate in its entirety. It included a mortgage-clear detached stone villa on Gallanach Road, overlooking Oban Bay and most of the town, as well as a 25 per cent share in a small fishing fleet of four trawlers that had worked out of Aberdeen on the east coast. All courtesy of Janice's divorce settlement from her first husband, Alexander McKay. More damning, at least in Gilchrist's eyes, was the fact that Crichton had also received one hundred thousand pounds from a life insurance policy which Janice had taken out three weeks before their wedding. It looked as if James Crichton had entered marriage with an exit strategy prepared in advance.

Calls to Will McKay, Alexander's oldest brother who now owned the fishing fleet, confirmed that Crichton had sold his share to the family at a price that *questioned his sanity*.

'Too high?' Jessie had asked.

'Just the opposite. Nowhere close to market price. But we were just glad to get it back, and get that bastard out of our faces.'

No love lost there, it seemed.

Within a week of Janice's funeral, the stone villa on Gallanach Road had been put on the market and sold to the first reasonable offer. The sale of both the matrimonial home and the stake in the fishing fleet told Gilchrist that Crichton had been interested in a sale for cash only, and once banked – which raised the question of where exactly it had gone – he had then moved from Oban to an unknown destination.

This was where Alice's notes became difficult to follow. They were clear enough to read, in concise statements like bullet points, but the flow of logic appeared convoluted. Her notes jumped forward in time, then back, casting up name after name, none of which seemed to be related to any other. How she had made the connection was none too clear, except for one constant that ran through each name – the date of birth.

Gilchrist scanned the list – seven names in total. So if each of these names was indeed Black living under a pseudonym, then he could see how it might become too much. You had to have an excellent memory to be a good liar, so it helped to intersperse the lies with a modicum of truth. A single birthdate helped memory recall.

But still . . .

The earliest date to appear on Alice's notes was fourteen years ago, which also had the first and only mention of the surname Kerr – a fairly common Scottish name as best he could determine. But a Robert Kerr had lived in Portree on the Isle of Skye, and married Norma Kintyre, a wealthy lifelong resident of the village. As in the case of James Crichton and Scott Black, Robert Kerr appeared to have turned up from nowhere, fully formed, in the shape of a successful building contractor. Also, just like James

Crichton, Kerr was married for less than a year before his wife, Norma, drowned after falling into the harbour during a heavy downpour.

The PM report concluded that Norma had too much alcohol in her system – four times over the limit – which on top of medication for a sore back, would have made walking in a straight line difficult, if not impossible. Hence the accidental fall into the harbour.

Newspaper articles at the time noted that Robert Kerr had been questioned under caution by the police, but been released without charge when Margaret McFarland had given a written statement that *Bobby and Norma had invited me over for dinner, and that Norma got too drunk and went for a walk on her own. Bobby had tried to talk Norma out of it, but you couldn't get through to Norma when she was drunk. No one could.*

'Who is Margaret McFarland?' Jessie said.

But Gilchrist was already flipping through his notepad. It took him a few seconds to find what he was looking for. 'Got you,' he said, and shoved his notes over the desk to Jessie so she could read them.

'Martha *Margaret McFarland* Kerr,' Jessie said. 'The bitch. So she *is* his sister?'

'I'm not convinced yet,' he said.

'But she gave him an alibi, while he took his wife out for a walk during a storm and booted her into the harbour.'

Gilchrist felt troubled that the local police hadn't questioned Martha more thoroughly. Now, they would likely never know for sure, but Jessie's theory sounded as strong as any.

Jessie said, 'It seems that Alice Hickson didn't know that Margaret McFarland were Martha Kerr's middle names. Did she?'

Gilchrist shook his head. 'I'm intrigued as to how she made the connection from Robert Kerr to James Crichton to Scott Black, with a few names in between.'

'Maybe Martha can answer that,' Jessie said.

'We have an interview room set up?'

'We do indeed.'

Gilchrist slipped his mobile into his pocket. 'Right, let's go.'

Glenrothes HQ on Detroit Road is the Force Contact Centre for Fife Constabulary, and is distinct from Glenrothes police station on Napier Road, which has custodial facilities and interview rooms.

Gilchrist parked in the police station car park and switched off his mobile. He hugged his collar to his neck as he and Jessie scurried towards the station, a fierce wind whipping his hair, iced beads of rain stinging his face.

He reached the door and pushed inside.

'Bloody hell,' Jessie said. 'Glasgow's weather might be shite, but this is pure Baltic.'

Well, he couldn't disagree with her on that. They introduced themselves at reception then headed to the Interview Suites. He opened the door to Room 2, and let Jessie enter first.

Martha was seated next to her solicitor – someone other than Tom McGarry – her lips tight, her face pale. She could have aged ten years since they'd last spoken to her.

They took their seats opposite, Gilchrist facing Martha, Jessie facing the solicitor. Once Jessie was satisfied that the recorder was switched on and working, she went through the introductions, reading off the solicitor's business card – William Thorncroft of Becket Leeds & Associates – and confirming that, 'Martha

Margaret McFarland Kerr is being interviewed under caution, on suspicion of being complicit in the murders of Janice Hickson and Norma Kerr.'

Martha's eyes widened at the mention of Norma Kerr.

Thorncroft leaned forward. 'Who's Norma Kerr?'

'We believe her to be your client's late sister-in-law,' Jessie said.

'I thought my client was to be questioned on matters relating to Janice Hickson.'

'We've come across fresh evidence we believe links your client to an earlier murder,' Gilchrist said. 'When she gave an alibi for her brother, Robert Kerr.'

Martha's face hardened.

'We note with interest,' Gilchrist said to her, 'that your police statement was signed Margaret McFarland, which are your two middle names.'

Martha blinked, as if in confusion.

'Why did you use those names, and not Martha Kerr?'

'No comment.'

'You told us earlier that you and Bobby are brother and sister. Why did you not tell the Oban Police that in your statement?'

'No comment.'

Gilchrist sat back. 'You're not doing yourself any favours,' he said. 'This is your chance to clear your name, your chance to tell us what happened. We know your brother's a bully and a misogynist. We know that. But what we don't know, although we suspect we do, is that he forced you to do what he wanted you to do.' He waited a beat. 'Against your will.'

Martha lowered her eyes.

'Because that's what he's like,' he said. 'He's killed two women recently – Kandy Lal and Alice Hickson. And two of his previous wives, Norma Kintyre and Janice Hickson, died in suspicious circumstances within one year of being married to him.'

'Is there a question in there somewhere?' Thorncroft said.

'All of it's a question,' Jessie said. 'Your client can speak any time she likes. All she has to do is say yes or no.'

Gilchrist eyed Martha. 'Let's go back to the night your sister-in-law, Norma, drowned in Portree. Your statement said that Norma got so drunk no one could persuade her not to go for a walk in a downpour. You remember that?'

She shrugged. 'No comment.'

Jessie slid a batch of photocopies across the desk to Thorncroft. 'This is a copy of your client's statement,' she said. 'I've highlighted the relevant sections.'

Thorncroft glanced through them, then said, 'My client had nothing to do with Mrs Kerr's unfortunate accident. That's clear from her statement. So what's your point?'

Gilchrist said, 'The point is, that your client gave her brother an alibi while he went about the business of murdering his wife.'

'Are you implying that my client lied, that she falsified her statement?'

'I am.'

Thorncroft turned to Martha. 'Is this statement false?' he asked.

Martha shook her head. 'No.'

'Were you coerced by anyone, including your brother, and or the police, to write anything in your statement that you did not believe to be true?'

'No.'

Thorncroft gave a triumphant smile, and shoved the statement back to Jessie. 'I don't know what you intend to do with that, but it simply strengthens my client's case.'

'Except that she's lying.'

'Not according to my client.' He turned to Martha again. 'Are you lying?'

'That's it,' Jessie snapped. 'Here are the rules. You're here to advise your client, not to question her. We'll do the asking, and you do the advising. You got that?'

Thorncroft eyed her as if she'd shot him.

Jessie rapped her knuckles on the table. 'Hello? Earth to Thorncroft? I said, *have you got that?*'

Thorncroft looked away and appeared to find interest in his notes.

'Carry on, sir,' Jessie said to Gilchrist. 'I think the message got through.'

'What did you get out of it, Martha?' Gilchrist said.

Martha looked at him and blinked.

'You're not married. You live by yourself.' He struggled to find some inoffensive way of saying that her cottage was rundown and that she dressed like a tramp, then settled for, 'And you appear to live modestly. So I'm thinking it's not money.'

She lowered her gaze to the table again, but for just that fleeting moment, Gilchrist thought he detected the covering up of a lie. He waited until she lifted her gaze and her eyes settled once more on his. 'Or maybe it *is* about money,' he said.

Nothing.

'We've instructed our Financial Investigation Unit to apply for a warrant to carry out a search of any bank accounts in your name.' He puzzled at the merest hint of a smile, the tiniest twitch at the corner of her lips.

Was he on the wrong track?

So far, they'd found nothing in Scott Black's accounts, other than a few hundred quid to fund day-to-day living. Even the most recent bank account uncovered by Matt Duprey's forensic search of Black's Facebook account held no huge amount. Money came in from his contracting business, and went out in the form of direct debits or standing orders – utilities, council tax, on-going business expenses. But a detached stone villa in Oban, and a share of a small fishing fleet – albeit sold cheaply for cash – had to have been worth six figures at least, fourteen years ago. Not to mention Norma Kintyre's estate a few years earlier – another six-figure sum? He was sure of it.

So, what had Black done with the money?

Or more correctly, where was he hiding it?

He leaned forward and stared hard at Martha. 'So tell me,' he said, 'what will we find when we perform a forensic analysis of your bank accounts?'

She returned his gaze for several seconds, then said, 'Nothing.'

Her spoken response pricked his senses. Not what he'd been expecting. Not at all. Another blank look, or shrug of her shoulders, or a *no comment*.

But instead, she'd said – *Nothing*. Which told him everything.

Well, not quite everything. But it did let him see what he'd been missing.

He offered a smile, a prelude to his coffin-nailing question, because that was what he was about to do to her, this sister of a serial killer, this cold-hearted woman with no sense of remorse for the women she'd betrayed: he was going to bury her.

If he could, that is, because he was still working on instinct, still trying to wheedle the truth out of someone who didn't want to talk, who when she did, spewed out nothing but lies. He would have to nudge his way forward, step into the swamp with care.

For if he got this wrong, he could be the one being sucked into the clammy depths of deepest shit.

'We've also applied for a search warrant,' he said. 'For Raven Cottage.'

Martha stilled, as if her breath had caught in her throat.

'What do you think we'll find?' he asked, one sane person beseeching another.

Her eyes slid left, right, left again, then lowered to the table.

'Want to tell me?'

He knew he was homing in on her weakness, the one thing she thought no one would ever find – money. Not hers, he thought, but Scott Black's. But it worried him that he could still be wrong, that his assumptions were nothing more than blind stabs in the dark, no matter how much he thought her body language betrayed her.

He eased into it with, 'Wherever the money's hidden, Martha, we'll find it. It's what we do. It's what we're good at.' He cocked his head, tried to catch her eyes. But she was having none of it. 'And once we do, it'll be a major problem for you. Because if Bobby denies all knowledge of it, or more correctly *when* Bobby denies all knowledge of it, because that's what he does, isn't it? Takes no responsibility. Then you're on your own.'

Even though her eyes still focused on some spot on the table, he had a sense of her vulnerability, an inexorable stripping away of her protective layers. 'Then guess what?' Five seconds ticked by, but she could be mute for all the response she was giving. 'When Bobby denies it, Martha, you'll be taking the blame. All that money you can't explain away. You'll be who we're coming after. And believe me, Martha, there'll be no turning back when that happens.'

He pushed his chair back. Together he and Jessie stood.

Thorncroft looked up at them, as if not knowing what to say.

Jessie said, 'Interview suspended at one thirty-five.'

Gilchrist gathered his notes, and glared at Thorncroft. 'We're taking a break. But you should spend the next ten minutes advising your client of the seriousness of the charges she's about to face. If she continues to blank us, then that's it. No deals. Nothing. We're going the full way, and she's on her own.'

He followed Jessie from the Interview Room, aware of Martha's eyes on his back.

In the hallway, he switched on his mobile and groaned when he saw he'd missed three text messages, within ten minutes of each other, and a missed call – all from Maureen.

'*Shit,*' he said.

Jessie jerked a look at him. 'Problems?'

'You could say.' He walked away for some privacy, and opened her messages.

Tried calling but cant get u. R u coming?

He cursed. He'd known last night that he probably couldn't see her off at the airport, and should have told her so. But he could at least have given her a call that morning, spoken to her, wished her and Tom a safe trip, told her he would see her when she got back, told her that he loved her.

The next message only worsened matters.

At the gate. Can u pls call.

315

Ah fuck it. He checked the time – twenty minutes ago – then thumbed on to the next message. But he shouldn't have bothered.

Boarding now.

'No,' he moaned. 'Not like this.' He dialled her number and stared at the message as he waited for the connection. Typical Maureen. Short, curt and to the point. No *goodbye*. No *see you soon*. No *miss you*. No *love you*. Nothing. Just *boarding now*, her way of shutting him out, letting him know what she thought of him.

The call connected to voicemail.

'*Fuck*,' he said, and hung up. He pressed redial. Getting through to voicemail meant she hadn't switched off her mobile for the flight yet – didn't it?

'Come on, come on. Pick up, Mo. For crying out loud, just pick up, will you?'

But the call went to voicemail again.

'Shit.' He struggled with the almost irresistible urge to hang up, but instead listened to the recorded message, waited until the line beeped. He took a deep breath. 'Hi, Mo. It's me.' He'd found a spot in the corner, which gave him a view of the outside world through a rain-clouded window. He stared at grey skies, heavy and thick enough to threaten snow. Nothing like the weather Mo was heading to. 'I'm sorry, Mo. I know you've heard it before, but . . . well . . . work got in the way. It's not an excuse. I should've made the effort – well, more of an effort.' He closed his eyes. He was rambling, not getting to the point.

He took another deep breath, tried to collect his thoughts.

'I should've been there. At the airport. I know. I'm sorry. But I

316

couldn't make it. Give me a call when you get to sunny Oz. Even if it's just to let off some steam and tell me how annoyed you are with me. Reverse the charges. I'm happy to pay.' Fuck it. He was gibbering again. 'Anyway, what I wanted to say was, that you're doing the right thing marrying Tom and moving away from here. All this weather will get to you in the end.' He chuckled to let her know he was joking, but even to his ears it sounded flat. 'But I'll miss you, Mo, and I'm sorry we didn't connect this morning. My fault, I know. But I want you to know that I love you. And I wish you and Tom the very best. Can't wait to see you again. Stay well, princess. And stay in touch.'

He ended the call, puffed up his cheeks, and exhaled.

What would she do when she listened to that little lot? Probably ignore it, and delete his contact details from her mobile. Who could blame her. He'd disappointed her. No, worse than that. He'd failed her. He'd let her down so badly. How had she felt when she'd tried to contact him from the airport and couldn't get through? What had she thought of him? What father would do that to his daughter – let her fly off to the other side of the world without a parting word? Who else had been there to see them off? Had Jack made the effort? Well, Jack didn't own a car, didn't have a licence, so that was unlikely. But Jack would at least have spoken to his sister before she left.

Of that, he was certain.

His stomach curdled at the thought of Tom's parents being at the airport. How would Maureen have felt then, saying farewell to them, all the while wondering where her own father—

'Best I could do,' Jessie said.

Gilchrist jolted at the sound of her voice.

'Not the greatest coffee in the world.' She handed him a Styrofoam cup. 'But it's wet and hot. What can I say?'

He took a quick sip. 'Wet and hot it is.'

She eyed him over the rim of her cup. 'Nothing serious, is it?'

He let out a defeated sigh. 'Maureen's emigrating to Australia.'

She mouthed a whistle. 'Boy, I just knew Stu Pierson was a looker.'

He smiled to let her know he got her joke, then said, 'I didn't make it to the airport to see them off.'

'Ouch.' Jessie raised her eyebrows. 'You tried calling?'

'Can't get through.'

'Well, that's always a problem.' She nodded to his coffee. 'Want to finish that out here, or take it in with us?'

That was Jessie's way of dealing with the problem – put it behind you, and get on with something else. She was right, of course. What else could he do?

'Let's give Thorncroft another five minutes,' he said. 'Maybe he'll have talked some sense into her by then.'

CHAPTER 37

Five minutes?

It wouldn't have made any difference if they'd given Thorncroft five weeks. No matter how Gilchrist and Jessie poked and prodded and tried to tease answers from Martha, she gave a silent shrug, or a *No comment*. His scare tactics hadn't worked either. Threats that she could receive a custodial sentence fell on deaf ears. For all the attention she was giving them, they could be rambling on about last year's weather forecasts.

It seemed that Martha Kerr had shut down for good.

But even so, something niggled. No one could sit back with such casual disregard for the serious trouble they were in without showing signs of worry or nervous tension. Gilchrist had carried out hundreds – make that thousands – of police interviews, but never before had he come across someone so disinterested in it all. He wondered if she might be suffering from some mental impairment that prevented her from comprehending reality, some psychiatric disorder that kept her in a fantasy world of her own making. Of course, on the other side of that coin, she could be much smarter than she was letting on, smarter than Gilchrist, smarter than Jessie, so smart in fact that she was not just one step ahead of him, but half a dozen. Or maybe Gilchrist had become too cynical in his old age, for he couldn't rid himself of the feeling that they were being made fools of.

Just before 3 p.m., he scraped his chair back and stood. They were getting nowhere. Even though he was tempted to charge Martha with obstructing the course of justice, he couldn't shift the sense that, by her continued silence, she was trying to lead them to the wrong conclusion.

And Thorncroft wasn't making it any easier. He seemed to have gone from silent spectator to courtroom defender of the weak and helpless in the space of a few questions. 'It seems patently clear to me,' he pronounced with legal gravitas – or so he thought – 'that you have absolutely nothing that connects my client to the deaths of Janice Hickson or Norma Kerr.'

'Other than the fact that she spent the evening with her brother and his wife on the night his wife was murdered by—'

'*Drowned*,' Thorncroft barked. 'Nothing more than an accident involving a woman who'd had so much to drink she could barely walk. All backed up by the post mortem *and* the police report *and* my client's statement.' He slapped the desk to emphasise his point, which had Gilchrist raising his hand to prevent Jessie from responding in kind.

Gilchrist leaned forward and again tried the voice of reason. 'Not once has your client given a satisfactory explanation for signing her statement using her middle names, nor for not advising the police that Robert Kerr was her brother and Norma was her sister-in-law.'

'It wasn't up to my client to provide such information. It was for the police to interview her. If they failed to ask the appropriate questions, my client was under no obligation, legal or otherwise, to inform them of their own shortcomings.'

'Even so,' Gilchrist said, 'if your client was innocent, she would have willingly provided any—'

'I simply fail to see the logic in that.'

'That's because you're stupid,' Jessie said.

'I beg your pardon?'

'Ditch the selective hearing,' she said. 'You heard.'

Thorncroft tugged his jacket, gave a throaty *harrumph*. 'My client has been in police custody for over four hours. What do you intend to do about that?'

'We haven't decided yet,' Jessie said.

'If you're not going to charge her, I insist you let her go.'

'We've got twelve hours to hold her before—'

'This is preposterous. I'll be filing a formal complaint.'

'File all you like.' Jessie gave him a deadpan smile. 'But you know the law as well as we do. At least, you should. Although I'm beginning to think you haven't a clue.'

Gilchrist did not intervene. He let Jessie and Thorncroft mouth off at each other, while he kept his eyes fixed on Martha, aware of her tiny smirk. If he didn't know better, he'd say she was enjoying the whole affair.

When Jessie raised her voice, Gilchrist raised his hand. 'That's enough.'

She pressed herself back into her chair.

Thorncroft shuffled his shoulders. 'Well, I have to—'

'You too,' Gilchrist snapped.

Thorncroft adjusted his tie. Martha smiled.

If Gilchrist had to look back on that interview, he would say that Martha's smile to her solicitor had been his moment of epiphany, when a spark of intuition let him see another possibility, one he'd never considered until then. There had been no reason for her to smile. A shrug of her shoulders, another blank stare at that same spot on the table, or even a nervous tic might have gone unnoticed – but not a smile. And certainly not a smile directed at a barely competent solicitor. Thorncroft hadn't been deep into the intellectual throes of winning some complex legal argument. Far from it. He'd been making an arse of himself, as Jessie had pointed out to him.

It seemed that it didn't matter to Martha whether she was released or kept in custody for the full twelve hours, or even charged with being complicit in a pair of murders. He was developing a sense that it mattered to her that they kept their focus on her, kept wasting their time with her. Because that's what they were doing – wasting their time.

Which was the whole point of her silence. He thought he saw that now.

He'd been asking the wrong questions, looking in the wrong direction.

And she had smiled because she believed her ploy was succeeding.

It was only when he took a step back and asked the question – what ploy? – that he thought he saw the shadow of some different outline. But he needed more than gut instinct or intuitive reasoning. He needed answers, or more precisely, he needed to see how she responded to one specific question.

So he pulled himself upright, then laid his hands flat on the table in the area where Martha had been focusing her blank stare. Then he looked at Thorncroft and said, 'Here's what we're going to do. We're going to keep your client in custody, and tomorrow morning we'll make a decision on whether or not to press charges.'

A glance at Martha confirmed the smirk was still there.

'So, Martha,' he said, 'just to be sure we're not missing anything, you say you don't know where your brother might be hiding.'

Thorncroft cleared his throat again, as if preparing to say something, but Gilchrist cut him off with, 'That's not a question. Just a statement of where we are with respect to your client's lack of knowledge of her brother's current whereabouts.' He slid his hands across the table, closer to Martha, and watched her eyes widen. He slid closer still, pleased to see her push back in her chair, as if she feared that he would suddenly make a grab for her.

He kept his tone level, his voice quiet. 'I know where your brother didn't go to.'

Thorncroft coughed.

Jessie said, 'Shut it, you.'

Gilchrist kept his eyes on Martha's. No longer fixed on that thousand-yard stare, but struggling to recover that spot on the table. 'Your brother didn't go far,' he said. 'That's why we found no sign of him on the CCTV system. He'd not gone far from Raven Cottage.'

Martha seemed to still, as if she were holding her breath.

'Because he'd already holed up by the time we went looking for him. Not that we'd ever likely find out where he's hiding,' he said. 'The Scottish countryside is a big place. He could be anywhere. But that doesn't matter.' His hands had almost crossed the table, and he took care to place one on top of the other. 'What matters is that he didn't go far. And you, of all people, you know *why* that matters.' He pulled himself back, settled into his seat and glared at her. 'Don't you?'

Martha looked at him, no longer smiling.

He returned her dead gaze. 'It matters, because he has to come back.'

Her mouth opened as if to speak, but he beat her to it.

'He's not going to leave without the money, Martha. But you knew that, didn't you? As long as we were interviewing you, you thought we weren't looking for him. But he knows we're on to him now. He knows it's over for him, there's no turning back. So, what options does he have?' He let a couple of beats pass, then said, 'He's about to leave the area, Martha, maybe even the country. But before he does, he's going to come back for the money. He has to.'

Her eyes smouldered.

'And he'll be heading to your cottage,' he said. 'Because that's where it is.'

'It's not,' she said.

Jessie said, 'She speaks after all.'

Martha's eyes flared for a fearful moment, then settled on Gilchrist. 'There's nothing there,' she said. 'He's got bank accounts everywhere. All over the world.'

'No, he doesn't.' Gilchrist didn't know that for sure, but he was intrigued by the way her mind seemed to work through the movement of her eyes. 'He would leave an electronic trail whenever he accessed foreign bank accounts, and I can tell you with absolute certainty that our IT experts have found no such trail.' Again, he could not say for sure, but sometimes you just have to press.

'You're wrong,' she said.

He took pleasure from her discomfort, the way her gaze darted around, how her fingers curled into weak fists. 'He has a number of bank accounts, we know that. But they contain nothing close to the sums he inherited from two wives.' He smiled, hoping to portray a confidence he didn't feel. 'So, what did he do with all that cash? Where did he keep it?' He shrugged his shoulders. 'I'm willing to bet we'll find it in Raven Cottage.'

'You'll find nothing.' Her eyes gleamed.

Gilchrist's antennae sparked alive. Wrong answer. No denial that the cash wasn't there. Rather a statement that it was, and they'd never find it. 'And I'm also willing to bet that you're bluffing,' he said, 'because after all these hours of *no comments* you're talking to me now. Telling me I'm wrong. Telling me I'll find nothing.' He gave a victory grin. 'Which, when you think about it, Martha, says that I've hit the nail smack dab on the head.'

She bit her lip, as if to ensure she couldn't say anything more.

But she was too late. The damage was done.

Gilchrist nodded to Jessie. 'Charge her with obstructing a police investigation and attempting to pervert the course of justice. We can discuss other charges in the morning.'

Thorncroft spluttered in defiance, but Jessie said, 'You had your chance. You were warned,' then pushed on with the formal charges.

As Gilchrist left the interview room, he glanced at Martha as he closed the door, and thought he caught the glimmer of tears in her eyes.

CHAPTER 38

Gilchrist walked across the car park, remote fob in his hand. His plan was simple, at least he hoped it was: to pick up the search warrant for Raven Cottage, then strip the place if they had to, searching for what he hoped would be the *hidden stash*. Of course, there was always the worry he was wrong, that he'd misinterpreted Martha's body language, even her spoken answers. So the fewer people who knew about this sketchy plan of his, at least in its early stages, the better.

He would play it softly, proceed with the utmost caution.

And for the time being, stay well away from Smiler.

He switched on his car's engine, turned up the fan and let the cabin warm up. As he waited for Jessie, he tried to work through the pluses and minuses of moving forward.

He didn't think that Scott Black, or whatever his name was, would be armed if he turned up at Raven Cottage. They'd found no firearms certificates under his name, although that was never a guarantee. So it seemed reasonable to carry out an authorised search of the cottage unarmed. And besides, securing firearms would need to be authorised by a senior officer, so any plans he had for that, whether or not he tried to keep them quiet, would wing their way back to Chief Superintendent Smiley.

Still, it would be prudent to wear body armour.

But first things first.

He phoned Mhairi. 'What's the latest on the warrant for Raven Cottage?'

'It's not been approved yet, sir.'

Bloody hell. This was the problem when you followed protocol – too many people could insert too many spanners into your works. 'Can you push it through for me?' he said.

'Already tried, sir, but it's still on Smiler's desk.'

He gasped a curse, and said, 'What the hell's *she* doing with it?'

'I don't know, sir. I'm sorry.'

A surge of anger zapped through him. There was no reason for Smiler to be involved in the application for a search warrant, other than to be kept in the loop. But he berated himself for his naivety. Their relationship had got off to a rocky start, and this was Smiler's way of trying to rein him in, control that maverick side of his – on and on with petty admin processes until she ground him into submission, or issued the final ultimatum: retire or be fired.

'Would you like me to try again, sir?'

'No, Mhairi. I'll take care of it.'

He got through to Smiler straight away.

'Good evening, DCI Gilchrist.'

'Why haven't you processed the search warrant?'

'I had some questions—'

'Then why haven't you contacted me about them?'

'I'm not sure I care for your tone, DCI Gilchrist.'

'Well what tone would you like me to use when time is running out?'

'If time is running out, then the sooner you get in here, the sooner your warrant will be processed.'

Gilchrist had more chance of hammering his head through a brick wall than Smiler signing off on his application over the phone. 'This isn't working for me,' he said.

'Nor for me, DCI Gilchrist.'

Well, there he had it. Her endgame in sight. The line died before he could come back with some biting quip. But if the truth be known, he was just about done with it all. He tossed his mobile into the back just as Jessie opened the passenger door.

'Bloody hell,' she said. 'This weather would freeze the balls off you.'

'That's more information than I need to know.' He slipped into gear, reversed into the travel lane, then powered across the car park.

'So you think Black's really going to come back to the cottage?' she said.

What could he tell her? That it was another stab in the dark? But if they had a search warrant, at least they might find the money – if it was ever there in the first place.

Bloody hell, what a mess.

'What do you think?' he tried.

'I think you drive too fast.'

He tried to slow down as he exited on to Napier Road, but the tyres slid on the slush, and he had to give a hard tug of the wheel to avoid hitting the kerb.

'See?'

He accelerated to thirty-five, then set the cruise control. 'Is that better?'

'Getting there,' she said. 'So you're saying Black's been hiding close to the cottage so that he can come back and recover a stash of hidden money?'

In plain language, his rationale sounded weak, even to his own ears. He managed a smile, and said, 'It's possible. Yes.'

'And he's going to come back when, exactly?'

Again, it all sounded iffy. 'The sooner the better, I'd say.'

'As soon as today?'

He eased into traffic. 'As soon as tonight.'

'You want me to organise a team?'

'No team. We don't have a search warrant.' He drove on, conscious of Jessie's eyes on his, her silence demanding an answer. 'It's stuck on Smiler's desk,' he explained.

'Shit. So we're going to have to wait until—'

'I'm not waiting.'

'*What?*' She stared at him. 'Jesus, Andy. You could get into serious trouble for this. Not to mention that anything we find would be inadmissible.'

He chanced a look at her. 'We?'

'You're not doing this on your own. And that's non-negotiable.'

'This is my mess, Jessie, so don't get—'

'What about baton guns?'

He shook his head. 'Forget it.'

'No,' she said. 'Baton guns wouldn't work. Smiler would stop us.'

'Us?'

'Get over it, Andy. I've told you. You're not doing this alone.'

He tightened his grip on the wheel. Jessie was right. It would be folly to risk tackling Black alone. He knew Jessie could handle herself, but without baton guns, they might be at a serious disadvantage. With a show of reluctance, he said, 'OK, but we'll pick up body armour, just in case.'

Jessie glanced at her watch. 'If your theory's right,' she said, 'then that bastard might come back to the cottage as soon as it's dark.'

Gilchrist already had his car's sidelights on. In another thirty minutes, it could be dark enough for headlights. It would take over an hour to collect body armour then drive to the cottage. Time was indeed running out.

'Phone Mhairi and have her organise body armour.'

'If I know Mhairi, she'll want to come with us.'

'Two sets only,' he said. 'And *that's* non-negotiable.'

They met Mhairi in the car park close to the East Sands, in a corner devoid of streetlighting, courtesy of local vandals. She opened the boot of her car and removed two sets of Kevlar body armour. She handed Jessie her set first, then Gilchrist his, and waited for him to strap his on securely before saying, 'I would like to come along, too, sir.'

'No chance, Mhairi.'

'I could help—'

'No, Mhairi. I'm not dragging you into this. It'll get you into trouble with Smiler,' he said, and opened his car door.

'I'm already in trouble, sir.'

He froze, the door half-open. 'What do you mean?'

'When I was leaving the Office, Smiler saw me. She called out, but I just ignored her and kept on walking.'

'Did she see the body armour?'

'I think so, sir. All three sets.'

Jessie said, 'Well, you can't return a set to the Office now.'

Gilchrist had to agree. They would need to face the consequences in the morning.

'I could be a lookout, sir. Let you know as soon as anyone's coming.'

Even in the darkness, he could make out the glint of youthful expectation in her eyes. What was she hoping for? A hands-on struggle and a hard-fought arrest? A wild chase through dark country roads? But in all likelihood, his plan was a waste of time, with them all sitting around in the freezing cold, waiting for Black to turn up and being disappointed, or maybe relieved, when he didn't.

Perhaps his plan was nowhere near as treacherous as he feared.

'Lookout it is, then,' he said. And even though it was likely nothing was going to happen, added, 'And no heroics.'

'No heroics, sir,' she said, and winked at Jessie as she took her seat in the back.

Gilchrist parked outside the third to last house on the road to Raven Cottage. The three of them then walked briskly up a shallow incline that steepened as they neared the cottage. A covering of snow – threadbare thin in parts, wind-drift thick in others – troubled Gilchrist. Their footprints along the road could be noticed by anyone, meaning Scott Black. But they managed to skirt the worst of it, picking their way with care in single file, and a glance behind assured him that their tracks were more or less hidden.

In the pitch black of a windswept countryside, Raven Cottage looked as if it had been abandoned for decades. The slated roof lay white with snow. A north wind had stiffened, shovelling clouds

331

across the sky, offering glimpses of a gibbous moon and sprinkling the ground-frost with a million diamonds.

Gilchrist's heart was racing, his breathing laboured. Jessie puffed hard in the cold, but Mhairi could've finished a casual stroll down the street for all the strain she was showing. As his heart settled, he took his bearings. He had intended to inspect the cottage, to make sure it was locked up, and importantly, that Black had in fact not been and gone. It would have been helpful, too, if they could break in – leaving no trace of having done so, of course – and begin a search for whatever stash he hoped to find. And if that proved successful, he would gladly face Smiler's wrath in the morning, secure in the knowledge that a late-approved warrant would provide positive results.

But as he eyed the area, he realised they had a problem. They could not get close to the cottage without leaving fresh footprints. If Black turned up, he would know they'd been there, and could turn and run. So, rather than risk it, they positioned themselves in the woods around the property, and settled down for the wait.

But now they were there, sheltering against the bitter cold, this plan of his had to be the most stupid he had ever devised.

Time crept past. Minutes turned to hours.

And the cold set in with a vengeance.

Frost pressed through his clothes and gnawed at his bones. Ice nibbled his nose and ears, and bit into his fingers. He eyed the length of the road leading to town to confirm that it still lay clear. Black was not on his way. He pulled his mobile from his jacket again, taking care to conceal the light from its screen, and checked the time – 11.34. He tried to work out how long they had been there – three hours? four? – but his mind seemed to have frozen, too.

He shielded his mobile's screen, and dialled Jessie's number. He thought he caught the flicker of her phone's screen high in the woods to the side of the cottage. Then it settled into darkness again. He had warned both of them that even the tiniest flicker of light could appear magnified in pitch blackness.

'Any thoughts?' he asked in a low voice.

'Plenty,' she said. 'Mostly about jumping into a hot bath.'

He blew into his hands, but even his breath seemed to have chilled. 'We'll give it until midnight,' he said, 'then call it a day.'

'Or a night.'

From where he stood, he couldn't see Mhairi, who had positioned herself on the other side of the cottage from him. But they each had an unrestricted view of the road into town.

'Have you heard from Mhairi?' he asked.

'Spoke to her a few minutes ago. She's thinking of a hot bath, too.'

He gave a silent groan. Not only had his plan been idiotic, it had failed magnificently, and frozen the three of them senseless. He was on the point of calling it off right there and then when Jessie said, 'Hang on, Andy.'

'What is it?'

'Sshh.'

He pulled his jacket collar up around his face to smother all light from his phone, then eyed the cottage. 'You still there?' he said.

'I see something moving.'

'Where?'

'In the fields.'

He peered into the darkness. 'A fox?'

'Bigger.'

'Sheep?'

'Man size,' she said. 'And it's walking.'

Of course. How could he have been so stupid? Black would not approach the cottage from town. He would walk across the fields, take the same route he'd driven the motorbike, the same way he and Jessie had walked a couple of days ago. But an acid nip of worry stung his gut at that thought. Black was approaching where Mhairi had positioned herself.

'What about Mhairi?' he said.

'I don't see her.'

'Is she anywhere near—?'

'Can you see him now?' Jessie interrupted. 'He's almost at the corner of the cottage.'

'Alone?'

'Looks like it.'

He thought of telling Jessie to check with Mhairi, make sure she was OK, but Mhairi's mobile's screen might light up and give the game away.

'You see him?' Jessie hissed.

Gilchrist focused all his senses on the corner by the fields. But he could be looking at a black screen. His sight seemed to shimmer and fade, but it was only the clouds shifting in the sky. The moon burst through at that moment, and for just an instant he caught movement by the gable end.

'I see him,' he said.

'You think it's him?'

'Don't know yet. I'm switching off. Check with Mhairi. Not by phone. Make sure she's OK.'

'Will do.'

'I'm moving in.'

'*Andy.*'

The sharpness of her voice stopped him. 'What?'

'If it's Black,' she said, 'don't tackle him alone.'

He suspected that Jessie was worried not only for his safety, but for hers and Mhairi's, too. 'Call the local Office for backup,' he said. 'If it's not Black, then it's somebody else trespassing.'

'Just one thing.'

'What's that?'

'There are no trespass laws in Scotland.'

'Shit, Jessie. We'll catch him breaking in, then.'

He ended the call and crawled out from behind a copse of shrubs that had provided protection from the wind. A gust cold enough to strip flesh from bone hit him face on. It had to be ten below, with a wind chill of God knew what. He fought off the urge to clap his hands, stomp his feet, work some warmth into his freezing body.

Instead, he crouched lower and crept towards the cottage.

The figure was clearer now, black silhouetted on grey, working its way along the front of the cottage towards the steps where they'd first seen Martha. He tried to judge the size of the figure; man-sized and man-shaped, no doubt about that, wide shoulders, too.

But was it Black?

Silent, he watched and waited.

CHAPTER 39

Gilchrist held his breath as the figure crept with slow deliberation – two steps, then still as a statue for a couple of beats, and on again. From where he watched, everything about the figure's shape matched his memory of Black – its bulk that hinted of hard muscle, the careful approach that spoke of stealth and guilt.

Was he looking at Scott Black?

He could not be certain. He needed to move closer.

He crept into the open, keeping his head low, his body close to the ground. Out of the shelter of the woods, he felt exposed, vulnerable, as if all the man had to do was cast a glance his way and see him. The wind seemed to strengthen at that moment, whipping off snow-frosted fields with Arctic ferocity. Behind him, branches bristled and trunks groaned from the frigid onslaught. The moon lit up the skies for an instant, only to be extinguished by clouds that tumbled through the night as if on a rising tide.

The figure stilled, and seemed to cock its head at the woods.

Gilchrist held his breath. Had he been seen?

He resisted the urge to drop on all fours. Any movement might be noticed. He kept his gaze fixed on the stationary shape, little more than a shadow, grey on grey, and prayed the moon would stay hidden, the winter night remain dark.

Nothing seemed to move. Only the wind.

Ice stung his face. Tears froze his eyes.

The figure took another step, and the world rebooted.

Then two more to reach the front entrance, and face the door as if to open it.

Gilchrist saw his chance. And took it.

He scurried into the open, half ran, half crawled across the road, and almost threw himself into a beech hedgerow that edged the property. He lay still, catching his breath, thankful to be out of the wind.

From behind the hedgerow, his view was restricted to the front of the cottage, the hut to the side where the motorbike had been garaged, and the snow-frozen area of gravel beyond the entrance. He slid his hand inside his jacket for his mobile. Once the door opened, and the figure – call him Black – entered, he would call the local Office, report a break-in and secure backup, if Jessie had not already done that. Well, that was the plan, and like most plans it was easily disrupted, in this instance when the figure turned away from the front door and continued to creep along the face of the cottage.

What was happening? Was he going to walk around the back and try the rear door, or break a window at the side to gain access? Or did Gilchrist have it wrong, and it wasn't Black at all, but some other lawbreaker looking for easy cash or removable furniture from a derelict house? And at that moment, as if to answer his fears, the moon broke through.

The night sky glittered alive. Fields glistened like a frosted carpet. And the silhouette slipped from shadow and glanced into the woods, tilting his head back as he did so, to reveal a shorn head and a clean-shaven face.

And in that frozen instant, Gilchrist recognised Black – not bearded and thick-haired like he'd been a couple of days ago, but face shaved and skull polished from a recently shorn disguise. Then Black turned and strode to the corner of the cottage, no longer creeping, as if he'd only just realised that no one in their right mind would venture into such desolate country on a night like this, and that he was alone.

Or worse – and this is what set Gilchrist's heart racing – he had spotted Jessie.

Gilchrist glanced up the steep slope at the back of the hut, searching for Jessie in the moonlight. But the woods and shrubs looked thick and impenetrable in the shifting shadows. Then Black surprised him by leaving the protection of the cottage wall and trotting across the side yard.

Gilchrist's heart leaped into his mouth.

Black had seen Jessie – he must have – and was now about to climb the slope at the side of the cottage and tackle her head-on. But how could he have spotted her? How was that possible? As if on cue, the sky blackened as clouds shifted, and the night settled once more into winter darkness.

But not before Gilchrist caught Black standing at the hut door.

The shadows were too dark for him to see what Black was up to. Then the wind shifted, carrying the clinking of metal his way, and the hard snap of a padlock.

The hut door swung open, and Black slipped inside.

Gilchrist had his mobile in his hand; he called Jessie.

'Do you see him?' she asked.

'He's gone into the hut.'

'What for?'

What for, indeed? Gilchrist trawled through his memory, trying to pull up what he'd seen when he'd been inside earlier. But other than the motorbike, he came up blank. Was that why Black was here? Not for the money, but for his motorbike? Was he intending to drive off somewhere else? It just didn't seem to make any sense, unless . . .

Then the answer struck him.

'The money's not in the cottage,' he said. 'It's in the hut.'

'Jesus, Andy. You think so?'

No, he wanted to say. He'd been wrong too often before. Instead, he said, 'Check with the backup, Jessie. And get hold of Mhairi. Make sure she's OK. I'm going in.'

'Andy, don't—'

But he was already scarpering towards the hut, shoes crunching on the snow-covered surface, the rough-edged gravel giving him grip. He had no idea how long Black would take to recover whatever money he'd hidden there – and it struck him that it might not be money at all, but a stash of weapons.

Too late now. No turning back.

Ten yards from the hut, he heard movement inside, the heavy scraping of something being dragged across the floor, the dull thud of it being dropped. Five yards to go, and the gravel changed to iced grass and frozen mud. His feet skidded from under him, and he found himself on his back, stunned.

The movement in the hut stopped.

But he had no time to consider that. He sprang to his feet, shoes slithering on the frozen mud, and managed to reach the hut as Black's figure filled the doorway. On instinct, Gilchrist rugby-tackled him with a shoulder into his midriff, powering them both inside. Black crashed against the side of the hut with a force that threatened to break it. But before he could regain his feet, Gilchrist pushed himself upright.

Black scrambled to his knees, face twisted, eyes blazing.

Gilchrist booted him on the chin, then stepped out of the hut.

A glance at Black as he closed the door almost stopped his heart. Black was back on his feet – how had he done that? – and was already diving for the door, his intent clear in maddened eyes. Gilchrist slapped it shut, fumbled with the padlock and just managed to secure it as a force like a demolition ball thudded against it.

The hut shuddered. The door shook. For a moment, Gilchrist feared the weakened hasp would tear free from the onslaught. But the metal lock rattled securely. A roar from within could have been an animal in pain. Another brutal thud rocked the hut to its foundations and had Gilchrist backing away.

He tried to get through to Jessie, but her number was busy – likely checking on backup. He tried Mhairi's number and gave a sigh of relief as she answered.

'Are you OK, sir?'

'For the time being,' he said. 'Where are you?'

'Making my way towards you, sir.'

Gilchrist jerked a glance at the hut again. The door seemed to bulge against its hinges, as if from some terrific force within. If Black broke free, Gilchrist was no match for the man, he knew that – and now saw how stupid he had been to think he could have arrested a man of Black's strength by himself.

Thank God backup was on its way. At least he hoped it was.

'Stay out of sight,' he said. 'And that's an order.'

'Sir?'

'Wait until backup arrives. I don't know if the door is going to hold him.' He ended the call and faced the wooden hut, troubled by the sudden silence. What was Black up to?

He ventured a few steps closer and eyed the door.

Still closed. Padlock still secure.

Nothing but silence from within.

He stepped closer still.

What the hell was Black up to? He'd heard no glass breaking, so the small window at the back was still secure. Was Black taking a breather, recovering his strength between door-battering episodes? Or had his heart given out from his explosive rage, and he was now lying unconscious? Or was it all just a ploy to get Gilchrist to unlock the padlock and chance a look inside?

Not a hope in hell, he thought.

He stepped away and walked to the hedgerow for a better view of the road into town, when an explosion of splintering wood drowned out the wind. He turned in time to see the head of an axe wriggle in the moonlight as Black struggled to pull it free from the split wood.

Then the axe head vanished.

Another crash of wood splitting and cracking had the hut door at a wild angle, one of its hinges torn out by its screwed roots. A guttural howl and a kick to the door almost burst it free from its padlock hasp. Gilchrist looked around – nowhere to hide. He speed-dialled Jessie's number as he hustled towards the far corner of the cottage, by the edge of the fields. It didn't matter that his footprints could lead Black to him. He only hoped that Jessie would answer and tell him that backup was on its way.

In the meantime, he had a madman to keep at bay.

Behind him, wood cracked and disintegrated as if being crushed by a bulldozer.

He slipped around the corner of the cottage and turned in time to see Black boot the remains of the door to the side, and pull himself from the ruined hut into the cold wind like an inchoate devil emerging from its shell. Gilchrist half expected smoke and fire to belch into the night, and a prehistoric roar fill the air . . .

'*Andy?*' Jessie's voice exploded into his ear. 'Where are you?'

Her question puzzled him. She should be in the woods at the top of the hill, in a position to see everything. But his mind couldn't work it out, and he said, 'Back of the cottage. Have you called for support?'

'On its way.'

'About bloody time.' He pressed his back against the roughcast wall, eyed the length of road into town. But it lay clear. 'Christ,' he hissed. 'Where the hell are they?'

'*Gilchrist.*' Black's bellow was loaded with rage and hatred, and fuelled with adrenaline from bursting free from his wooden prison. 'You're going to pay for this, Gilchrist. I'm going to find you and chop you into little pieces.'

Gilchrist whispered into his mobile, 'Stay hidden, Jessie. And make sure Mhairi stays hidden, too. You got that? I'll keep his attention until backup arrives.'

'Jesus, Andy, what the—'

He killed the call, dropped his mobile into his pocket, then strode out from behind the end of the cottage. Black stood in front of the hut ruins, an axe in one hand, some other tool – a sledgehammer, he thought – in the other.

Gilchrist stood with his arms by his side. 'You're under arrest,' he shouted.

Black grinned as he strode towards him. 'Sure I am.'

CHAPTER 40

Gilchrist shouted, 'Don't make it worse for yourself, Bobby.'

Black stopped in his tracks at the sound of his name. 'She tell you that, Martha? Did she?'

'She told us everything,' Gilchrist lied. 'She coughed it all out, Bobby. Told us about Norma and Janice. How you killed both of them to inherit their money.'

Black cocked his head, as if he'd heard something, which had Gilchrist praying that Jessie and Mhairi were doing as ordered – staying hidden, and out of sight. Then Black faced him again. 'How did you know I'd come here tonight?'

'As I said, Martha told us everything.'

'*Liar*', Black snarled. 'You're a *fucking liar*.'

Gilchrist tensed, troubled by the change in Black's tone. He thought he could keep him occupied until help arrived. But he'd missed something, some small detail that had set Black off.

'Why do you say that, Bobby?' he tried.

'She never knew I was coming here tonight. I never told her that.'

'But this is where the money's hidden.'

'But she never *knew*.'

Gilchrist still didn't get it. Martha never knew what? About the money? About where it was hidden? About when Black would come back to collect it? 'She knew enough,' he said, and hoped he'd hit the mark.

But Black guffawed at the sky for a surreal moment. Then he lowered his head and stared at Gilchrist. 'Martha's a stupid wee cunt.'

A quick glance down the road into town told Gilchrist that support was still not on its way. Surely the local Office hadn't got lost, or didn't know the address. He had no idea what was holding them up. But what he did know was that Black was standing no more than thirty feet from him, armed with a sledgehammer and an axe, and had now turned the full heat of his hatred Gilchrist's way.

Without another word, Black walked towards him.

Gilchrist backed away from the shelter of the cottage, into the dark night and the full force of an Arctic wind that stung his face with specks of ice. 'Why did you kill Kandy?' he shouted. 'You picked her up from the airport and drove her home to kill her and stuff her body under the floor. You didn't need to kill her. That was careless, Bobby.'

'She was beginning to put two and two together. Said she would see me in jail. Couldn't let that happen.'

'That's where you're going now, Bobby. To jail. But you'll get a fair trial.'

'That'll be fucking right.'

'Kandy knew you'd killed Alice,' Gilchrist said, more statement than question. But he needed answers. 'How did she find that out?'

'She was friends with Alice,' Black shouted, as if that explained everything.

'And she kept a backup copy of Alice's files,' Gilchrist said, as the pieces slotted into place. 'Which you found when you refurbished her bathroom.'

Black stared at him, as if seeing Gilchrist in a different light.

'You didn't need to kill Alice,' Gilchrist said. 'You could've moved away and set up home someplace else. You could've taken up a new identity, just like you'd done in the past.'

'But Alice knew. She knew too much.'

'She was a freelance journalist, always after a good story. And you were her story. Is that it?'

'She was nothing but a money-grubbing leech. She wanted to write a best-selling book about me. Can you believe that?'

'But isn't that what *you* are, Bobby? A money-grubber? At least Alice didn't kill anyone to earn her money.'

But Black didn't rise to the bait. He just kept walking, his steps slow and deliberate, his intention clear from the posture of his body. 'Alice was another stupid wee cunt. I told her she'd got it wrong. I told her I wasn't who she thought I was.'

'But she didn't believe you, did she?'

'No.'

'And she wasn't wrong either, was she?'

'No,' he said, confessing for the first time to his murderous past.

'So how did she find you?'

'Her and Janice kept in contact. Skyped themselves stupid.'

'And you overheard Janice saying something about you?'

'I did, aye. That was the end of it right there,' Black said, 'when Janice said she was frightened of me.' He stopped at that, as if to question the stupidity of that remark – *why would my wife be frightened of me?*

Gilchrist stopped, too. 'Well, she had good cause to be frightened of you, Bobby.' He tried to gauge the distance between them – fifteen feet, less? – and work out how to keep him at bay if backup didn't arrive within thirty seconds. But the problem didn't compute, at least to an answer that gave any hope of survival. He now wished they'd brought baton guns along with them, or better still, a Taser.

Without either, his only hope was to keep talking, keep the clock ticking.

And keep his distance.

But a few more backward steps would put him up against the boundary fence, and he felt his heart move to his mouth as the gap continued to narrow. 'After all, you murdered Norma, and—'

'Nobody can prove a thing,' Black sneered.

'But Martha can. Martha was there. She saw it all.'

Black seemed to freeze, then chanced a quick look behind him.

Gilchrist peered into the darkness beyond Black, to the wreck of a hut and the steep slope to the woods above, relieved to see that Jessie and Mhairi were still out of sight. 'She was there the night you killed Norma,' he said. 'She covered for you on her police statement. What do you say to that?'

'She's still a stupid wee cunt.'

'Maybe so, but Martha's now in custody spilling her heart out.'

Black shook his head. 'No, she's no. She's no spilling anything out. She knows better than that.'

'She knows not to cross you, Bobby, is that what you're saying?'

Black lowered the sledgehammer to the ground, balancing it upright on its head. Then he hefted the axe from his left hand to his right, and widened his stance.

Gilchrist could not fail to catch the change in attitude, as if Black had realised that time was running out and he had to take action before it was too late. Even if help arrived now, it would be too late for Gilchrist. Another glance along the road had him wondering what the delay was. All he could do was continue to try to confuse Black, as bits of the puzzle slotted into place.

'You're not worried about what Martha will say,' he tried, 'because once you've taken the money from the hut, you've no need of her any more. Do you?'

Black tightened his grip on the axe.

'That's what she did,' Gilchrist said. 'That's why she lived here. She was your safe bet, your keeper, someone you trusted enough to keep an eye on your hidden stash. But what did she get out of it, Bobby? Living out here, in a run-down cottage, wearing rags for clothes, as if she didn't have two coins to rub together, while she's looking after your nest-egg?'

'As I said, she's a stupid wee cunt.'

'So now she's outlasted her usefulness, what are you going to do?'

Black picked up the sledgehammer with his free hand, and moved closer.

Gilchrist sensed an urgency in his actions now, no longer hesitant, but deliberate and purposeful. 'That's far *enough*,' he shouted.

A grin slid across Black's face like a shadow.

'There's no escape,' Gilchrist tried. 'The local police are on their way.'

But Black said nothing. Instead, he lowered the axe and swung it backwards and forwards like a pendulum, each sweep becoming greater until one forward swing continued in a looping arc over his head. Then down and up and over again, and again, getting faster with each revolution until the axe seemed to be swinging in time with Gilchrist's racing heart.

You had to be strong to do that. But Black was powerful, and with each revolution he edged closer. Gilchrist kept his eyes on the spinning axe, waiting for the moment of its release. He would have to be lightning fast to step aside in the time it would take – only a fraction of a second – for the axe to cross that ever-shortening distance between them.

'You're only going to make matters worse,' he told Black. 'Killing me isn't going to help. Think what you're doing.' But trying to reason with a madman in full maniacal heat was worse than useless, and Gilchrist found himself backing deeper into the garden – one step, two steps, three . . .

His heels caught on a hard tuft of grass, and he tried to shift his stance at the moment Black took a step forward and released the axe with a raging howl. He had time only to twist away as the axe head clipped the side of his body armour beneath his left armpit. But the handle caught his unprotected arm on the passing, and a pain like a bone snapping shot through him with the force of an electric shock.

He grunted, clasped his arm, and felt his heart stop as Black walked towards him, sledgehammer now gripped in two hands, raised above shoulder height, the look in his eyes telling Gilchrist that he was about to have his head driven into his groin.

'*Don't*,' he gasped.

But Black was beyond listening. Nine feet, six feet, three . . .

Gilchrist turned to run, but his shoes slipped on the snow, kicking his legs from under him. He fell on his back as Black reached him, and only just managed to roll to the side as the sledgehammer buried itself into the ground by his head with a force that could have started an earthquake—

'*Scott Black.*'

Gilchrist's world froze at the high-pitched scream. He watched Black remove the sledgehammer from the ground at the same time as turning to the sound of Jessie's voice.

'Yeah, *you*, you fucking psycho.'

Black grunted, 'What?' as disbelief twisted his features.

'That's right, you demented wanker. The lot's going up in flames if you don't put that hammer down.'

Black roared like a wounded animal, than hefted the sledge-hammer in both hands and strode towards Jessie.

'*Stop*', she shouted. '*Stop. Or it's going up. I'm not kidding.*'

Gilchrist could hear the raw panic in Jessie's voice. He raised his head off the ground in time to see Black running along the front of the cottage towards the ruin of the hut, sledgehammer high, voice trailing after him in an unearthly howl.

Jessie stood beside the battered hut door, a lighted roll of paper as thick as a medieval torch held head-high, flames whipping and flaring in the bitter wind. She showed no signs of the panic Gilchrist had detected in her voice, but just stood there, as if fear-less, as Black ran towards her. Then with fluid deliberation, she threw the torch into the hut, and stumbled back as the hut exploded with a roiling orange *whumpf*.

Black howled like a dying wolf.

'*Run*', Gilchrist shouted. '*Run, Jessie.*' He struggled to pull himself upright, managed to stumble against the roughcast wall. He cried out again, but his voice was as good as lost in the wind.

Jessie had recovered from the shock of the explosion, and stood shielding her face from roaring flames that cast an eerie glow over everything. She then noticed Black bearing down on her, and she backed off from the unstoppable advance of a sledge-hammer-wielding madman.

'*Run, Jessie,*' Gilchrist screamed.

But she just stood there, deaf to his cries.

Black reached the far end of the cottage, arms rising higher, ready to deliver the blow that would surely open Jessie's skull like a ripe tomato splitting.

Gilchrist stumbled on the snow-covered gravel, shouting for all he was worth. But again, his words blew away on the wind. He could never reach Jessie in time to help her. From behind, off in the distance, he thought he heard the high-pitched wailing of police sirens while a voice in his mind whispered, *They're too late. They're too damn late.*

Just like he was.

Too damn late to save Jessie—

Something whipped out from the gable end of the cottage.

Black stopped in his tracks, staggered to the side.

Mhairi stepped out from the gable end and hit him again. This time, Black dropped the sledgehammer. Another blow to the head sank him to his knees. Two more steps and she stood over Black's body, her arms raised as high as an executioner.

Gilchrist shouted, '*Don't!*'

Mhairi seemed to hear him, for she glanced at Gilchrist, but for only the briefest of moments, before turning her attention back to Black and despatching him with a blow that could have split rock.

Black thudded face-first to the ground, and Mhairi stood back to let Jessie take over.

She kneeled on the snow and cuffed Black's hands behind his back while rattling out his rights: 'You're not obliged to say anything, but anything you do say will be noted and may be used in evidence . . .' Not that Black could hear any of it, with a bleeding skull that told Gilchrist he was unconscious, or worse.

When he reached Black's prostrate body, he pressed a finger to his neck to confirm he was still alive. But from the way Mhairi had hammered him, it must have been a close thing. A quick examination of Black's skull suggested it was nothing more than a head wound, but they would need to have him checked out in hospital.

He reached over Black's body for the sledgehammer, threw it beyond his reach – just in case – then pushed to his feet. His arm throbbed from the pain of a broken bone, but it could only be a fracture at worst, he was sure of that.

He said to Mhairi, 'What did you hit him with?'

She held up her weapon. 'Sledgehammer, sir, without the hammer.'

Gilchrist eyed the wooden handle, then turned to the bonfire. By the time the fire brigade arrived, if they ever did, the hut would be nothing more than blackened ash, with everything it had once stored beyond salvage.

Jessie pressed her hand to his shoulder. 'Are you all right, Andy?'

'Just about,' he said.

She frowned at something on his side. 'You're bleeding.'

He looked down at his body armour, and saw that the axe had sliced it open as it had hurtled past. He tried to take his jacket off, but a stab of pain in his arm stopped him short.

'Want a hand?' Jessie said.

He said nothing as she examined the cut, then helped him remove his body armour.

'Looks like it didn't go right through,' she said. 'You're lucky.'

With the body armour off, the wind chill hit him anew, and he stepped closer to the blazing hut, seeking warmth. 'Quite a campfire we've got here. What did you use?'

'Plastic container of petrol that was lying in the hut. Just poured it over everything.'

He waited for her to explain how she'd set it alight, but he sensed reluctance. 'So it lit itself, did it?'

She put her hand into her pocket and removed a packet of cigarettes – Rothmans King Size, ten pack – and a plastic lighter.

'What?' he said. 'You're smoking again?'

'Bought them after telling Robert about his operation. And this cheapo lighter.' She cupped the cigarettes and lighter in one hand, as if weighing them, then shrugged. 'Lost the urge now. Must be an omen. Somebody up there's watching over me.' She tossed the lighter and ten pack into the flames.

Gilchrist gave a wry smile, then closed his eyes for a moment. Heat bathed him like a burning sun, returning warmth and life to his frozen limbs. 'Would've been useful to have saved the hut's contents for evidence,' he said.

Jessie nodded to Mhairi, who said, 'Sir?'

He frowned when she held out a red and white sports bag with both hands. He took it, surprised by its weight. 'What's this?'

'The evidence you were talking about, sir. Money. Lots of it.'

Jessie said, 'Stacked with rolls of fifty-pound notes, security bonds, memory sticks, CDs and other stuff. We removed three bags in all, before I set it alight. Best guess?' she said, screwing up her face. 'Several mill. Maybe more. Who knows?'

The distant sound of wailing sirens had the three of them turning in unison to look down the road that led to town. A string of four mobile police units, as best Gilchrist could tell, were racing up the hill towards them, lights flashing.

'Here comes the cavalry,' he quipped.

'Just in time to put the kettle on,' Jessie said. 'I hope they've brought the biscuits.'

He nodded to Black at his feet, who was stirring awake. 'Let's get him taken care of first, and while you're at it, get hold of the fire service. We need to get this fire under control. There might be more in there that's worth salvaging.'

'Already on it, sir,' Mhairi said, mobile to her ear.

He tried to retrieve his own mobile from his pocket, but grimaced from a jolt of pain that fired the length of his arm. He eased his hand to shoulder height, attempted to flex his wrist, move his arm about, but the pain in his biceps burned like a torn muscle.

Defeated, he returned his hands to his pockets and walked towards the road entrance. Away from the blazing hut, the winter wind hit him with a vengeance. By the time he reached the entrance, the cavalcade was slowing down, doors opening in readiness to spill the team out.

They would want to speak to him, but his bones hurt, his arm throbbed, and a dull ache behind his eyes was doing what it could to sharpen itself into a migraine. Just thinking of asking what the hell took them so long had him gritting his teeth.

He was through. He was done with it all.

Jessie and Mhairi could debrief whoever was in charge.

He barely acknowledged them as he shuffled past, heading to his car.

CHAPTER 41

8.10 a.m., Friday

By the time Gilchrist had driven back to St Andrews, filled out a report on the arrest, then headed home to his cottage in Crail, it was after four in the morning when his head finally hit the pillow and sleep sucked him into unconsciousness.

When his alarm went off at 8 a.m., he'd had to unfold himself from bed.

Under a gloriously hot and restoring shower, he scrubbed life back into his aching body, taking care around a raw graze on his left ribcage. If Black's spinning axe had hit him an inch to the side, he would have been in serious trouble. He positioned a square of antiseptic gauze over the wound, secured it with a couple of strips of Elastoplast, then put on his clothes with some difficulty. A walk down the garden path in a frosted sea haar had him shivering from the cold by the time he filled Blackie's bowls.

It really was time for a holiday in the sun.

Back indoors, he phoned Jack who, to his surprise, picked up on the third ring.

'Hey, man. What're you doing up so early?'

'I should be asking you the same question.'

'Jen's an early riser. What can I say?'

'Is she there?'

A pause, then, 'No, why?'

'Just wondering why she's up so early.'

'She's getting her studio ready to exhibit my stuff, man.'

'Shouldn't you be helping her with that?'

'I'll head down there later in the morning.'

Gilchrist saw his opportunity. 'I'll see if I can squeeze in half an hour before lunch and swing by and take a look at it all.'

'Whoa, cool, man.'

'Catch you then.' Gilchrist hung up.

He found the business card for Tinto Gallery and dialled the number.

The call was answered with, 'Jen Tinto?'

Gilchrist faced his kitchen window and stared into a November dawn as dark and cold as his feelings for this woman. 'This is DCI Andrew Gilchrist of St Andrews CID.'

Silence for two seconds, then, 'Oh, hello, what can I do for you this morning?' in a voice that sounded chirpy and cheerful.

But she wasn't fooling anyone. Least of all Gilchrist.

'You are required to present yourself at the North Street police station today,' he said.

'What for?'

'We have concerns over the legitimacy of the Tinto Gallery in London.'

'Oh.'

'Do you drive?'

'Eh . . . yes. Why?'

'Good. Bring your driving licence with you. We need to see that.' He let a couple of beats pass, then said, 'Ten o'clock this morning. You know where the police station is? It's just around the corner from the Central Bar.'

'I . . . eh . . . I . . . what type of concerns?'

'We'll discuss that when you get here, Ms Tinto.' He hoped the formal address would have the effect he was looking for, but just to be sure, added, 'If you have a solicitor, I would urge you to bring him or her along with you. And one other thing . . .'

'What's that?'

'Don't be late.'

He ended the call, and stared into the garden shadows.

He didn't think she would call Jack. And he didn't want to open an investigation into Jen Tinto, or whoever the hell she was, or the Tinto Gallery for that matter. Nothing to do with the current lack of resources. Rather, doing so would harm his relationship with his son. No, he thought, he'd put money on Jen Tinto slipping out of Jack's life without a word of thanks or a backward glance.

He placed his mobile on the kitchen counter and switched on the TV.

9:45 a.m., Glenrothes police station

Gilchrist entered Interview Room 1.

Despite his earlier concerns, Black's injuries turned out to be superficial. X-rays and a CT scan confirmed his skull to be intact, not even fractured – a result that astonished Gilchrist. A cut to the back of the head, from the last of the four blows administered by

Mhairi, needed ten stitches, which striped his shorn skull like a misplaced zipper – no subtle butterfly stitches for this murdering bastard. His face, on the other hand, looked as if it had been used as target practice for the Scottish kick-boxing team – no longer sculpted like a statue, but puffed and swollen purple-blue. Tape was strapped across a flattened nose with nostrils blackened from dried blood. Eyes as thin as gun-slits tracked Gilchrist as he followed Jessie to the table on which lay a couple of business cards, courtesy of Black's solicitor – Dominic Haggerty of Haggerty and Associates.

As Gilchrist and Jessie took their seats, Haggerty sat tight-lipped, a pin-striped tailor's dummy with a bald pate and white moustache that somehow reminded Gilchrist of a WWII Spitfire pilot. He looked the picture of health beside his client.

Without introduction, Haggerty said, 'Do you really intend to proceed with this charade for an interview?'

'Charade?' Gilchrist said.

'My client should be in hospital. Not here. He's in no fit state to be interviewed.'

Jessie slapped open a folder and fanned a spread of colour photographs across the table. 'Your client's victims are in a worse state.'

'That's not the point.'

'No. They're dead. Your client's alive.'

Gilchrist raised a hand to take control, and waited until he had everyone's attention. 'We can do this now,' he said, 'or we can come back and do it later. It makes no difference to me.' He nodded to Black. 'Why don't you let your client decide?'

Haggerty twisted in his seat, put a hand to his mouth and whispered into Black's ear.

From all the reaction Black gave, Haggerty could be talking to a mannequin. Then he sat back, and scowled at Gilchrist. 'I would advise you again, that my client is in no fit state to be interviewed, and that if you proceed with this travesty, I will seek to have the entire interview struck from the records for having been obtained under duress.'

Gilchrist signalled to Jessie. She switched on the recorder, noted time and date, and announced the names and appropriate titles of everyone present.

Introductions over, Gilchrist said, 'The interviewee, presently known as Scott Black, is being represented by his solicitor, Mr Dominic Haggerty of Haggerty and Associates. Mr Haggerty, do you practise medicine in any form or capacity?'

'What?'

'Just answer the question, please. For the record.'

As the penny dropped, Haggerty grimaced and said, 'No.'

'So, as a legal practitioner you have no professional medical experience or knowledge and are therefore in no position to say if your client is medically fit to be interviewed, or not.'

'Strictly speaking, no,' Haggerty said. 'Although it should be clear to everyone present that the significant injuries sustained by my client during his arrest are—'

'Save that for court,' Jessie snapped at him.

'I really must object—'

'You just did.'

Gilchrist gave Haggerty a deadpan smile, then removed a sheet of paper from his files – a handwritten report from the A&E doctor, Dr Julie Cardon, who had examined and treated Black at Ninewells Hospital in the small hours that morning. He read it out for the record, a statement that confirmed Black's injuries were not life-threatening, that he'd remained conscious and coherent throughout her examination, and had suffered no apparent mental impairment from his injuries.

It didn't matter to Gilchrist that Haggerty would raise objections in court, nor that they might be overruled by Dr Cardon's testimony. What he wanted was to put pressure on Black now, let him know that they had him for the murders of Alice Hickson and Kandy Lal, and were looking into his past, too. But after his first question, 'Can you confirm your name for the record?' he knew his efforts would be a waste of time. In response, Black stared at him in silence, not even offering so much as a *No comment*.

Fifteen minutes later, with Black having not uttered a word, Gilchrist knew they were getting nowhere – at least for that morning. He excused himself, and let Jessie carry on with the interview formalities. Black's silence might not help them at that moment, but his continued refusal to co-operate would do him no favours later in court.

And all was far from lost.

Black's non-co-operation stiffened Gilchrist's resolve to focus all his team's efforts on finding damning and irrefutable evidence of Black's murderous past.

10.52 a.m., St Andrews

Gilchrist turned left into South Street, tugged his collar up against a blast of snow-laden wind. Flakes fluttered against his face like weak hail. As he passed the Criterion, he glanced inside and saw Jack seated at the bar, phone to his ear, hair ruffled as if he'd just risen from bed, or was recovering from a night on the binge.

Gilchrist pushed through the door. At the bar, he squeezed Jack's shoulder.

Jack's face lit up with surprise, then slipped into disappointment. 'Hey, man.'

Not yet midday, and his eyes were already spinning. Alcohol had always been Jack's first response to disappointment, and Gilchrist had no doubt that this instance was due to the unexpected disappearance of his girlfriend and art aficionado, Jen Tinto.

'I was just walking to the studio,' Gilchrist said, 'when I happened to see you.'

Jack removed his mobile from his ear, and slapped it on to the bar.

'Problems?'

Jack shoved his fingers through his hair, downed a shooter – double vodka, Gilchrist would guess – and signalled the barman for another. 'Can't get in touch with her.'

'Who?'

'Jen.'

'Downing vodka like there's no tomorrow's not going to help you find her.'

Jack smiled, an odd twisting of his lips that didn't suit him. 'Yeah, well, she's not up for the finding, is what I'm thinking. She's gone, man.' He made a sliding motion with his hand. '*Pooph.* Just like that.'

'She's not answering her phone?'

'Disconnected.'

'Nothing bad's happened to her, has it?' he asked, just to gauge a reaction.

Jack picked up his mobile, tapped the screen. 'Here's how it's done, man. Heartless.' He pulled up a text, and read it. 'Sorry,

Jack. New York has crashed and I can't get funding. It's over. Bye. Sad face. Kiss kiss.' Jack snorted in derision. 'Can't get fucking funding? What's she on about? The studio was covered for a month.'

Gilchrist put his hand on his son's arm. 'You'll find another studio,' he said.

'I already *had* a studio.'

'And now you don't.'

'The master of the understatement, I must say.'

'Just remember, Jack, that there are two sides to every coin.'

Jack snorted. 'Like that's going to help me exhibit my stuff, man.'

Gilchrist knew from experience that his son was beyond listening, and would have to run the full course of getting drunk, feeling sorry for himself, getting drunk some more, then recovering with fresh ideas for sculpting or painting.

He squeezed his shoulder again. 'Catch you later, Jack.'

'Yeah, sure, man. Whatever.'

Outside, he turned his back to the wind, took time fiddling with his scarf while eyeing Jack through the window. His son had his mobile to his ear again and another shooter in front of him. Tough love was always hard to dish out.

But sometimes it was the only way.

Gilchrist ruffled his scarf and headed back to the Office.

6:45 p.m., Friday

Jessie swung her Fiat into her driveway, and gasped with surprise.

Her house lay in darkness, not a light on in any of the rooms.

She switched off the engine and stepped into the night.

Something was wrong. Terribly wrong.

A tremor gripped her legs as she twisted her door key and pushed the door open.

As she stepped inside, the heavy silence told her that something had happened. Panic sucked the air from her lungs. She almost spilled her takeaway – a special fish, and a half-chicken supper from PM's; Robert's favourite – as she rushed into the living room.

The curtains were open, the TV off.

Her heart thudded in her chest, stifling the cry in her throat. 'Oh no, Robert.' She dropped the takeaway on to the coffee table and staggered into the hallway.

Upstairs, Robert's bedroom door lay open, his room in darkness.

She flicked the light-switch, and a lamp lit up the bedside table.

Robert lay on top of his bed, on his back, eyes closed.

'Oh God.' Jessie pressed her hand to her mouth as she stumbled into the room towards her son's motionless figure. 'Oh no, God, please, no.' Her voice was no louder than a whisper. She sank on to his bed and reached out to him.

He jerked awake, pulled himself free with surprise.

She gawped at him.

What's the matter, Mum? he signed.

All the lights were off. I thought something had happened.

He shook his head. *I couldn't sleep last night. I was upset. I was thinking about my operation. I was tired, and I fell asleep this afternoon.*

Tears welled in Jessie's eyes. *I'm so sorry. I wish there was something I could do.*

Don't worry, Mum. It doesn't matter if I can't hear. I'm going to write a book, a funny story. I started it last night after you went to bed, and I wrote some more today. That's why I was so tired. He gave her a smile that warmed her heart. *Do you want to read it?*

Jessie choked out a giggle. *Will it make me laugh?*

Robert grinned. *It's so funny it'll make you cry.*

'Oh Robert,' she gasped, and reached out for her son and hugged him with all her strength. 'I love you, I love you, I love you.' She thought he tried to say I love you, too, but she wasn't sure. It didn't matter. All that mattered was that her son was going to be all right.

He was going to be all right.

10 p.m., Friday
Fisherman's Cottage, Crail

Gilchrist took the call on his mobile – ID Dainty.

'You didn't hear this from me,' Dainty said, 'but Victor Maxwell's on the rampage.'

Gilchrist frowned, confused. 'About Tommy?'

'About Jessie.'

'*What?*'

'Don't fucking ask,' Dainty said. 'Apparently word's got out that Tommy has a list of names, and that bastard Maxwell's going ballistic. When his back's to the wall, he comes out fighting, and he's been putting it about that he's going to have some fucking heads for this.'

'But he doesn't know for sure that a list exists, does he?'

'This is Maxwell we're talking about.'

'Even if he knew the list existed, he can't know that Tommy gave it to Jessie, or that I gave it to you.'

'Under normal circumstances I'd agree with you. But Maxwell's not normal, Andy. He's got fucking eyes everywhere. So all I'm saying is – watch your back. And tell Jessie to do the same. Until that nutcase of a brother of hers turns up more likely dead than alive, then we all need to steer clear of Maxwell and the rest of his fucking team.'

Gilchrist stared into the darkness of his back garden, his heart heavy with the weight of it all. What kind of a world were we now living in where you had to tread with fear around the very people who were there to protect you and keep you safe . . .

'That's the wife calling, Andy. Got to go.'

'Keep me posted, Dainty.'

'Will do.'

The line died.

Gilchrist decided he would talk to Jessie in the morning, pass on Dainty's concerns, and take it from there. In the overall scheme of things, the likelihood of his and Maxwell's paths crossing was slim to zero. But if Maxwell ever found out that he'd seen Tommy's list of names, well . . .

Christ, it didn't bear thinking about.

CHAPTER 42

11 a.m., Monday
North Street police station

Three days later, evidence was quickly piling up against Scott Black.

A velvet bag containing miscellaneous articles of jewellery had been recovered from one of the sports bags removed before the hut was set on fire. One piece in particular grabbed Gilchrist's attention, a diamond necklace that looked similar to one worn by Janice Crichton in the photograph of her seated on the bonnet of her car – since identified as a 1995 Jaguar XJS Sovereign. If confirmed to be the same necklace, then that was powerful evidence that James Crichton and Scott Black were one and the same.

Gilchrist had each item of jewellery photographed, and copies sent to Senior Sergeant Stu Pierson in Australia with a request to find out if any pieces belonged to Alice Hickson. Kandy Lal's family had been contacted with a similar request. As of that morning, nothing had come back, but Gilchrist was convinced it was only a matter of time before they had a positive response.

More encouraging, Matt Duprey of the IT section had managed to access two memory sticks, and discovered hundreds of voyeur videos ranging from thirty-second clips to a full twenty-four-hour coverage. A first review had failed to convince Gilchrist of their criminal value, until Matt was able to link a series of images to a number of Internet romance sites used by Black for blackmail and extortion. Disappointingly, or so Gilchrist thought, none of them provided any connection to Martha Kerr.

Still, it was early days.

Bank details, too, uncovered four separate Channel Island accounts in excess of three million pounds in total; but more importantly, they provided pseudonyms believed to have been used by Scott Black. Two new addresses – one in Inverness, the other in Fort William – led Gilchrist to contact the local police offices to establish historical ownership of these properties.

Northern Constabulary had confirmed earlier that morning that Mrs Mary Jamieson, wife of Dean Jamieson – second marriage – and lifelong Inverness resident, had drowned in a tragic boating accident twelve years earlier, having fallen overboard in wild seas. Although her children inherited the family home, her husband Dean had inherited a two hundred and fifty thousand pounds life insurance payout. He had subsequently left the area, and no one had heard from him since.

With Dean Jamieson's Channel Island account being found on Black's flash-drive, the file on Mary Jamieson's accidental death was reopened and scheduled for reinvestigation by Northern Constabulary as murder. Gilchrist emailed jpeg files of all the jewellery, with a request to let the surviving family members review them. You never could tell.

With Mary Jamieson's death likely to be added to Black's list of victims, Gilchrist was quietly confident that he would hear a similar tale of suspicious death and inheritance fortunes from the Fort William property.

Talk about the noose tightening.

CS Smiley surprised him with a rap on his door and a curt, 'My office.'

Once again, Gilchrist trailed after her, puzzling over her perfume, trying to place it, before realising with an intake of breath that Cooper wore the same fragrance. He entered her office and had a sense that the space was taking shape, that Smiler's presence was slowly but surely replacing the ghost of CS Greaves.

Three new bookshelves lined the walls with hardbacks as thick and colourful as sets of encyclopaedia. Two houseplants – devil's ivy and a large-leaved philodendron – stood in opposing corners. In another couple of weeks, he might expect to see the place wallpapered. It seemed that Smiler was imposing her personality on her office, after all, which told him she was settling in for the long haul with Fife Constabulary. Of course, the worrying converse of that equation was that his own time with the Constabulary might now be shorter-lived.

Maybe retirement was worth reconsidering.

Smiler held out a hand, not for shaking, but as an invitation for him to take one of two seats that fronted her desk.

As before, he remained standing.

'You do realise that without a search warrant you could have compromised evidence found in Kerr's property,' she said.

Despite Colin and his SOCOs stripping the cottage, they'd found nothing damning to Black. On the other hand, the hut had

367

been a treasure trove. A plastic bin, dug into the ground beneath it and accessed through a removable floor panel – the sound Gilchrist had heard when Black entered the hut and opened it – had yielded invaluable evidence.

Gilchrist shook his head. 'We didn't enter the cottage, ma'am, only the hut. And that was to apprehend a suspected serial killer.'

'You're manipulating my words, DCI Gilchrist. You entered the property *per se*, the land registered in the name of Kerr. And you did so without a search warrant.'

'Not to perform a search of the property, ma'am, but to apprehend a suspected serial killer who had already attacked an innocent member of the public and stolen her car. With a suspected history of violence against women, we couldn't risk losing him again.'

'So you were concerned for public safety?'

He realised her questions were not being asked to criticise his or any member of his team's actions, but as Devil's Advocate. She wanted to know how he would answer in a court of law if – better make that *when* – Black's defence argued for wrongful arrest and dismissal of all evidence on the grounds of inadmissibility.

'I was concerned for public safety, ma'am, yes.'

'And you believe you apprehended Mr Black without the use of undue force?'

'He was beyond reasoning, was armed, had already attacked one police officer with intent to kill, and was threatening to attack another. He was prevented from doing so by DS Mhairi McBride acting in self-defence, ma'am.'

'With four blows to the head?' She raised her eyebrows. 'That could be argued as undue force.'

368

'Anyone can argue what they like, ma'am, but it took four blows to the head before two female colleagues were able to disarm and handcuff this alleged serial killer.'

She nodded, as if to acknowledge the end of her interrogation. Then darkness seemed to fill her eyes. 'Next time you need to enter a suspect's property, DCI Gilchrist, be damned sure you first have all appropriate documentation in place. Is that clear?'

'It is, ma'am, yes. And it won't happen again.'

'Good.'

'Because I'll make sure you never have an opportunity to sit on it again.' He gave her one of his deadpan smiles. 'Ma'am.'

She glared at him for five cold seconds, as if trying to work out how best to suspend him – not from the Constabulary, if he had to guess, but by his balls, from the rafters. Then the moment cleared – like clicking a switch – and she leaned forward and slid a sheaf of pages across the desk to him.

'This came in the other day,' she said, 'from Blair Stevenson's solicitors.'

Well, it had been only a matter of time, he supposed. 'Which other day?' he said.

'Last Wednesday. Confirming Stevenson's intention to file a complaint of physical abuse and wrongful arrest against this office, and you in particular.'

He looked down at the paperwork. 'Is that my copy?'

She grinned at him then, an odd down-turning of her lips that showed white teeth and somehow conveyed a sense of amusement, which puzzled him.

'I take it you never heard from Complaints and Discipline?'

'Not yet, ma'am.'

'Good.' She then slid a separate manila folder across the desk to him.

He stared at it, strangely reluctant to pick it up. 'Ma'am?'

'It's a statement from a Mrs Deirdre Cook.'

He frowned. The name meant nothing to him.

'You should read it,' she said.

He opened the folder and removed two sheets paper-clipped together and covered in sprawling penmanship. He noted the date as Thursday – the day after the letter from Blair Stevenson's solicitors – and the address as the same street as Jehane Marshall, Blair's girlfriend.

Although I am retired ten years from school-teaching, I always set my alarm for seven-thirty every morning. At around eight-ten in the morning of Thursday, 24th inst., my breakfast was interrupted by shouting and swearing coming from across the street. On looking out my window, I observed a young man assaulting a woman, pushing and shoving her to the ground, and shouting abuse at her. I was about to phone the police when a car stopped and the driver got out and said something to the young man, who immediately leaped across the fence and attacked the driver. At first I thought the driver was physically outmatched, but he very quickly overpowered the young man with skilful expertise, and to my surprise handcuffed him to the fence. The driver then attended to the young woman. He helped her to her feet, placed his jacket over her shoulders like a true gentleman, and very gently led her indoors. Shortly after, a police van arrived and removed the handcuffed young man. On being shown photographs, I am able to identify the young man who launched an unprovoked assault on the driver of the car, as Blair Stevenson, and the young woman who was being abused, as Jehane Marshall. In my opinion, the driver of the car risked his life, and should be awarded a medal for his extraordinary bravery.

Deirdre Cook

Silent, Gilchrist scanned the statement again, then returned it to the folder.

'We sent a copy of this to Mr Stevenson's solicitors,' Smiler said, 'along with a copy of the hospital report. No broken ribs, no ruptured spleen. Bit of bruising. That's all. We've yet to hear from them. But in light of this statement, I would suspect they'll drop their case. I'm almost tempted to charge him with wasting police time.' She frowned at him. 'You look puzzled.'

'Who took Mrs Cook's statement?'

She offered him a flicker of a smile. 'Everyone was tied up in your investigation,' she said, 'so I took her statement.'

'You knew Mrs Cook?'

'Far from it. I knocked on a few doors, and struck lucky.' She shook her head. 'You seem to forget that I worked my way through the ranks. I've done my fair share of door-to-doors, and I'll be damned if I'm going to let anyone bad-mouth the Constabulary, or any of its staff, without good reason.' She stood up, walked round from behind her desk, and stood before him.

'When I accepted this position,' she said, 'I was well aware of your reputation. I have to confess that I came prepared for confrontation, but I'm pleased to say that I seemed to have summed you up wrongly.' She held out her hand, a bit clumsily, he thought.

'I owe you an apology,' she said.

371

He took her hand, and shook it. 'Ma'am.'

'Right.' She slid her hand free. 'I'll let you know as soon as I hear from Stevenson's solicitors. Then we can decide how to proceed.'

He nodded. 'I wouldn't think we'd have anything to gain by counter-suing, ma'am.'

She gave his words some thought. 'Not sure I agree with you on that. But we'll see what they come back with.' She walked behind her desk. 'That'll be all, Andy.'

He failed to keep his surprise hidden. 'Ma'am?'

'Diane,' she said. 'At least, not in front of the team.'

He thought her smile suited her. It took years off her, made her look less formidable, and gave him a fleeting glimpse of what she was like in private. He smiled in return, gave a silent nod, then turned and walked from her office.

Midday, The Central Bar

Gilchrist had just taken a sip of his pint of Deuchars, when his mobile rang. He picked it up – ID Mo – and took the call walking through the bar. 'Hi, princess. How's Australia?' He pushed through the door on to Market Street, and turned his back to the wind.

'Dad?'

Even from that one word, he knew something was wrong. An iron clamp squeezed the breath from his lungs. He pressed his mobile tight to his ear, tried to keep his voice calm, his tone level. 'I'm here, Mo. Is everything OK?'

She sniffed. 'Not really, I suppose.'

'I'm listening.'

The line fell silent for a couple of beats, but when her voice returned he thought she sounded more like herself. 'It's Tom,' she said. 'He's different.'

Hairs rose on the back of Gilchrist's neck like hackles. 'What's he done, Mo. Let's have it.'

'It's not like that, Dad. Settle down, for God's sake. Why do you have to take everything I say the wrong way?'

He chuckled at that. There was nothing wrong with Mo. She was fine. 'Well, you know me,' he said.

'Look, Dad, you don't have to go off on one, you know. I'm all right. It's just . . .'

Silent, he waited.

'It's just that . . . I'm not sure I want to live in Australia, after all.'

He frowned. The pieces didn't fit. She was holding something back. 'So how does that make Tom different?' he asked.

'We've been here less than a week, and he's already talking in an Australian accent. Shrimps on the barbie this. Sheila that. Fridge stocked with Fosters. I mean, what does he take me for? And now he's talking about driving all the way to the east coast and camping out under the stars.' She let out a heavy sigh. 'It's scary. I don't like it.'

'What about his new job?' he asked. 'How is that working out?'

'He's not sure he likes the company any more.'

Not good. Not good at all. Now that Tom had arrived in Australia, it seemed as if he had discovered a new sense of freedom. How Maureen fitted into that was anyone's guess.

'You still have a return flight, right?'

'Yes.'

'Well, don't let Tom push you into anything you don't want to do, and don't make any long-term decisions on a whim. Maybe best to wait until you come back to Scotland.'

'You make it sound easy.'

'It's as easy or as difficult as you want it, Mo. It's your life. It's your decision.'

She sniffed again, let several seconds pass, then said, 'Thanks, Dad. I love you.'

'I love you, too, Mo. See you soon?'

She chuckled, a pleasing sound that tugged at his heart. 'See you soon, Dad.'

He sent a kiss down the line, and ended the call.

Then returned to the bar to finish his pint.

ACKNOWLEDGEMENTS

Writing is a lonely affair, but this book could not have been published without help from the following: Jon Miller, former superintendent with Tayside Police; Gayle Cameron (retired), Police Scotland; and Kenny Cameron (retired), Police Scotland, for their invaluable information on police procedure. I would also like to thank Heather Holden-Brown and Cara Armstrong at hhb agency for their advice and encouragement; Joan Deitch for her professional copyediting to the nth degree; Rebecca Sheppard, Amanda Keats, Helen Upton and many others at Little, Brown who put in great effort behind the scenes to give this novel the best possible start; and especially Krystyna Green, Publishing Director, for her tough-love editorial advice and for once again placing her trust in me. And finally, Anna, for putting up with me, believing in me and loving me all the way.

AUTHOR'S NOTE

First and foremost, this book is a work of fiction. Those readers familiar with St Andrews and the East Neuk may notice that I have taken creative license with respect to some local geography and history. The North Street Police Station has closed, but its proximity to the town centre with its many pubs and restaurants would have been too sorely missed by DCI Gilchrist for me to abandon it. I'm also pleased to note that the Criterion has recovered its original name from Lafferty's Bar. Any resemblance to real persons, living or dead, is unintentional and purely coincidental.

Any and all mistakes are mine.

www.frankmuir.com